THE FALL FROM PARADISE VALLEY

Virginia Nosky

Sev stood over her. "1602. I'll wait for you." He laid a key card on the table and was gone.

Christina stared at the little white card. She wouldn't go to him. He was gone and she could walk away. It was only when he was with her that she weakened. Felt so overpowered. 1602. She got up, leaving the plastic card on the table.

She waited for the small elevator to the parking garage, pacing nervously, her eyes on the ugly blue carpeting. Behind her two men got off one of the big, brass elevator doors to the upper floors. The door stayed open. Christina turned and stared at it, then slowly walked over. Her head buzzed. She stepped in. She heard the ding of the garage elevator as its door slid open at the same moment the brass doors closed behind her.

1602. Her hand trembled as she pushed the sixteenth floor button. She could no longer deny she was aroused. She'd caught fire the moment he'd touched her down at the table and now she couldn't bear waiting to be with him. She paced in the elevator in an agony that someone would stop its rush upward. Wind whooshed in the airshaft, and then the car slowed and stopped, the doors sliding open silently. Frantic she searched the number printed on the walls. Which way? Which way?

1602.

She had left the key card on the table in the bar. She raised her hand to tap on the door. There was one more chance to stop the insanity. She rested her head on the door, breathing in short gasps.

Then it was open and he was there and she was in his arms, opening her mouth to his, wanting him more than she'd ever wanted anything. Her fingers tore at his tie, unbuttoned his shirt, her mouth drinking in the taste of his throat, the black springy whorls on his chest.

He took her face in his hands. "Shhh. We have time. We have time for it all," he whispered.

He slid her jacket from her shoulders and began to unbutton her blouse.

All those buttons, she thought frantically. "Tear it," she begged.

Virginia Nosky

**BLUE ISLAND
PUBLIC LIBRARY**

Champagne Books Presents

The Fall From Paradise Valley

By

Virginia Nosky

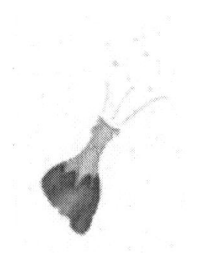

This is a work of fiction. The characters, incidents and dialogues in this book are of the author's imagination and are not to be construed as real. Any resemblance to actual events or persons, living or dead, is completely coincidental.

No part of this book may be reproduced or transmitted in any form or by any means, electronic or mechanical, including photocopying, recording, or by any information storage and retrieval system, without permission in writing from the publisher.

Champagne Books
www.champagnebooks.com
Copyright 2011 by Virginia Nosky
ISBN 978-1-77155-050-5
March 2011
Cover Art by Trisha FitzGerald
Produced in Canada

Champagne Books
2-19 Third Avenue SE
High River, AB T1V 1G3
Canada

Dedication

To Richard

Virginia Nosky

The state of matrimony is the chief in the world after religion: but people shun it because of its inconveniences, like one who, running out of the rain, falls into the river.

Martin Luther, *Table Talk*

Virginia Nosky

ONE

CHRISTINA

Everybody came. Everybody who counted in the city. If you didn't go, Christina Cross knew, it was thought that you weren't asked. Nobody turned down an invitation to this glittery *affaire*. It wasn't as if it was a charity ball—anyone could go to one of those if they had the money and the inclination—or even a society wedding. Those could be crashed easily enough. This was a *grand* celebrity wedding, engraved vellum invitations checked at the door. Who would have thought when Christina Cross was growing up that a Phoenix chef's marriage would be the hottest event of the year?

The local press swarmed around the guests, *Good Morning, America* had sent a camera crew and *Bon Appetit* planned a full story, complete with recipes from the menu. *People* magazine had come and the buzz had it that *Town & Country* sent a reporter and photographer for a big cover spread. That may have been, to the people who cared about those things, overly optimistic. They hadn't shown up yet.

The sun had dipped below the sharp ridgeline of the Phoenix Mountains a half hour earlier, but the sky remained tinted with plumes of liquid rose and gold. The green and white striped tents set up for the wedding and reception were still washed with color. An orchestra played in the largest of the tents. The guests drifted over the lush Arizona Biltmore golf course grass that was still fragrant from the morning's mowing, forming and reforming into groups to its romantic strains. A low hum of conversation was punctuated with bursts of laughter and the pops of corks being liberated from bottles of the *vintage-est* champagne. The groom had chosen the year. He had overseen the preparation of the food. It was perfect, of course. That's why everybody was here.

It was cool for a May evening. Christina wished she'd worn the foamy mohair sweater that looked so good with her dress, a sheer pink linen Carolina Herrera. Well, she hadn't brought it tonight and now she was shivery. Too bad, because now she'd have to find something else to go with the sweater because she couldn't wear the dress again in this crowd. They'd all remember it. Everybody always remembered what Christina Cross wore.

The prattle of the horse-faced woman seeped in and out of Christina's consciousness. "…well, of course we're usually gone this late in the year because I simply can't take the heat at all my dear when it gets close to a hundred but Arnaud was so precious when he just begged Barney and me not to possibly think of deserting him on his wedding day so here we are but not for long all I have to do is whisk the geraniums into the Suburban they simply love it at the beach house…"

Christina knew her eyes were glazing over. They always did when she got stuck with Alicia Bentham. *How does Barney put up with it? Well actually, he doesn't, really. Not all of the time. Everybody knows that. Alicia probably does, too.*

Alicia stopped her monologue and let her eyes follow Laise Brock with undisguised disapproval. Christina smiled pointedly and moved away, calling after the tall beauty with the mane of wild red hair. Laise and Barney Bentham? Was that why the sour look on Alicia's face? No way. Laise had better taste than that.

Laise turned at Christina's call and waited, half-smiling, her head cocked slightly.

Laise always looks so wary, thought Christina. Just what was up with her and Preston? It wasn't the first time Christina had wondered at the sudden change about five years ago in the faces that Laise and Preston Brock presented to the world. Was Preston with her tonight? One never knew any more. If they showed up at the same time one always got the feeling it was by accident. Strange. Not that Laise would ever tell anybody anything. She'd always been a loner, even when she'd still been involved with the fund-raising committees. Christina smiled up into the not unfriendly, noncommittal gold eyes of her friend.

"God, you look fabulous, Laise. I tried on your Versace. Absolutely loved the chartreuse leather with the chiffon. I looked absolutely awful in it. It needs somebody tall. It's perfect on you." Christina laughed. "Now that I've got you eating out of my hand with the lavish compliments…you are eating out of my hand, right?"

Laise smiled, seemed disarmed by Christina's little joke. "Why, you can see that I am."

Christina was relieved. She liked Laise, and they'd been close once, before Laise got preoccupied with…what? She went on, "I want to ask a favor of you."

Laise shrugged. "Sure, if I can do it."

"David's got this French trade delegation coming. There's going to be a big dinner with the governor and all. They want to make a presentation of some sort to the delegation. In French. Would you write up something appropriately flowery? My French isn't good enough. I'd make some god-awful *faux pas* and cause an international incident. Hey! I should ask you to make the speech. Would that ever knock those Frenchmen over."

Laise made a face. "Oh, Christina. You know I hate doing that sort of thing. But sure. I'll write something up for David. Does he know what he wants to say?"

"Pretty much, but he'd welcome any suggestions—some French frills. He can call your office at the university. What's a good time?"

"I'm there every weekday for office hours between nine and ten. Next week is finals week, though, and I'll be giving exams. I'll probably be in my office grading papers from, say, two 'til five or six."

The two women strolled across the grass toward the buffet tents.

"The wedding of the town's favorite chef would have to be a *tour de force*," Christina commented. "His staff has outdone itself. Have you ever seen such a feast?"

Long tables, set under a one hundred-fifty foot tent on the number three fairway of the famous old hotel's golf course, gleamed with silver, spotlighted ice sculptures—and food: barons of roast beef, duck *confits*, shrimp tamales, poached salmon, smoked mussels and trout, tiny deviled quail eggs topped with a dot of truffle, barbecued oysters, lobster and chipotle pasta, bowls of pearly caviar nestling in shaved ice, and, and, and…

Everywhere there were sprays of white everything: roses, peonies, iris, French lilacs, tulips, antherium, orchids, carnations, ranunculus, freesia. The bride carried a single calla lily. There couldn't have been a white flower left from South America to Honolulu to the east coast. The perfume was intoxicating.

Christina surveyed the extravagant table and remarked, "I never can eat this stuff. It doesn't look like food. Too gorgeous. Too perfect. Too much. Like a painting—a still life. I like to look at it, but it doesn't make me hungry."

Laise smiled and scooped a ball of caviar onto a toast round. "Not me." She closed her eyes, licked off the caviar and popped the toast in her mouth. "God, that's heaven." She took another. "Some decided personality quirk—I like to be the first and spoil the perfection."

"Alicia Bentham glared at you a minute ago."

"Yes. She wanted to use the ranch for some barbecue bash for the party national committee. I told her no."

"Well, that's certainly your privilege. Political festivities can get pretty wild. I don't blame you. They'd probably stampede your cows."

"Yeah. You really should try this caviar. Got to be beluga and how many times do you get a chance to make yourself sick on that? Bless Arnaud." She licked her fingers. "Alicia's such a bore. Told her I didn't want a herd of elephants thundering over my spread and frightening my horses. Or are they donkeys? Never could keep the political beasties straight." She winked. "Not very tactful. You know me."

Christina laughed, but said nothing. Laise was notorious for her candor. She truly didn't care what people thought of her. Funny. That hadn't always been true.

The two women talked casually. An ABC cameraman moved close with his light and started to take their picture, but Laise abruptly turned her back to him. He shrugged and focused on Christina, who smiled agreeably into the camera. Laise moved away.

A black-tied waiter eased to Christina's elbow with a tray of champagne flutes. She shook her head. Why did everybody else adore champagne so? Even the good stuff went to her head and made her thirsty. She looked around for a bar, suddenly needing a solid-type drink.

She crossed the lush fairway, trying not to sink her pointed heels too deeply into the turf. Was there even a prayer the pink silk Manolos would come through the party unscathed? She was afraid to look. Probably not with the rain this week, she thought ruefully, wincing inwardly at the almost eight hundred dollars down the drain—sacrificed to the privilege of being at Arnaud's wedding with everybody who was oh-so-important.

There were a lot of foodie stars from all over the country, the local biggies, of course—the governor, both senators, three of the state's congressmen. There were even some real celebrities from TV and the movies. No real A-listers, but a respectable covey of B's. Arnaud was one of a group of chefs talented not only in the kitchen, but at self-promotion. He'd won several national awards, including the James Beard, cooked for a lot of bigwigs all over the country, including the White House, and developed a very *in* following.

Christina's husband, David, had helped, of course. Everybody knew David was more versed in wine and food than most of the professionals in town. When David found Arnaud's first restaurant, that was suddenly the place to be seen. He suggested that Arnaud start giving cooking classes to the food aficionados. It was a novel idea then, but now all the important chefs did it. Then he began a cooking show that picked up syndication. Back then there were only a few on television, not like the present mob, and Arnaud became famous. Even though there were lots of stars now, his shone very bright.

Christina didn't begrudge him any of his success. He was a good friend and had helped her out more than once. There were a lot of people here tonight who owed their successful fundraisers and parties to Arnaud.

She eased into the crowd clustered around the bar.

"I see you needed a stronger libation as bad as I did, babe." Miriam Merriman's throaty voice curled over her shoulder through the noisy conversation.

Christina took the martini from the bartender and turned to Miriam, her good friend and David's partner's wife. "God, yes. I've got the champagne thirsties. Why do I succumb and drink the toasts with the stuff? I'm a sheep."

Miriam grinned. "I find that nobody seemed to notice me honoring the happy couple in gin. I just have the bartender put it in a flute." She raised her glass. "Cheers."

"Amen."

"Did you get a load of the cake? Big white replica of Arnaud's signature dessert chocolate tower. Migawd, it's as tall as I am. No little bridesie and groomsie on top, though." She sighed. "Just a white orchid. Kinda too bad. Always thought it a rule that you had to have the little dollies. Tradition is dead. Say, have you seen Ting Cartwright? She's brought the most gorgeous black man you've ever seen. He looks like a diplomat or an African prince."

"Yes, I saw them. Wouldn't you just love to hear what Jake is saying?"

"That prick. I adore it that he came home and found she'd moved everything out. He's simply livid. Huffing and puffing he'll re-do the whole house and—" Miriam swept her arm in a great gesture. "—have great, lavish parties there. As if he could even approach Ting's parties."

"What a joke. He didn't ask you to decorate the place, did he?"

"Can you believe he did? I told him to fuck off. Oh, he'll find somebody. He'll go through a lot of poor suckers who think the rich Jake Cartwright is going to spend a fortune. By the time they realize he's stingy as hell, as well as being a big blowhard, they'll have been driven slowly nuts, wasted two years, and lost three quarters of their reasonable clients."

"Good for you."

"Anyway, Ting doesn't give a shit what he does, so all his bragging is for naught. She's got her own money. I don't know how she put up with him as long as she did. To celebrate being rid of the bastard, she bought herself a new Porsche. The salesman was Jenks something-or-other, the guy she's with tonight. He's some sort of promoter of rock groups as well. Anyway, you know Ting. She does what she wants. And she wants this Jenks, I guess. Don't you love it?" Miriam stopped and waved her arm. "Oh, there goes Jack. I want to run ask him how long he can stand all this socializing. Plus I want to be gone before the rock band comes on and blows out my ears.

We've got to be up early to teach that mountain-climbing class down on Papago Buttes. Let's get together next week, okay? I might even cook if you'll put up with something elementary like mac and cheese. I refuse to let David's delicate palate intimidate me."

Christina laughed. "Good. But let's go out. You don't need to slave over a hot stove after you've been coddling clients all day."

"Who was going to slave? But I was hoping you'd say that." Miriam waggled her fingers goodbye and ran after her husband, her straight, silver hair swinging cleanly around her small head.

The lithe, athletic figure disappeared into the crowd. Miriam hated these affairs. Jack Merriman did, too, but Miriam *really* hated them, and her language, never good, got raunchier the longer she had to stay. Some people thought she'd probably had too much to drink, but that wasn't it. Miriam actually drank very little. Her impatience with the "beautiful people" simply took over. Christina judged that Miriam was at the end of her rope, social-wise. The *fucks* would be coming thick and fast if Jack didn't get her out of here.

She spotted David, his graying blond head bobbing above the crowd, then she narrowed her eyes. He was laughing with Halcyon Justus. He always seems to end up with Hallie Justus. She wondered if their affair had heated up again. Probably not, but thinking about it? She felt a hot pang of jealousy. She'd been so understanding before and David so contrite. And then, her reasonable concession, that since they had to see Sev and Hallie in the ordinary course of their lives, they would simply behave as if the liaison had never happened. David assured her it had been nothing serious for either of them.

Oh, why was she letting all this past stuff bother her? David loved her. Of course he did.

Christina felt the possessive hand on the back of her

neck before she realized anyone was close to her. Shocked, she spun, struggling to keep her balance as the heel of her rose silk sandal spiraled down into the grass.

Severance Justus reached to steady her, eyes black and amused in the dusky light. Unnerved, she brushed back a lock of hair. "Sev, why don't you just say hello, like everybody else? I was a million miles away and you startled the hell out of me."

"A million miles? Or fifty yards." He gestured with his drink at David and Hallie. "They do enjoy one another, don't they?" Abruptly he turned and grinned at Christina. "But I did want to startle you. I always want to startle you, because you blush, and hardly anybody does that anymore." His teeth were bright white in the gathering twilight as he rubbed her arm where he held her.

She *was* blushing, furious with herself, hating the way Severance Justus kept her off-center. Sometimes he seemed scarcely to remember her name when they met, then other times he'd do something...something like this. But always, after a few minutes with him, her palms were damp and she felt tight and coiled inside.

It always surprised Christina that Sev Justus wasn't extraordinarily tall, maybe just under six feet. But there was a solid mass about him. Or power. And assurance. That was it. His hair was dark, nearly black, and beginning to gray at the temples. He was tanned, of course. And fit.

We all work at it so, thought Christina.

"And why is the lovely Christina Cross by herself on this happy occasion? A little bored, perhaps, among our fascinating friends?" he drawled.

Christina looked away from the sleepy dark eyes. "Not at all. I was wishing I had a sweater."

Sev smiled and wrapped his arm around her shoulder. "Ah. You're cold. We must do something about that."

He took her hand and pulled her along through the

crowd toward the green and white tent where music from a small orchestra floated out into the night. The dance floor was beginning to get crowded as the evening cooled. Christina tugged at her hand as Sev circled her onto the dance floor and brought her solidly against him. Involuntarily her back stiffened and she tried to move away, but his hold on her back tightened.

"Always loved this song," he murmured into her ear. His body moved with hers to the music.

She glanced up to find his eyes on her face. Her breathing was shallow and tense and she scolded herself. *Why do I always feel this man is taking all my oxygen away?*

"Look at me a minute…no, straight on." He turned her chin up, not letting her look away. "I've never been able to figure out the color of your eyes."

"Sev, you've never given the color of my eyes a thought," she snapped.

"Is the lovely Christina accusing me of…now let me see…?"

"Stop calling me 'the lovely Christina.' Why do you feel you have to tease me?"

"Yes, I am teasing you. What I want is for you to look at me. Really look at me. I can't figure you out. You have a beautiful face. A lovely body. Your makeup is perfect. Your clothes are always the latest and the best. You dress to make people look at you…men to look at you. Then, when they do, you get uneasy. You edge away. Admire, but don't touch, is that it?"

Christina looked into the mocking black eyes. Is that what she did? Was he right?

"That dress you're wearing. It's very low cut." His eyes dropped to her breasts. "And when the light's in back of you, you can see through it. When you walk, your skirt opens and shows your leg quite nicely…up to here." He moved his hand and rubbed her upper thigh. It was a possessive, suggestive caress and Christina gasped at the shock of it. "You're the one who's teasing me, and every man here."

Christina was speechless with anger.

"They're gray sometimes, but right now they're a very frosty blue."

Dimly Christina heard David's voice behind her. With a half-smile, Sev let her go. She tore her eyes from his face, her cheeks hot, her pulse pounding in her ears. With an effort she arranged her features and turned to find David and Hallie Justus looking at her and Sev carefully.

Christina had always thought Sev and Hallie looked more like brother and sister than man and wife. Her hair was black and glossy, short and windblown. Her eyes were dark and intense, her body athletic and strong, the physique of a first-rate tennis player and golfer. Her clothes were usually simple, but she had a taste for ruffly dresses that didn't suit her. Like the flowered number she had on now.

The two couples exchanged automatic pleasantries. Christina and Hallie said they must get together for tennis. David had some contracts ready for Sev to look over. Then, to Christina's relief, they moved apart as the orchestra began to play. David swung her smoothly around. They danced well, one of the many things they did well together. Christina felt her tension easing, but she was still annoyed.

"What were you and Sev in such deep conversation about? You looked upset."

"Oh, nothing really. You know him. He's so sure of himself and opinionated. He was talking about women's fashions. He didn't like my dress. It pissed me off. Let's get the car. I'm cold."

David hailed a golf cart to take them back to the hotel parking lot.

God, what a relief it will be to get home, she thought. *Why don't I enjoy these affairs anymore?* She thought of what Sev said about the way she dressed. Yes, she enjoyed clothes.

Is that all she found stimulating these days? Shopping? God. When had her life gotten so shallow?

She slid onto the soft beige leather seat of the Mercedes as the boy held the door open for her, his eyes lingering appreciatively as her skirt fell open. Let him look, she thought wearily. It's probably been a long, boring night for him. Then, with a pang, she looked down at the smooth exposed thigh where Sev had touched her. She flipped her skirt over her leg. *I won't think about him, about the things he said. I don't need that kind of aggravation in my life.*

She put her head back and breathed in the expensive, new-leather smell.

The Mercedes was still a new toy for David and had more gadgets than the last one. The car surged out onto 24th Street with suppressed power. David looked over and winked at her as he floored the accelerator.

She smiled. "Better watch out for Foto-Cop when we hit Paradise Valley. They already have three great shots of the lead-footed David Cross on file. They might get ouchy at number four."

"Spoilsport." But he slowed the car slightly.

To the north, Squaw Peak was silhouetted against the night sky, to the south the sparkle of millions of city lights and the evening stack-up of planes landing at Sky Harbor Airport.

David turned onto Tatum Drive. "Jack and I are taking the plane up to Sedona in the morning. There's a piece of property opening up near the Tennis Ranch. Might work for another resort. The timing could be right. Great location, box canyon. We'll go take a look."

"Tell me when's a good night for you. Miriam wants us to have dinner this week."

"Why not Tuesday when Jack and I get back?"

"I'll call her. She planned to cook something elementary she said. Macaroni and cheese. She didn't want you to think you intimidate her food-wise. Anyway, I told her we'd go out."

"Not much intimidates Miriam." David laughed. "God, I'm glad Jack found her."

Miriam was Jack's second wife and he adored her. They'd met when she took some classes that Jack taught at one of those mountain climbing/wilderness survival schools up in Colorado. Each was licking divorce wounds. She was an interior designer and Jack offered her a job with Cross & Merriman Holdings as a consultant in the firm's development projects. Of course, as Jack said, he'd been in her sleeping bag from the beginning.

Once Miriam moved to Phoenix, only a matter of months went by until she became Miriam Merriman. Even she laughed about the name—said it took her a year to keep her mouth from sticking together when she said it, but she let it be known that she would not put up with Mim, or Mimsy, or some such cutesie nickname. Jack, however, she allowed to call her Mac. Sometimes he called her Pinto, but not very often. A private endearment like all married couples have.

David turned the car into Clearwater Hills as the gateman waved them through. They wound their way through the lavish desert houses and began the ascent up their own mountain. The climb didn't much bother Christina anymore, but it had at first. Heights terrified her, but the house had been so spectacular, the view so incredible, that she made herself get used to the three hairpin turns and the final shot up the driveway. It was worth it. For miles in every direction the valley stretched to take her breath away.

As David pulled the car into the driveway, they could hear Rosie and Gil—Rosencrantz and Guildenstern—the two golden retrievers barking joyously over their latest safe return.

The door from the garage opened on a small passageway that led to the big chrome, granite and stainless steel kitchen on one side. Rosie and Gil trilled and spun and barked. David herded them out the back door and went out to wait for them.

Christina went up a level off the living room and down the long hallway to the children's rooms. She could hear the TV in Caroline's room. David, Jr.'s room was quiet, which meant he had music crashing in his ears through his headphones. No question what this generation will be called, she thought. It will be the Deaf Generation. She opened his door, saw that she was right and gestured that she wanted to communicate with him. He lifted the earphone a crack and a guitar riff seeped into the room.

"Daddy and I are back, Davey. Time to turn the light off. Don't forget you have Junior Assembly tomorrow."

He pulled his mouth wide with his fingers and stuck out his tongue, making a gagging noise. "UghHKKKKkkk."

"Well, only one more time after tomorrow, then you'll be a certified gentleman and can wipe everything you learned from your head and be a comfortable barbarian again."

Her eyes surveyed her son's lair. "My God, Davey. This room is a pigsty. Lupe has enough to do without trying to get through this. At least pick up your dirty clothes before you go to bed. It's starting to smell like bears live here."

David nodded and snapped the earphones back in place. Christina sighed. Eleven-year olds. She closed the door and turned to Caroline's room.

"Hi, darling. Did you finish your report?"

Christina saw her own blonde hair and blue eyes gaze back at her. "It's all done. I just have to print it out. I can do that in the morning before the bus comes." Caroline gave her mother a pussycat smile.

She's playing perfect child tonight, Christina thought. Caroline had several favorite roles. Perfect child came into play when David, Jr. had been criticized by his mother or father, thus highlighting her superiority to her sibling. "Make sure you get up early enough, then. And don't forget you have a riding lesson tomorrow after school."

Caroline rolled her eyes to the ceiling. "Mother, I'm not Davey. When have I ever not gotten up on time or forgotten my lesson?"

Christina grinned at her daughter. This nine year old child/woman was a little frightening. If she and David were to produce a president, Caroline would be it. She had great political instincts.

She came down from the children's wing of the house into the living room and began to turn off the lights. David came in with the dogs and went to say goodnight to the children. Christina crossed to the opposite end of the living room and went up a level to the master suite. She popped the tiny snaps down the side of the pink linen dress and slipped it over her head and kicked off the silk Manolos, frowning at the grass stains on the needle heels. Naked she went to her closet to put her jewels away and spun the lock of the built-in vault. Her hands went to the clasp of her diamond necklace.

David kissed her shoulder. "Don't take that off yet."

TWO

LAISE

"Miss Spenser, you've done something quite new. The course you've designed in vernacular French has quite excited other Language departments. Expect some questions." The dean polished his spectacles. "I like to think the university is open to offering students a little...um...spice." He smiled primly, proud of his open-mindedness.

Sex, you mean, my dear Dean. Laise chuckled to herself. *Spice, indeed. Anything to pull a few more students into this impoverished department. Just doing my bit to X-rate the halls of académe for the home team to bring in hordes of students waving money.*

When Laise started her academic career at the university, she'd sensed that the same faculty had been teaching the same subjects the same way for years. Dusty, that's what she called it. And wouldn't it be interesting if some new breezes blew through the halls of the Language Department? Maybe if she could teach the kids to talk as dirty in French as they did in their own language they'd have a better time when they went to France and met up with *les etudiants francaises* in the cafés. *And won't it be fun to shake up the cobwebs in this department. And I'm not only thinking about the students.*

She smiled sweetly at the dean. "You're very forward thinking. It will be an interesting experiment if nothing else."

She broke away from the dean's office before she started to giggle. *I'll probably be drawn and quartered before the next semester's up.* Merde. *The kids will love it.*

Laise wasn't unaware that heads turned as she hurried along the Mall, crowded with students rushing to final exams. Six feet tall, with her flying blaze of hair, she stirred freshman hormones as well as geriatric ones. Laise Spenser Brock was unquestionably a dish. Also loaded. In other words incredibly and irrevocably rich—an heiress three times over. In the groves of *académe* this made her a very rare bird. Her fellow faculty members didn't know how really rich she was, since those funds were pretty much beyond the comprehension of the Foreign Language professoriate. But they knew she was different.

Actually they knew her as Laise Spenser. She had dropped the Brock when she went back to school for her doctorate. After the awful confrontation with Preston. Something about a new beginning, a new self-assertion would ease the transition away from wife and mother. That's what she'd hoped anyway. And for the most part it had separated her from her former life. Whether she was any happier could be debated.

She and Preston Brock were still married and she used his name socially. She could hardly help it since she hadn't divorced him. She just didn't want that part of her life associated with her university life. At the huge school she could hide. She kept her clothes simple and her mouth shut, and trusted, rightly, that the insular academic world never thought to connect her with the Laise Brock whose name occasionally cropped up in the society columns. But really, Laise didn't care what her colleagues thought. She didn't care what anybody thought. That's how she'd gotten through it.

Her bizarre marriage to Preston Brock was the subject

of endless whispers and speculation among their friends. It had been normal enough the first ten years. She'd been young, Junior League, and doing her volunteer hours and hours raising money for organizations medical and cultural. That's when she'd come home unexpectedly one evening after a museum board of trustees meeting and found Preston in their bedroom with Bartlett Savage, devoted husband of Claire Savage, Laise's fellow art museum board member. One couple of their "crowd." A nude Bartlett was kneeling over her white silk chaise, Preston bent over him.

With Preston's expression of horror as he looked up and saw her etched into her memory, she walked carefully down the long hall to the living room, sat down and waited. Moments later she heard the French doors to their bedroom open and a motor turning over softly. An expensive car sounded like that, she thought idly. Why hadn't she noticed a car?

Preston emerged, finally, his face ashen; but at least he hadn't been craven.

Laise was curt. She sat, long legs crossed, hands clasping and unclasping the chair arms. "Don't sit down, Preston. This will not take much time. I thought, up until a few moments ago that I loved you. I find to my surprise that I don't. You may leave if you choose. You don't have to. Pay attention to what I'm saying. My mind is quite clear on this. I can stay married to you. You will, of course, sleep elsewhere in the house. You are a kind and loving father, probably more than I as a mother. The boys adore you. I am not inclined to raise them by myself.

"There are only two mild conditions if you stay. You will be discreet, which I assume—except for tonight—you have been. And you will not bring your lovers to my house. Find someplace else. And you will be here when you are needed as head of this family. I say all this as things stand now. I am not interested in divorcing you. Other men have not appealed to me. That can change, of course, in time. If these arrangements don't suit you, you can leave now. Tonight."

Preston spoke in a whisper. "Is there nothing I can say to you? Explain..." He raised his hands helplessly, then dropped them.

"No. Nothing. Not now. Perhaps, sometime. I imagine this...situation has caused you some pain. I don't want to hear about it. Now, go away."

Preston stood, anguished, then turned silently and left the room.

That had been five years ago. That was when she decided to go back to school. To do something concrete with her life. End the charities, the teas, the committee meetings. She did not just want to change her life, but to replace it. She was fluent in French, Spanish and Italian. She had a master's degree in nineteenth century French poetry. She liked the academic world—it was parochial. The huge Arizona university had over sixty-eight thousand students, a faculty in the thousands. She could get lost there.

She quit her charitable obligations abruptly. It took her three semesters to get her doctorate. She wrote her thesis on the sensuality of André Breton—the irony of his homosexuality amused her. Her work was well-received and the university offered her a job. Her teaching schedule wasn't arduous, no one particularly knew or cared who she was, and the university gave her ample vacation time. Laise was accustomed to shopping in New York, Paris or Milan, or catching an exhibit at the Tate in London, or flying to a party in Malibu, or skiing in Gstaadt. The school year curtailed her traveling some, but she found teaching suited her. For longer than she thought it would.

But it looked like she'd be stuck in town this semester, at least until August, when she'd have three weeks to escape from the scorching Phoenix summer. Of course, there'd be weekends with the boys at the ranch up near Globe, where it was cooler. In August she would go to France.

~ * ~

Laise's great-great-grandfather had moved to Arizona when it was still a territory, had worked as a prospector and had been lucky with claims to several copper and silver mines. Her great-grandfather branched out into cattle, then land. Her grandfather orchestrated the real expansion of the family fortunes until the Spensers were one of the most powerful families in the Southwest. Laise's father was elected to the United States Senate and it was during those years that Laise was educated in the exclusive preparatory schools in the East. She spent two years at Le Rosey in Switzerland and got to know the children of the royal and wealthy of Europe, polishing her already excellent French and Italian. Spanish was really her first language rather than English. She'd been raised by Mexican nurses and underfoot of Mexican ranch hands from the time she could crawl.

Laise was an only child. When her parents were killed in a light plane crash north of Durango in Mexico, Laise inherited her father's half of the Spenser holdings and her mother's estate, most of it in San Francisco real estate. Before her grandfather died, it had been decided that of his two sons, John would run the family businesses and Laise's father Jeremiah would make a career in politics. The brothers were close and never had any serious disagreements about their father's plans for them or the running of the family affairs. The big boom was in land, the mining holdings dropping off with the fall of copper prices, environmental concerns, and labor problems. When Jeremiah and Rose Spenser were killed, Laise became a very rich young woman. She returned from their funerals to Europe, alone, grief-stricken and lost.

Preston Brock was the Chief Operating Officer of the family holdings. Laise was woefully inexperienced when it came to finance and she came to depend heavily on him for advice and guidance. He was kind and responsible, and when

Laise came dejectedly back from Europe, she fell in love with him. He was fifteen years older than she. They were married quietly at the family ranch near Globe, Arizona. She loved the ranch. She'd spent her childhood there, and when she asked her uncle if it could be all hers, he signed over sole ownership as a wedding present.

From the beginning Preston was a considerate lover, and though Laise was vaguely disappointed at the lack of fire in their love-making, she told herself it was just her schoolgirl ideas of wild romance, fired by the steamy stories and hormonal speculations of her pubescent schoolmates at the school in Switzerland.

If Laise was inexperienced with money, she was even more so with men. She had always been tall for her age and felt awkward around boys. She towered over the European males, and though they were fascinated by this willowy American heiress, she imagined herself even more ungainly. When she came back to Arizona and met Preston Brock, he was four inches taller than she, ruggedly handsome, and gentle and solicitous of her as she tried to get her life together. It had been natural that she would turn to him.

As she matured into her dazzling twenties and their two sons arrived, Laise and Preston seemed a beautiful and ideal couple. It was after ten years of marriage that their lovemaking began to taper off. There were fights. She accused him of liaisons with other women; he accused her of being over-sexed. They were becoming openly hostile. The revelation in their bedroom that night came almost as a relief as Laise considered it in retrospect. It explained so many things.

THREE

PRESTON

Preston Brock had been a tense and lonely child. His mother died when he was an infant and he was raised by a series of indifferent housekeepers. His father was the chief accountant for a ranching conglomerate near Barstow, California, with offices in that bleak Mojave Desert city—absorbed with his endless columns of figures, a remote and undemonstrative figure to his son.

Preston spent his summers working at the company ranches and by the time he finished high school he could cowboy with the best. He toyed with the idea of staying with the company, working his way up to foreman someday, but he was an excellent student. When he was accepted at Stanford University, he left the town where he had grown up with a sense of relief that surprised him. He had never expected to leave it.

In his sophomore year at Stanford his remote father's heart faded away entirely, leaving Preston with a modest inheritance and the house in Barstow. He sold the house, and with the money had enough to finish school. He majored in finance and graduated summa cum laude. After graduation he took a job as an accountant with Spenser Land and Mining in Arizona. He found he had chosen the right field. He understood money. He was intuitive and resourceful and it wasn't too long before he came to the attention of John Spenser, who gradually increased his responsibilities until he was doing much of the day-to-day decision-making.

When the bereft young Laise arrived from Europe after her parents' deaths, the lost, red-haired girl touched him deeply. He was deeply sympathetic, remembering his own lost parents. He had been so intently absorbed by the Spenser business affairs that thoughts of a family for himself he had relegated to a vague *later*.

Now, when Laise turned to him in a bewildered need, he found himself responding to her as he had no one else in his life. He was fifteen years older than she, but as he reflected on her situation, he thought this not a bad thing. Of her great wealth, he did not consider it, other than that he would be able to guide her wisely. That said, he scarcely noticed. It had come to be an abstraction. His fascination was in fitting the pieces together to make them work. That their life was one of luxury—well, it just was. When Laise presented him with two sons, he joyfully set about giving them the loving attention that had been lacking in his own life.

He didn't know when his interest in their sex-life began to wane. He had never been a particularly passionate man, but he enjoyed the tenderness between Laise and himself.

One day he played tennis with Bartlett Savage. They had a regular weekly game, whatever the temperature, and that day was a searing one hundred thirteen degrees. It had cooled slightly by six o'clock in the evening, but it was still too hot for any but the most dedicated players. Preston and Bartlett had been the only ones on the courts. They played hard, as usual, and went down to the locker room to shower and change.

Towels wrapped around their middles, they sat on the benches in the locker room, rehashing the match with cold beers. It was an easy and relaxed moment. Conversation became desultory. Preston became aware that Bartlett was looking at him oddly. He found he couldn't look away. Bartlett stood and walked slowly down the bench. He stopped in front of Preston.

What had he seen? How had he known? Had it always been there? Preston asked himself these questions endlessly. Bartlett had put his hand under Preston's chin and looked at him for a long moment, then bent and kissed his lips hard, his thick, sensual lips closing over Preston's as he darted his tongue between his teeth. Preston was stunned and thrilled at the same instant at the sexual surge in himself.

And that was all. They had parted and dressed quietly. Preston left first. He didn't go straight home. He drove distractedly, then stopped at a ratty bar. He sat for a long time staring at his face in the fly-specked mirror, his mind a turmoil of exaltation and horror.

Bartlett called him not long after and invited him to a party. He didn't go that time, but the next time Bartlett called, he went.

He remembered the dark, high-ceilinged apartment, filled with handsome, stylish young men. Air heavy with the smell of marijuana. His shock at a group gathered around a fireplace snorting lines of cocaine, he guessed they called it, from the mantel. As soon as Bartlett became involved with a tall, dark-haired boy, Preston left. He promised himself that was as far as it would go, but the next time he and Bartlett played tennis, they left together,

He stayed away from the drug scene. He knew that Savage went to parties, but Preston avoided them. When he saw Bartlett it was in private. He took a lease on a small apartment on the west side of town where it wasn't likely he'd ever see anyone he knew. He kept that shadowy part of his life separate from his day to day existence and only returned to it when he couldn't stay away.

Laise was cool to him in the beginning, after the night she found out. But their relationship developed a pattern. He was deeply wrapped up in the lives of their two sons. He had always been determined that they would have the paternal affection that he had not. They went to ball games and rodeos. When the boys could hold a rein, they were taught to ride. Preston had infinite patience with their homework. Long before they were old enough to get their drivers' licenses, they learned to handle pick-up trucks, tractors and horse trailers on the ranch. Laise was right that they were closer to him than to her. Earlier she expressed worry to him that she didn't feel terribly maternal. She sometimes thought it was because she never had siblings. Her parents had always treated her as a small adult. She really didn't know what one did with boy children.

The next years Preston and Laise continued their social life, and though it was difficult to conceal that there had been some fundamental change in their relationship, they hid the exact extent of their estrangement.

Preston did not know if there were whispers or suspicions. He did know that Phoenix was a city where it was hard to keep a secret. So he had been careful. Until that night Laise found him and Bartlett. It had been Bartlett's impulse to go to the bedroom. The boys were away on a camping trip. Laise never came home before eleven the nights she went to the Museum Board of Trustees meetings. Bartlett had drunk too much brandy and had laughingly pushed it. Then, the brandy racing through him as well, the idea of making love to Bartlett in Laise's bedroom had excited him, and he gave in, positive they'd be safe.

That had ended the lies. What he feared most of all was that Laise would find someone she wanted to marry and she would divorce him. He knew she wouldn't take the boys, but he loved her in his way, and he found their détente comfortable. So far, he guessed, she must have had a few affairs, not that he knew for sure. It would just seem natural, considering that she seemed to need sex; they fought so much about it before their estrangement. He still loved so many things about her, it was just the physical side of their marriage that he hadn't been able to face any longer.

And Bartlett had sensed it.

FOUR

LAISE

The affairs Preston imagined didn't amount to much. After the grind of getting her doctorate, Laise realized there would have to be some sex in her life sooner or later. But she hadn't gone looking for it and refused to consider anyone from their social circle. She had squirmed around with that splendidly sleek fraternity boy from her Seventeenth Century Drama class. He had earnestly asked her to have coffee with him to discuss his fascination with Racine's *Phèdre*. She had looked into those sassy cornflower blue eyes and at the bulge in his tight jeans, shrugged and agreed to meet him after her last class. She hadn't even made him bother with the coffee, much less *Phèdre*. He led her to his Porsche and drove to a remote spot in the stadium parking lot. Then it was all mouths and tongues and thrusting, squeezed into the expensive leather bucket seats.

"*Cherie, ma cherie,*" he'd panted over and over as he slipped off her panties with remarkable expertise. "*Mon amour,*" the young voice crooned with twenty-year old assurance.

So he had the wonderful audacity to call her *cherie* and *amour*. She met him three more times, and though she loved licking his springy blond hairs, she decided her legs were too long for grappling in a Porsche. She gave him an *A,* which was what he was after. He only deserved a *C*, but she really did want him to know that she appreciated what his rigid young penis had done for her. And after all, he had tried to make love to her in French and had even gotten his modifiers right. A *C* for *Racine* and an *A* for fucking. She turned in her grades with a clear conscience.

Occasionally she thought of him with a kind of bittersweet regret. He'd smelled like sunshine and tasted like honey and their orgasms were long and noisy.

There was the owlish, skinny, incredibly hairy teaching assistant. That had been kind of an accident. At the time she'd just needed something between her legs and his had been really something. Unfortunately he was so inept with it that it just turned out to be an uncomfortable thrashing around against his desk to be endured. How had that even started? She couldn't remember. She had no idea what became of him and she couldn't remember his name. He just vanished, unregretted, into some black hole.

Then, there was the long-haired poet who had been booked for the lecture series. She had introduced him to the gathered crowd. She had impulsively gone back to his hotel with him simply because he asked her. Well, it wasn't quite like that. He'd moved over to her at the reception after his reading and whispered, "Is there anything to do around here but fuck?"

She said, "No."

He'd recited his poetry to her while he pumped away and she took him to the airport the next morning. They went at it one more time in the parking garage before he autographed a collection of his poems for her, kissed her, promised to dedicate his next book to her, waved good bye, and got on the plane.

And that was it. Not much for three years.

She'd checked at the book store when the poet's next

book came out and smiled when it was dedicated to somebody called Kerry Ann.

~ * ~

"Ah, *la bellisima,* where are you going in such a hurry?"

It was Gianluca Lucchese calling to her as they descended the sunny steps from the entrance to Hayden Library. He fell into step beside her.

"Oh, *ciao,* Gianluca. I'm on my way over to Administration. I haven't gotten the printout on my classes for this summer and I want to make sure they're filled before I do a lot of work for nothing."

"*Bene,* this is a good surprise. I will be teaching this summer, too." He laughed, showing a perfection of even white teeth. "That is not a surprise. I'm the new kid in town, *vero?* I am assigned the summer classes nobody else wants, eh? And now you will be here, too. I am a lucky man." Gianluca clasped his hands dramatically over his heart.

Laise laughed. Gianluca was new on the Foreign Language faculty this year. He had all the females aflutter, from the teaching assistants to the tenured full professors. He had the charming but exasperating assurance of the Italian male that he was utterly irresistible, except Gianluca very nearly was. He was dark and slim, tall for an Italian, though not as tall as Laise's six feet. His eyes were a limpid brown and heavy-lidded, with a kind of sleepy Mediterranean eroticism that made women touch their hair and check their lipstick.

Laise didn't know much about him, just that his family had sent him to the United States to visit an uncle who taught downstate at the university in Tucson. She did know that Gianluca's clothes were expensive and fashionable, and he had the elegant ease that comes with being raised around money. He was kept on a tight budget, for whatever reason, because he often complained about his lack of funds. And he certainly couldn't be earning much with the university. Language faculty was right down at the bottom when it came to salaries.

"Well, come along, since we're fellow slaves this summer. We'll find out how much work we have to do." Laise's spirits rose. Maybe this summer would be a little more fun than she thought.

FIVE

MIRIAM

The call came just after eight on the Friday evening of the Memorial Day weekend, from the Maricopa County Sheriff's Office. Jack reached over Miriam to get the phone. Miriam became attentive to his cryptic replies. They were on call for the long holiday weekend for rescue work if they were needed. Accidents always spiked over the holidays, but for some reason Memorial Day was the worst. Maybe the first long weekend before summer vacations made people crazy. And careless.

Jack repeated the particulars. "We'll pick up the posse at 4 a.m. at the entrance to the park. We'll have our horses and food and water for a day's search. Check. Righto, Jeff. Well, the little girl hasn't been gone that long and the nights are warm. We'll find her." He hung up and rubbed his face. "God, I hate these little kid things."

Miriam turned toward him. "What is it, Jack?"

"A little girl, lost out at Saguaro Lake. Three years old. She wandered away from the family campsite. Same old thing. Everybody thought she was with someone else. You know the story. Family's hysterical. I just want to wrap my arms around these frantic people. Assure them we'll find their little ones." He paused. "Sometimes we don't."

"Poor little thing. So scared. Wondering why her Mommy isn't there. How long has she been missing?" Miriam tucked her shoulder under his arm and curled against him.

"Since about two this afternoon they think. They started looking in earnest around two-thirty, combing the desert around the campsite. They called the sheriff at four. They didn't find her, but they didn't have an organized search party. The sheriff's men have just pulled all the volunteers. Too dark. They want to start a systematic search again at first light. You know what it's like out there at the lake. The terrain gets pretty rugged. We'll take Nightmare and Dropcloth. Bimbo and Ace went last time." He rolled over and turned out the light. "We'd better set the alarm for two. Good thing we went to bed early."

Miriam giggled. "We didn't go to bed early. You poked me while I was leaning over the dishwasher. You would not be denied, sir."

"Poked! God, Mac," he whooped.

"That's exactly what you did," she said serenely. "Just poke, poke, poke." She reached down and tweaked him three times. "Of course, I loved it."

He turned quickly and pulled her over him, but she kissed his shoulder and climbed off the other side of his hip.

"Don't go," he complained. "Let's do a quickie. I'll turn the lights back on. You've got me all horny again."

"Animal. I've got to wash my face and brush my teeth. Set the alarm."

He made a grab for her but she squealed and darted away.

~ * ~

It was still dark when they unloaded the black Nightmare and the gray and white roan, Dropcloth, though the sky was lightening perceptibly in the East and the stars were beginning to wink out. They'd tacked the horses up at home, leaving only the bridles to be slipped on when they got to the lake. There was a clatter as the horses backed out of the trailer, reluctant to leave unfinished hay bags.

A group of about twenty men and women waited quietly while the deputy explained the procedure. Only the chink of metal bits and spurs and the creak of leather could be heard under the nasal western voice, along with the early morning birdcalls—mockingbirds, mourning doves, cactus wrens and an occasional water bird. The air was humid off the lake, a hovering dankness characteristic over these man-made lakes that had swallowed up whole canyon systems to provide storage water for the thirsty metropolis of Phoenix, thirty miles to the west.

"We'll fan out from the family's trailer until we get just in sight of the rider on our left and right. Don't separate any farther than that. Keep your neighbor in view as best you can. It'll be hard when the ground begins to get uneven and you start to climb. Shout from time to time. Call the little girl's name. Belinda. Criss-cross the terrain looking and listening. Anybody see or hear anything, fire off a shot—into the ground. Everybody got a weapon?"

There was a low murmur of assent.

"Remember now. Little girl's name is Belinda. She's three. Had on a pink T-shirt and white shorts. Pink tennis shoes. Too bad her clothes aren't brighter, but watch for the pink. Mr. Nolan, the little girl's father would like to say a word to you."

A distraught man stepped out of the gloom. "We…my family and I… want to thank you for coming out to look for our little girl. I guess we just want to say we're all grateful…and…we pray you find her soon." He rubbed his unshaven face nervously, then stepped back to embrace his wife.

"I wish I could let you ride with us, sir, but you not bein' familiar with horses, well, you'd just slow us down."

"I understand, Deputy."

His wife nodded, her face gray with worry and fatigue.

"Now, you all can search the campgrounds again. That'll be a real help, Mr. and Mrs. Nolan," the deputy said kindly. "Sometimes little ones just curl up and go to sleep somewheres."

"We'll do that. We'll keep looking."

The deputy gave the family a small salute and turned to his posse. "Anybody got any questions? Think you've all done this before." The sun-burned young man looked over the group. "Okay. Let's move out."

The posse stirred, the leathery creaks and metallic clinks grew louder, the horses blew and snorted in the fresh morning air.

Jack and Miriam rode side-by-side for a few moments, then pulled apart as the search party fanned out over the rocky desert dotted with creosote bush, spiny cholla cactus, and the tall desert sentinels—majestic saguaros silhouetted against the sun-blushed morning sky, their waxy white flowers iridescent in the early light.

~ * ~

The sun was ten o'clock high and so far there was no sign of the little girl Belinda. There was plenty of wildlife to see, however, though the night hunters had taken cover as the sun rose.

Nightmare shied at a warning rattle. Miriam spotted the diamondback and made a wide detour as the snake curled away. She watched the ground carefully to make sure she didn't encounter any of his friends. The warm spring days brought out the snakes and, though they were shy, it paid to be vigilant. She prayed the little Belinda didn't meet up with anything dangerous.

Miriam moved Nightmare up to a trot for a few moments, then slowed to a walk. The sun blazed on the yellowish soil and the dirty green of the creosote bushes sporting their lemony flowers. She took off her brown felt cowboy hat to wipe the perspiration from her forehead, the thick silver strands of her hair dark with sweat. The warm, pungent smell of horse rose to her nostrils.

She leaned forward and patted Nightmare's withers. The sky reflected its blue in the mare's glossy black hindquarters. The horse twitched her ears nervously, still uneasy about the snake. Miriam murmured comforting words and shifted her weight in the saddle. She was halfway wishing she and Jack hadn't gone at it again when she went back to bed. She was paying for it today. He probably was, too. She smiled and glanced to her left where she could just see him reappearing after going down into a gully.

How lucky she'd been to have found Jack. He'd saved her life. Had it been only a little more than two years ago?

Miriam urged the horse on, her eyes sweeping the dazzling landscape, alert to any motion or sound. But on another level her mind began to play out the beginning of the miracle her life had become after the…other. After Jonas Laird had beaten her for the last time.

~ * ~

"I'm sure you won't be disappointed, Mr. Laird. It will be a wonderful museum and I certainly want it to reflect your taste. That, I think, is surely what you have in mind." Miriam rolled up the sheets of plans and drawings she'd spread out on the table in Jonas Laird's glass-walled office with the sweeping views of Denver and the distant Rocky Mountains.

"Exactly, Miss Gentry. That's why I'm making my collection available to public view." The dark, angular face lightened a little. "That and the fact that I've got to have some place to put all this stuff so I can continue expanding my collection. Broaden its scope. I've been wanting to branch out into the twenty-first century British wave, and that stuff can get big." He gave her an appraising smile.

Miriam Gentry had to admit she was terribly impressed with someone so rich they could build their own museum, much less have the money to fill it. Jonas Laird had taken over an old building in downtown Denver and gutted it, then sponsored a competition to design the interior for his largely contemporary art collection. It was an extraordinary accumulation of twentieth century works, chosen with a remarkably accurate eye for the artists who would be the stars at the close of the century and beyond.

And he had hired her to design the entire, monumental exhibition space, library and offices. She had never done anything like it before and hadn't even dreamed of winning the competition, but she'd entered on a lark and let her imagination soar.

It was art that Miriam loved, and it showed in the exhibition space she conceived. Jonas Laird had chosen her proposal over thirty-five others, and it was only natural that he and Miriam would see a lot of each other in the course of the museum project. In retrospect it wasn't difficult to see how Miriam Gentry could become mesmerized by Jonas Laird. She was very young, just twenty-three, with not a whole lot of experience with men. Just some panting high school boys, then pawing college boys. Jonas Laird's wealth, worldliness and sophistication thrilled her.

Miriam had been raised in a little town in central Ohio, daughter of a high school principal. Her mother was an art teacher. When Miriam was ten years old, she looked around at the somnolent little town she'd been born in and made up her mind that she wouldn't spend an hour more than necessary in Sunbury, Ohio.

She went to Ohio State University and majored in art and interior design. She graduated and went straight to Chicago to the Art Institute to pick up courses she thought she needed. Satisfied she'd armed herself with all she needed for her design career, she packed her bags and set off for Denver. The whole idea of the Rocky Mountains excited her after the flat, prosaic corn, wheat and soybean fields of central Ohio.

Her first winter she discovered a passion for skiing. The

skiing went wonderfully, but her design business sputtered, until she had her proposal miraculously accepted for Jonas Laird's museum.

Jonas Laird was a three times-divorced bachelor, thirty-six years old when Miriam first met him. He was charming, witty and urbane. She had never known a man like him. He was not what could be called handsome, but he had a dark, poetic look, and deep, searching eyes. He had a vast fortune, only half of which was inherited, and he used it to collect not only paintings and sculpture, but fine furniture, antiques, wines, sleek automobiles and Arabian horses. His taste in everything was exquisite and, as he came to pay her more than a professional attention, she was overcome by the sheer perfection of his life.

The night he'd kissed her and taken off her dress it had not even crossed her mind to say no.

~ * ~

Miriam could feel Nightmare favoring her right front foot and knew she had picked up a rock. She stopped the horse, swung out of the saddle and pulled the hoof pick from her back pocket. The sun beat down directly overhead. Soon it would be time to turn back and re-search the ground they had covered. Three-year-old legs could travel only just so far, even if Belinda hadn't stopped since she wandered away. You had to be careful you didn't overshoot and waste precious time looking beyond where a lost person could possibly be. Miriam prayed the little girl had found some shelter. The sun was very hot and dehydration was at the danger point.

Miriam picked out the rock jammed in the frog of Nightmare's foot, then gave her a drink from the water bag and hooked it back on the saddle. Nightmare's tail switched at a fly. Miriam yawned and stretched—relieved to be out of the saddle for a few minutes.

Something caught her eye at the periphery of her vision. Miriam blinked and looked again. She was sure of it. Then

Nightmare nickered and her black ears pricked forward. A tiny flash of pink, wasn't it? Miriam's eyes had been straining since early morning and now she couldn't be sure she'd seen anything. It could be a late cactus flower. Her eyes flew to the distance to see if Jack were visible, or the man on the other side. But she had moved into a cluster of small hillocks and could see neither.

She mounted and moved Nightmare up to a trot up the rocky incline where she thought she'd seen something. There. Again. Then a glimpse of something else. Tannish, almost the color of the desert, but moving.

Then she knew that tannish flash. Coyote. A coyote didn't bother humans as a rule, but they would attack a small child. Miriam unholstered her revolver. She didn't want to fire until she felt sure it was the little girl, but if it were a coyote, the shot would frighten it away. She fired into the ground. The shot made a sharp crack in the shimmering hot air and the sound reverberated off the rocky terrain.

Nightmare scrambled up the loose rock and then Miriam could see the coyote, red tongue lolling, tiny yellow eyes focused on the shadow of a large rock. The animal paced, nervous now, but reluctant to leave. Miriam thought about shooting it, but hated the thought of killing an animal only acting instinctively in its own territory. And it was risky. A bullet could ricochet if she missed. She fired another shot into the ground and the coyote gave in and slunk off. She heard another volley to her left, and another on her right. Jack would be on his way. And others.

Miriam rounded the large rock. The little girl huddled in its shadow, thumb in her mouth, her blue eyes wide and frightened. In one motion Miriam jumped to the ground, her canteen in her hand.

"Hello, Belinda. My name is Miriam and I've brought you a drink of water. Then I'll take you home. Your Mommy and Daddy will be so happy to see you."

SIX

GIANLUCA

To Gianluca, the Language Department appeared at first to be indifferent to Laise's life unconnected to the university. But as the weeks passed he began to think that wasn't entirely true. They vaguely gossiped among themselves that she had money and that she was "social", but since she didn't discuss her life with them, he realized it was simply a not very interesting part of her. Gianluca was astonished at the snobbish indifference to money in academia.

As the semester progressed the talk dropped off. Eventually there circulated just the desultory whispers that handsome people generate as a matter of course.

But Gianluca Lucchese had listened avidly and as the days of his exile from Italy and his family wore on, he became very interested and wondered if, in Laise Spencer, he might find his salvation. The department thought that Gianluca had been sent to the United States for "seasoning" before he joined the family business—some clothes factory in Italy—and as far as that went, true enough. A better term might be that he was put "on ice."

There had been an unpleasantness over a girl in Rome. She had been badly injured and a young man had died. There was some family talk of self-defense on Gianluca's part, but the whole episode became so clouded in contradictions that the talk sputtered, then finally went out, almost as if the scandal never happened. Sums of money were exchanged and Gianluca was sent away to visit various overseas relatives until, his father said, memories faded and his son learned the ways of self-discipline. Twenty-two at the time, he was now twenty-five.

In the three years of exile Gianluca tried a number of frivolous pastimes. His allowance, at first, was generous. But he fell in quickly with a crowd of young, spoiled European aristocrats who drank, drugged and partied from Ibiza to New York. He found himself early one Sunday morning wrapped, in his Ferrari, around a Long Island oak tree. The police took a dim view of the amphetamines in the car, but intervention by his Italian relatives in New York City got him off with a mild warning and he kept his passport. The Lucchese family had important "connections" in the U.S.

The generous allowance, however, stopped immediately. In desperation he tried selling his services as an escort and, given his seductive good looks, strong appetites and beautiful wardrobe, he did fairly well at it. The work was not arduous and his "clients" were often generous. And so occupied, Gianluca waited out his exile from the bosom of the family. He expected his penance over the Ferrari incident would be brief. Donatella Lucchese, his mother, made the trip to New York and disabused him of this optimism. In light of his youngest son's unsavory escapades, Ugo Lucchese had proved to be unyielding to the pleas of his wife.

Not only was he still in disgrace with the dark affair in Rome, his mother told him he was doubly disgraced in his father's eyes by his antics with the fast crowd he'd run with. Donatella would give him a small allowance that she would be able to conceal from his father. But until he showed himself to be contrite, mature and dependable, he'd not be allowed back in the family.

Donatella suggested Gianluca get away from the east coast and try to make his fortune farther away from its temptations. Her uncle Leonardo was a respected astronomer working under the auspices of the Vatican at the big university in a place called Tucson, Arizona. She wrote and received a reply within days. Leonardo Firelli would welcome his great nephew and give him guidance and a place to live. No money, Donatella assured her son. Guidance and a home.

Gianluca headed west. He vaguely remembered the uncle in question as kind but distracted, who had been somewhat alarmed at the exuberance of three small Lucchese boys. He hadn't seen the gentleman in years and now chafed at the idea of another "father" telling him he was good-for-nothing.

And so, reluctantly, he made his journey west in fits and starts. Raised with fine foods and wines, he worked as a waiter in Chicago until his insolence angered the chef. He sold men's clothing at an upscale store in Kansas City, but lost his temper with a rude customer and was fired. Gianluca loved beautiful clothes and found it was so easy to charge those expensive shirts and ties and jackets to his store account. When the store owner found out how indebted Gianluca was, he threatened to have him arrested.

When his second hand Chevy broke down in northeastern Arizona, Gianluca hitched a ride with a group of University of Colorado college students on their way to summer jobs at the Grand Canyon. The students cheered him loudly as he left the steaming car by the side of the road without a backward glance.

Vulnerable in his desperation, he was sensitive to the stark, wild beauty of the vast canyon and the sense of peace that its majestic spaces gave him. He lingered. He began to fill in as a waiter at the historic El Tovar Lodge. Gradually he became friendly with the tightly-knit service community at the national park. He got to know the wranglers who handled the mule trains that descended to the bottom of the canyon. He enjoyed their easy company and began to accompany the trains whenever he had time off. Gianluca had been good with horses as he grew up, though these stolid, crafty mules were a far cry from the elegant animals he'd known in Italy. He developed a fondness for their stoic, dependable, cranky independence. The headaches that had plagued him since the incident in Italy gradually eased, then disappeared.

    He was soon conducting tours into the canyon and proved popular with the young, unattached women. The attached, as well. Gianluca's sympathetic, moist dark eyes and insouciant charm eased many a female fidgets and uneasiness over the long, heart-stopping ride deep into the gorge.

    His life moved along pleasantly until one day he took a group of Italian tourists down to the Phantom Ranch at the bottom of the mile-deep chasm. As they sat around the campfire in the evening, laughing and joking, singing old, familiar Italian songs, he became consumed with homesickness. He decided it was time to go see his mother's Uncle Leonardo in Tucson and seek his advice. He needed to go back to Italy and his family. His work at the canyon had been responsible and uneventful. After a stay with his uncle, he felt sure he could convince his father to let him go home.

    Gianluca bought himself a small, serviceable Japanese car. Not a Ferrari, to be sure, but it didn't use much gas. He said his goodbyes to his Grand Canyon friends, packed his belongings into the little car and headed south to Tucson.

    He drove along the south rim of the canyon and stopped to fill his mind with a last glimpse of the majestic gorge, wondering if he would ever be back. He had been at peace here, but it was time his life moved on. He was twenty five.

    With a pang of regret he turned from the soft peach and lavender spires, with the morning sun still casting shadows on the striated rock formations that recorded a billion and a half years of the earth's history.

The Fall From Paradise Valley

~ * ~

Gianluca drove all day, crossing first the high plateau of northern Arizona, into the central mountains. The high country behind him, he began the long, gradual descent into the stark, skeletal beauty of the Sonoran Desert, with its cactus, mesquite, and creosote bushes. To his eyes it was a harsh, forbidding landscape.

Highway I-17 led into Phoenix and it seemed to Gianluca that the great desert city sprang from a nearly lunar landscape. From the interstate, Gianluca stared at the glowing red glass and steel as the giant cranes and skyscrapers reflected the fiery setting sun. Traffic was heavy—he'd hit the evening rush hour. The air conditioner of his little car wasn't efficient, and though it hummed importantly, he was aware of the breathtaking heat that shimmered up from the roadway.

I-17 curved east and picked up I-10 to Tucson. Two and a half hours later he was looking for his uncle's house in the foothills of the towering Santa Catalina Mountains—picture book *papier machè* peaks turned mauve, then a deep purple in the lingering summer twilight. He stopped at a convenience store for directions and caught his breath at the physical assault of the August heat when he left his car. The desert's typical anvil-shaped cumulonimbus clouds had been visible from late afternoon on, with ominous black interiors and flashes of interior lightning. Gianluca thought it would surely rain torrents. There'd even been an occasional fat droplet or two on his windshield. But that was all, in this part of the country where rain can evaporate in the upper atmosphere before it reaches the ground.

His great uncle Leonardo answered the phone, very glad to finally hear from Gianluca. He was just in time for dinner if he didn't mind sharing a few things from a campus delicatessen that he'd picked up on the way home. Gianluca assured him that anything would be welcome. Buying the car had depleted his resources and since morning he'd had only a disgusting package of orange crackers glued together with something salty, warm and sticky that he'd bought from a gas station vending machine.

Gianluca remembered little of his great uncle, who had left Italy as a young man. About all he could recall was that he was the Firelli intellectual, not obsessed with power or money as the Luccheses were. Gianluca's father Ugo had sneeringly called Leonardo a dreamer and therefore, of no consequence. It would have astounded him to discover that his wife's mild Uncle Leonardo was far more famous than he, Ugo Lucchese—a globally respected and influential astronomer. Several celestial phenomena bore his name, as well as long bookshelves of books, articles and treatises on astrophysics.

~ * ~

Leonardo led a studious and insular life. He had been expecting Gianluca for some time with a mixture of anticipation and trepidation. He had come to feel, with some relief and some regret that his nephew wasn't going to show up.

After the two men had eaten what could be generously described as an antipasto, and finished a bottle of a rather good California red, Leonardo sat back and cleared his throat.

"Your mother has told me something of your…um…difficulties. I wish you would stay with me a while, if for no other reason than I would like to get to know at least one of my great nephews. I always think I will take time to go back to Italy and touch my family again, but my work always steps in, and the years have drifted by. I'll not have time in my life to finish the work I want to do. It never seems to come to an end…my work." He smiled ruefully. "Everything seems to be a beginning." He distractedly raked his fine hands through a wild corona of silver hair. "Stay with me. You've been away from Italy for three years now, and as hard as your father is, he loves you, and he'll be softening before too long, I think." He tapped his wineglass thoughtfully and looked at the empty bottle with a small expression of regret. "We'll see if we can't hurry up the process of his forgiveness."

He stood and rubbed his hands together. "And I think we can open another bottle of wine, eh? It's not every day I welcome my great nephew." He disappeared into the kitchen.

~ * ~

Gianluca looked after the old man gratefully. Maybe things could be worked out after all. He wondered what his uncle had in mind. He watched Leonardo come back with the wine, beaming as he turned the corkscrew. He was a small man, probably in his late sixties, with a narrow face set in a large head, eyes dark and luminous with intelligence. His crinkly hair fanned around his head, uncut and unruly, with an air of neglect about it.

Leonardo went on as he filled their glasses. "It will be pleasant to have you here. I've never married. An astronomer's hours are not conducive to marriage. We don't have to stay up all night anymore. The computers do that for us. But it wasn't always so, and now I wouldn't know what to do with a wife. However, I confess to being a little lonely. I have my friends, but they're just as dull as I am." He lifted his glass in a small toast. "Well, perhaps we can find something for you to do. First we must let Donatella know you are here. She has worried. Is your visa still good?"

"Yes, Uncle."

"You can get it renewed, yes? You have a green card?"

"That hasn't been a problem. Father knows people."

"Ah, yes. I guessed that. What was your specialty at university?"

"Economics."

"So. The dismal science. But, of course your father planned for you to go into the business and be the financial genius." He chuckled, more at his own innocence of monetary matters than at Gianluca's intended slot in the family fortunes.

The concerns of Ugo Lucchese were as distant to him as quarks and interested him a whole lot less.

~ * ~

Ugo Lucchese had left the poverty-wracked Calabrian city of Reggio, at the toe of Italy's boot, when he was barely eighteen. He was fiercely determined to break out of the structure of that poverty and the strangle-hold of the *'Ndrangheta*, an organization similar to the Sicilian *Mafia*, and the *Camorra* of Naples. Calabria was the land of the *'Ndrangheta*, a word stemming from the ancient, Greek-based dialect that the Calabrians still spoke. A close translation would be *prowess*.

Ugo left his harsh, mountainous home, a sterile land tortured with earthquakes and natural calamities, and went north to find his fortune. He went first to Rome, but an unfortunate street brawl attracted the attention of the police, so he moved farther north to Turin. In that foggy, gray, industrial city he worked for a time in the giant Fiat works, learning mechanics and how to curb his temper, then got a job with a small, family-owned textile factory. He worked relentlessly and caught the attention of the elderly owner, who was happy to turn more and more responsibility over to his intense employee. They both discovered that Ugo had a genius for the business, with innovative ideas that led the way into mass-producing high-style, high-quality, high-priced knitwear, just when the snobbish designer label phenomenon burst upon the cash-rich boomer generation. Within seven years he bought the family out.

Ugo met the aristocratic Donatella Firelli at a dinner party, and after seducing the panting young heiress, had married her over the fierce objections of her elegant family, who were horrified at the prospect of this dark, frightening southerner among the genteel Firellis.

In the north, southerners are known as *terroni,* earth people. Peasants. Ugo Lucchese looked every inch the southerner. Powerful and swarthy, with black curling hair and black flashing eyes. His mouth was thick and sensual and to many people, cruel. His overt virility made the innocent Donatella weak with desire. They had three sons quickly: Antonio was the oldest and closest to his father in business skills; Paulo was brainy and his mother prayed he would go into the church, but Ugo had other plans for him; and the youngest was Gianluca.

After assuring the male descendency of himself, and singularly uninterested in siring daughters, Ugo began to frequent Donatella's bed less and less, finding more exciting diversions for his powerful appetites in the tall, slim beauties who modeled his factories' clothes.

All of the sons inherited their father's dark handsomeness, but it was Gianluca who had got his mother's dreaminess, albeit with his father's volatile Calabrian temper.

All three of the boys were expected to work in the company and were schooled to fill certain slots that Ugo had ordained for them.

Ugo Lucchese swore the company would always be a family concern, as so many Italian businesses were. Antonio knew from childhood that he would be his father's heir, sent to the United States for an MBA from Wharton. Paulo was to be second-in-command and trained as an engineer. Gianluca was to learn finance and take over the money-management of the company.

Gianluca turned out less than ambitious. He loved expensive clothes, fast cars, parties and gambling. And above all, girls. Beautiful girls. He resented his father's disapproval of him and they clashed often, with his mother's intercession the only brake to open warfare. Donatella adored her youngest, and as Ugo's ardor cooled, she focused all her maternal and feminine instincts on her last-born.

When the unpleasantness in Rome occurred, Ugo was more than ready to give Gianluca the lesson he'd been courting. He made no secret of his bitter disappointment in him, convinced that the overly-refined Firelli DNA had polluted the Lucchese genes in his youngest son.

SEVEN

GIANLUCA

Gianluca had been at his uncle's house only a week when Leonardo came home one evening, excitement filling his face.

"Oh, my boy, I think I have found just the thing for you. I have a colleague at the university up in Phoenix who called to ask if I knew an Italian who could take over some beginning Italian classes for an ailing faculty member. The fall semester is beginning in two weeks and there is some desperation to filling the job."

Gianluca began to protest, but his uncle rolled on. "It might be only temporary, but it is an opportunity. Your father would be greatly impressed, you know, with a university post."

Gianluca knew that was true. Like many self-taught men Ugo respected letters; however, Gianluca had no experience whatsoever at teaching. "Why, I think it's out of the question, uncle. I couldn't teach anybody anything." The thought of it seemed so outlandish he made a face at Leonardo.

His uncle threw back his head and roared with laughter. "I will coach you. You will find American students are not critical. You will have a text to follow. These are not advanced courses."

So Gianluca found himself on the faculty of Arizona

State University teaching Italian 101, 102, and 103. It was like his uncle said it would be. The Italian Department, grateful to have him fill in on such short notice for the absent professor, furnished him with past lesson plans and exams.

Surprisingly, Gianluca turned out to be a good teacher. The work wasn't too taxing and there were a lot of pretty girls bewitched by the dark, romantic good looks of the young Italian instructor.

With his success at teaching came self confidence. His father would approve of him. He began to think of going home. He would no longer be in disgrace. But he needed a clincher. Slowly Laise Spenser began to figure in his plans. He would take home a rich American wife. Or a fiancée would be almost as good. He remembered the large cash wedding gifts Ugo had given his two brothers when they married.

Gianluca had known immediately that Laise was rich. He knew an Armani shirt when he saw one. And the way she moved, the attitude she had with other people—that don't-give-a-damn assurance that comes of having money all one's life. She was a little older than he, but that didn't matter. His father would like that, that he was mature enough to attract a mature woman. His father would be impressed with him.

He began to spin dreams, make plans around her until they became very, very real. He would take home to Italy the tall, beautiful, aristocratic and, above all, rich American and show them how brilliant Gianluca Lucchese was. He would lie awake at night creating the scenarios of his homecoming.

By the time the fall semester was drawing to a close, he was on a friendly basis with Laise—isn't it a beautiful day, I like your dress, I'm trying to understand American football, aren't there ever any Italian movies here? Casual. She'd stop to say a few words to him from time to time.

He had hoped to make a stronger impression by the Christmas holidays, but ended up going skiing with one of his prettiest students who, while being both charming and joyously libidinous, was not rich enough. No, he was right to focus on Laise Spenser. The money was very important. Beautiful, elegant, highly educated *Profesora* Laise Spenser. All of that. But rich was the most important of all. How pleased his father was going to be.

The skiing girl had to go back to California and he still had tedious days to kill during the long semester break. He began spending hours in the library researching Arizona history. Someone had mentioned that Laise came from an old Arizona family and he needed a subject with which to approach her on more than a casual basis. If he seemed very interested in Arizona, perhaps she would be impressed. One day he came upon a reference to the Spensers, so began to study old newspapers in hopes of discovering the answers to some of his questions about Laise.

When he read about the death of her parents and subsequent inheritance, he became excited. Until he read about her marriage to Preston Brock. She didn't wear a ring, had never mentioned a husband...

But by this time he was so convinced he would prevail in his plans for her, he told himself this was only an inconvenient detail. She must be divorced. This would distress his mother, but his father would be impressed with her family, her money and her beauty. Divorce wasn't that uncommon in Italy these days. He just wouldn't mention it at first.

When the spring semester began in February, Gianluca began to put himself into positions to run into Laise. She spoke fluent Italian and seemed to enjoy the opportunity he gave her to speak it. It seemed natural for him to drop by her office, and if he saw she wasn't busy with someone else, he'd drop easily into the armchair by her desk and find things to say to make her laugh. He knew he had enormous charm, was genuinely funny, and had a sexuality of which he was extremely confident. He knew she enjoyed his visits and noticed that her face lit up when he appeared at her door. He had tried to impress her with tidbits of Arizona history, and he thought it odd that she brushed these comments aside. He gave up going to the library. It had bored him anyway.

As the weeks passed, Gianluca found Laise more and more bewitching—thought of her constantly, dreamed of her. Her flawless white skin, her wild red hair mesmerized him. Sometimes when he'd made her laugh, she'd throw her head back and her long, pearly throat made his teeth ache he so longed to sink them into it. If she noticed his erections, she gave no indication.

He was able occasionally to get her to have coffee with him in the Student Union. He'd not gotten her to go off-campus with him.

Every once in awhile, when the weather was lovely in February and March, they'd get coffee at the stand on the mall and stretch out under one of the olive trees along the walk. He knew she found him handsome; in fact she often teased him about his good looks and the loaded glances he got from coeds and faculty alike.

So, impatiently he bided his time. When he found out she was teaching summer semester, he volunteered as well. It hadn't been difficult. Nobody wanted to stick around Phoenix in the summer. He'd get her in bed before July. He knew it. The corner of his mouth twitched in a smile of anticipation.

In the meantime there was a German exchange student with a wonderful tongue.

EIGHT

MIRIAM

Miriam had hidden her life with Jonas Laird from her friends. Even Jack didn't know all of it. She had almost succeeded from blotting it from her own mind. She had married Jonas with such innocence, such naiveté. Her commission to design Jonas's museum had immediately led to a burst of clients for her interior design business. At last Ohio was behind her, the future golden. She had truly believed that. Her creativity blossomed, her design work was the talk of Denver society. And the praise was deserved. What she had accomplished on her own she could look back on with pride. Then, of course, Jonas had stepped in.

~ * ~

"There is no reason you shouldn't marry me, Miriam," Jonas said, "and a lot of reasons why you should. For one, after tonight's opening, no one who is anybody will have her home done by anyone else. I'll make sure of it."

"Oh, Jonas, how would you ever do that?"

He smiled. "You don't have to worry. I can do it. But let me go on. Two. We like the same things, though I must admit you're a better skier than I."

It crossed Miriam's mind that this was hard for him to say.

"There are things, however, I can teach you—the things that come with having money, a great deal of it. Three, you seem to like the things I do to you in bed." He gave her breast a small, hard squeeze.

Miriam caught her breath and blushed. She did like what he did to her in bed, though some of it was a little beyond what she'd imagined. Of course, her experience had been somewhat limited to the few groping students and an occasional young Denver businessman who didn't appeal to her enough to lose her virginity over.

"I'd feel really funny having you push my business, Jonas. I can make it on my own. Look, you picked me. Others will, too."

"Don't be foolish. Never refuse anything that will help business. You will have the most exquisite studio in the city. We won't discuss it any further. Now, there will have to be a financial agreement before we marry. You understand that, don't you?"

"I don't understand that at all, Jonas. That really hurts my feelings. I'm not after your money. I don't even think about it, except that you're very generous with it. With me. It sounds so…so…greedy. Tacky even."

But Jonas simply brushed aside her hesitant objections.

"Nothing to it, Miriam. It's done all the time when there's a lot of money involved, particularly on one side. I've promised you your studio will flourish. Money will not be a problem for you. And I will teach you to spend it on the right things, the best things. The only things that count."

So she pushed aside the hurt, and when the time came, she signed the prenuptial agreement. She was still dazed that this worldly man wanted to marry her. Maybe he would tire of her in a few years. She would really try to develop the sophistication that seemed to mean so much to him. Then she was ashamed that she even considered that their marriage would not last. Just because Jonas had been married three times before didn't mean she couldn't make it work. She would learn all he could teach her and make him proud of her.

For the first two years of her marriage their lives went smoothly enough. Miriam was disappointed that there wasn't a great deal of warmth in their relationship, though their sex life was exciting. Jonas had a vivid imagination and taught Miriam things she never dreamed people did in bed.

Then he began asking her to do things she got edgy about. Like tying her up, spanking her, wearing strange painful devices. She didn't like it when he hurt her and said so.

"I will simply not do that, Jonas. That's really sick. And you can knock off doing things that hurt me. I swear I'll slug you if you do that again."

She could see Jonas becoming annoyed that she had a mind of her own.

About that time that he slapped her for the first time. She'd talked animatedly with the husband of a client one night at a party, laughing over some witty ideas he had for the couple's guesthouse. When they'd gotten home Jonas accused her of having an affair with the man. She was astonished, then stunned when he hit her.

"That hurt. What the hell's wrong with you? I did nothing to be ashamed of. You want me to be gracious to all these friends of yours. I was just having a nice conversation with the guy. He's a client. He had some fun ideas."

"I'll bet they were fun ideas," he sneered. "I saw the way he was slobbering over your tits."

"You're crazy."

He hit her again. "Don't...you...*ever*...call ...me...that...again."

After that began the gradual descent into a hell that she still marveled that she had had the strength to break away from. She really knew no one to confide in. Denver was a new city to her when she had met Jonas, and acquaintances had all been his after they married. Acquaintances, not friends. She realized more and more that Jonas had no real friends.

She bore his accusations, his increasing cocaine abuse, the beatings, the spiraling down into a world of self-loathing and self-accusation. She had been tempted to ease her pain with drugs. They would have been easy to come by; indeed, Jonas continually pushed them on her. But somehow she knew she would lose every shred of herself if she succumbed and she fought the impulse with the strength she had left.

One day Miriam sat in her office, staring at the wall, mindless tears running down her cheeks. Her young assistant, Charles, hurried in the door and stopped when he saw her. She glanced at him as he stood, hesitant, looking her over carefully. She looked at her hands, picking at a damp handkerchief. Some minutes passed before he spoke.

"Sweetie, I think you should listen to me. Crying…well, it helps sometimes, but I think you need more than that. When I'm flat on the floor, there's a man who helps me an awful lot." He went behind the desk and rummaged for her phone book. "Here. Now I won't say another word about it. But, we'll just look up his number, shall we?" He riffled through the pages. "There's a good girl. Ah, here we are."

Miriam went back to staring at the wall while Charles looked up the number and wrote it down for her. He picked up her hand and curled her fingers around the piece of paper and kissed the top of her head before he left.

Miriam didn't know how long she sat there, tears still streaming down her cheeks, but finally she opened her hand and smoothed out Charles's note. There was a number for a Dr. Aaron Shulman. She looked at the open phone book. Aaron Shulman was a psychiatrist.

~ * ~

Surprisingly, Jonas didn't object to her seeing Dr. Shulman. "Actually, I was going to suggest therapy for you, Miriam. You're much too high-strung lately, imagining so many things. Perhaps you will discuss your frigidity with him.

It's becoming a burden to me. There really should be no constraints in the bedroom between a man and his wife. Perhaps I'll go with you."

Dully Miriam thought if he did she'd either not go, or go to someone else. But Jonas seemed to forget the idea when she didn't bring it up again.

It took her several months to be openly honest with Dr. Shulman, but he was patient and she began to not be so ashamed to talk about Jonas's perversions.

The night he brought the young man into their bedroom had been the end. When she became hysterical, Jonas hit her again and again. Miriam bolted from the room, the two men's laughter exploding in her ears. She pulled a raincoat over her nakedness and ran, praying Jonas wouldn't follow her to her car.

She drove for several hours. When she had calmed, she called Dr. Shulman. The psychiatrist put her up for the night and the next day she went back to the house when she knew Jonas wouldn't be there and packed a few belongings.

Jonas was reason itself for awhile, agreeing that he'd probably gone too far, too fast with her. She should really get over her silliness and come home. He'd had a long talk with Dr. Shulman and had clarified a few of her wildest imaginings. The psychiatrist had been quite helpful, he told her. The two of them had mapped out a course of treatment for her. Miriam didn't believe Dr. Shulman would do that, after the things she'd told him,

Instead, Miriam rented a small apartment and furnished it with things from her studio. Then she filed for divorce.

It wasn't long after that her business began to fall off. Clients didn't pay their bills. Then she knew Jonas meant to strangle her financially.

Miriam's self-confidence in her ability to survive was shaken. She had been with Jonas five years and insidiously been stripped of her self-esteem. But Jonas seemed to have lost interest in her, other than a residual vindictiveness. Her business fell to practically zero.

Dr. Shulman had miraculously not fallen for Jonas's "clarifications" and became her only shoulder to lean on. But, despite his encouragement, she was in despair.

One day he suggested she go on a mountain wilderness survival course in the northern part of the state. At first she refused.

"Look, Miriam. You love the outdoors. You're an excellent skier, you know the mountains. Maybe you've never done anything like this, but it's helped a number of my patients enormously. I've taken the course myself, so I'm not suggesting anything I don't know about. Your biggest problem now is learning to stand on your own again. Finding out within yourself that you can survive these past few years. You can flourish again, I promise you. You can take charge of your own life, Miriam my dear. You're strong. You can be happy again."

In the end, she agreed to go.

And met Jack.

NINE

JACK

Jack Merriman surveyed the group sitting on the ground in front of him and Bill Brokaw. It was Bill's course, really. Jack was here to instruct the rock-climbing part. His eyes rested on the small young woman with the odd, silvery hair. She slumped cross-legged, worrying a rock in her fingers, looking absolutely miserable. One of Aaron Shulman's people, he guessed. So many of them had that lost look. Or rather the few he'd had in the course. He'd only done this four or five times for Bill. He liked teaching and the course got him up in the mountains, away from the business in Phoenix. He needed to get away a lot since Joanna walked out last year, taking the girls with her.

He hadn't really been surprised about Joanna. She'd always hated the West. He met her when he did some graduate work at MIT and had been smitten with her fine-boned beauty and patrician manners. They had been married in Boston in an impressive Episcopal ceremony befitting the status of Joanna's blue-blooded Massachusetts family.

Joanna had tried. He honestly thought she'd tried. But she wilted in the baking Arizona sun, constantly lubricated her fine fair skin to combat the ravages of the parched air, and grieved for the fierce northern winters of the Atlantic coast, the fog, and the cool Cape Cod summers. Her delicate coloring seemed to bleach in the desert sun and made her seem colorless and over-refined. He fretted over her lassitude, attempted distractions to bring a spark, but in the end the southwest climate, the distance to her beloved Atlantic sea coast defeated them.

Joanna bore him two daughters—pale, rarefied replicas of their mother.

No, he hadn't been surprised that she'd left, despite both their tears. He still felt the loss, but knew that it had not been a happy union. He missed the girls, but admitted his visits with them back East didn't excite them all that much. Once his presents were opened they smiled sweetly and asked to be excused. He always left them with a heavy heart.

He found his gaze resting on Miriam.

The young woman turned an enormous pair of hazel eyes to him, frowned and bit the corner of her mouth. Jack felt a clunk in the pit of his stomach. He pulled his eyes away, squatted on his haunches and picked up a stick, tracing a small design in the sandy soil by the streambed as he listened to Bill's familiar opening remarks to the group.

"This course won't be easy, and I won't coddle you. That's not what you're here for. But you'll learn things you never thought you would, and accomplish things you never thought you could. I'll tell you this. You'll leave here a different person. Stronger. More at peace with yourself. It doesn't matter how many times I've come out here, I'm renewed. For whatever reasons you've chosen to be here, you will be, too.

"Now, we'll just go around and everybody tell your name and anything else you feel like. If you don't feel like anything else, that's okay, too. We'll get to know each other quick enough."

Jack watched Miriam as the group introduced itself, twelve in all. Some gave descriptions of what they did in their normal lives, but when it came to Miriam, all she said was her name. She was curt and she didn't smile.

"Miriam Laird."

Jack raised an eyebrow. Laird was a big name in Colorado. Was she one of those Lairds?

When they had all been introduced, Bill pointed to Jack. "That's Jack Merriman. He'll instruct you in the basics of mountaineering and rock climbing. In your solo exercise there'll be a time when you'll need those skills."

Several in the group looked around uneasily.

"Now." Bill rubbed his hands together. "Let's get down to business. In your five-day exercise at the end of the week, you'll have a rope, some carabiners." He held up an aluminum snaplink. "And a knife, a few matches, water purification kit, and that's it. With those you'll have to find your way out of the wilderness area, feed and shelter yourself."

There was a murmur and some laughter.

"Don't get all excited. After a week you'll know how to do it. Now. Food. It's the least important of the three needs for survival. The first is water, the second is shelter. If it's extremely cold, that moves to first, but it's not that cold yet, so you'll be fine. The body can survive about ten days without food, three without water—in the desert, less, but humidity is high here, so you should have your three days. Get mighty thirsty, though, before that's up.

"There's no lack of food. It's our prejudices against what's edible and what's palatable. The line will begin to blur depending on the desperateness of your situation. You really can eat bugs." He grinned. "I can promise you that you will."

A groan swept over the group.

~ * ~

After a couple of days the group split into two sections and Jack took six for the mountaineering work. Miriam was in this first section. She'd been attentive and quick to learn, but she was stand-offish and abrupt when people made advances to her. She was viewed as unfriendly and wasn't liked.

One day Jack had them working on a rock face, teaching the technique of belaying, when climbers are roped together for mutual safety. Jack instructed them in twos, leading them up the cliff face, a fifty foot, nearly vertical limestone wall. They had spent the morning learning the techniques of climbing and rappelling, the method of quick descent down steep rock by sliding down a rope. He was leading the last twosome up, Miriam and a thirty-six year old furniture refinisher from Sante Fe. Miriam was third on the belay line and last up. She didn't seem to be paying close attention to signals and Jack shouted at her a couple of time to answer her position. When she pulled herself over the top, Jack snapped at her, his voice angry.

"Dammit, Miriam, this is a cooperative group effort. When I tell you to listen for signals, I mean it. You've got to let your buddies know where you are."

Miriam stood against the sky on the lip of the cliff, the nylon rope in her hand. "Fuck you," she said, and slipped over the side, rappelling swiftly down the sheer rock face, jerking the anchor rope sharply.

Jack stood, stunned. The rest of the group looked at each other uneasily, murmuring among themselves whether he was going to do something about this sulky, unlikable member.

He steeled his chin, adjusted the rope at his waist and went over the edge, his face grim.

When he scrambled to his feet at the bottom, Miriam was disappearing into the trees. He took off after her, cursing under his breath. What in the hell was she thinking of? She could have killed herself back there.

Her red T-shirt would flash through the shadowy pine and aspen woods, then disappear again, but he knew he gained on her, even as quickly as she ran. When they came into a clearing he was almost up with her. He lunged at the red shirt and brought her down to the ground, knocking the wind out of her. He flipped her on her back and glared down at his gasping quarry, his own breath coming hard.

"What in the hell do you think you're doing? You could have killed yourself with that dumb stunt back there. I've just about had it with you, you spoiled little bitch. Everybody's been tip-toeing around you for three days and we're all sick of it. Nobody said you had to enjoy this, but it was one of the agreements. Ironclad. You follow the rules. Not some of the rules, or the ones you feel like, or think you agree with. All of the rules. Do you understand me? And when I'm in charge, you'll do what I say or you can pack your gear and get out." His voice was strangled with rage. "Today."

Miriam still struggled to catch her breath, but she mouthed the words as her chest heaved under his weight. "Fuck you."

Her eyes reflecting the blue sky turned them to yellow green as they blazed back at him.

He glared down at her and the only sounds were the heavy rasps of their breathing. He felt her struggle underneath him and he realized he was probably crushing her. She wasn't very big. The movement unleashed a hot rush at his vitals. In a blind reflex he crushed his mouth to hers, bruising, muttering against her lips—"Yeah, that's just what I've been wanting to do to you since the day you walked in here."

Her breath came in dry sobs as she jerked her face away.

With enormous effort he calmed the roar in his ears, knowing if he didn't he'd have her clothes off and going at it as hard as he could. God, he wanted her.

Slowly he rolled off her and sat up, his arms still around her, brushing twigs from her hair. She started to cry, long, jagged scrapes of some untold grief. He held her until her sobs lightened, then finally stopped.

He tipped her face up. "Where'd you learn to talk dirty that way?"

She snuffled. "My father."

He raised an eyebrow. "Your father?"

A hiccup. "He was a high school principal and he had to be so nice during the day he just let it go when he got home." She gave a watery grin. "It kinda rubbed off on me, I'm afraid."

He held her and rocked her for a while longer. "We'd better get back. The others'll be getting worried."

"Yeah. Worried that you didn't kill me."

"Well, spanked, maybe."

She winced and he felt the recoil in her.

"I'm sorry. That wasn't funny."

Miriam moved away from him and stood up slowly, her eyes averted, brushing pine needles and leaves from her jeans. She shrugged. "Don't worry about it."

But he noticed the tears starting down her cheeks and wondered. And it did worry him. What made her so hostile? Had she been raped? Beaten?

~ * ~

Night in the forest is never still and Jack lay in that limbo between waking and sleeping, listening to the occasional night bird, the whisper of water over rocks, the soft, mysterious sounds of nocturnal creatures. The group camped in a clearing a little way from the stream and the dark shapes of the sleeping bags were faintly outlined in the little light that came from the quarter moon, now just visible over the treetops.

He started at the faint rustle near his bedroll. Miriam, her face obscure with the moon behind her, sat on her heels watching him, her hands nervously toying with a small rock. When she saw that he was awake, she caught her breath softly. He raised himself on an elbow, wishing he could see her face.

She began to speak, swallowed, and began again. "What...what you said...back there. You know. On the ground. Did you mean that?"

He could feel her tension. "Yes."

"I just wanted you to know that…that I would like that."

He started to reach for her, but she put out her hand. "I mean, after this." She gestured at the surroundings. "I…I don't think it would be a good idea for now. I guess. You know. Here."

"I guess not," he said, not at all sure that it wouldn't be a wonderful idea.

"I live in Denver." Her voice sounded breathless in the dark.

"I know."

"Oh?"

"I asked Bill."

"Are you ever…in Denver?

He grinned. "Why as a matter of fact I have to be there as soon as this is over."

Her fingers feathered his face and then she slipped away.

Jack lay back down slowly and crossed his arms under his head. He felt wonderful. A nice little ache in the balls. He didn't think he wanted to wait until Denver at all.

TEN

MIRIAM

The helicopter dropped Miriam off about ten in the morning to begin her five day wilderness solo. True to what Bill Brokaw had told the group, all she had was a knife, some waterproof matches, a rope with a couple of yards of webbing to anchor a rappel line, several carabiners, and finally, one of those ceramic water filters. The last was a grudging accommodation to the state of the water in even the remotest wilderness regions of the world. Bill had recited the horrific microbes and parasites infesting crystalline springs, as well as muddy ponds and fast-moving streams and rivers everywhere. There lurked terrible sounding diseases like giardiasis, amoebic dysentery, hepatitis, salmonellosis. They had all promised fervently that they would never, never not use their filters so they would all be in robust health when they got back to tell everybody how wonderful he was. Everybody laughed, but the point was made.

Each of the survivalists also wore a tracking device, so in the event somebody really got lost, he or she could be traced easily. The devices were space-age technology—Global Positioning Systems, or GPS receivers, that transmit three simultaneous signals from U.S. satellites to fix the user's longitude and latitude at a precise moment. Miriam fingered the GPS receiver attached to her belt. It was comforting, even though it wouldn't do anything to get her back to the base camp. The information went to Bill. She was on her own unless she got so hopelessly off-track that they had to come and get her. She was determined they wouldn't and took the simple map out of her pocket to look over casually, then stuffed it back in her pocket.

They'd been told that everyone beginning the solo exercises reacts differently to that first realization that they are alone. Some people scurry around immediately, setting to work on the course back. Others might panic and lose their way, swallowed in the trees and undergrowth.

Miriam sat down.

It was very peaceful in the clearing, with a sort of fine, downy grass carpeting the small area. The copter's rotors had flattened it and now it looked like a delicate green watered silk. The aircraft's noise had silenced the wildlife, but finally a small animal chittered, a chickadee called. Miriam looked up. A red-tailed hawk soared against the deep blue sky. The forest was mostly pine, some oak, and aspen. Their white trunks glistened as streaks of the morning sun filtered through the verdant canopy of the forest.

Miriam stood up and looked at her shadow, then walked around the edge of the clearing until she found a straight stick. She went to the center and picked up a fist-sized rock, then pounded the stick into the ground and carefully marked the end of its shadow.

Then she sat down to wait.

Under her scrutiny, small wildflowers began to make themselves noticed. She recognized, what was it—bistort? Bill said she could eat that. The roots and young leaves, okay to eat raw, but better boiled. Miriam smiled. She'd been here twenty minutes and already she'd found lunch. Not exactly gourmet fare, but she'd have to get used to that. Her eyes traveled to a pretty plant with red berries. Baneberry. Don't eat that, they said. Even a little bit. As few as six berries would make you very sick.

She saw valerian, which she could eat, though it smelled terrible and tasted worse. It was better if it was cooked. She spotted white phlox and yellow dog-toothed violets, daisy-like fleabane. Nothing to eat there.

This was fun. She got up and marked the shadow from her stick. With her finger she drew a straight line in the soft grass from the end of the old shadow to the end of the new. That line would be east/west.

She pulled the sleeve of her flannel shirt back to see her watch. She pointed the hour hand toward the sun, knowing that halfway between the hour hand and twelve would be south. All her findings agreed. After lining up landmarks she could see in the distance, she worked closer and closer to her position and marked them on her map. With luck she could keep her bearings. Her line back to base camp was almost due north.

Pleased, Miriam sat down and leaned back on her elbows. Roughly twenty miles from camp she would need to travel four or five miles a day over rough terrain—detours, up, down. It would be hard work to get that far every day. Not impossible, but Bill had been honest. They weren't being coddled.

Almost all American mountain ranges course north and south, so her route would be fairly obvious if she could familiarize herself with the peaks that could be seen over the treetops. She studied her map again, added a few more details. It was time to get started. She hadn't panicked. She would be okay.

~ * ~

Miriam coiled the rope over her shoulder; though the rope wasn't heavy, it would be likely to catch on things. She would need to have her hands free. She hooked it to the aluminum carabiner and clipped it to her belt, took a deep breath, squared her shoulders and moved into the forest. The trees closed around her, confusing her sense of direction.

Miriam went back to the clearing that now seemed a safe haven. She checked the trunks of the aspens, which were supposed to be darker on the north side. Was this one darker than that one? A film of perspiration sprang to her upper lip. Yes. If you didn't look directly at the pearly bark, but off to the side, it was easier to discern a deeper shading. It checked with her reckoning. With several means to check direction, she set off with more confidence.

Miriam took off her outer shirt. Hiking was hot work in midday though it cooled very quickly in the mountains in late afternoon. Her plan was to stop around four to make camp. How long would that take? She didn't want to run out of daylight this first night, before she'd made her shelter. The fewer mistakes made the first day would pay off in the end. That was the important thing they'd been told—be careful, pay attention and don't make any major mistakes the first day.

About three o'clock she came to a small stream and was tempted to make camp near it. But it was too early. She could catch a fish for her dinner, though, then push ahead and stay close to her planned schedule.

The fish proved to be harder than she imagined. Miriam could see the little speckled trout darting by, but they were elusive streaks of silver, their tiny red spots winking at her through the glassy water. At one point she jumped up in exasperation and shouted, "You motherfucking little bastards!"

In frustration she heaved a rock into the forest, loosing a flurry of protests from the local birds. Knowing it was foolish to waste her energy on such outbursts, she crouched down and tried to calm her temper. Patience. Lots and lots of patience. That's what was called for.

She spied a low hanging rock downstream. Stretched out on her stomach, she eased her arm down into the achingly cold water. She calculated she'd have some minutes before it would numb her hand into uselessness. Her fingers relaxed and gradually began making small movements. When the first fish nosed curiously against a finger she squelched the powerful urge to grab it. She became absorbed in the watery world around her hand and it was with reluctance that she told herself she would have to act soon or her hand would be too cold and clumsy.

It was almost easy when she concentrated. She'd just closed her hand and there it was. She quickly tossed the fish to the ground and hit its head with a rock. There was a moment of almost unbearable exhilaration that she'd caught her dinner, but when she looked down at the pretty fish that had been swimming so freely only moments before, tears stung her eyes.

"Oh, shit," she gulped. "Good old Miriam, great white fucking hunter."

Catching the fish had taken over an hour. She would have to make camp there.

She studied her situation. Night mists by the stream would be too damp. About twenty yards up the slope she spotted a rocky overhang. With a lining of leaves and pine boughs it could be made comfortable.

Miriam set about gathering the materials for her shelter, as well as the all-important kindling and firewood. Her dozen waterproof matches would have to last the entire assignment. If she used two each night, there would be four in reserve. The fifth night should put her back in camp.

She found some pitchy sticks under the pine tree that would make readily flammable tinder. She set about constructing her fire. She tugged an old log over toward her rocky shelter to keep her fire out of any wind and to help reflect its heat, then made a small teepee of kindling and tinder. She sat on her heels and regarded it carefully, suddenly feeling nervous. What if she couldn't get it going? She'd never done this before. Oh, she'd watched Bill and Jack, even been given matches to do it herself. But she'd needed more than a dozen to get it going and Bill had only said, "Now you see what you did wrong. Nurture. That's the name of the game. You must nurture a fire. Be patient and nurture your fire."

Right. Nurture. Miriam wiped her hands on her jeans and took out her matches. Hands shaking slightly, she struck one against a rock, sheltering it quickly with her hand and bending to the small pile in front of her, poking the small match into the little opening that held an old bird's nest and the pitch-scented sticks. The match went out.

"Shit!"

Miriam moved the rock over to the teepee, then stretched out on her stomach, the match in her hand only inches from the potential fire. She struck the match quickly and poked it into the tinder. It went out.

The string of her imprecations shrieked at the smoking perfidious match echoed back at her mockingly.

Miriam lay back down and rested her chin on her hands, glaring at the pile of sticks that looked less and less like a fire. What had she done wrong? Maybe she should get the match going first.

Holding her breath she struck the third match and tilted it, letting the tiny flame lick up the shaft. Tense and shaky she watched it burn, then holding her breath, she eased the match with great delicacy into the opening in the tinder. It caught slightly and she blew softly, willing it to burn. There was a curl of silvery smoke, then a tiny point of flame. It had caught, oh hot damn, it had caught. She breathed on it, then blew on it, exulting in each petal of flame.

Carefully she added a stick at a time, terrified that she would smother her fire, but it continued to burn, then grow. She became aware that her face was fiercely hot, that concentrating so hard she'd stayed too close. She moved away and sat Indian-style, admiring her handiwork, feeling a goofy kinship with the long-ago-men who had discovered fire.

Miriam cleaned the fish, trying to keep her stomach quiet at the warm slipperiness of its entrails, then threaded flesh along a skewer. When the little trout looked done she controlled the urge to jump up and down. My God, she'd done it. She'd caught and cooked her dinner over a fire she'd built herself!

The fire burned low, but Miriam had stacked wood to replenish it. Full night had fallen when she went down to the stream, tempted to strip and take a real bath, but she was still uneasy in the woods and somehow didn't want to part with her clothes. Maybe tomorrow, though the thought of that icy water hitting her belly brought a shiver. She splashed her face and arms and feet, then washed her socks. They'd be damp still in the morning, but clipped to her belt they would dry. She wished they'd been allowed to bring more than one extra pair.

"Take care of your feet, folks," Bill had said. "They're what'll bring you home."

There were small patches of sky above the treetops and the stars seemed very close. An owl hooted. A night hawk screeched. Miriam lay on her back, hands crossed under her head, assessing her first day. Jonas and his world seemed like something from the remote past. Irrelevant. She knew she was on course, then worried that she might get overconfident. She would re-evaluate that in the morning. She had eaten, she had shelter. She had water, and wasn't worried that would be a problem. The area was full of mountain run-off streams and snow still dusted the high peaks. But she hadn't gone as far as she should have. And she'd used three matches. She must use only one tomorrow. She must keep her reserve of four in case it rained and she had difficulty starting a fire. Yes, tomorrow she would only use one match. She knew how to do it now. She hoped.

Relaxed and weary, she was still wakeful. A night alone in the forest was fairly daunting, though the past week had gotten her over her edginess at a lot of the night noises that sounded so spooky. It had been comforting to have other people nearby back at the camp. She knew Jack had moved his sleeping bag closer to hers, though he'd given no indication that their words the night she'd spoken to him had ever happened. But he always seemed near, and if her fingers fumbled something, his hands seemed always ready to guide hers, or touch her shoulder reassuringly. Unconsciously Miriam licked her lips.

She had tried not to look too much when Jack had his shirt off, but it was difficult. His back was broad, his chest covered with a mat of thick dark curls that Miriam wanted to rub her face in. Jonas had a skinny, hairless body that looked graceful in his elegant clothes, but with the exception of an oversize penis, he had an androgynous delicacy. Jack's almost overpowering masculinity had made her breathless on more than one occasion. He had warm brown eyes and a wide forehead, made wider because he was beginning to lose his hair. His mouth was wide, with a ready smile that had cut deep creases in his cheeks and made crow's feet around his eyes.

Before sleep began to steal over her, she thought about trailing her fingers through Jack's luxuriant pelt from his chest on down, across his belly and below. Maybe if things went well she would get back to base camp a day early. She was anxious to see him again. Well, of course it was doubtful that she could make up that much time, but it was cozy, lying here on her bed of pine boughs, with small pops and hisses from the fire.

Thinking about it.

~ * ~

The next morning, Miriam squatted at the top of the cliff and surveyed her situation, the dense wood behind her. A small gorge with a tumbling stream was about sixty feet below. Getting back to camp a day early was out of the question. She'd gotten into a box canyon yesterday and it had taken several hours to get herself straightened out. She knew the stream ran by the base camp. All she had to do was get down to it and follow it.

She stood. "Well, babe. Better get at it. It ain't gonna go away."

She paced along the rock table looking for a firm anchor to tie her webbing. The webbing would make a loop through which she could pass her rope, doubling it down to the foot of the cliff. When she reached the bottom, she could pull the rope down after her. She tossed the rope over and eased it to the ground, then pulled it up to see if she had enough rope to make a double line. It was nearly long enough she decided.

On close inspection, a needle of rock proved embedded and solid so she fastened the loop, anchoring it with a ring bend knot, then pulled the rope through the loop. Carefully she played the double line down close to the ground under the cliff. She backed up to the edge of the cliff and straddled the rope, bringing it forward over her left hip, across her chest and backwards over her left shoulder. She had made what Jack called a *dulfersitz,* a kind of sling to maneuver down a rock face.

The doubled rope now hung behind her. She grasped that with her left hand, the rope above with her right, for balance, then leaned backward on the rope, knees bent slightly, took a deep breath, and stepped off the cliff.

Miriam looked over her left shoulder to see where she was. The friction on her hip and shoulder became evident almost immediately, making her worry that the rope would burn through her shirt and jeans. Her heart pounded in her chest as she placed her feet against the rock, trying to remember not to get excited and go too fast. Heat radiated from the wall of rock and its warmth was comforting as she played the rope out in her hands, concentrating her mind on everything that Jack had taught them.

"Don't hurry. You might lose contact with the wall and dangle. You can correct it, but it's scary. Watch, watch, watch where you're going!"

She came to the end of the rope about fifteen feet off

the ground, a little farther than she expected. She'd used too much rope anchoring it to the rock.

There was nothing to be done. She hung momentarily, then slipped off the rope, careful to hold on to one end, pushing off the rock face in order to fall free.

She hit the ground with an uncomfortable smack and rolled quickly, hoping she hadn't damaged anything. She banged her head on a rock and saw streaks and stars before she came to a stop, vaguely aware of damp, sandy soil under her cheek, the watery murmur of the stream very near. Still gulping for air she thought she'd just lie there for awhile and relish the thought that she'd just rappelled down a sixty foot rock face.

The self-congratulation passed and her breathing calmed. She groaned and sat up.

Jack was crouched beside her, his head cocked. "You sure know how to scare the hell out of a guy."

Her mouth dropped open.

"Close your mouth. You okay?"

She nodded, eyeing him carefully. "What are you doing here?"

"Waiting for you." He grinned. "We keep an eye on our people."

"You *follow* us?"

"Well, not exactly. Just check on you from time to time."

"I see." She remembered her various naked bathings and splashings after she'd gotten over her reluctance that first day. After she felt relaxed in the woods. "You must get to see an awful lot of interesting stuff," she said, her words more huffy than she felt.

His eyes crinkled. "The best."

Her voice was cool. "I'm not sure that that's ethical."

"Oh, come on. I'm teasing you. We follow you with the tracers. Know pretty much where you are, how good you're following the map. I got uneasy when I saw you headed for this cliff. I didn't want you attempting anything this high. But I knew if you got here you'd do it. I hate to say it, Miriam, but you can be kinda...um... rash. Turned out I was right."

He reached for her hand and helped her to her feet.

She pulled out of his grasp and stepped back. "Well, it was sweet of you to worry about me being rash and all. But I'm all right." She studiously brushed herself off.

Jack stood, his thumbs hooked over his belt loops, then stammered. "Uh, well, you're okay then. I guess I'll be heading back. You've only got a little way to go. Camp here tonight, you'll have a short hike in the morning."

She glanced up at the sky. "What about you?" The sun had dropped and dusk was coming on.

"Oh, I know my way in the dark. I'll get back to camp tonight."

Miriam rubbed her boot in the sand, making a small square. "Oh."

"You've done a good job."

"Thank you. I've enjoyed it. I think."

He laughed. "Good. Well. See ya."

He turned to go.

"Jack!"

He turned back

"Uh, well...I mean...wait. Maybe you don't need to go right away? I'm...I'm good at catching fish. Would you like to...uh...stay for dinner?"

His slow grin made her feel fluttery somewhere around her pancreas.

"Why, thank you. I'd like that a whole lot." They stood smiling at each other. "I know where there are some wild strawberries," he said finally.

He sat back from the stream and watched her catch the fish, admiring her adroitness. He knew she was proud of her ease at making camp. She didn't want him to help her build the fire.

"It wouldn't be fair, you know. I'm supposed to do it all by myself..." She smiled. "...or I won't graduate with honors."

But he did help her gather moss and pine boughs. By the time they'd arranged the branches, both of them were strung taut with expectation. It was fully dark and the fire turned their faces a soft bronze. They were self-conscious on their knees, not knowing how to stop fiddling with the pine boughs that they both knew to be their bed.

He touched her shoulder and turned her face to him. "Miriam, I lied to you. I came here because I wanted to make love to you tonight. I haven't been able to think of anything else."

"I know," she whispered, her eyes looking somewhere beyond his left ear.

"Waiting to find you in Denver seemed like such a terrible waste of time."

His voice was rough and made her catch her breath. Her eyes moved to his face. "What if I hadn't asked you to stay?"

He grinned. "I thought you probably would."

"Yes." Had she even made a sound as she said it?

He reached up and touched her face, tracing a finger around her eyes and then her mouth. She held her breath and her eyes closed and she was filled with relief when his mouth closed on hers, warm and soft and sure.

He made love to her gently, sensing she had been wounded, and he trembled with restraint, though when he came it was explosive.

She burrowed against him, right in her expectations. How his chest would feel under her cheek. "Jack?"

"Mm?"

"When we make love again, I'll...it will be...fine for me. I was nervous. I won't be the next time."

He squeezed her. "Well, we've got all night to get the hang of it. I been kinda out of practice."

She lay encircled in his arms. He had known just the

right words to say. As she thought about it, he had from the very beginning. When she'd rappelled down the cliff and run from him, he'd chased her, pulled her to the ground, lay on top of her and given her hell, but he hadn't frightened her. He'd held her while she cried and the time with Jonas faded. She had thought she could never be with a man again, and Jack had made her forget in a few short days. She smiled to herself. Some "never."

After a while he got up and put more wood on the fire.

He came back and knelt between her legs, his eyes traveling over her.

She squirmed under his scrutiny. "You're embarrassing me."

"You shouldn't be embarrassed. Not the way you look." He reached out his hand. "I thought your white hair was natural."

"Um, well, it is." Her hand fluttered to the hair at her temples. "It just didn't change anywhere else."

Jack stroked her gently. Her tension drained away and she closed her eyes. Her fingers curled around the pine boughs. Distantly she heard the fire crackle and could smell the ignited pine pitch.

The damp night air cooled their sweat-drenched bodies.

"Is this what they mean by rutting?" she mumbled against his shoulder.

"Ah. Are you referring to the sexual excitement of the male deer? As in: The stag is in rut? Biology 101. I don't think it applies to the doe. To me? Well, Professor Merriman says yes." He nuzzled her neck. "I feel very staggish. Good of you to notice."

"Leaves and pine needles are stuck all over me. I feel like I should go splash in the stream. Wanna go?"

"Yeah, let's do that, Pinto. In a minute." He kissed the top of her silvery head.

She looked up at him. "Pinto?"

She felt a rumble in his chest. "I had a black and white horse once…"

She buried her face. "Don't ever call me that in front of anybody or I'll die. I'll know exactly what you're thinking."

He whooped. "And you'd be right. I'll find this very hard to forget. You want to do it again?"

"Well…yes."

"Then I better not freeze my balls in the stream."

ELEVEN

CHRISTINA

"What time will you boys be home?" Christina asked the two Davids. "Is it a doubleheader today?"

"Yeah," her husband answered. "We're going to try to get in that game we missed with the Yankees because of the storm last week." He tossed off his orange juice and put the glass in the open dishwasher. "C'mon, Davey. We'll be late. Go get your glove." David, Jr.'s eleven-year-old memory was selective. He might set off to play baseball and remember his cell phone but forget his bat and glove.

Christina took the orange juice glass from the dishwasher and rinsed it under the faucet, then replaced it. "Are you pitching today, darling?" she asked her son, now absorbed in a chocolate and coconut cereal. She'd weakened and bought it because he whined so piteously in the store that people had begun to give her disapproving looks. He'd be better off eating the box, she thought.

"Billy Bentham is starting, but I'll probably have to go in relief and pull the game out," he said importantly. "Only had one day's rest, too."

Christina looked at David. "I thought he was supposed to have at least two."

David looked defensive. "We're getting close to the

playoffs, Christina. Every game counts."

"If your arm feels sore, you make Daddy let you quit, do you hear, Davey?"

He rolled his eyes at his father. "Sure, Mom."

Male collusion, Christina thought. Davey would pitch today if his arm was falling off.

David Senior looked his watch. "Come on, Davey. Eat the rest
of that mess and finish your juice. It's our turn to line the field. Did you remember to wear your cup and jock strap?"

"Daaaad!"

His father gathered up the baseball paraphernalia. "Davey, take the bats. Get the water bottles out of the fridge in the garage. Okay, everybody .We'll be back about two, I expect. You going to Pilates class?" His eyes traveled over Christina's jogging bra top and bicycle shorts.

"Mm hm."

"I hope you don't have an accident. Those outfits get smaller every year. Especially in the ass."

Christina frowned and glanced at her son. "David!"

David Junior snickered.

Caroline looked in the kitchen door, her voice impatient. "When's Mrs. Cartwright picking me up, Mama? You know Kay hyperventilates if I don't have the horse tacked up right at nine." Then she added, "And don't forget I have to have a check for a hundred and seventy-five dollars for Moonmist's new shoes."

David groaned, "Sometimes I think I get up in the morning just to support that horse. What in the hell does the guy put in those shoes? Platinum?"

"Moonmist needs *corrective* shoes," Caroline said patiently.

"Mrs. Cartwright'll be along. Don't forget the new reins." Christina rummaged in her handbag for her checkbook.

"My God, Mama. You always think I'm going to forget

stuff. I'm not David."

"I know you're not and don't say 'my God.' It's not attractive in a young girl. There's Mrs. Cartwright now. I'll see you about noon or so." She tucked the check in Caroline's back pocket and gave the heavy blonde ponytail an affectionate tug as she followed Caroline to the front door.

~ * ~

It was after ten when Christina got home from her Pilates class. She and Lupe made out a shopping list. They were having a few couples in for dinner that evening. Just casual, but it was really for close friends to meet Jenks Jameson. Ting Cartwright was getting serious about the handsome black man and it seemed the friendly thing to do for her friend. Arnaud was doing the food and his staff would come this afternoon to set up tables around the pool. Martinez would see to the flowers. She hoped it wouldn't get windy, always a possibility in July. And she hoped the misters would make it cool enough.

"You'd better stop and put gas in the Jaguar, Lupe. Take the Texaco card. Oh, and I forgot to put Campari on the list. Get a bottle, will you? It's what Mrs. Cartwright drinks, though I can't imagine why. It looks like the red medicine you put between your toes for ghastly funguses, and tastes worse."

"Some people might say that about whisky and gin," Lupe said mildly, adding to the list.

Christina laughed. "Touché."

Lupe was a widow with grown children. She'd come to work for them ten years ago. David was putting two of her daughters through the university in Tucson. He'd set her son up in a business decorating hotrod cars and low rider trucks. Lupe worshipped the whole family but it didn't stop her from making droll comments about their activities.

After Lupe had gone Christina went upstairs and peeled off her workout clothes, then absently pulled a bikini from a closet section of swimming wear and pulled it on.

"Rosie! Gil!" She stepped out of the bedroom door onto the wide deck as the golden retrievers tumbled out the door. Rosie had had the foresight to snatch up a tennis ball from the basket by the door and dropped it at Christina's feet. She stopped the ball before it rolled down the curving stone steps and gave it a wide toss down into the pool. The dogs were a gold blur as they hurtled down the curving steps and sailed into the crystal aquamarine water.

Christina laughed. Gil got the ball, of course. Rosie always let him have it if there was only one. Gil had established himself as alpha dog when they were only puppies.

A small waterfall spilled into the square, tiled, zero-edge pool on a deck lower than the house, blasted out of the mountain rock, overlooking the valley. Christina walked to the end of the diving board, gazed for a minute at the view she never tired of—the papier-mâché like McDowell and Superstition Mountains to the north and east, planes landing and taking off from Sky Harbor Airport and the White Tank Mountains to the south. She dove into the water. After twenty laps, she got out and threw a raft into the water and collected an armload of tennis balls from the deck.

"Game time, guys," she called, but the dogs were already quivering with excitement.

Christina took off her bikini top and threw it over a deck chair, jumped into the water and wiggled onto the raft, stretching out on her stomach. She floated around lazily, tossing balls to the dogs. It was their favorite game and they were in and out of the water barking with delight.

She flipped over onto her back. The warmish water felt silky on her skin. She reminded herself to turn on the aerator to cool it off. Idly she continued the game with the dogs, enjoying the sun on her body. The heat felt good. It had been a hard workout this morning. She dozed.

Dimly she realized the tone of the dogs' barking had changed. More excited. Was Lupe back already? She opened her eyes and saw Sev Justus leaning on the wall that surrounded the pool, his head on his arms, grinning at her. She sat bolt upright on the raft, which promptly folded in half and dumped her in the water. It floated away, leaving her treading water and sputtering. She dragged her hair out of her eyes and swam to the edge of the pool where there was some cover.

She sputtered in her anger. "How long have you been there?"

"'Bout ten minutes." He hadn't moved and was still grinning at her.

"Ten minutes! That's rotten of you. A gentleman wouldn't...stand there... staring at somebody like that without warning them. Skulking around like, like a...a...."

He roared at this, his white teeth gleaming in the sun. "You might take a poll asking for words to describe me. 'Gentleman' probably wouldn't come up with a great deal of regularity." He beamed at her. "I was enjoying the splendid view...of the valley from here."

She glanced helplessly at her bikini top, dangling on the arm of the deck chair.

He followed her glance, and grinned even more broadly. Slowly he took his elbows off the wall and disappeared. She heard the gate unlatch and then he was walking over to the deck chair. He was dressed for tennis and the sun dazzled off his white shirt and shorts.

Rosie and Gil were beside themselves with this new diversion. They barked and wagged and panted. "Good boys." Sev scratched their wet ears then threw a ball in the water. Gil sailed into the pool and Sev looked for one to throw for Rosie. After a minute of this, he casually walked over to the deck chair, picked up the bra and strolled over to where Christina was clinging to the side of the pool.

"I guess this was what you wanted." He dangled it over her.

She hugged her arms over her breasts, glaring up at the

heavily-muscled, darkly-furred legs, and then up to the amused black eyes.

He lowered the bra and she snatched it awkwardly, trying to keep her breasts covered, then struggled to get the brief top on under the water. She was all thumbs and the hook kept sliding through her fingers.

"Oh, for God's sake, Christina. Come on. Get out. I'll hook it for you before you drown."

"Why don't you just go away!"

"Well, now, I can't. You've got to sign something."

"Just put it in the kitchen. I'll figure it out."

His face was sincerity itself. "Why, as your legal advisor I couldn't let you sign anything without me explaining it. I'd be remiss if I didn't make sure you understood it perfectly."

She knew he wouldn't go. He was enjoying himself too much. Mad and miserable, she swam over to the steps and clutched the bra together in the back. She felt the bikini bottom slip, but she didn't have a hand to tug it back up.

"Turn around. I won't look."

"It's a little late now for gallantry, isn't it?" she hissed through clenched teeth.

He chuckled.

She tossed her head and turned, tan and slippery in the bright sun.

She could feel his breath on her back as he hooked the suit. "There now. All covered up. Aren't you going to ask me in?"

"You are in." She flounced toward the steps to the balcony that ran the length of the house.

"Got any coffee?" he called after her.

She paused, not turning, knowing his eyes were all over her. She gritted her teeth. "There's some nice bitter stuff left over from breakfast probably. Help yourself." She wished she weren't wearing her briefest bikini and what in the hell was he doing here anyway, damn him, on a Saturday morning? She stifled the instinct to tug the bikini down over her derrière.

In her dressing room she jerked a white terrycloth robe of David's out of the closet and wrapped herself in it. She glanced in the big wall mirror, touching a hand to her wet hair. *I look a sight. Well, too bad. I wasn't expecting company.* She wished she could slick on lip-gloss, but that would make it look like she cared.

Barefooted, she went down to the kitchen. Sev was rummaging around in the refrigerator. He poked his dark head out. He had an apple in his mouth.

He mumbled something that sounded like, "Starving." He bit into the red apple and strolled to the breakfast corner and sat down at the smoked glass table.

Her voice dripped with sarcasm. "Are you sure I couldn't make you some breakfast?"

"Hey, that'd be great! Thanks."

She clenched her teeth. "Would an omelet do? Waffles, perhaps? Soufflé? Crêpes? A quiche?"

He closed his eyes in thought. "Waffles…hmm. No, omelet, I think. Yes. An omelet would be perfect, since it's so close to noon."

"I'm so glad. Would cheese be all right? Mushrooms, perhaps?"

"Just cheese, I think. I really don't care for mushrooms with my eggs."

"Just cheese, I think. I don't really care for mushrooms with my eggs," she mimicked throwing open the big built-in refrigerator door. She pulled out the eggs and cheese. "It's Wisconsin cheddar. Is that all right?"

"Great."

"Do you care for chives? Fresh dill?"

His eyes closed in ecstasy. "Christina, you spoil me. Let's see. Both, if I may."

She padded over to the back door and disappeared. In a

minute she was back with a handful of dill and chives. She made her face expressionless as she chopped the greens. She bent and pulled open a cupboard door, extracted a pan, and slammed the door shut with her foot. The pan clattered onto the stovetop. Two tablespoons of butter slapped into the pan and began to sizzle as the rich aroma filled the kitchen. She whisked the eggs in a bowl. Sev continued to smile while she grated the cheese and poured the eggs into the pan.

"I have Perrier. Tomato juice? With a touch of lemon? Perhaps you'd prefer lime? Or would you like me to squeeze some fresh orange juice for you?" Her voice was murderous.

Sev gave her a look of wide-eyed innocence. "You'd really do that for me, Christina?"

She grimly got four oranges out of the refrigerator, cut them in half and yanked the juicer out of its corner on the counter. "Some people like ice. Some don't. Would you like ice? I could strain it if you don't like it pulpy. We want it to be *just* as you like it."

He tipped his chair back against the wall, his eyes half-closed. "I love ice." He licked his lips. "And pulpy," he whispered.

She could hardly stop from grinding her teeth. "Cubes or shaved?"

"Shaved, please."

Christina flipped the switch on the icemaker and ice ground noisily into the crystal glass. She poured the orange juice over the ice, walked over and handed it to Sev.

He made a silent toast to her and drank. "Ah, nothing like fresh orange juice after a tennis game, don't you think, Christina? All those electrolytes, right?"

She didn't answer, but walked over to the stove and flipped the omelet, glaring at it, willing the eggs to be done. "You'll want toast with that, of *course*. Sourdough, whole wheat, rye, or English muffins? I also think there are some blueberry muffins left. I'd be *more* than happy to warm those for you."

"Oh…let me think. English muffins. Yes. English muffins toasted would be perfect. On the light setting. With blueberry jam, if you've got it."

"I have plum," she said evenly. "Would that do? Or strawberry. Or marmalade?"

"Why, I haven't had plum in a long time. My mother used to make it when I was a boy. Plum would be good."

"Somehow I can't picture you as a boy. Or having a mother."

Sev looked taken aback. "Christina, I think you've hurt my feelings."

"Oh? You have feelings? Salted or unsalted butter?"

"Getting a little bitchy, are we? Unsalted, please."

"I have been provoked." She pulled the English muffins out of the toaster, burning her fingers in the process. She gripped the counter, ready to explode. Why had she allowed him to goad her into this ridiculous charade? Angrily she slapped butter on the muffins, took the glass pot of jam from the refrigerator, slammed the door with her hip and banged the muffins and jam down in front of Sev. She slid the omelet from the pan, got silver out of the drawer with a clatter, yanked a linen napkin from a cupboard and set the table.

"I apologize about the provoking because this looks wonderful! Sure you don't want anything?" Sev rubbed his hand together with a jovial enthusiasm that made Christina want to throttle him.

She poured herself coffee and leaned against the counter and glared at him over the rim of the cup. He ate at a leisurely pace, savoring each bite. He could have been dining in some elegant hotel. At last he leaned back and sighed.

"That was delicious."

Silently she walked over with the pot and poured him a cup of coffee, then went back and leaned against the counter. He watched her as he tipped his chair back, the cup in his hands. She could see the corners of his mouth quivering.

Christina spun around and busied herself, moving dishes around the counter. But she couldn't stop the pinpoint of laughter that had started to bubble up in her chest. She tried to swallow it and maintain her sulk, but it got the best of her. Helpless, she started to laugh.

When she turned, tears were starting down her cheeks. "All right, Sev. Why are you here? Skulking."

He was wheezing, doubled over. "Christina," he sputtered, "Again I do apologize. I've really been pulling your chain. I couldn't believe it when you let it go so far. I was almost sure you'd dump the orange juice on my head." A fresh sputter of laughter shook him. "I don't know what got into me. Truly, I wasn't spying on you for ten minutes. Well, two, maybe. I'm not that strong. Anyway, David needed some papers dropped off on the Trailway's deal. You have to sign, so he told me to bring them to the house. I guess I've been kinda rotten, but breakfast was delicious. Are we friends again?"

"You really are a bastard, you know."

"Well yes, but other than that. Friends?"

"Bastard."

"Aw, c'mon. Friends?"

"Oh, all right. Friends. But you're still a bastard."

He grinned. "Oh, I know that. Shake on it."

He held out his hand then, and she felt she had to walk over and take it. His fingers were tight against her palm too long, until she tugged away and backed up to the counter again.

"For the record I had a wonderful mother."

"That wasn't very nice of me."

"No." He watched her for a moment. "Hallie wonders what to wear tonight," he said at last.

She cleared her throat. "Oh... casual. Tell her I'm wearing cocktail pajamas."

"What in the hell are cocktail pajamas?"

"She'll understand."

With relief Christina heard the dogs bark and the car pull into the garage. The two Davids talked excitedly as they came up the stairs. She smiled. "They must have won."

~ * ~

Later, after she took a shower, she'd stood in front of her full-length mirror, trying to see herself objectively. She remembered Sev standing over her as she held the side of the pool. She stared at her reflection and turned slowly to see her backside. How had she looked to him? She saw herself flush at the thought of his eyes going over her. Had she truly been angry? Or had it been mixed with something else? Could she admit that Severance Justus had an unsettling effect on her? That he made her edgy and uneasy—and he knew it.

Sev was the go-to lawyer, they said, if you were guilty. He'd get you off. Several years ago he'd convinced a jury his client's young wife had fallen on a butcher knife thirteen times getting out of bed. The client walked away from a murder charge. That was only one instance of how persuasive, and yes, seductive the man could be. Everybody whispered about him. Some people said they'd seen him in other cities with women. But nobody seemed able to pinpoint his conquests. Like everything else about him, it excited speculation. Speculation. Sev Justus let people know only what he wanted them to know.

Sev had been Attorney General a few years back and it was thought he was politically ambitious. But he served for two terms and then went into mostly defense work—said to David once that he ran into a better class of criminal than the ones in government. But he was active in politics behind the scenes. He had gotten Jed Holliman elected governor. He also handled the legal work for Cross & Merriman Holdings.

Christina's thoughts were interrupted by the phone ringing in the bedroom, but David must have picked it up. She sat down at the vanity and unwrapped the heavy peach towel from her wet hair and became engrossed in pulling a comb through the tangle. She looked up to find David looking at her, a strange expression on his face.

"What's the matter?" she asked.

"That was Barney Bentham. Doug Purcell died this morning. The governor wants to appoint me to fill his Senate seat and be ready to run in November."

Christina slowly put the comb down and turned to stare at David. "What did you say?"

David had a bemused look on his face. "I told him yes."

Christina looked at him for a minute, then slowly turned back to the mirror to work on a tangle. "You didn't tell him you wanted to talk to me first...or anything? To see what I had to say?"

"Well, no. I thought you'd be thrilled. Really Christina, I'll call him back and tell him no. I can't do it if you object. I just didn't think you would."

"Oh, I don't, David. It's wonderful. Really." She smiled and turned to him again. "You just caught me by surprise. This does turn our lives upside down. Give me a chance to get excited."

David sat on the vanity and took her hands in his. "It still hasn't sunk in yet for me either, but think of the challenge, Christina. Washington. I've been thinking about running for office. We've batted the idea around for the last year."

Her eyebrow went up. "Oh? Who's we?"

"Sev. Barney Bentham, Jake Cartwright, Jed Holliman...the party bigwigs. Everyone agrees new blood is needed."

"How in God's name will you be able to run a campaign in November? It takes months, more, to get a campaign off the ground."

David's face was alive with excitement. "We can do it! It'll take work, and it will be hard on you and the kids. But we can do it. I know it. Doug Purcell's staff and war chest are intact. The campaign's mapped out. It's just that David Cross will be the candidate. I'm not unknown in the state."

Christina bent her head and kissed his hands. "Yes. You can do anything, David. I know that. And you're not to worry about me and the children. It will be a wonderful and exciting challenge. An opportunity for us, too."

After David had gone, Christina looked at herself in the mirror. She hadn't even dreamed that he'd considered running for office. He hadn't talked about it to her, not once. And there was a time he wouldn't have said yes without automatically asking her what she thought. It didn't seem that long ago.

~ * ~

Sev wasn't finding the morning easy to forget. He'd driven up to the house, hadn't gotten an answer at the door, which surprised him. Lupe was usually there. He'd heard the excited barking of the golden retrievers, so he'd wandered down the flower-edged walk that led from the driveway down to the pool. He'd been about to call out over the wall when he saw Christina in the pool, lazily throwing tennis balls to the dogs. She was topless, which was how she must sunbathe all the time because she was a smooth, even tan. Her legs were apart, trailing in the water off the sides of the blue raft. Her stomach muscles would tighten as she threw the tennis balls. He felt a stirring in his balls, knowing it was lousy to be watching her, but he couldn't pull his eyes away. He was just going to call out, but the dogs spotted him and dashed over to the wall.

He had enjoyed her confusion and it was all he could do to control the impulse when he walked over to the pool to give her the bra—to reach down and pull her out of the water, wet and slippery. She probably would have slugged him, but God, it would have been worth it.

He knew she was self-conscious walking up the steps to the second floor deck. Women. With a body like that. Her waist was small and her hips curved roundly down to sleek thighs and beautiful legs. There were deep dimples above her buttocks that made his teeth ache. And he knew he wouldn't forget those breasts in a long, long time. But he knew he wouldn't wait a long, long time. It was going to be fun making love to Christina Cross. He'd waited long enough.

It had been an effort to get his body under control before she came downstairs bundled up in that terry robe. He'd wondered what she'd decide to put on. She'd covered up from her chin to her polished toes, but he remembered what was under that robe.

~ * ~

The early June evening had cooled enough to be pleasant. The Cross's guests were lingering over coffee and liqueurs on the patio's rattan chairs and couches. The lights of Paradise Valley winked against the distant dark mountains. The scent of roses and spicy petunias hung in the air.

"Senator Cross. Has a nice ring to it." Jack grinned as he offered a toast of congratulations to his partner. The dinner party was winding down, the excitement over David's announcement had quieted and people were beginning to stir, thinking of leaving.

"Will you go to Washington right away?" Miriam asked.

"I think I have to. There are a couple of votes coming up that are important to the state. That's why Jed Holliman was anxious to appoint someone right away."

"Will you go, too, Christina?" Laise Brock asked.

"I don't think so. If David wins in November, then we'll have to find a house there, I guess. God, Laise. I don't know. I still am not used to the idea. And the kids are fritchy about leaving their friends. We've got all that to figure out."

People began to move around, making their goodbyes. Christina began to clear the coffee cups away. She'd told Lupe to go to bed, she would finish in the kitchen. Ting followed her out.

"Thanks a million for this evening, Christina. It meant a lot to me. Jenks, too. He was not convinced he'd fit in."

Christina looked up from putting saucers in the dishwasher. "Everybody loved him. He's such fun."

"I'm trying to talk Jenks into marrying me. What d'you think?"

Christina stood and put her hands on her friend's shoulders. "If it makes you happy. I can't say I can imagine what your life with Jake was like, but I would guess it's your turn to be happy."

Ting spun a wineglass in her fingers. "No, you can't imagine. I know nobody understands why I stayed with him." She shrugged. "But he was a good father, oddly enough."

"What do the boys think of Jenks?"

Ting laughed. "They think he's 'cool.' He manages some rock groups, you know. And he knows all about cars. What else matters at that age?"

"Well, then." Christina smiled, then her voice grew serious. "You'll set the tongues wagging, but I suspect you're already aware of that. That never bothered you much."

"Not really. Oh, Christina, I'm so happy. Jenks makes love to me with such ...*joy*. He's a lovely man. I've wasted a lot of years."

"Well, for what it's worth, tell Jenks for me that he ought to marry you."

Ting hugged her. "I will."

When Christina left the kitchen, she saw David emerging from the study with Preston Brock, Sev Justus and Barney Bentham. She knew David was going to ask Preston to be his finance manager for the fall election. It looked like he had said yes. She had asked the Brocks to come tonight on an impulse, surprised when Laise had called and said they would come. It had been a fortunate impulse. David always said that Preston Brock knew more about money than anybody else in the state.

The Benthams were the last to leave and Barney draped a heavy arm across Christina's shoulder. "Well, now, Christina, what do you think of this husband of yours? He's going to be a fine Senator, whatta y'say?"

Christina slid the arm off her shoulder. Barney had had too much to drink, as usual. Still, he seemed to be able to function. "Yes, yes, of course he is." She smiled and took David's hand.

TWELVE

LAISE

The sounds of students changing classes seeped under the door into the French classroom. Laise looked at her watch. It was 11:53, past time to end her French Civilization class. "That will be all for today. If you have any questions, save them for tomorrow. For any other reason, you have my office hours. *Á demain.*"

Several students milled around her. They always did even when she told them to save it or go to her office. She didn't mind for herself, but the Spanish professor who had the classroom after her got so huffy if it wasn't vacated promptly. He was out there now, glaring at her through the small glass window. A prissy little pink rooster. She sighed. God, their turf was so small. So little, to protect with such ferocity.

She gave him a dazzling smile as she inched out the door with her questioners still milling about her. "*Buenas dias, Señor Juarez. Cuanto lo siento.* So sorry."

Señor Juarez harrumphed and bustled into the room, flushed and prim. Laise suspected he longed for this semester to be over. The daily brush with her seemed to so unnerve him it must take him half the period to get himself together.

Classes were changing so the elevator was crowded. Laise exchanged pleasantries with several former students as the elevator poked its way up to the fourth floor. She stopped at the department office and collected her mail and messages. Not that there was ever anything interesting, but her box had to be bailed out daily to keep ahead of the junk.

The building was quiet. Language professors and students traveled in the summer, so there was no more than a skeleton faculty. She glanced through her mail as she made her way down the ugly beige and pea green corridor. Stuff from publishers mostly, touting the newest miracle edition of their books. And the books only got worse. Loaded with pretty colored pictures and diagrams. And, of course, every latest edition meant the student couldn't use the last one; all the used books were obsolete and the new books were invariably more expensive. She'd gotten so fed up she printed her own handouts and told the students not to buy the book. It didn't work. She was told by the dean in no uncertain terms the students had to buy the book and use it. She smiled politely, used her handouts, and apologized to the students about buying the book. It got around fast enough that the professor looked the other way if they didn't.

Laise unlocked her office and pitched the pile of mail into the banged-up green metal waste basket. It was a plain room, about twelve feet square, with scuffed, regulation yellow oak furniture. Laise had no inclination to personalize it other than hanging a few travel and art posters. Some of the wall space on either side of the window she'd filled with books. It had taken her three years to get that window. When one of the language professors died, she simply moved in. She had done it so quickly that bad feelings hadn't a chance to develop, though she still got a snide remark from time to time. Out the window the tops of a grouping of palm trees were just visible. She loved the un-tree-like clack and rattle of the fronds on those breezy pleasant days when she could open the window. Pigeons cooed throatily year round on the window ledge, but Laise found them rather fun to watch, particularly when the babies hatched. She'd even named a few: Captain Hook had a black patch around one eye; Boaz was black and white; Desdemona fluffed pretty silvery feathers; Lady Chatterley's plumage shone a reddish brown; Iago had a particularly deep coo. Laise's names were indiscriminate, since she didn't know how one told the difference between pigeon males and females. So far none had ventured into her office if the window was open.

Today everything was closed up against the fierce heat and July monsoon humidity. There promised to be a storm later and the palms hung still in the heavy air.

She slipped into the creaky desk chair and opened her notebook. She still had to write up the test she was giving Friday. There was a light tap on the door. "Ah. *Ciao,* Gianluca. *Come va?"*

He smiled and entered her office. *"Molto bene, grazie. E lei?"*

"Oh, everything's fine. I'm getting anxious for the semester to be over. It'll be good to get away. I'm suddenly very tired of summer."

"That's what I want to talk to you about. You're going to be in the south of France, no?"

"Yes. I'm meeting a couple of my old school friends in Cannes. We get together every year. I plan to leave as soon as I get my grades turned in after the final."

Gianluca leaned over the desk, his face animated. "Then you must come to visit me and my family for a few days. I have heard from my father. He wants me to come back for a short visit." He laughed. "At least it is a beginning. We have a villa near Portofino. Oh, it is so beautiful. You will love it there." He pushed away from the desk and paced excitedly in the small confines of the office. "It will be August. There are always many guests. We have dinner parties. Take the boat out. We have a fantastic boat. You could bring your friends as well. Yes. That would be perfect. Bring your friends and we will all be gay and carefree. Your friends and my family."

"Oh, Gianluca, I don't know. But I'm so pleased for you. Everything will be fine for you now, you'll see." Laise knew how much this overture from his father meant to Gianluca. He had told her how he loved the Arizona desert, crediting his father's Calabrian genes, but he longed for the rains and mists of the Piedmont, and he missed his family passionately.

Laise was familiar with northern Italy and had spent some time in Turin, or *Torino*, and Gianluca had gotten into the habit of dropping in to her office to talk about the lovely arcades of his native city, the shops, the *Piazza Vittorio Veneto*, with its massive buildings. The largest piazza in Italy. He talked dreamily of the great, narrow late-nineteenth century tower of the *Mole* and its lift that takes one almost three hundred feet above the city, with a view of the river Po and beyond, of trees, of villas, of countryside. This, of course, if it wasn't raining and a breeze had blown away the dense, industrial smog. It was all beautiful when the sun shone; but he loved the mists, too, and the low, slate gray skies.

"You'll come. I know you'll come. *Per favore!*"

"Well, it sounds wonderful, Gianluca, but my plans are a little unclear. My friends like to keep everything a little vague, so each of us can..."

Gianluca chortled with delight. *"Perfetto!* You can come. It's all settled. I will write to my mother."

He crossed behind her desk and spun her chair around, grabbing her by the shoulders. He bent his head quickly and caught her fully on the mouth. Laise started to laugh under his lips, expecting the impulsive kiss to end in a joke or a lighthearted remark. But it didn't end. His soft mouth covered hers, warm and sure. His hands moved up to her face and held it as his kiss became more urgent. Her astonishment gave way to an unexpected rush of heat. He pulled her up, pushing her against the edge of the desk with his hips. He covered her face with kisses, murmuring, "*Bellisima,* how I adore you, how I want you." Laise found herself responding to his urgency. Her lips parted, her breath came in gasps. He was hard against her legs. He pulled her skirt up and his fingers pushed aside her panties, probing, insistent.

She struggled back to reality. "Gianluca, please stop. The door is open. This is crazy."

Slowly he stopped his caresses. "You are right. This is not the place for us." His eyes burned into hers for a long moment, then he turned and abruptly left her office.

Laise leaned weakly against her desk, panting, her whole being centered at the hot ache where he had touched her. Her legs had turned to water. She fell into her chair and ran her fingers through her hair, over her hot cheeks. She couldn't erase the feel of his mouth on hers, and the possessive imprint of those tantalizing, demanding fingers that had brazenly known just where to touch.

Her breathing gradually slowed. Distracted, she gathered her notebook and bag. She couldn't bear to be in the office another minute.

It was just after noon as she left the building. The sun was a white-hot incandescence in the lapis sky. The mountainous afternoon monsoon clouds were beginning to billow on the horizon and the humidity was oppressive. The sodden air intensified her agitation, as sunlight danced around her and off her skin, a palpable presence. It shimmered off the olive trees just beginning to drop hard green fruit in anticipation of the dusky, lustrous deep brown crop of autumn.

Heat and glare radiated from the lot where she parked her white BMW. The broiling asphalt burned against the soles of her sandals and perspiration trickled between her shoulder blades and under her breasts beneath the soft white linen shirt.

He was waiting by the car. Her heart began to pound as her footsteps slowed. She walked toward him. He held out his hand.

"I will drive," he said.

She handed him her keys, avoiding his eyes. What in God's name was she thinking of? Had she lost her mind?

They drove to a small complex of garden apartments.

"Viva sola?" She barely recognized her voice.

"Yes, no one will interrupt us."

He parked the car, came around and opened her door. He held out his hand.

She knew she had a moment. A moment to make the decision. A pause to back away.

She looked up at him and took his hand.

As soon as they were inside they were in each other arms, all mouths and tongues, pulling impatiently at buttons and hooks and zippers and always his soft Italian words of love. He moved her through the small apartment and they fell together on the bed, his mouth everywhere. Then he was over her, his impudent dark eyes daring her to stop him.

Then he pushed into her roughly, possessing her with a certainty that swept her away. She had not known how ready she was for this and wrapped him in her long legs, meeting his plunging hips with her own.

~ * ~

Gianluca nearly sobbed with relief that she came so fast. He'd been ready to explode ever since he'd kissed her in her office; but he wanted her to love it. Wanted her to need him with the hunger that savaged him every time he thought of her.

He lay still, imprisoned within her legs, nuzzling her breasts. "Ah, Laise, *bellsisma, ciero.* I knew it would be like this. How I've wanted this. So long. From the beginning." He began to kiss her slowly.

Triumph soared through him as she sighed and he felt her arousal begin again. He struggled to tamp down his mind. He knew how to satisfy a woman. Reflect later on what he had won today, he told himself. Slow, he told himself. This woman would not be easy to tame if he pushed too far too fast.

Thoughts of bringing this rich American back as a prize to show his father receded as the heat in his loins took over.

~ * ~

She dozed on her back trying to figure out what this complication was going to do to her life. She certainly didn't feel regret; she'd never been made love to like that. This young Italian had played her with an incredible finesse.

There was a greenish cast to the light in the room when Laise awakened. The sun was losing to the afternoon storm clouds. Gianluca was leaning on an elbow over her, smug and smiling.

"I love your eyes. You have eyes like a tiger. Gold. Untamed. But I tamed them for a little while, *adesso?*"

"Now? Yes. Now I feel very tame." She smiled languidly and brushed a dark, damp curl off his forehead and traced her finger around the beautiful mouth that had seduced her back in her office.

"I love your hair. Flames. The weather makes it wild, too." He stroked her hair.

He was right. The humid weather made it unruly and their exertions made a tangle on the pillow.

"Here, too."

She caught her breath. She couldn't be, she thought, but she was ready for him again, throbbing for him.

He moved seductively. "I will make love to you again. And again. Then I will make love to you tomorrow. Over and over."

"Gianluca," she groaned. "This is…complicated."

"This is not complicated." He moved down over her. "This is very simple. I will make love to you every day."

She tried to twist away. "I'm leaving in two weeks. You're going away."

He held her hips. Her mind drifted away from impossibilities to the scorching immediacy between her legs and his hungry words.

"I will make love to you every day for two weeks. And then I will make love to you in Italy. I will…love making love…to you…in Italy. Say you will come to me in Italy. Say it. Say it, *bellisima.*" His rhythm was insistent. "Say it. Say yes to me. *Si. Si.*"

"I…"

"*Si…Si…Si.*"

"*Si…yes…yes…*

THIRTEEN

DAVID

It was eight o'clock in the morning and nine members of the team that would oversee David Cross's election to the United States Senate were assembling in the conference room of Merriman & Cross Holdings. It was a dramatic room, on the eleventh floor of the lavish Esplanade office complex on Camelback Road and 24th Street. One side of the room was a glass wall that looked at Camelback Mountain, Squaw Peak and the Phoenix Mountains directly to the north. The other walls were paneled in rosewood and hung with three large English paintings of horses, red-coated riders and dogs in elaborate gilded frames. A rich blue, red and gold Oriental covered the parquet floor under a fifteen foot walnut conference table.

Martha Banks, David's secretary, was serving coffee from a silver service on an antique credenza, as they began to gather around the conference table. There were: David; Jack Merriman; Barney Bentham, State Party Secretary; Preston Brock, campaign finance chairman; Severance Justus, campaign legal advisor; Ash Ford, pollster; Larry Dawson, press secretary; Jaime Carbajal, minority liaison.

David spoke as he pushed a button to lower a map of Arizona. "I think we can begin. Margot Jensen isn't here, but she said she'd be a little late. She had a meeting with the guy she wants to do the copy for the TV ads. Martha, let everybody get their own coffee. We need you for the minutes."

"Righto." Martha, small, with severely-cut black hair, had been with David and Jack for ten years. She sat and turned on her laptop.

David sat in the middle of the table. Jack sat at his right. David had asked him to be his campaign manager, much to Jack's surprise, and though he protested that he knew nothing about running a campaign, he was enormously pleased that David had that confidence in him. David had brushed aside Jack's misgivings, saying he needed him to keep Barney Bentham in his place. Jack had agreed. Nobody knew more about Arizona politics than Barney, but he could be an ass and he drank too much. Besides, it was better to run your own show. David could hire the experts; he needed a confidante to run things.

"As you all know, I've just got back from Washington. I've had a chance to look into Doug Purcell's office operation. He's got good people and things should go along without too much disruption. I'll be taking Martha with me on my trips back, and she can work with Doug's secretary until we can get a handle on things. If I win the election, there'll be time to work into some changes. Martha has consented to go to Washington in that event. Thanks again, Martha." He sat back in the big, high-backed leather chair and placed his hands flat on the table. "So. How do we go about letting the people of Arizona know David Cross should be their permanent senator?"

Jack took over. "Here's our thinking. David's got two votes coming up important to the state—the one on Colorado River water, the other the closing of Luke Air Force Base. All the work's been done on those. Our important objective now is to get David elected in November. Doug Purcell didn't face strong opposition. Cameron Brown was kinda a token candidate, but he'll be spending more money now, and pushing his advantages. He'll be strong in the rural areas. That's where we have our work cut out for us. Purcell never cultivated that vote and it dropped off more because he was ill and wasn't as vigorous in keeping fences mended."

Barney Bentham leaned forward. "We just need to get David known more. A lot of areas don't even know you're running, David. Hell, as far as that goes they might not even know Purcell's dead. We have to change that and the sooner the better. Have to get some early TV. That'll cost." He turned. "Sev? You're familiar with the disclosure laws. You getting David's affairs straightened out?"

Sev Justus looked up from a pad he was covering with elaborate doodles. "We've got a coupla months 'til deadline. I'm getting the blind trust set up. Don't worry. I'll make sure we don't break any laws. There are no big debts in his business and nobody's mad at him, far as I know."

"We've got to set up a campaign headquarters," Barney said. "Get you away from this ritzy office, David. Can't use Purcell's…you know…new man, new office."

The meeting wore on. Jaime discussed the minority vote. Margot Jensen came in and discussed the campaign literature and TV ads. Preston gave a financial report. One by one the staff left until there was only David, Jack, Barney, Sev, and Preston.

Barney cleared his throat. "While there are just the few of us here, I'd like to bring up a delicate matter. David, your appointment was sudden, and though I'm not saying it was an impulse of the governor's, there are a couple of questions that need to be asked." He shifted uncomfortably in the tall leather chair.

"What is it, Barney? Don't beat around the bush," David said.

"If we get deep into this campaign and somebody should come up with some killer something out of your past, we better know about it. You got anything that might cause any problems?"

"I don't think so. Like what? I haven't killed anybody, been in jail. I've gotten a speeding ticket or two..."

"You know what goes on now. The papers jump on anything. Ever gotten involved with drugs...even in college?"

"I tried pot once or twice...and, yes, I did inhale. Didn't like it. I was a jock. Football and baseball. Coaches would have killed anybody if they found out they used anything. And I wasn't interested. Got drunk some...off season." He shrugged.

"Pot we get away with these days. Got any problem with booze now?"

David felt a hitch of irritation that Barney Bentham would be quizzing *him* about booze. "No. I can take it or leave it."

"Sev handles your legal affairs. You're in business with Jack. Any disgruntled people out of the past who might get vindictive?"

"I know why you have to get into this, Barney, but you don't have to worry," Jack interrupted. "We really are honest-to-God honest businessmen."

"Legal affairs all on the up and up. David is a model citizen." Sev grinned.

"Now I live in the same town, and I've never heard any scandal, but I have to ask. Any trouble with the ladies?"

"Good God, Barney," Sev jumped in. "David's got a fine reputation in this town. Nobody's going to come out of the woodwork and accuse him of anything."

"Hey, settle down everybody. I gotta do this. It's routine. The press crucifies anybody these days."

"It's all right, Barney. You're quite right," David said.

Barney sighed. "Just for the record— anything anywhere you can think of? Your kids are almost too young to get you into trouble. Kids can drive you nuts getting arrested, drugs, raping girls, it's terrible—"

David cut in. "My children are no problem. I have no drunken brothers or shady cousins. My father is a judge back in Lansing. My mother is dead. My grandparents were all teachers or doctors. I have a nice, rather dull, ordinary family."

"And Christina?"

"Oh, for God's sake, Barney. Christina's raised money for three quarters of the charities in this town," snapped Jack.

"Okaaay, okay, okay. Just doing my job. We'll leave it at that," Barney said defensively. He leaned back in his chair, clearly relieved to have the discussion put to a close. "I'm sure you understand, David. If anything came up, we're the people who'd have to handle it. We have to know."

"Don't worry about it, Barney. It's a difficult responsibility for you. I'm not offended. You're just, as you said, doing your job."

Barney stood and rubbed his hands together. "It's going to be a great campaign. We can't lose that Senate seat. I'm very confident."

After they had all gone, David went to stand at the window, absently staring at Camelback Mountain. Funny, he thought, Sev jumping to my defense like that. I always thought he knew about that fling Hallie and I had. Apparently not. Well, it's certainly just as well. It was a while back and neither of us took it very seriously. It was just one of those things. Water over the dam.

FOURTEEN

LAISE

Laise closed the book in her lap and looked out of the window. The plane had just crossed the coastline of Normandy and would be at Charles de Gaulle in about forty-five minutes. She took the hot towel the flight attendant handed her, then fished a lipstick and mirror from her travel tote. She looked awful. She slicked a gloss on her mouth and snapped the mirror closed. It was the best she could do until she got a bath at the hotel and could start from scratch.

Her first class seat gave her as much room as any but her arms and legs were long and difficult to get in a comfortable position on a long flight. She and her tall seatmate spent the night bumping knees and elbows, muttering apologies.

The man had spent a lot of time on his laptop so Laise assumed he was some sort of businessman. He was good looking and had tried a bit of flirting during mealtimes, but Laise was too preoccupied with thoughts of the last two weeks, and besides, she never talked to people on a plane. One couldn't get away if the company proved annoying. It had been her experience that it generally did, though this man looked interesting. But, she had decided to keep to her rule. She had plenty to think about.

Out the window, the small patchwork fields of the French countryside moved below her: greens and browns punctuated by the startlingly yellow colza. Cottony mist clung in hollows and lowlands, and periodically the ground was obscured by wispy clouds, but all in all it looked like it would be a nice day. Hot. Paris in August could be very hot, and though the city didn't close up for the entire month like they said it did, there was still a rush to the seaside resorts. Well, she wasn't spending a lot of time in the steamy city. She was heading to the sea, too.

And Gianluca? As she had promised him? Her promise had been made, she smiled to herself, under duress. Great duress. Her gasping, "*Si, si, si,*" came back to her in a rush.

She and Gianluca hadn't made love every day, despite his pleadings, but she'd gone to his apartment a half dozen times. The rest of the time she'd gone around in a red haze of, no other word for it, lust. She'd felt swollen with desire.

She'd never had a lover like Gianluca. Not that she'd had that many, but he was incredibly passionate, almost insatiable. He was also tender and fun. Back when she and Preston had been having their quarrels, he'd accused her of being over-sexed, when actually she'd thought herself the opposite, even more so in the past few years. The sex in her life had not ever touched her very deeply, even with Preston, if she was to be honest about it. Now she could think of nothing else but the next time with Gianluca.

She never tired of letting her mind's eye go over Gianluca's body. His skin was like gold silk. He was perfectly proportioned and loved to have her look at him as he strolled naked around his bedroom, growing more tumescent with every step. Even now she could feel the pinpoints of desire and she unconsciously shifted in her seat and recrossed her legs. In her mind she ran her hands over the muscles in his back and buttocks, her lips over his thighs and calves, the crisp hairs and hard muscles between her teeth. She saw his dark, glossy hair as she watched him rove over her body, his hot dark eyes that held hers as she climaxed.

A small gasp escaped her throat. Yes, her whole body was involved in their lovemaking. *I have missed a whole lot 'til now*, she thought, then smiled again to herself, warmth suffusing her.

Her erotic trance was broken by the announcement for landing. She leaned to replace her book in the travel bag and glanced at her seatmate, to find his eyes on her.

He seemed bemused. "You're a very beautiful woman and I'd like to take you to bed and make you look at me that way."

Laise looked into intense blue eyes, fringed with thick, sandy lashes. It took a moment for it to register what he'd said, then she turned toward the window and watched the lush French countryside rush up to meet the plane, her heart pounding with shock at his words, her body still keyed up by her thoughts.

Why not? She could always change her mind, and right now the thought of spending the night alone in Paris seemed a waste. She turned. He still studied her. "I'm at the Meurice. Mrs. Spenser."

Out the window she saw the runway blur and slow. She'd been right. It was a beautiful day.

They didn't speak again. When the passengers reached the concourse he vanished into the crowd. When Laise pulled her luggage claim checks from her bag she found his card. *William Fowler, Fowler & Black Investments, San Francisco.* When had he put it there? She tapped the card on her thumb. What should she do if he actually called her? He was very nice looking, and he'd gracefully accepted that she didn't want to talk on the plane. But then that perfectly outrageous thing he'd said. So entirely out of character? At least he looked like it might be.

The corners of her mouth curled up. He'd sure tuned

into her mood. And he was right. Had she seemed like an animal in heat to him? Had her erotic reveries sent out mating pheromones? Gianluca had turned her into a sexy broad, all right. So much so that she didn't want to spend the evening alone. But did she really want to spend it with the unknown William Fowler from San Francisco?

Laise collected her two Hermès suitcases from the carousel and motioned to a porter. The long ride into the city went quickly with her anticipation of what William Fowler was going to do.

At the hotel, the bellman let her into the high-ceilinged room, with its soft green silk walls and red velvet draperies. On a small *chinoiserie* chest was a huge arrangement of the fattest, long-stemmed red roses she had ever seen. She crossed over and found what she was looking for. After she tipped the bellman, she tore open the small vellum envelope engraved with the name of that obscenely expensive florist on the Rue Royale.

If I remember the Meurice rightly, these should go well in your room. I hope you'll have dinner with me tonight and let me apologize for my inexplicable lapse of sanity. Wear something special. Eight o'clock. Will Fowler.

Laise began to laugh. Will Fowler knew how to get a fabulous bouquet of roses delivered in the time it had taken her to drive in to the city. And he hadn't called. Hadn't given her the chance to refuse. He was getting more interesting by the minute. Was he really embarrassed by his "lapse" as he called it?

Here she was, in Paris barely more than an hour and already she'd been propositioned. So far she'd said maybe. Now, was she going to say yes, or no? Wear something special, he'd said. She was beginning to think she didn't have anything special enough. Well, that's what she was in Paris for, to shop before going south to meet Agathe and Olimpia in Cannes. It was guaranteed you could find something special on the Rue

Faubourg St. Honoré, or in any one of dozens of couturiers on the fashionable streets around it.

Laise picked up the phone and made an appointment at Carita. The trip would catch up to her today and a massage and facial would give her a chance to nap. Then Michel could do something wonderful with her hair. Yes, she was going to look special for William Fowler. The prospect was beginning to excite her. It had been a long time since she had dressed for a man. Gianluca liked it that her clothes were expensive, but he didn't really care what she had on as long as it came off in a hurry.

That evening the phone rang at exactly eight o'clock. His voice was as nice as she remembered it.

"Mrs. Spenser? Will Fowler. I hope you've decided to give me a second chance." He didn't sound embarrassed. Maybe faintly amused.

"I'm looking forward to dinner."

"I'm delighted. I thought we might have a drink here in the salon. It's very pleasant and the piano is wonderful. I'm afraid I didn't mention I must make a stop before dinner. At the Kuwaiti embassy. Do you mind much?"

"Mind? Oh, no. Not at all. It sounds interesting."

"We'll not stay long. It's a business courtesy. Our dinner reservation is for ten."

"Are you here in the hotel?"

"Yes. Would you like me to come up to your room to get you?"

"No, I'm ready. I'll be right down." Laise hung up and mused. *How very formal this all is. Is this the same outrageous man on the plane? How is this evening going to end? I wonder if Mr. Fowler has lost his nerve. What a shame if he has.*

Laise turned to the cheval mirror. She'd found the dress almost immediately—a simple, black chiffon slip that frilled at the hem of a short skirt. It was very expensively sexy. It looked like it cost a fortune, and it had. The black Christian Louboutin silk sandals were dangerously high and made her legs look yards long. Taller than a lot of men. Laise usually thought nothing of it. But tonight she wanted to look every inch her six feet. The stiletto heels would add even more. To intimidate William Fowler? Maybe, though he was very tall himself.

Michel had tossed her hair into a wild tousled mass. She clipped on her diamond earrings, gave herself another pouf of her specially mixed perfume—a heady mixture of tuberose and freesia—and without another glance in the mirror, picked up her key and evening bag. What would the end of the evening bring?

She could hear the piano as soon as she got off the elevator. American show tunes. There was nothing like them and they were played all over the world. She crossed the marble floor and entered the elegant cream and gilt salon. The piano player was the same one who had been playing here even before the renovation. He smiled and gave Laise a small bow of recognition and approval.

Étienne. Yes, she was sure that was it. She would try to stop and tell him she was glad he was still there.

Laise saw William Fowler the same instant he saw her. She crossed the marble floor, feeling the gossamer skirt brushing softly around her thighs. He rose to meet her and she could tell she was a success when she saw the look on his face. After all, the last time he had seen her she'd been disheveled and travel-weary, with dark circles under tired eyes in a just-scrubbed face. Even then he'd thought that she looked good enough to want to take to bed. What did he think now that Carita had recreated her? Ha!

He was dressed in beautifully-tailored evening clothes. Expensive. He was even better looking than she remembered, but he'd been tossing around all night in an airline seat, too. About forty, she guessed—straight, dishwater blond hair, eyes not quite as blue as they seemed this morning. Maybe it was the light. Hard to tell.

They smiled but neither spoke as he held out his hand and guided her to a place on the sofa beside him. Nice mouth, she noticed.

He looked at her for several moments in unselfconscious admiration. "I'm afraid you've quite taken my breath away. Would you like a drink?"

"A Scotch, please. Something single malt."

After he'd ordered, he turned to her and cleared his throat. "Um...about my remark this morning...I feel I must say something. I don't quite know what. I can't really say I'm sorry, because you're here..."

"Please. You saw something. I wouldn't ordinarily have answered the way I did. Let's just say we were both in a receptive frame of mind and leave it at that."

He was silent, searching her face, then laughed deeply. "Yes, let's do that. You've let me off the hook rather generously."

"Now, tell me why you've been invited to the Kuwaiti embassy."

"I do a lot of business in the Middle East...you know, I can call you Mrs. Spenser all evening, but I'd rather not."

"It's Laise."

"Very pretty. Unusual."

"It was my great-great-grandfather's name."

Amused, he said, "I started to think you were going to say great-great-grandmother."

"I was supposed to have been a boy. When it didn't turn out that way I think my father thought by invoking his great-granddaddy's name that it would turn the trick."

"You a boy. That would have been a terrible waste. I've got a lot to find out about you, Laise Spenser. I do know for sure that you are definitely not a boy."

They continued to talk, liking each other. The piano insinuated its romantic songs into the low murmur of conversation in the room, and the discreet, bell-like sounds of expensive glassware.

What a charming man, Laise reflected, witty and easy to be with. She began to look forward to the rest of the evening very much.

There was a limousine waiting to take them to the reception. Laise glanced at Will and he winked. "The Arabs are not favorably impressed if you arrive in a taxi, though with you along, I could arrive on a bicycle."

She smiled, pleased with the compliment.

"This was also to impress you. Somehow I don't think you are very."

"Oh, but I am. Particularly if it was for me." She squeezed his elbow slightly.

When they were settled, he said, "I promise you we won't stay long. Do you speak French? It will be more interesting for you if you do."

"I'm a French professor."

"You're a what?"

"I teach French. At Arizona State University."

"Well, I'll be damned. I would have thought you were in show business or something. Something incredibly glamorous."

She turned wide, innocent eyes to him. "You don't think professors are glamorous?"

"It has not been my experience." He laughed and touched her hand. "I must revise my ideas about professors."

Laise didn't look away. "I promise you I'm not absent-minded."

He leaned back against the seat, studying her, before he answered. "Neither am I."

A tacit understanding passed between the two of them that neither had forgotten the remark of Will's that had led them here.

The iron gates to the Kuwaiti embassy were massive. They were open for the reception, but Will had to show a heavy vellum, engraved invitation to a uniformed guard before the car was allowed through the entrance.

A doorman with elaborate epaulettes and imposing mustaches greeted them and held the door as they left the car. Another man in a sort of combination uniform and formal dress escorted them into the main hall and handed Will's invitation to yet another functionary at the head of the receiving line, made up entirely of males in Arab dress. After they had gone through the line, Laise looked around curiously. The décor was lavish—silk-paneled and gilt walls, frescoed ceilings, waterfall-like Baccarat chandeliers. And the carpets. Everywhere the jewel-toned carpets of the Middle East.

There was a mix of nationalities, a typical embassy reception. Laise had accompanied her parents to these functions occasionally, when they were in Washington. She'd been a teenager then, but she decided things hadn't changed measurably in the intervening years.

Will moved through the crowd with Laise, pointing out various notables. Then, a man caught his arm and Will introduced him as an oil company official. He and Will became involved in conversation and Laise let her eyes wander over the room.

"Laise Brock! What are you doing in Paris? It's been ages."

Laise recognized the voice and turned. "Hello, Janice, how very nice to see you." She held the other woman's hand with affection. "Is the Senator around? I'd love to say hello."

"He was a minute ago. I'll go find him. He'll be so pleased. But what are you doing in this place? I didn't think Preston had much to do with the Middle East."

"No. I sat next to a gentleman on the plane. He asked me to come. It sounded interesting. Otherwise I'm just in town to shop a bit, then meet friends in Cannes."

Laise glanced around, feeling she had to introduce Will, but the crowd seemed to have swallowed him. She was relieved. She didn't want tonight to have anything to do with her life. When Janice Kilmer went off to find her husband, Laise drifted away. The Kilmers had been Washington friends of her parents, and she saw them occasionally when she was in town. She'd have to drop them a note and tell them she was sorry she'd lost them in the crowd tonight.

Where was Will? She edged toward a wall where she would have a view of the room. He was taller than most in the crowd. She knew she'd spot him soon. As her eyes swept the room her attention was caught by a large, inlaid basin resting on an ornate side table. There had been an Iranian man in the French department at the university and he'd gotten her interested for a time in Middle Eastern art when there had been a big show at the Phoenix Art Museum. She recognized the piece as a fine example of fourteenth or fifteenth century metalwork. She moved closer, bending her head in order to examine the intricate gold and silver inlay. There were elaborate inscriptions on six exterior panels in the graceful Arabic script.

"Do you read Arabic?"

Laise straightened to find a pair of dark, glowing eyes on a level slightly below hers. A Kuwaiti—or Saudi maybe.

"No, but it's a lovely piece. Is it Mamluk?"

"You are knowledgeable as well as beautiful. Would you like to know what it says?"

"Very much."

He invited her to look more closely as they leaned over the basin, his fingers indicating the inscription as he translated. Laise noticed that he barely glanced at what he was reading to her, and she thought he must live or work in the embassy to be so familiar with the piece. He was Kuwaiti then.

" 'Glory to our master, the king, the royal, the learned, the just, the defender, the champion, the warrior, the protector, pillar of Islam and of Muslims, the protector of the weak and paupers, crowns of kings and sultans, reviver of justice among all, defender of truth and proof, and glory and prosperity to the owner.'" The man smiled with very red lips and very white teeth. "There are five additional panels, but I think you get the idea." He looked at her intently. "I'd like to show you a finer piece, since you're interested. It is quite spectacular. Would you like to see it?"

She hesitated. "I would, of course, but I'm with someone and I've lost track of him. I really shouldn't disappear."

"Ah yes, William Fowler. Someone will find him for you."

The teeth gleamed in his neat black beard as he raised a finger. A man appeared immediately at his shoulder. The two spoke softly.

He seems important, she thought. *But he wasn't in the receiving line. Who is he?*

"It is done. Come."

He took Laise's arm and they moved through the crowded room toward a pair of heavily-paneled double doors. Another man materialized to open the doors wide. The room was some sort of study or meeting room—large, book-lined, with cabinets full of art objects, and tables covered with carved woods, ceramics, and more metalwork. On a table in the center of the room, by itself, illuminated by an overhead spotlight, was a large, inlaid basin similar to the one Laise had admired. This vessel was much larger and more ornate—with gleaming gold and silver animals combined with human figures and weapons. Elaborate geometric borders glowed with cabochon rubies, emeralds, and sapphires.

"In this case the craftsman is known—Muhammad ibn al Zayn. He has signed it here. You see? 'Work of the master Muhammad ibn al-Zayn, may he be forgiven."

"Forgiven?"

"By God. In Islam, everything is dedicated to God in our quest for forgiveness." He led Laise around the basin, pointing out scenes and inscriptions. "This is the finest piece in the embassy. It is quite lavish, don't you think?"

"It's truly a magnificent work. You were very kind to show it to me. I'm quite honored." Laise didn't quite know what to do next, and the man was watching her carefully.

"I am leaving for Kuwait in two days time. Would you like to come with me?"

Laise was startled. "I'm sorry. I'm afraid I don't understand." Suddenly she felt uneasy and stepped back involuntarily, her eyes wary. The man seemed to be waiting for an answer. With a flood of relief, she turned at the sound of Will's voice.

"Ah, here you are." He stopped, puzzled at the expression on Laise's face, then turned to the Kuwaiti. "Your Highness, I'm happy that you met…uh…Dr. Spenser. I very much wanted you to."

The dark-eyed man raised an eyebrow, then turned to smile at Laise. "Ah, it is Dr. Spenser, is it? And I didn't introduce myself. Very careless, yes? I do get rather carried away. I am Prince Sabah." He turned to Will. "I have enjoyed our little talk. Perhaps I can show Dr. Spenser other treasures in my country another day." He smiled at Laise. "Now, I have kept you too long, I'm afraid. William is an old friend. He will forgive me." To Will, he said, "We will be meeting tomorrow."

He left the room quickly, the big doors opening magically before him.

Laise turned to Will, bemused. "He wanted me to go to Kuwait with him."

Will grinned. "I'm not surprised. Are you going?"

Her mouth parted. Then she saw the gleam in his eye and began to laugh. "So, I'm Dr. Spenser, am I?"

"Aren't you? And I knew it would impress the prince."

"Do you always have to impress people?"

"You bet. You have increased my status enormously. Now, let's go to dinner, Dr. Spenser."

The Fall From Paradise Valley

In the car he told her, "We're going to Tour d'Argent." He paused. "Do you think I'm overdoing all this?"

She laughed with delight. "Oh, there's no question. But I'm having a wonderful time. Tour d'Argent is perfect—it's the most romantic spot in Paris."

"Absolutely. I'm glad we agree."

They drove down the Seine past the Tuileries and the Louvre, crossed the Pont Neuf, the majestic façade of Notre Dame spotlighted against the night sky. The Quai de Montebello changed into the Quai de Tournelle and the car pulled up to No. 15. They rode up the small elevator to the famous old restaurant on the sixth floor.

"Ah, bon soir, Monsieur Fowler…"

Will chatted with the maitre d' a moment and then they were led to their table. They were by a window with a view of the flying buttresses of Notre Dame.

"Will, I can't think of a lovelier place to be on my first night back in Paris."

He was pleased with her reaction. "I hope you don't mind…I went ahead and ordered the duck for us. I thought it might be special to have our own duck number."

She laughed. "No, I don't mind. That's wonderful. You've thought of everything." She glanced around the elaborate, tasseled, circular room, with its curved windows looking over Notre Dame Cathedral. In the center of the room stood a raised platform with its ornate silver duck press ritualistically preparing the famous *specialité de la maison, canard à la presse,* each bird given its own individual number since the 1890s. "They seem to know you. You must come here often."

"A fair amount…the Arabs and the Japanese are…"

"…impressed."

"You got it. It's my job to separate people from their money. A lot of it. I've got to look like I know what to do with it." He chuckled. "Even if I don't always."

"Are you married?"

He paused, then picked up her hand. "Yes." He rubbed her fingers distractedly a moment. "But I want to know more about the professor. You're a Spenser from Arizona. Any connection to the late Senator?"

"He was my father. I'm surprised you'd remember. He and my mother were killed fifteen years ago. Did you know him?"

"I met him a couple of times. I was just out of graduate school and working for a firm that did a lot of lobbying. You go by your maiden name...and yet you use Mrs."

It was a question she supposed she would have to answer now that he knew who she was. She looked at her hands that he held and drew a breath. "Yes. My married name is Brock. I use it socially in Phoenix. My husband, Preston, manages the Spenser interests. We...aren't close...anymore. He's a nice man and a wonderful father. We haven't divorced because there hasn't been any overriding reason to."

She looked down at the tablecloth, focusing on the pattern in the heavy damask. "Will, I wish you didn't know who I was. I suppose that's silly. I think I'd rather have stayed a question mark." She looked up and smiled. "The mystery woman."

"Forgive me. I didn't mean to be personal. It's hard for me not to be curious about you. You fascinate me. You must admit a six foot, ravishing red-haired professor in a fabulously expensive couture dress, with traffic-stopping legs would excite any man's imagination. But we'll talk about something else and you can be as mysterious as you like. Now...how long will you be in the city?"

"Four more days. I'm meeting old school friends in Cannes on Saturday. And you?"

"I'm scheduled to leave on Friday, but it may be sooner." He paused. "I'd like to see you again."

"Yes, I'd like that, too."

"What do you like to do? Museums, art galleries, shopping, cathedrals, the theater?"

"There are a couple of exhibits I'd planned to see. And some shopping. Mostly I just came to get in touch with the city again. To walk the streets, stuff myself every morning with croissants…"

The evening passed quickly. Laise's brief regret at Will's knowing about her passed.

As they left, their waiter presented them an embossed card with their duck number: #1,984, 762. Will laughed. "We almost made it to the two millionth bird. We must come back."

The spell woven by the food and wine in the hushed ambience of the restaurant affected them both. They were quiet riding down in the elevator. Outside the soft summer night brushed over them.

"Would you like to walk?"

She nodded.

Will spoke to the driver. While they walked, the car moved silently down the street behind them. They went down the steps to the river, intoxicated by the night. There were other couples strolling along, small groups of revelers, lovers in the shadows. Moonlight winked on the surface of the dark, moving river. The smell was damp, mossy, decaying. The smell of centuries.

Will stopped and turned her toward him. "Let's get the car."

"Yes."

In the car, Will's arms went around her and his kiss was gentle at first, but became more insistent as she opened her lips to him. He murmured in her hair and into her throat, "Laise. I meant what I said, you know. I want you. You know that. Tonight. Now."

She whispered, "I know. Yes."

Back at the hotel, Will dismissed the driver. They rode up in the elevator, not touching, but their eyes locked in anticipation. As the door to her room closed behind them, Laise was in his arms. His mouth sought hers, then moved down her throat, as his hands slipped the straps of her dress from her shoulders.

His voice was husky. "How do you get this off?"

She reached back and slid the zipper down and the black chiffon slithered to the floor. Her body was flushed and her breasts trembled under his caresses.

Together they threw the heavy brocade coverlet off the bed. She pulled his tie off and managed the cummerbund and two studs, enough to find the sandy pelt on his chest. She worked his suspenders over his shoulders, then pulled the pants zipper and pulled him over her.

"Don't wait, Will. Please."

He filled her with a sharp groan. It couldn't have lasted more than a few minutes. He was still shuddering on top of her as her head cleared.

He lay still with his eyes closed as she finished undressing him, pulling out studs and cufflinks, working his arms through his sleeves. She slipped off the black patent pumps.

"Do you always make love with your shoes on?"

"I don't think I've ever been in that much of a hurry," he muttered. "And you're really turning me on again, you know that."

She pulled off his long silk socks, then tugged his pants free. He was very turned on. She sat on the side of the bed and picked up his leg and ran her fingers up and down the long bones. He made small noises in his throat.

"You have pretty legs," she said.

His eyes flew open and he threw himself up and grabbed her. "Pretty legs!" he whooped.

"Well, you know what I mean. Nice. Long and strong."

He flipped her over on her back and straddled her. "You're getting distracted by unimportant things. We need to get back to the basics. Like I have something very basic that's long and strong and I don't think I've heard you beg for mercy yet. Let's work on that."

"Why, I don't think I was even close to begging," she murmured.

But the light-hearted moment was over. Will's eyes were intense. He watched her face as he moved into her. "This time will be slow. I want to feel every inch of you around me, pulling me into you."

~ * ~

It was nearly morning when he dressed quietly and left. She was so soundly asleep that even the riotous Parisian garbage trucks didn't waken her. He wrapped a note around one of the fat red roses, laid it on her pillow and slipped out the door.

A pale, silvery light, not quite dawn, suffused the city as Will left the Meurice. The bangs and crashes of the garbage trucks were beginning to recede, the shouts of the crews lingered on the morning air. Will took a deep breath. He felt wonderful. He wondered when Laise would wake up. He was strongly tempted to go back and waken her himself, knowing it was out of the question. He had early morning meetings and he wasn't dressed for business, with his tie and cummerbund in his pockets and his evening shirt touched with lipstick.

There were several taxis parked near the entrance to the hotel. He walked over and tapped on the window of the first one, waking the sleeping driver and his enormous black dog, some kind of French shepherd mix.

"Rue Malasherbes, *s'il vous plait.*"

"*Oui, Monsieur.*" He turned on the meter as Will climbed in the back. The big dog gazed over the seat at him with sky blue eyes, then curled up again on the seat beside his maser. Will never tired of the charming impulse of Parisian taxi drivers to take their dogs on their rounds with them. Or the French to take their dogs anywhere, for that matter.

The driver eyed Will's evening clothes in his mirror. *"Une soirée couronée de succès, eh, Monsieur?"*

Will laughed. The French. They loved love. *"Oui, Monsieur. Un grand succès."*

FIFTEEN

LAISE

It took more than the intrepid garbage men of Paris to waken Laise. The bedside clock showed nearly nine when sleep drifted away. She slowly became aware of the silky linen sheets, the humid fragrance of roses, and bright, bright sunlight nudging her closed eyelids.

Will was gone. Sunlight was pouring brightly into the room. She had not had the night maid turn down her bed last night and pull the draperies, not knowing exactly what to expect. The sheers were pulled on the long windows, but the heavy red velvet draperies were open. Neither she nor Will had given them a thought last night. Laise smiled. They'd given thought to only one thing last night.

She rolled over onto Will's side of the bed, burying her nose in his pillow. He hadn't worn cologne, thank God, but he'd smelled nice—soapy and shampooey. She could pick up small whispers of his scent. She was disappointed he wasn't there. She felt sexy, smelled of sex, the stickiness of him still between her legs. Sighing with regret, she got out of the big bed. The rose that had been on her pillow had fallen to the floor. She picked it up and nuzzled its velvety wilting petals against her mouth. She unrolled the note wrapped around its de-thorned stem and walked over to poke the rose deep into the water of the vase. Maybe the lush, burgundy blossom would revive.

Laise—I hated to leave you. What a special evening it was for me. I hope for you, too. I have meetings this a.m. near the Bourse. The Café de la Paix is nearby. Can you meet me there at two? We'll have lunch, then do something you like. I can't wait to see you. Will

She smiled. *He's very sure I'll be there. He was sure I'd go last night. Of course he's right. I can't wait to see him. It was heavenly last night and I can't wait to do it all over again.*

Naked, Laise walked into the big bathroom, with its gilt mirrors and crystal wall lamps. She grinned at her image in one long mirror. "Sexy broad. Propositioned twice in one day. Once by a prince yet. I wonder what would have happened if I'd said I'd go with him to Kuwait. Been a concubine? Do they still have harems with eunuchs? Wow! Wouldn't that shock old Phoenix."

The shower was a big marble affair with a dozen adjustable jets. The Meurice, in its major overhaul, had replaced the eccentric French plumbing. Michel's wild hairstyle went down the drain as she washed away the night's residues of love. She gritted her teeth and flipped the handle to Cold, making desperate moans as the icy cascade sliced across her stomach.

Later, Laise emerged from the hotel into a bright blue day, with three hours until she was to meet Will. She bought two buttery croissants and walked along the paths of the Tuileries gardens, inhaling the city. She admired people's dogs and watched them swell with pride at her compliments. An aloof Parisian melted when one spoke to his dog. It was a game Laise loved to play. It was even better if you had a camera and requested a photograph. She had a wonderful collection of French dogs and their beaming masters and mistresses. It was a toss-up which was the more delicious, man or beast.

She stopped at a spirited game of *pétanque*, a close

relative to English lawn bowling, though played on a dirt surface. The players began to preen and show off their fanciest moves, putting elaborate spins on the heavy metal balls. She moved away when she realized she'd become a distraction to their game. Laise didn't have any illusions when it came to how she looked.

Laise had some favorite boutiques and shopped for the two evenings she'd have with Will before he left. Again, she thought, she hadn't had the fun of dressing for a man in ages. She signed the bill at the last shop and directed the *vendeuse* to send it all back to the Meurice.

It was near two o'clock when she cut across to the Avenue de l'Opéra. Her heartbeat quickened at the thought of meeting Will. Yesterday she'd been excited about meeting an intriguing man. Today she had a *rendez-vous* with her lover. How surprising the accidents of fate.

About a block from the Opera House she caught sight of Will across the street, walking parallel to her. She easily kept pace with him and enjoyed the opportunity to watch him unobserved. He wore a gray suit, English, judging by the cut of it. Somehow this pleased her, that he would have an English tailor. He had an easy, athletic stride and his sandy hair ruffled slightly as he walked.

As if he knew he was being observed, he glanced across the street and saw her, smiled and waved, quickening his pace. By the time Laise reached the busy plaza in front of the Opera, she was trying not to run, trying not to collide with other pedestrians. He made a sign to wait for him on the corner and she paced along the curb, impatient for the light to change.

Then he was there and pulled her out of the crowd and spun her toward him as they both talked at once.

"You're even more beautiful than I remembered."
"I'm glad you're here."
"The meeting dragged on forever."
"Did you get any sleep at all?"

He grinned but didn't answer and tucked her hand under his arm as they began to walk toward the Boulevard des Capucines.

"We can go to the Bois if you want. There are several wonderful places. The Café de la Paix came into my woolly head this morning. It's not too far and it's been restored within the last couple of years."

"Yes, I know it. Let's go there. It's charming."

He glanced up at the sky. "Do you have an umbrella in that suitcase you have over your shoulder? It looks like it might rain."

"No, it was beautiful when I left the hotel," she said.

"Maybe we'll be lucky. I'm starved. How about you?"

"Famished. I bought some croissants to eat in the Tuileries, but the effects are all gone. I'll embarrass you I'll eat so much."

"I won't look. Now, tell me what you've done this morning while I was trying to concentrate on a dull business deal and all I could think of was topaz eyes and hair the color of an Irish setter."

She laughed with delight. "A setter. How wonderful. No one has ever said that to me before."

"I have two of them. And you even move like a setter, kinda lopey and loose. Like now."

"Now I'm self-conscious. I've forgotten how to walk."

"I'll help." He put an arm around her waist.

At lunch she wanted to hear about his morning and his business. He raised an eyebrow in surprise at her understanding of the complicated workings of the project he described.

"The French professor has a head for business," he commented.

"I make myself. It doesn't interest me terribly, but when my parents were killed, I was so totally helpless. I was completely dependent on other people, especially...my husband. He was the financial brains of the family's holdings.

Of course, I was very young then, but I realized I wouldn't always have that excuse."

"Was that when you married?"

"Yes."

He hesitated, then changed the subject. "So, back to Kuwait. They're still rebuilding refineries nearly twenty years after the Gulf war. We're heavily involved, competing with Europe and other Middle Eastern companies. The war in Iraq has complicated some things. There's an incredible amount of money involved and it's a juggling act, that's sure. I have to make some calls this afternoon, but I can do that anywhere. We'll do whatever you want."

"There's a special show at the Palais Royale of Seurats. Let's do that."

The waiter poured the last of a bottle of a white Bordeaux and Will made a silent toast to Laise. She solemnly returned it, then lowered her eyes. "Will I see you tonight?"

"Of course. Would you like to go to the theater? There's not much going on in August, but we could find something to see."

"Anything, really. Will, why don't I just let you go back to your hotel now. When did you last sleep? Two days ago? I can go to the Palais Royale alone. Truly, I don't mind."

"I'm not at a hotel. My company keeps a flat here. It's easier and cheaper in the long run. It's on the Boulevard Malasherbes, near the Madelaine."

"That's not far."

"No. It isn't."

"Oh." She watched her finger go around and around the rim of the wine glass.

He reached over and stopped her hand. His voice was rough. "Would you like to see it?"

She looked up. "Yes."

When they came out of the restaurant, it was pouring and traffic was in a rain-drenched snarl. Will tried to hail a cab, then grabbed her arm.

"Come on. It's only several blocks. We're getting soaked anyway, and you'll get chilled with just that silk shirt."

It was a warm rain and soon they began to laugh just for the sheer pleasure of splashing through the slanting silver sheets of water.

He took her into a small entrance tucked between a jeweler and an expensive men's store. The foyer was small, with several fine antiques and brass and crystal wall lamps. A tiny elevator took them to the fourth floor.

In the apartment Laise wiped her face with her hands and looked around. "You made it sound like a cold water walkup. This is very elegant. And I'm dripping all over your beautiful Oriental."

"Did I make it sound like that? I didn't mean to. We entertain here some, so it has to be presentable." He cupped her face in his hands and kissed the rain beaded on her eyelashes.

"The bedroom's through there. Take off your wet clothes and I'll find some towels for your hair." He ran his fingers through the wet curls. "I think there's a hair dryer somewhere in the guest bathroom."

She rested her arms on his shoulders, smiling. "I'm afraid your beautiful English suit is ruined."

"No, an English suit doesn't get ruined in the rain. With good reason." He turned her toward the bedroom. "Run along. I don't want you to catch cold."

In the old-fashioned marble bathroom, Laise sat on a small gilded stool and peeled off her wet clothes. Will came in with extra towels and she turned to him, her skin pearly and damp in the gray light of the rainy afternoon. He wore only blue boxer shorts. He walked over slowly, his eyes intent on her body. He wrapped the towel around her hair and began to rub the soft terry against her head, down her shoulders and breasts. The towel fell to the floor as he raised her chin with his thumb. His erection brushed against her cheek as he bent to kiss her.

"You're too damned big for me to carry to bed unless you help," he murmured against her mouth.

She turned her head and whispered. "In a minute."

They slept, made love, then slept again. They woke to find the rainy afternoon had turned to evening, then night.

"This bed," she sighed. "I feel like Madame Pompadour." Laise traced a finger around the elaborately carved headboard.

"Actually, I think she did spend a bit of time in it. According to the dealer."

Around midnight, they dressed. Will found a raincoat in a closet, too big around for Laise, but she pulled the belt tight. They had bowls of bouillabaise with a bottle of dark red wine at a dim, aromatic café near the apartment. When they came out of the restaurant, the rain had stopped and the air was warm and heavy. They walked through the deserted streets drowsy and content.

"I hate to be so sleepy because I'm very happy and I hate for the day to end," she said.

"I know. I'll get a cab and take you home. We have tomorrow."

When the taxi pulled up to the Meurice, Will kissed her. "I won't come up. I'll call you in the morning. And think about you the rest of the night."

"I'll be awake early." She opened the taxi door. "Don't bother to get out."

~ * ~

The ring jangled insistently, breaking into her morning dreams, nagging like a mosquito. Laise uncurled and groped for the telephone. What time was it? It seemed very early—the light filtering through the crack in the red velvet draperies was very pale.

"Laise, it's Will. Something's come up. The wheels are coming off the whole deal I was working on. I have to fly to

Dubai. Come with me, Laise."

She rubbed her temple, trying to focus on what he said.

"Laise, are you there? Did you hear me? I want you to come with me."

"Will...oh, Will. That's impossible. I can't. I have to be in Cannes day after tomorrow." She sat up, full of dread now. "When will you be back?"

"I don't know. Laise. I can't let you go."

Her mind was clearing, the reality beginning. She wasn't going to see Will again. But it hadn't ever been going past tomorrow. She thought they would have one more day. There was never going to be anything else. They had both known that. She felt hollow.

"Laise, answer me. Say something to me."

Her voice was dull. "I can't. Will, there's nothing to say. Paris was a wonderful moment. It's just over sooner than we thought. That's all."

"I'll come to Cannes when I can get away."

"No, Will, these two days were all there was ever meant to be for us."

"I'll find you in Arizona." His voice was desperate.

"That would be a mistake. Will, you're married."

"Laise, I never got a chance to tell you about that."

"It doesn't matter." She didn't want to cry.

"Will you come to Paris again? Promise me we can see each other in Paris. When will you be here again?"

"I don't know. Oh, why am I saying this? Thinking it? Will, it's got to be over."

"It isn't unless you want it to be. Do you want it to be?"
"Don't."

"Laise, I have to go, the plane will be leaving. Won't you let me pick you up? Just throw a few things together. We can send for the rest of your things."

"Goodbye, Will, I..."

"Take this number. It's the apartment on Malasherbes.

You can leave a message. You have my card. You can reach me in San Francisco. Take this number, Laise, please. Please, Laise," he begged.

"Just a minute." Her fingers trembled as she wrote the number on the hotel pad.

"*Au revoir, Laise.*" There was a small hesitation. "*Je t'aime.*"

"*Au revoir, Will.*" Her voice was full of tears. "*Je t'aime.*"

She heard the click as he hung up. *Je t'aime.* It was so much easier to say than "I love you." Did she love him? She put her face in her hands. "I can't cry. It was not meant to be something to cry over." She was stupid to think they could ever be together. Will Fowler was not a viable possibility in her life.

She cried. Fate had been so unfair.

Later she dressed and walked aimlessly. She bought a croissant, but it stuck in her throat. She found herself at the bookstalls along the Seine and bought an old book on Versailles and an Art Nouveau picture frame. Carrying something made her feel more in control.

Walking the Champs Elysées didn't bring the old elation. At Le Drugstore on the Place d'Étoile she tried to think if there was anything she needed, but the loud music began to confuse her and the bright, glittery displays were things she didn't want. On an impulse she sat down at the long lunch counter and ordered a glass of wine and turned it in her fingers as she tried to sort out the muddle in her head.

"You're American, aren't you? The tall girls are always American."

She turned to the young man on the stool next to her and smiled vaguely, then went back to contemplating her wine. The young man was dark and intense. He reminded her of Gianluca.

"Do you like this place?" He edged a little closer.

"Why, no. Not especially."

"I don't. But I like to meet Americans. And so I come here when I'm off duty. To have a glass of wine." He grinned engagingly. "And if I am lucky I will meet a beautiful American girl. I'm a medical student. My name is Christophe."

Laise sighed. *"Bon jour, Christophe."*

"I would like to show you Paris."

Two days ago, she thought, I might have gone with this young man. To his flat after he had "shown" her Paris? Probably. He reminded her of Gianluca, after all.

"Je sais Paris." I know Paris. Then, sorry she had been so abrupt, she touched his hand. "I'm sorry. It's just that you're two days late."

He shrugged and smiled, his face full of regret.

Laise fled Le Drugstore. The rest of the day and the next she spent in a fever of buying—St. Laurent, Chanel, Celine, Dior, Hermès. Wonderful jewelry at Jarr's. She needed luggage to carry it all and bought that, too. And still Will wouldn't go away.

With a sense of relief she took the taxi to Orly for the flight to Cannes on Saturday morning. The weather in Paris had remained hot and muggy and she was weary of being reminded of Will at every turn. It was only a romantic fling. That's all that it was ever meant to be.

But, no. It had been more. Much more. Maybe Cannes would put it behind her. There were so many things to put behind her. Maybe it would help her forget, too, to go to Gianluca and his family in Portofino. She would persuade Agathe and Olimpia that it would be an adventure.

SIXTEEN

CHRISTINA

The flower beds of white, purple, and pink lisianthus were beginning to look a little weary of summer, Christina thought, as she hurried up the steps of the Phoenix Art Museum. Humidity was high today and her dress felt damp and mussed. Not only the flowers were weary of summer at the end of August.

Fumes from dozens of school buses choked the parking lot and made her eyes water. Schools started in mid-August in Arizona and the field trips began almost immediately. Under palo verde trees swarms of children chattered like starlings over brown bag lunches on the central courtyard grass.

She really didn't enjoy touring groups any more, but she found it hard to say no, she'd done it for so long. Now, since David took over the Senate seat and was campaigning for the fall election, it was almost a given that she would keep up her civic activities. With a sinking heart, she knew it was too late to quit.

Barney Bentham, the state party chairman, had implied as much the few times she had been in campaign meetings. He'd wanted her resumé and had been enthusiastic about her involvement with the museum, the Kidney Foundation, and Heart Ball Committee, Crisis Nursery, the Humane Society and the kids' school fundraisers. He'd rubbed his hands together, saying something about culture, health, compassion and education, as well as the dog and cat factor—all being a plus, plus, plus, plus, plus combination. The Senator's wife was a well-known civic leader who could bring in money and votes. Barney told her to "keep up the good work," just when she had gotten burned out with it all.

Christina got impatient with Alicia Bentham, but she really couldn't stand Barney. With dismay she realized she'd have to deal with him forever—or forever as long as David stayed in politics.

Christina greeted William, the museum's front door guard, as he opened the door, then called over to Annie, the receptionist. "I've got the noon public tour. Make a couple of announcements will you, and we'll see what turns up. I'll be down in a sec." She checked her watch. She was having a late lunch with Miriam and wanted to start her lecture and get out of here. These public tours were a crap-shoot because you never knew who'd turn up or tag along. Her mood brightened. Maybe nobody would show up on this hot day. No, no such luck. Even if one person showed up, the public tour would go on.

For awhile a couple of years ago there was a hooker who had found a classy place to solicit her "nooners." She'd done a fairly brisk business for several months before one of the guards caught on. Christina thought the girl had a brilliant idea. Too bad they shut her down. There had been an upsurge of businessmen doing the galleries and sales had picked up in the gift shop. The girl had been a knockout and well-dressed.

Then there were the crying babies, dotty old broads who wouldn't keep their hands off any of the art works, smart-asses who tried to make you look bad. She was even more of a target since David went to Washington. So many things had changed since then.

Seven gallery-goers were gathered at the front desk.

Christina was just beginning her introduction when she saw Sev Justus break away from a painting he was examining and amble over to listen to her. Her voice altered slightly as she thought, *oh, shit. Now, I've got him to make me self-conscious.* Then she hated herself for that uncomfortable tenseness she always felt when he was around. She gave him a tiny wave and smile, wishing he would go away.

But he didn't. He strolled casually along with her group, always at the back, always his lazy dark eyes studying her.

The show was the big Cowboy Artists Exhibit, and it was news in itself because it raised an enormous amount of money for the museum, over three million this year. Christina wasn't surprised to see a photographer and reporter from the *Republic*. But they began to follow her around and she realized the cowboy art wasn't the attraction. The director must have alerted them she'd be there today.

The photographer wandered along with the group and she smiled agreeably for him. He took a couple of pictures and left.

This was beginning to happen more and more, being recognized as Senator Cross's wife. It was unsettling, but she knew she'd have to get used to it. Next month, when the campaigning began in earnest, she would have to be very visible. Not vocal. Just visible. The rapturous candidate's wife who should, God forbid, not say boo in case she had any dangerous opinions. Christina wasn't used to filtering her words so she wouldn't offend anybody. She figured at her age she had a right to have a mind of her own.

Toward the end of the hour a well-dressed man caught her eye. "I'd like to know if you think this stuff is worth the prices being paid for it?" The challenge in his voice was clear.

The reporter began writing.

Here it goes, she groaned inwardly, but her voice was silky. "I think the most obvious answer to any question of monetary value is: It's worth what someone will pay for it. And you're quite right. People pay very high prices for these works."

"You're playing word games with me." The man had a pained look on his face.

"I don't think so. The art market is a shifting one. Tastes change. Prices fluctuate. Western art is popular now. In five years, maybe it won't be."

"Let me put it another way, Mrs. Cross…"

So he knew who she was. Didn't like David maybe?

The man indicated a large painting Christina truly thought was mediocre. "Would you pay $280,000 for that?"

She gritted her teeth. "Look, I'm sorry you think I'm being evasive, but pricing is not really my role. Maybe you didn't find anything here that for you was worthwhile. Perhaps the man who bought this will take endless pleasure in it and think he got a bargain for $280,000." She gave the man a dazzling smile and hoped he got hit by a school bus on his way out.

Was this the way it would be if David was elected—everyone knowing who I am all the time? Eyes on me always? Waiting to pounce on every falter, every stumble.

Out of the corner of her eye she saw Sev make a V for victory sign and wink at her. Then he strolled off into another gallery.

~ * ~

The luncheon crowd was clearing out when Christina got to Arnaud's. She saw Miriam waiting at a table. She spoke to the hostess. "Hi, Jeanine. I'm meeting Mrs. Merriman. I see her. Don't bother showing me the way." She could see Arnaud in the open kitchen and waggled her fingers at him as she made her way to the table, then sank down opposite Miriam. "Ah, I need a huge iced tea. All I want to do in August is strip off my clothes and float in the pool."

"Not much chance of that for awhile, is there? The next

couple of months are going to be tough on you. Then, if David's elected, you've got all that house hunting and stuff to look forward to. I sure don't envy you."

"It's going to be hard on us all. David put Jack in charge of the campaign here, and then the poor guy has the day to day running of the business as well. How did all this happen, Miriam? Life was going along smoothly enough. David's always been into politics and fund-raising, but I never dreamed he would ever take public office." Her smile was rueful. "Shows how little you can know a person you've spent years with."

"What about you, Christina? How do you feel about going to Washington? Being in the limelight? I know what a private person you are."

"I don't like that people always know who you are." She told Miriam about the man in the museum. The photographer from the paper. She didn't mention Sev. "But maybe it's good having something new in my life. I was feeling kinda dull and bored. Not enough challenges right now, I guess. Every day seemed just like the one before. It's energizing to think we might have different lives, even though I won't like all of it."

"Jack's loving it, too. You have no idea how touched he was that David would trust him with this campaign. I know Barney Bentham wasn't happy, but fuck him. And now that Cameron Brown has gotten his act together and it looks like he'll get some votes, Jack's excited. He was afraid it would be no fun if David were a shoo-in. Well, you know. Jack and David are both big, hairy-chested alpha males…piss on trees, stomp on chief of enemy tribe. Stuff his balls in his mouth." Miriam reached over and patted Christina's hand. "David will win, though."

"Do you think? David's afraid to count on it. Everybody is, I guess. David's been making speeches all over the state when he's not in Washington. There's no such thing as a relaxing weekend anymore. Then there'll be debates close to the election." She grimaced, then laughed. "So far all I seem expected to do is sit and look loyal and enraptured and stay out of trouble." She sighed. "I guess I can do that."

"You'll be fine." Miriam studied the menu. "Ann Savage is over next to the window trying to get my attention. Don't look like you see her. I'm redoing her bedroom and I need a few hours vacation from that. She wants it in shades of purple. But get this. I've got to find her matching nightgowns. Now how many purple nightgowns do you think were manufactured in the world last year. One? Maybe two. I've got to find her six. Sexy. All different." She grinned. "The things a designer gets to know about her clients. I've discovered over time that when the lady of the house gets the bedroom redone, the master of the house probably needs his libido goosed…or his attention. With Bartlett Savage I would guess it's his attention. He looks libidinous enough. Do you think he's ac/dc maybe? Just a feeling."

"Oh, Miriam, I don't think so. I've never heard a word. Anyway, why do you have to find her nightgowns? That's appalling."

"She's part of the décor, dear, part of the décor. Ann had another few tucks done last year, and got some even bigger tits, but I guess it didn't work on Bartlett, so now we're redoing the boudoir. Get this. She asked if I thought she ought to put in a pole to dance around. She's been taking lessons. Picture it, if you possibly can. It took all my self-control not to snicker as I babbled on about corrupting the integrity of the ceiling beams and maybe that would be a better idea down in her exercise room off the pool house."

Christina tried to smother a giggle. "Oh, Miriam. How absolutely awful."

"There's more. She's talking about dying the Shih Tzu lavender to match the adorable bed I'm designing for him. Migawd! What next? Poor little thing. I'm trying to head that off. Convincing her that the silvery dog is just the perfect counterpoint to all that ultraviolet. And maybe he wouldn't much match the rest of the house? Think she'll buy it?"

"Dear God, I hope so." Christina turned as a hand fell on her shoulder. She forced a smile. "Oh, hello, Jillian."

"Christina, darling," the voice gushed. "Haven't seen you in just ages, but we've been gone most of the summer. Haven't had the chance to tell you how absolutely thrilled Andy and I are about David. My, my. Senator Cross! We must get together so you can tell us all about Washington. We always loved talking to the Purcells and stopping in whenever we were in the capital. So sad about him dying and all. Well, must run. I'll give you a call. We must have lunch so you can tell me all your plans. Love to David. You be sure to tell him how happy we are for him."

Christina stared at Miriam. "Would you tell me what that was all about? I can't stand Jillian Anders, and she can't stand me. I wouldn't think of having lunch with her."

"Oh, that bitch. She probably wants to be on the White House Christmas list, or be invited to one of the important Inaugural Balls. And don't you love the bit about visiting the Purcells in Washington? Helen Purcell can't tolerate her either."

"That's what I mean, Miriam. People suddenly coming out of the woodwork with the aren't-we-good-buddies stuff."

"Comes with the territory, sweetie. Now, let's be total slobs and have the lobster crepes and that chocolate tower thing that brings tears to my eyes, mostly because of the three pounds more I'll weigh in the morning."

~ * ~

It was the following Saturday morning. Christina and David had been late at a school meeting the night before and she'd had to drag herself out of bed for her Pilates class. But it was important she stay in shape for these next months. This campaigning took an enormous amount of stamina. David had the party mobile headquarters this weekend to hit the shopping centers and then there was an Elks or something dance tonight. She'd have to go to that. Sometime soon she'd have to go shopping for some Elks-dance-type dresses David told her. Her clothes were a little over the top. There was a fine line between intriguing the voters and pissing them off, he said. Christina had swallowed her annoyance. She had promised herself she'd try to make David's life as smooth as possible. He had so much on his mind now and then the election loomed in the fall. She would have to figure out how to dress like an Elk-ess. The thought depressed her.

After her class Christina ambled from the spa, down the cobblestone alley of the Italian Renaissance Borgata, the upscale shopping mall copied after an actual walled Italian town. They'd done some redesigning for a couple of years and with more flowerbeds and fountains it had gotten even busier. She'd just about passed the window of Félice, one of her favorite shops, when she backed up and examined the mannequin in the window. Definitely not an Elks-dance-type dress, but definitely gorgeous. She glanced at her watch. They wouldn't be open for another twenty minutes. Oh, well, she was too sweaty to try it on. She'd have to come back. She swung her bag over her shoulder and turned—directly into Sev Justus.

"Oh…sor…oh, Sev, it's you." She backed up quickly.

"Sorry, my fault. Well, well. Look who's here." He took both her arms and stood back from her. "And looking ravishing, as usual."

"Come on, Sev. I've just been to exercise class. I'm anything but ravishing." She was acutely aware of her messy hair and not a shred of makeup. "You always seem to find me at my Saturday morning worst."

"Ah, Christina, you don't have a worst. Look, I've just finished tennis, and I'm hot, too. Why don't you come and have an ice cream cone with me. I've got to hang around until

Burnham's opens up. I'm picking up Hallie's birthday present. I'd like to see what you think of it."

"I really have to get back..."

"Oh, come on. Twenty minutes. Keep me company. Häagen Daz is right down there. We'll sit outside."

"Well, actually, that sounds good if you'll get me a rum raisin."

"Done. I'm a double Dutch chocolate man myself."

She sat under the little umbrella thinking she really shouldn't have said yes. What made her do it? And if somebody she knew saw her, sitting here in her skimpy workout clothes with Sev Justus, well. She watched him come out of the shop balancing towering ice cream cones, smiling that smile that always made her tighten up inside.

"Oh, Sev. You know you've totally annihilated my morning workout."

"No point in eating them if you don't make yourself sick." He swiped a lick at a chocolate ball, then winked at her and sat. "I didn't get a chance to tell you how much I enjoyed your lecture at the museum."

"You know, I really wondered why you were there. The cowboys and Indians aren't really yours and Hallie's taste, I didn't think."

"It isn't. I find it kinda hokey. But I've got a client...or should I say I had a client with a very large collection of some of the biggie western artists. It's going to figure in the estate. I needed a little education. You were really getting me turned on to the stuff." He grinned. "But then you always turn me on."

Christina studied her ice cream carefully, too aware of his remark.

"Anyway, I didn't expect to find you there. It was a nice surprise. You're very good at that, the stories and the drama. You should have been an actress."

"I was." She laughed, relieved to change the subject. "I did the whole starving, waitressing in New York thing when I got out of Penn State. I got a few off-Broadway roles, but I really wasn't good enough for the big time."

"My God. An actress who admits she wasn't good enough?"

"No, really. The competition is so unbelievably good. And I hated the rejection. When I lost a role I'd be devastated for days. Then I did a little television—commercials, voice-overs. Little by little I got into the writing end of it, which I loved. Then I met David. He was with one of the big brokerage houses. Neither of us liked the city all that much. We decided to head west. And wound up here. We got married. David began his business, et cetera, et cetera, et cetera."

"And did very well at it."

"Yes. It was very good timing."

"Still write anything?"

"I still do some free-lance, sometimes with David on the wine and food stuff. I'll find something that interests me, do the research, write about, then try to sell it. I keep thinking I'll write that novel one day, but..." She shrugged.

"I don't think I've ever seen anything of yours. Tell me where to look."

Christina laughed. "Next time you fly somewhere, go through the airline magazine. You might find something. I did a piece on the Cowboy Art Show for US Air. Really, this is not a major career we're talking about."

Sev was thoughtful. "Maybe you could help me with this art collection. I need an expert to tell me what's worth something and what's junk."

"Oh, Sev, I'm no expert. I know some, but you should get a professional."

"Oh, I will. But maybe you could give me some advice with the preliminary weeding out. The firm would pay you, though I don't imagine that's much of an inducement." He waited, then reached over and rubbed her arm. "Well, think about it."

"All right. Maybe. I'll think about it." She had no intention in the world of working with Sev Justus on anything. "I feel like a little kid with sticky hands. I think I even have rum raisin in my hair. But it was delicious." She looked at her watch and stood up. "Now, let's go see what you've bought Hallie for her birthday."

They walked toward the jeweler.

"I had to do something special. It's the big four-oh. She's not happy about it."

"Hallie's forty? I wouldn't have thought so."

"Well, we all work at it, don't we?" Sev said dryly. "And it still comes. It will to you one day before you know it."

Christina made a face as they stepped inside the shop. "Sooner than you might think."

Moments later, the jeweler opened the gray velvet box and took out the emerald and diamond ring. "Turned out real nice, Mr. Justus, don't you think?"

"Oh, Sev, it's simply gorgeous. She'll love it." Christina bent over the box and touched the glowing green jewel.

"Try it on," he said.

"Oh, no. I wouldn't." She knew Sev was showing off a bit, but it was Hallie's ring. "But I'm glad I got to see it. And I won't breathe a word. Now I've honestly got to go."

"Wait a sec. I'll walk you to your car." He signed the sales slip.

"No, really. I'm just down those steps to underground parking."

"Then you definitely need walking with. Underground parking lots are teeming with perverts in open raincoats lying in wait for beautiful women to come and get their Jaguars."

"Oh, Sev, you're impossible. I come to the Borgata practically every other day and no one's so much as *had* a raincoat."

Outside the shop Sev casually put his arm around her

shoulders and smiled down at her. "I've enjoyed this."

She moved away and said lightly, "Yes, the ice cream cone was fun. Thank you. And I love Hallie's ring."

Downstairs the lot was dark and gloomy. The shops had only just opened and there were few cars.

"See," she said. "Not a pervert in sight."

"You can't be sure."

When they reached her car, she could feel him close behind her. She fumbled for her keys, then turned the lock.

He went across her chest to her opposite shoulder and his mouth was at her ear. "You know I'm going to kiss you, don't you."

She felt the blood rushing in her ears and stood very still. When he turned her around and cupped her chin with his hand, She couldn't look away. He bent his head and brushed her lips softly with his own, so gently, so easily. Over and over, barely touching her. Her eyes fluttered closed, and though her heart quickened, a warm lassitude stole over her. His arms went around her. When her lips opened slightly, she felt only the flicker of his tongue. And then it was gone. He gradually became more urgent and her hands came up to his chest, but they didn't push him away. She sighed and her breath came out light and fast. His hands came down to her buttocks, then he pushed her against the car with his hips.

"Let me make love to you, Christina. I'm obsessed with you." His voice was harsh against her ear.

"Sev, stop," she panted. "Someone will come. See us."

He growled, "Is that all you're worried about?" Behind her he yanked open the back car door and pushed her onto the seat.

She lay under him, struggling against the heat that made her want him. He kissed her hard, then roughly pulled down the straps of her top, imprisoning her arms, murmuring against her breasts, "If you knew what you were doing to me when we were sitting upstairs. I was on fire wanting you, wanting to kiss you, taste you. I can't forget what you looked like that day in the pool. Don't fight me any more, Christina."

A car came down the ramp and passed them, pulling in several spaces down. Christina froze, her reeling senses dashed with the sound of voices. She pushed his head away and tugged up her straps. "Sev, don't. Stop. I'm…I lost my head. Please let me up," she pleaded.

Gradually he was still, then raised his head and looked down at her. His eyes were hot, and so close she could see the individual hairs of his thick black lashes. She was not sure if he would stop. Or that she wanted him to.

"Yes. Of course. I lost mine, too." He leaned down and kissed her lightly, then sat her up, pulled her from the back seat and opened the front door for her. She slid under the wheel, not wanting to look at him, and rested her forehead on the steering wheel. He rubbed the back of her neck for a moment, then she heard him walk away, his steps echoing on the cement floor.

~ * ~

By the time she arrived home she was fairly composed. She could answer calmly when David wondered where she had been.

"I was getting worried about you. I thought you'd be back right after your class."

"Oh, I saw a couple of things I wanted to try on. One that looked like it might work for that thing tonight. But it looked dreadful on me. Then I ran into Sev. He was picking up Hallie's birthday present and wanted me to see it. Show off. You know how he is. It's a beautiful emerald ring. Hallie's going to be forty. Can you believe that?" She felt herself babbling, but at least he seemed satisfied.

"No, she doesn't look it." He put down the morning paper. "I'll be leaving for the shopping center in a little while. Get me something to eat, will you?"

"Of course." All she wanted to do was stand under an icy, icy shower, but she walked to the kitchen and opened the refrigerator door, still feeling the hot ache of unsatisfied desire. She took an ice cube from the bin and rubbed it over her forehead and steadied her breathing. The contents of the refrigerator were meaningless and she had to shake her head to remember why she was standing in front of it. She threw the ice cube into the sink and wiped her hands on her bicycle shorts, then reached for a package of ham and a carton of milk.

SEVENTEEN

LAISE

The airport at Cannes teemed with arrivals escaping the torrid August cities to the north. Flatbeds teetered with luggage against a symphony of shouts from vacationers eager to hit the beaches of the Cote d'Azur.

Laise hugged her tiny French friend. "Oh, Agathe, how good to be here. Paris was a steambath."

"Well, of course, *chérie*. Nobody stays there in August. I couldn't imagine what you were thinking of."

Laise shrugged. "I missed Paris, and I wanted to shop. I went absolutely mad. Wait 'til you see. Also, it turned out, I had an...interesting interlude. I'll tell you about it later."

She signaled a porter.

Agathe Assante was sputtering with curiosity as Laise pointed out her luggage to the porter, knowing she was being maddeningly close-mouthed.

When they got to Agathe's Mercedes, the porter surveyed the groaning luggage cart, shrugged and rolled his eyes.

Agathe put the top down and it was decided that if Laise held a large shopping bag on her lap and some small packages at her feet, the car could accommodate the pile of suitcases. Agathe gave the man a lavish tip and they lurched away.

"Now! How do you expect me to wait after you say you had an interlude. A man, of course." She jammed on the brakes to avoid an elderly man and woman returning to their car. The old man shouted and waved his cane. Agathe called out a merry apology and blew him a kiss.

"Of course. Be patient with me. I'm not quite rational yet. This caught me by surprise."

As the years passed, Laise's heart no longer pounded at Agathe's operation of a car and the conversation continued uninterrupted.

"Patient! When was I ever patient?" Seeing that Laise showed no signs of elaborating, she sighed. "So it was a serious interlude, eh? I'm afraid you have no experience in these things, Laise, though Olimpia and I have tried. Tell me when you are able, *chérie*, as long as you don't wait too long." She grinned impishly. "Of course I must know before Olimpia." She occupied herself with the gears of the Mercedes as they shot out onto the autoroute toward Cannes.

The smell of the sea filled Laise as the choppy waves of the Mediterranean spread out to the horizon. The sleek red car whipped through the heavy summer traffic, the car seemingly controlled by no more than one long red fingernail.

Laise found it easier to watch her friend rather than their perilous progress on the autoroute. Agathe's large almond eyes were covered with jeweled cat's eye sunglasses. Her long dark ponytail was pulled out of a dazzling sequined sun visor and whipped around her head in the rush of wind.

"How are the girls?" Laise asked.

"Insane, what else! *Folles!* For the rock stars. Were we that awful? Punk this, rap that. What is 'New Age?' Do you have any idea what Goth is? It makes me feel 'Old Age.' And they all want to look like those vulgar American children singers and actresses, with their diamond navels and hard stomachs and harder faces. Chloé begins school in Switzerland in September, the twins next year. It will be an enormous relief."

Laise knew Agathe adored her three girls, as well as her dour banker husband, who Laise found a bore. She knew Agathe sometimes did, too, and when the ennui got too great she simply took a lover until the restlessness went away.

When, a couple of years ago Laise had confessed her marital situation to her two friends, Agathe had said, *"Chérie,* what an ideal situation! You have a handsome husband who looks after your affairs impeccably, is an attentive father to John and Jeremiah, escorts you in society, and you don't have to worry about being discovered when you have a little adventure. *Quelle bonne chance!"* Agathe sighed with envy.

Olimpia reacted differently, mainly because Olimpia didn't worry about being found out when she wanted someone else. If the husband of the moment didn't like it, well, it was a lot easier to divorce in Italy than it used to be. She liked being in love with her husband, whoever he might be, and she couldn't understand how Laise could stay with a man she had no desire for. Olimpia was on her fifth husband. She had several small children and since she remained on good terms with all her former husbands, she found it confusing to remember who belonged to whom, a trivial matter in any case. They were all simply Olimpia's dark-eyed beautiful family, a fluid arrangement that seemed to suit everyone.

They left the highway and climbed the Grande Corniche into hills spiked with dark spiraling cypress trees and riotous scarlet bougainvillea. Lavish villas seemed stacked on one another up the precipitous bluffs overlooking the Mediterranean. Agathe swung the car onto a drive that dropped down steeply to a chalk-white villa.

"I sent the girls down to be with Charles's family. He was eager for me to spend the week with you. Do you suppose he has someone? Hm? He is not so watchful of me when he has a mistress."

The stucco house, with terra-cotta tiled roof and graceful iron grillwork looked out on a panorama of multi-colored sea blues, the city of Cannes with its baroque hotels, and the tile roofs of the white and pastel villas below. The pinks and reds of oleander, mandevilla, bougainvillea, geraniums, and roses cast a rosy blush over the landscape of some of the most expensive real estate in the world.

Olimpia d'Orsini's Alfa Romeo was parked in the tiled courtyard. The front door flew open and a tall blonde loped up the steps. "Ciao! Ciao!" she shrieked and wrapped Laise in an eager embrace.

The three women fell on each other like liberated schoolgirls escaping from a chaperone. They staggered under the weight of Laise's luggage and in her bedroom flung the suitcases open in an orgy of delight as they fluffed out dresses, lingerie, shoes—the fruits of her shopping convulsion in Paris.

"Oh, *chérie,* you must have had a broken heart to have bought so much. Been so unhappy." Agathe swirled out the black chiffon cocktail dress Laise had worn with Will. "So *élégante,* so *soignée.* So perfect for you."

Laise smiled. "Yes. It was." She picked up the dress and ran it through her fingers. "I met a man in Paris. It happened before I knew it, that he was someone I could love. But, he's not free." She sighed. "So you see. It would lead nowhere. He had to leave. He wants me to meet him again in Paris. He's from San Francisco. I don't want some long distance sort of affair with no future. He didn't tell me about his wife." She shrugged. "So you see, it really is hopeless."

"You Americans, I don't understand you," groaned Olimpia. "If you love being with him, go to him. Wherever he is. If he has forgotten you, you still had a wonderful experience and you can go on to someone else."

"Olimpia is right. Maybe it will turn out to be a fabulous relationship that will last a long time. What luck you have! A platonic marriage and a lover you would see only when you felt like it." Agathe frowned. "Every time I think I have found an interesting lover, he turns out to be as predictable as Charles. I am beginning to think all men are alike."

"I took his telephone number in Paris. I called it at the airport. I was going to leave a message and tell him I would come back. But I hung up. I threw the number away. It would be foolish, very unrealistic of me to keep thinking it would work."

Later they lay around the pool stretched out on blue and white striped chaises that faced the changeable blue sea. Laise made a pitcher of margueritas.

"I swear, Laise, I don't know whether I look forward more to seeing you or your margueritas." Olimpia closed her eyes and darted her tongue around the salt-encrusted rim of the glass. "So deliciously bad for you—salt, sugar, and alcohol. What could be worse?"

"Nothing. Would you like another?" Laise asked.

"Of course."

"How is Preston?" Agathe asked.

"He's well. We're friends, I guess. We just stay the same from day to day. John and Jeremiah adore him. Their lives are stable and that's what's important. Right now they're all up at the ranch. The boys are spending the summer learning to rope and brand—all those cowboy things. The ranch hands are wonderful to them, and they're actually beginning to be some help." She studied the pale green drink. "If I had something I really wanted to do, a real reason to change the status quo, I suppose I would. They're twelve and fourteen. They're old enough to handle it if I divorced Preston. I know that Will Fowler can never be that reason. I really must try to forget him."

"If you knew how we worry about your sex life," Agathe said.

"There's more."

"Ah."

"Ah," Olimpia echoed.

"I'll have to go back to the beginning of summer. There's a young Italian teaching at the university. I want to ask you about him, Olimpia. Maybe you know his family and some of the circumstances. I gather he's in some sort of family exile for something that happened four, maybe five years ago. His name is Gianluca Lucchese. I think it's a prominent family, Amalfi Sportswear. Does the name mean anything to you, Olimpia?"

"Give me a moment to think. I know the family, of course. It's an important one in textiles, as well as the Amalfi line. Big in other things, too." She thought a moment, then went on. "The father, Ugo Lucchese is a Calabrian. He's rather looked down on socially even though he married a Firelli. Rather coarsely handsome. Virile." She grinned. "You know how we northerners regard the south. Anyway, he's crude, but smart. He saw a lot of trends before others did and it made him incredibly rich. He was a major reason that Italian style is so big internationally. He's very powerful—ruthless, I understand."

"I'd like to know anything you can recall," Laise said.

"Yes, I'm beginning to recall now. There are three sons. The youngest got into some kind of unsavory trouble, but it all was quieted down very quickly. That's not surprising. Ugo can do that. He has many connections. I could find out for you easily enough. Yes, Gianluca was the young one. He was closer to my sister's age. She'd know."

"Oh, it really doesn't matter, I guess. He's fun, and he's been very attentive. But... Oh, don't get so excited. Gianluca has been very sweet...and very romantic. What I wanted to tell you is that we're all invited to his family's villa in Portofino. It seems his father is beginning to relent and Gianluca has been allowed back into the bosom of the family for a few weeks. What do you think? Should we go for a weekend? I think we'd have a wonderful time. Gianluca's begged me to convince you."

"*Pourquoi pas?*"

"Why not?"

~ * ~

Since Laise had met Will, she had wavered in seeing Gianluca again, but had finally decided to assign Will to that part of her holiday that would be put behind her. She had met him by accident, loved him impetuously, and now he was gone. That was that.

But her interlude with him had made her view her relationship to Gianluca with a level head. He must now be relegated to a summer romance as well. He had done her an enormous favor, bringing her alive, so to speak, and now she was ready to find a man to share her life again. She didn't know where, or how, but she was emotionally ready to put Preston behind her.

She didn't know if Gianluca would be quite so libidinous in close proximity to his family. Well, he said there would be plenty of people around. How had he presented her to his formidable father? To his mother? As the wise and steady older woman, professor and mentor of the young Italian faculty member? She could hope.

Well, she'd find out soon enough. He was picking them up in San Remo with the boat he said was so beautiful.

EIGHTEEN

LAISE

Gianluca was fizzing with excitement as he eased the small speedboat up to the pier in San Remo. He had scarcely looped the rope over the pylon before he sprang from the cockpit onto the wooden planking of the dock.

"*Ciao! Ciao! Salve! Sono molto leto di fare la sua conscenza!*" He embraced Laise eagerly, then Agathe and Olimpia. "I am so happy, so delighted to meet you. Let me help you get your bags stowed. Did you leave your car where I told you? It will be all right there. I made sure of it," he said, clearly anxious to be away.

Olimpia whispered to Agathe, "If a Lucchese says your car will be all right, it will be all right. Nobody would risk touching it."

The speedboat skimmed noisily over the water out into the boat-filled harbor. Gianluca pointed to a sleek yacht just ahead as their destination.

Laise knew it was the most beautiful boat she had ever seen, and called out to Gianluca with delight. "Oh, it is, Gianluca. You weren't exaggerating. It's magnificent."

Olimpia gazed at the yacht, admiring. "I've only seen one other of these. They're built down in the Viareggio boatyards. I think there are only a half a dozen of them in the world."

The *Donatella* was a one hundred-forty foot craft and a marvel of space age aerodynamics. Gianluca swept his arm, explaining, "There are four decks, five bedrooms. We'll go down to Capri tomorrow...away from the coast and I'll show you what she can do."

Laise noticed as they cruised along that other craft came close to look at the boat. They waved back, as pleased as if they'd built the boat themselves.

Gianluca pointed to the green hills. "We're almost there. The villa is up on that hill. There are other guests, and my brothers and their wives. There are lots of parties. Portofino is very merry in the summer." He took Laise's hand and whispered in her ear. "But there is time to be alone, too."

How I love the Italians, she thought. *Life is such fun to them. I'm going to have a wonderful time. This is good for me. I'll stop brooding over Will Fowler. The whole thing was impossible from the beginning.*

The sapphire harbor of Portofino was crowded with boats of every type, with the iridescent sunlight illuminating the soft peach and burnt orange of the seventeenth century buildings along the quai, where busy cafes with bright umbrellas lined the cobblestone square. The deep green hills rising above the town were dotted with red-tiled roofs of white villas.

Laise turned to Olimpia. "You know, of course, Portofino isn't real." She swept her arm to encompass the magical scene. "It is all only an enchanted photograph."

"Even Italians feel that way about Portofino," Olimpia laughed. "Eh, Gianluca?"

Ashore, Gianluca loaded them all into a bright red Lancia and inched his way through the strolling tourists in the square, up past the dozens of stalls of fine lace vendors selling snowy delicate handkerchiefs, formal table cloths, curtains, bridal veils and christening dresses. Then there were the chic shops with their heartstoppingly expensive wares. Giuanluca shifted gears and they began the climb into the emerald hills.

About ten minutes from the town they came to a large iron gate that swung open as they approached. The long drive, lined with dark, twisted cypress trees, led finally to an imposing chamois-colored Renaissance structure. Gianluca pulled the car around the circular gravel drive and stopped with a stone-flying flourish. Wide steps led to an elaborately carved double-door entrance flanked by great stone urns filled with profusions of red geraniums and purple lobelia.

A servant came down the stairs, followed by a medium-tall, brown-haired woman with a regal bearing and a tentative smile.

His mother, Laise thought.

"*Bienvenuto.* It is good to meet Gianluca's good friend." She touched Laise's shoulder lightly, examining her face before she turned to the others. "Ah yes, Olimpia. I know your family."

"I'll take them up, Mama." Gianluca signaled to the servant who was bringing their luggage and directed them all to one side of the grand staircase that rose from a landing and split, both sides curving up to the second floor. The entrance to the house was through a sixty foot wide marble-floored Doric-columned gallery. In the center was an elaborately-carved table with a giant *chinoisérie* vase filled with flowering branches. From the two story ceiling hung a great chandelier of clear Venetian glass. The Luccheses had not chosen a simple vacation home. The house was formal, opulent and still.

A maid unpacked Laise's suitcase and put her clothes in a small dressing room lined with shelves and drawers. Another maid brought a tray with fruits, cheeses, and small buttery pastries. Laise began to understand Gianluca's sense of frustration at his reduced circumstances after being raised in such luxury.

She had been alone in her room only a few minutes

when there was a light tapping on her door. She went to open it. Gianluca stepped in quickly and closed the door behind him, pulling her into his arms and covering her face with small kisses.

"It was an eternity until you came. I long for you. We'll be together on the boat. I won't come to you here. My father…"

She put a finger to his mouth. "Hush, Gianluca. I understand. Of course, it's better. We mustn't offend your parents." She kissed his cheek. "Now, let's collect Olimpia and Agathe. You can show us the house and grounds."

It was late afternoon as he took the three out to the gardens. From the vantage point of a path that overlooked the house they could see the sun getting low in the west over the sea, turning it into a sheet of copper. The kew, kew, kewing of sea gulls floated up from the harbor.

Gianluca was in an expansive mood. "We should leave early in the morning for Capri. It's about four hundred kilometers. We'll take our time along the way, but I want to arrive before noon day after tomorrow so the tide will be right to get into the Blue Grotto. We will swim there. It's fantastic."

Night had begun to fall when he stood and they started back to the house. "Dinner will be at 9:30. We have drinks before, around the pool and you will meet everyone. My brothers and their wives are here. There will be twenty for dinner my mother says."

It was close to nine o'clock when Laise finished dressing after telling Agathe and Olimpia she would hurry and to go down without her. She had nearly fallen asleep in the mosaic tub in her bathroom, almost a small pool. The bathroom itself was huge, all marble and gilt mirrors. The bedroom was spacious as well, with tall windows that overlooked the gardens and the sea. The Venetian bed was wide, with ornate carving touched with gilt, with a cream silk and lace duvet and mounds of silk and lace pillows. Silk draperies hung from the ceiling over the bed, pulled back with a heavy twisted cord.

Laise gave herself a last look in the long mirror in the dressing room. She had decided to wear a peach silk Dior that had a silver lace overlay. It had tiny straps and was short—nothing to it really and she liked the color with her hair. She didn't know how formally these people dressed for dinner, but the house was very grand for a summer villa, after all. When she had asked, Gianluca had told her she would look beautiful in anything she wore. No help at all.

Down in the foyer Laise could hear sounds of conversation and laughter. An accordion played softly—the sound of the Mediterranean. But she was puzzled over how to get to the party. Gianluca had hurried them through the endless rooms of the house and now she was confused, facing the choice of several hallways.

Down one corridor the music became fainter, so she tried another. She found herself in a spacious loggia with walls lined with paintings they hadn't seen this afternoon. It apparently didn't interest Gianluca.

What a pity, she thought.

There was a skylight with filigreed wrought iron that ran the length of the ceiling, but tonight the room was illuminated with sophisticated track lighting that highlighted each work of art. And what works of art! Gaddis, Duccios, Giottos, a Botticelli, a Raphael, and more. There were several pieces of sculpture along the center of the gallery. She became absorbed in the paintings, knowing the importance of the collection. She was examining a large Piero della Francesca madonna when she felt someone watching her. She turned quickly, knowing she had lingered too long.

She felt almost an electric shock when she confronted Ugo Lucchese. She knew it was he. It had to be. And his physical presence was almost an assault.

"*Signorina* Spenser, I believe." He offered his hand. "I am Ugo Lucchese." There was admiration in the eyes that openly appraised her.

"Molto lieto. I am Laise Spenser. But it is *Signora* Spenser."

The black eyes widened slightly for a moment in surprise and he raised a thick eyebrow. "*Signora?* I thought...well, that doesn't matter, does it?" he said smoothly. "Gianluca did not mention that you are married. Are you traveling with your husband?" The inquiry was polite, but pointed.

Laise was puzzled. What had Gianluca told his father about her? "No, I'm traveling with friends."

Ugo Lucchese studied her face for a moment, then said, "I see you are admiring my della Francesca. Are you familiar with Italian painting?"

"Yes." She turned to leave, but he didn't move. She turned back. He was the host, after all, so she couldn't be considered late. "My grandfather was very interested in the *quatroccento.* He traveled extensively in Italy and became a collector of Italian painting and furniture. When my parents died, I inherited the collection. It is fairly extensive. I have a few favorite pieces in my house, but the major portion of the collection is on extended loan to our local museum. I have added to it from time to time but, as you know, good things don't come on the market much any more."

"Quite so. Perhaps because of all you American collectors?" There was a touch of sarcasm in his voice.

Laise felt a flare of annoyance. She measured Ugo, feeling her eyes narrow. Her voice was silky, but unmistakably angry. "Perhaps you believe I should give up my paintings so there would be more to hang on the walls of Italian villas."

His eyes, like obsidian, locked into hers. Neither moved as the gay music floated into the loggia from the party by the pool.

Laise's voice was tight. She did not take her eyes from his. "I live in a city where there isn't great opportunity for people to see fine Italian works. It pleases me to make my paintings accessible to others."

The rebuke hung in the air.

Suddenly Ugo Lucchese roared with laughter. "You insult me in excellent Italian." He took her arm and tucked it into his. "Come with me. Dinner will be soon and you haven't had the opportunity to meet the other guests. I will show you the way. And you will be next to me at dinner."

Laise's tension drained away, but she felt shaky. Her face was hot and her hands were cold. She wished he wouldn't notice, but she knew that he did. He had deliberately provoked her and she had allowed him to make her angry. And it wouldn't help Gianluca if she annoyed his father. How much he looked like him, she thought. But the son was softer, almost blurred, compared to the sharp *definition* of this man.

And she knew she had never met a man like Ugo Lucchese before.

They went through the open French doors to the pool where the company was gathered. The waterfall-fed pool was for swimming, but also served as a long reflecting pool for the marble columns that supported a gallery across the back of the house. There were tall stone fountains, as well as statuary and more stone urns of flowers and fancifully topiaried boxwood. A formal Italian garden.

Gianluca hurried over to them and exclaimed, "Oh, you've met my father. What did I tell you, Father? She is beautiful, no?"

"Yes, very beautiful." He bowed to her briefly. "Signora Spenser is sitting next to me at dinner, Gianluca. We will talk about painting." He gave her a small smile and moved off to his other guests.

"What is he talking about? That's not fair. I wanted to sit with you." Then his face brightened. "But, I'm so happy he likes you. Come, you must meet the others. Agathe and Olimpia are over with my brothers and their wives."

Agathe and Olimpia mingled with the guests around the pool. There were Gianluca's two brothers, Antonio and Paulo, both so close in looks, and their pretty, vivacious wives; an uncle and aunt from the Firelli side of the family, and three other couples—a minister of some government agency or other, a Swiss diplomat, a manufacturer, and their wives.

The long dining room was paneled with painted murals of the local scenery. There were two large Murano glass chandeliers over a long table with heavy Florentine silver candelabra filled with several dozen glowing tapers. The high-backed chairs were of heavily-carved dark wood and upholstered in olive moiré silk. The table sat on a long Aubusson runner in blues and greens that helped soften the sound in the tiled room; but it wasn't an intimate room for a summer retreat—cold and formal.

The company, however, was in high spirits. Laise noticed that Gianluca was subdued around his father, maybe nursing a sulk because he wasn't sitting with her? She also noticed Donatella's eyes resting on her briefly, then moving away. *Another Lucchese disgruntled about the seating arrangement?*

Ugo was the perfect host, charming and attentive to everyone. The wine had calmed Laise's annoyance, but she felt she had invisible threads connecting her to Ugo Lucchese that pulled at her imperceptibly. Actually he said little to her directly, but his hand might brush hers, or his eyes glittering in the candlelight would catch hers at an unguarded moment, making her look away from their sensual appraisal.

Laise tried to keep up an animated conversation with the diplomat on her right, a Swiss attaché to the legation in Rome. He was a portly man who obviously enjoyed the table and he tucked into the wine and various courses with gusto. Laise vaguely remembered his face from her long ago Washington days, but she didn't mention it. She didn't want her regular life here.

After dinner, the men and the women separated. Donatella took the women upstairs in a velvet-paneled elevator to a pretty sitting room off what Laise guessed was her dressing room. Laise reflected that the old custom, rarely done in America any more, was rather nice. She chatted with Gianluca's sisters-in-law. They were intrigued at how tall she was, sure they had seen her in some magazine or another because of it. They were full of questions about fashions and fads in America, and the latest films. Gianluca had told them she had a ranch, though she was sure she had never mentioned it to him. Well, it wasn't a secret. She was reluctant to say much about her family or personal life, but the ranch may have come up in her conversation.

And now she had been baited by his father to reveal her family's interest in Italian art and her own collection. Maybe she had been wrong to come. Maybe it had encouraged Gianluca too much. Their lighthearted lovemaking excited her, but that's all it was. It had awakened her, and now she felt open, even vulnerable.

Donatella served the small cups of *ristretto,* stronger even than the espresso the Italians love. She found the older women friendly and gracious, but occasionally, looking up from another picture of yet another beautiful dark-eyed baby, she would again catch Donatella's thoughtful gaze. As Agathe and Olimpia chattered with the other women about mutual friends, Donatella invited Laise to come sit beside her. She wanted to know about Gianluca's life in Arizona and Laise painted as glowing a picture as she could—how well-thought-of he was at the university. After all, she thought, she was here to prove that Gianluca had settled down—that he had a mature professor as a friend. *I'll give him a good report card. I can see why he is so intimidated by his father. I'm intimidated by him, and that hasn't happened to me in a long, long time.*

After about an hour the women went downstairs. They mingled with the men for perhaps half an hour, and then card games were being formed. Since it was after midnight and the cruise down to Capri was to sail early, the boat-trip people began to drift off to bed.

Laise, her friends and Gianluca strolled in the garden until Agathe said good night.

Olimpia agreed. "I'll go with you. Tomorrow will be wonderful so I must get to sleep."

Gianluca promised them he would not keep Laise long. After they'd gone, he turned to her, his eyes bright. He was elated. "The evening went well, don't you agree? My father's impressed that I chose you."

"Chose me?" She wasn't sure what he meant.

"To kiss!" He swept her into his arms and kissed her ardently, apologizing with sad Italian words that he couldn't make love to her tonight, as much as it broke his heart.

"Stop, Gianluca." She laughed. "You're smothering me. I can't breathe." But she felt a surge of heat as he massaged her buttocks and pressed himself to her.

Over his shoulder she saw the silhouette of Ugo Lucchese in the tall windows of the library.

~ * ~

In her room, Laise got ready for bed slowly, aroused by Gianluca's kisses, keyed-up by the strong *ristretto*, the flashes across her memory of Ugo's earlier patronizing of her in the gallery. His anger at her had been palpable then suddenly, surprisingly, he had laughed.

But it was later, with his intense glances at the table, the casual touches casting invisible wires that spoke, "I will have you," that made her will away the images of those dark, provocative eyes.

I'm glad we're going away tomorrow. I was naïve to think it would be a harmless interlude with Gianluca.

After she turned off the light, she went to the door of her small balcony and stood listening to the night sounds. She could hear a nightingale a distance away. A small dog yapped.

The night was fragrant with the scents of mimosa, jasmine and roses. The three-quarter moon, silvery and bright, had begun to lower in the sky.

It's late, she thought. *I must try to sleep.*

The bed linens smelled faintly of lavender and the scent drifted in and out of Laise's consciousness as sleep eluded her.

She heard the door open softly and came fully awake. "Gianluca?"

It wasn't Gianluca. She had known all evening who it would be. Wanted it to be.

Her mind reeled. *Laise, Laise, you fool. You fool. Don't do this.*

Ugo stood over her, his black eyes opaque in the moonlit room. He said nothing, but abruptly pulled her up and brought his mouth down hard on hers. His kiss was unequivocal in its demand.

She struggled against the ache that throbbed between her legs. She forced her face away from his hungry mouth, gasping, "You mustn't. We can't."

His hand roughly jerked her face back to his and the demanding lips silenced her protests. He yanked his robe off and tore her nightgown to her waist. She was flung down as he suckled her breasts and his knee thrust her legs apart. He plunged into her then pulled out and slammed into her again. She whimpered, then sobbed. He was enormous. He filled her. He surrounded her and she was aflame, her slickness pouring around the relentless iron prod. Her first orgasm resonated through her, a second, a third, and still he bucked over her, controlling her. She begged for his thrusts when he withheld them. Sobs tore at her throat. Finally he brought her to a summit and let his own orgasm burst, flooding her with his hot juices. His hand was hard on her mouth to smother her cries.

He withdrew the battering ram from her, leaving her exhausted and sated. She felt the bed move as he stood and she opened her eyes. He was standing, looking down at her, his face unreadable. In the light from the moon she could see the sweat glistening on his muscled body and in the mat of thick black hair on his chest and stomach, and in the nest that surrounded his thick, partially erect penis.

"So. Now the *putana* of the son is also the *putana* of the father," he sneered.

The word cut through her like a razor. *Putana.* Whore. Stunned, Laise heard the door close. Her mind reeled. She sat up then flung herself to the bed. She raged, she pounded the lacy fragrant pillows, clawed at the mattress.

And she knew that the next time he came to her she would open her legs and beg him to drive into her again and again.

NINETEEN

LAISE

Laise examined herself critically, holding the magnifying mirror close to her face. There were blue circles under her eyes, which she could always count on if she slept badly. Had she been able to doze off for any more than an hour? No more than that. From physical prostration if nothing else, she thought bitterly. Her lips felt bruised and swollen and her teeth had cut the inside of her mouth from Ugo's crushing kisses. Her cheeks and chin, scraped by his coarse beard, were red and irritated. Well, it would have to be a masterful makeup job. She set to work.

She smoothed foundation over her face. She started to put the cap on the bottle, but looked at her face again and smudged more under her eyes, then whisked a translucent powder over it. With each step—blush, mascara, eye shadow, she felt it more a mask. Finally she rubbed a soft peach gloss on her lips and studied the results. Maybe it wasn't too bad. She knew she looked better than she felt. Coffee and sea air would help. She'd try to nap on the boat.

What had happened to her? Gianluca had touched some unknown button in her, unlocked a sexuality she'd never dreamed lurked there. Will had picked up on it and made a pass at her. But that wasn't what he was all about. She knew that.

He had moved her emotionally like no other man. With Gianluca it was just sex, joyful and carefree. She had loved Will for only one night and an afternoon. How naïve to think there could be more.

And last night? She longed to say that Ugo had raped her, but she could not hide it from herself that it had not been rape. She had cried out, "You mustn't. We can't!" while her eager body had opened to him, thrilling with the lust that humiliated her now. What she had done with Ugo had a base so elemental and savage, so mindless, so devoid of emotion. It was pure, violent, sexual gluttony and her body had responded to it instinctively and hungrily. Was it because of the aching emptiness that losing Will had left? Were her emotions so raw that she would respond in such a primal way to Ugo's assault?

Yes, an assault. That she had been complicit in it did not change what it was. But why? It was more than that he simply wanted her. That she was married had surprised him. She knew he had watched Gianluca's caresses in the garden after dinner. Was that why he was so vengeful and angry? That she was an unfaithful wife? Was it because she had defied him earlier? He said she had insulted him, but he had laughed and taken her arm. Surely he wasn't so irrational as to despise her for that. Was he? It made no sense. Unless he only wanted to humiliate Gianluca's mistress? His married mistress? Was that how he saw her? Was that what she was? Why didn't she run? Now. Today.

It would be awkward if she left the villa, she reasoned. She had gotten Olimpia and Agathe here. Plans had been made. It would embarrass Gianluca and he had had nothing to do with last night. He would be hurt if she left with some lame excuse or another.

Laise angrily scooped her makeup into a large straw bag and ripped the zipper closed. All the reasoning in the world wouldn't hide the real reason she wouldn't leave. She wanted Ugo Lucchese again.

The cruise group assembled in the cool foyer. Laise looked around quickly to see if Ugo was there. She wondered if he would want to see how she looked this morning, see how she behaved.

He wasn't there, but Donatella was, regal and serene, though Laise felt the tiny undercurrent she'd felt last evening in the watchful dark eyes. *Does she know? Can she tell? Does she know what he does? Am I the only one? I can't think of it.*

The yacht *Donatella* glistened, brass fittings like gold in the clear morning light. The fairytale harbor bustled with returning fishermen. Hard to believe this was not only a rich man's playground, but a working fishing port as well.

Gianluca stood on deck, reveling in his duties as host, directing the loading of luggage, describing the activities of the three-day trip with such effervescence that his older brothers began pummeling him back and forth between them.

"What are we going to do with the *cucciolo,* Paulo?" cried Antonio.

"Throw him overboard so we can all go back to bed!"

Everyone roared their approval, and the brothers picked up the "puppy" and swung him back and forth threateningly. They obviously adored their young brother and he was almost bursting with delight at their teasing.

"You'll see! We'll sing and eat and dance. Who will make you do all these things if I drown?"

Puppy, thought Laise. *How very like a puppy he is.* Charming, undisciplined, exuberant. His brothers were more serious, but what Italian is totally serious? Then she thought of last night.

One.

The captain greeted them, then went to the bridge to get underway. Laise could feel the powerful engines under her feet. She, Olimpia and Agathe leaned over the rail and marveled at the rocks shimmering up through the glassy water.

"How could it be so clear this far out?" exclaimed

Agathe.

"The land is very rocky," Olimpia explained. "No sediment washes down to despoil the water. Not much grows on those rocks either."

The skirl of gulls was loud in the still morning air and the few boats out cut through the silky surface of the water, leaving quiet chevrons to mark their passage.

After the yacht was some distance out to sea, Gianluca took the three women up to the wheelhouse. The captain was clearly delighted to show off the latest gadgets. There were batteries of dials, warning lights and signals to monitor every system on board. They went up to the flying bridge where there were more control panels that duplicated all the essential systems. Gianluca and the women looked down from their airy perch and waved to the others sunbathing on the stern deck.

Agathe casually draped her arm around Laise's waist. "Are you all right, *cherie?*"

A twinge of anxiety shot through Laise's stomach. Did she look ill? She had thought she was behaving well. Was it just that her friends knew her so well? "No, I'll be fine. Just a touch of vertigo the first few minutes when we hit open sea. Isn't this just the most glorious day." *Oh, please, let that reassure her. I must find a couple of hours to sleep. I'm exhausted.* The emotions of the night washed over her and she turned away from the expression on Agathe's face.

The skipper raised his eyebrow at Gianluca, who nodded, grinning with suppressed excitement. The skipper opened up the throttles and the *Donatella* accelerated to twenty-five knots. High above the water as they were, the boat detached from the sea. The silence was eerie. The swish of the bow wave was all they could hear; the engines only a distant hum as they rushed through choppy water amid two foot swells topped with lacy frills of white.

"Take it down, captain," Gianluca said with regret, "or we'll be in Capri by this afternoon. Let's go down and eat."

The chef had set up an elaborate buffet in the saloon. Paulo teased Gianluca. "He's been talking of nothing but showing you the boat, Laise. You'd better be impressed."

"Impressed! This is another world for me. I live on the desert, remember."

She felt revived by the excitement of the speed run and breakfast. She had less success keeping thoughts of last night at bay. As soon as her attention drifted away from the company, the soreness between her legs and the cuts inside her lips brought unwelcome pictures: the gossamer curtains undulating in the silvery moonlight, the dark brocade of Ugo's robe as he threw it aside, the glistening mat of his chest, the blackness of his eyes lowering to her. With great effort she tried to be part of the conversation.

They dropped anchor in a secluded cove to go swimming. Laise was in her stateroom changing into the suit she'd bought in Paris. There was a soft knock on the door but Gianluca didn't wait for her to answer. He slid into the room, his eyes hot and amorous. Dressed only in a white Speedo, he displayed a healthy erection. He kicked the door shut and went to embrace Laise, slipping off her suit and edging her to the bed.

"*Mia bellisima,* don't make me wait another moment."

Laise found she was still in an aroused state from the night and welcomed his ardor in spite of the raw soreness between her legs. He plunged into her joyfully, soft Italian words tumbling from his lips in time with his rhythm.

She kept her eyes open and emptied her thoughts of Ugo.

Gianluca, raised on an elbow, smiled down at her. "Now I have made love to you in Italy." He jumped up and pulled her after him. "Put your suit back on. It's very pretty. You look like the Botticelli Venus. We must put you on a seashell, my love goddess. We will swim and I will make love to you again and again."

Paulo wanted to water ski, so they winched a little sixteen footer from the aft cockpit and spent the rest of the morning skimming over the deep blue water.

After an on-deck luncheon, Olimpia dropped onto the U-shaped settee next to Laise. Her smile was bright, but her voice was low and troubled. Laise, caught by her tone, glanced to find Gianluca, satisfied that he was far enough away.

"Laise, last evening I saw something. Maybe I am wrong, but I know you pretty well. Ugo Lucchese is an overpowering man. Don't let yourself be drawn to him, I beg you. He will try. His...conquests...are no secret. And Italian families can be unforgiving." She paused. "There. I'll not say any more." She squeezed Laise's knee. "Isn't this a divine trip!" She touched Laise's shoulder as she rose to move away and join the others.

Laise was uneasy as she watched her friend. Was it so obvious? Or was Olimpia just overly tuned to her? But her words were a warning to Laise. There was no question about that. And did Olimpia know that it was already too late?

The others were arranging themselves for siestas and sunbathing. All at once Laise was exhausted, depleted. She stood and stretched, wondering if she could even make herself walk to the stateroom. "I'll leave you sun worshippers and take my siesta below before I turn into a big red lobster."

Gianluca rose to go with her. When they reached her stateroom, she turned to him with apologies. "Gianluca. I didn't sleep well. I really need a nap. "

"Ah, *mia cara,* I think only of myself. Sleep well, *tresora.*"

She wakened two hours later, feeling the soft motion of the boat and the almost imperceptible engines. Gianluca was nuzzling her neck, licking her ear, fondling her breasts. She knew this was Gianluca, but this time when he entered her she didn't open her eyes.

He was Ugo, and her body exploded again and again.

Gradually her awareness spiraled up. Reluctantly she opened her eyes. Gianluca smiled down at her. *"Fantastico, mia appassionada,"* he murmured

He unwound himself from her and stood, his body tawny in the reddish glow of sunset from the porthole. He moved over to gaze out to sea. "The sun is setting, we must go up and watch. Everybody will be in the saloon for cocktails. Dinner is very casual tonight." He smiled with delight. "The chef and I have arranged a surprise. You will love it. Everybody will love it. You will see I haven't lived in Arizona for nothing." He turned to her with boyish pleasure.

She laughed, catching his mood. "Gianluca, you're gorgeous. If I'm Venus, you've got to be a god. What god will you be? I know. Apollo!"

He preened under her gaze and she saw he was becoming aroused. "No, Gianluca. No. I've got to shower and dress." She dashed into the pink marble shower and adjusted the gold fixtures, then held her face up to the cooling, cascading water.

Gianluca's surprise was a western-style barbecue. Laise was astonished that he would know how to do this. Then he explained about his Grand Canyon days with the tourists. A wonderful part of his life. It had been part of his job to help with the barbecues at Phantom Ranch in the bottom of the canyon. The *Donatella's* chef had risen to the occasion and had created an excellent facsimile of cowboy beans, barbecued ribs, and corn on the cob. The corn was fine and white, but it tasted almost the same, only a little sweeter.

~ * ~

In the morning they were anchored off the harbor at Capri. The town itself, high on the precipitous dolomite bluffs and reached by funicular from the harbor, was almost painful to the eyes in its dazzling whiteness against the amethyst sky. Small rowboats clustered around the yacht, entrepreneurs eager to take passengers to the Blue Grotto, one of many that dot the island, home of the Sirens who tempted Odysseus. Gianluca and his brothers haggled athletically with the boatmen, obviously eager to get many customers before the tides swallowed up the entrance to the cave.

The entrance looked impossibly small, but the boatmen shouted for them to flatten themselves on the bottom of his boat. The weathered old man gauged his timing and miraculously they surged through the entrance on a wave, into an eerie, still world. Laise felt she had been transported into a large, bluish-green jewel. It was quiet, and though there were other boats with people, voices were hushed and awed. They all slipped over the side of the boat into the water and swam briefly, the incandescent blue light that shone up through the water giving their bodies an otherworldly glow. They didn't stay long. The grotto was not large and the boatmen didn't linger when there were more euros to be made.

They returned to the *Donatella,* still spellbound by the blue glow of the cave. The sixteen-footer rode alongside the yacht, ready to take them into town.

The funicular carried them to the top of the limestone cliff, the gears and cables whining as they climbed. They watched the *Donatella* get smaller until it was a white toy in the deep lapis water of the harbor.

The two towns on the island—Capri at twelve hundred feet and Anacapri at sixteen hundred feet—were both saturated with tourists. The big summer festival, *Ferragosto,* when a procession carries the Madonna through the central plaza of Capri, had been the week before, but the crowds were still there. They swarmed over the *Piazetta,* the main square, and through the narrow streets where the shops held not only tourist souvenirs, but the most luxurious of the world's goods—couture clothes, furs, jewels and more jewels, fanciful shoes, luggage, fine paintings, priceless antiques and more clothes. The women spun off to the shops. The men groaned.

Antonio, noting his wife's fascination with an

extravagant alligator handbag, spoke first. "We promised we'd go to the ruins first. Ruins, then lunch, then shop. You agreed, Gianluca."

So they visited the ruins of the palazzo of the Emperor Tiberius, predecessor to the ruthless and deranged Caligula—and one of the most glorious views in the world. Small to the eye before, the *Donatella* was a tiny bright charm in the dark sea that stretched before them.

Back in town Laise wondered if they could possibly find a table in the tourist-stuffed town, but she hadn't reckoned on the Lucchese name. At the restaurant *La Capannina*, heads were put together and with streams of Italian shouts over the noise, miraculously a table for ten appeared in the middle of the dining room. A feast followed, course after course of the local specialties, and bottles and bottles of the potent red Caprian wine.

After leaving the restaurant they ambled through the streets. Laise found a dress at Versace—very short, with a dramatic matching fringed shawl, the print of different varieties of red and pink roses. Gianluca loved it and insisted she wear it that night. She found shoes at Ferragamo with huge red roses on the toes that surely had been made with the dress in mind.

While Gianluca tried on shirts in the Ferragamo shop, she slipped away into Bulgari. She wanted to get him something special and he adored jewelry. She found a heavy gold bracelet. She would have it engraved later, she thought. As she left the store, a young man moved very close and began to walk beside her. He was darkly handsome, with a gleaming smile, and flirtatious as only the supremely confident Italian male can be.

"*Posso offrire qualcosa da bere?* Can I offer you a drink? You must let me show you Capri. I will show you things tourists never get to see." He winked. "Someone as beautiful should not be alone. It is *una perdita.* A waste."

"But I'm not alone." She laughed, charmed at his sassy

approach.

Suddenly Gianluca was there. He spun the young man around. "Get away from her, *bastardo,*" he snarled, his face ugly and distorted with rage.

Laise was stunned. She thought he would strike the young man, who was as astonished as she. "Gianluca!" She grabbed his arm. "Stop it. What are you thinking of? He meant no harm. What on earth is wrong with you?"

His eyes remained blazing and furious, his body coiled.

The young man backed away, glanced at Laise and shook his head, then hurried away.

Laise took Gianluca roughly by the shoulders. "Gianluca, look at me. Stop it!"

Slowly his eyes focused on her face and his body began to relax. *"Mi scusi.* I am just so jealous for you. Forgive me, please. I...I didn't know what to think. Please forget this."

They walked along in silence. After a few minutes, Laise slowed her steps to look in windows and make small comments, trying to ease the tension. Gianluca slouched, his hands in his pockets, answering in monosyllables. She knew he was ashamed of himself. Gradually they collected the others and started back to the harbor.

All Italians are hot-headed, jealous, she thought. *I was laughing, flirting with the young man, too. He saw that. He didn't mean to lose his temper. It was really partly my fault. I should just put the whole thing out of my mind.*

And she tried—tried erasing the ugly image of Gianluca's face, flushed, twisted, his eyes bulging with rage.

When they gathered in the saloon for cocktails, Laise gave Gianluca his bracelet. He was delighted and took it that his outburst had been forgiven. Then with a small flourish he placed a small box in her hands. Everybody had been shopping and soon they were all opening gifts, shrieking with surprise at some treasure, seen and loved but not bought, and now owned. Laise opened her small box and stared, speechless. Large topaz earrings, flowers that glowed against the black velvet—the amber centers surrounded by layers of diamond baguette petals.

She looked up dismayed. "Gianluca, they're exquisite. But...I can't accept these. Truly. They're far too expensive." Where had he gotten the money for a gift like this? In Phoenix he was always strapped for money. God, he must have borrowed it. From whom? Not his father, surely. His mother?

His eyes darkened with disappointment. "It doesn't matter. They are for you. They match your eyes. You must have them. Put them on or I will be very hurt."

Laise caught a glimpse of Antonio and Paulo exchanging glances.

Uneasy, she slowly took the earrings from the box and put them on. *I'll wear them tonight*, she decided. *We'll talk in private tomorrow. We've had enough scenes for one day.*

The next day they dropped Olimpia and Agathe in San Remo and turned toward Portofino. Olimpia didn't speak of Ugo Lucchese again, as she'd promised, and when Laise waved goodbye to her friends, she knew she should be with them. She approached Portofino with dread, though a frisson of arousal swept through her when she thought of the night ahead. Olimpia had not needed to warn her about Ugo Lucchese. The air around him was explosive with risk.

The family and several guests were dining at the *Splendido,* the old hotel that boasted the most magnificent view in Europe. Gianluca was going to be knocking on her door in minutes, expecting her to be ready to go. She shook her hair back and held up the topaz earrings. If she wore them, she should sweep her hair back. Her cotton lace dress was studded with tiny rhinestones. She didn't need earrings, and besides she was giving them back. Gianluca would be hurt, but he shouldn't have given them to her in the first place. She was leaving in the morning. If he were angry with her, that would be the end of it.

Her time in Paris with Will had made her aware that she had been marking time in her life. Gianluca had broken into her shell, but he was nothing more than an interlude. Laise again felt the scalding pang that nothing had come of her encounter with Will. The trip to Portofino had not eased her heartache. She found herself spinning recklessly in the bitter emptiness left by Will, longing to erase it, to drown herself one more time in the cauldron that was Ugo Lucchese.

When Gianluca knocked on her door, she gave a final brush to her hair, put the earrings in the box and snapped it shut with finality.

"*Ah bellisima,* what a dress. You are a vision. Your hair a sunset. But you don't wear your gift. You must."

"Gianluca, I told you, I can't wear them. I can't accept them knowing you can't afford them. I don't want to hurt your feelings, but I don't wish to discuss it any more."

She put the box in his hand and curled his fingers around it.

His face relaxed. "Is this all that is worrying you? Then it is perfectly okay." He was smiling broadly, teeth white and dazzling. Relieved. "My father made me a gift of the money to buy them for you. He called Bulgari the morning we left and ordered them especially for you. He said the topaz would match the brilliance of your eyes. So, you see? It is all right." He opened the box. "You can put them on."

It was a moment before she could speak. Her voice was hoarse as she tried to keep it under control. "Gianluca, then they are a gift really from your father, not from you. What can you both be thinking of?" Trying to keep the fury from her voice she said, "I will not wear them, I will not accept them. I will not discuss it further. Period."

His liquid dark eyes were puzzled. "But why are you angry? Father only wanted me to give you something beautiful. The money is nothing." He opened the box. "Here. Please put them on. They look wonderful with your eyes."

She snatched her evening bag from the dressing table. "To hell with my eyes. Let's go. The others will be waiting."

~ * ~

Again Laise was placed next to Ugo at dinner, though the party was seated less formally at a large round table. She kept a grip on her composure and for most of the evening with her sheer rage at the implications of his gift to steady her, she could maintain the façade that it was simply a family dinner.

Ugo was perfunctory in his attitude toward her, gracious enough to be correct, but there was an undercurrent of cynicism in occasional glances, the knowing black eyes that belied the light, easy charm.

Laise focused her conversation on the others. She'd gotten to know the brothers and their wives on the trip to Capri and they were easy to be with. The whole family was talkative, with the exception of Donatella, so the evening passed.

But after the wine glasses had been filled and emptied several times, Laise felt Ugo's eyes on her more often and she could feel the heat in herself, the flush on her skin—knew there was a brightness in her eyes that she could not conceal.

Antonio was making a toast to her, regretting her departure tomorrow and the pleasure the family had in welcoming her. "Our little brother has brought a beautiful addition to the Luccheses."

There were enthusiastic murmurs and, bewildered, Laise smiled, not sure what she had just heard. She saw Ugo raise a glass to her, a ghost of a smile playing around his mouth. Donatella occupied herself with the man on her right.

Later, Laise and Gianluca walked in the garden before going to bed. Her agitation made her snap at him. "Just what, Gianluca, did you tell your family about me? About our relationship?"

"They are modern people, Laise. They know that we are lovers." His eyes slid away from hers.

"I'm sure they know that. But what else did you tell

them? I got the distinct feeling tonight that they think there's more to us than just being lovers."

"Well, *bellisima*, I...I implied that one day we might be married. Now don't be angry with me. I know I have never said anything to you. But I hoped...perhaps I said too much..."

"Too much! Gianluca. I'm married. I have two children."

"But you don't love your husband. How could you? You don't use his name."

"That has nothing to do with you. My relationship with my husband is a private affair."

"Please, don't be angry with me."

"Gianluca, you've misled your family. Your parents. Look, I'm leaving in the morning. Please straighten this all out. I don't want to be angry with you." She put her arms around him. "We've been such good friends. We'll still be seeing one another back at school. You're important to me, Gianluca. I'm very fond of you. You were a good thing to happen to me at this time in my life. I want us to remain close."

"Yes, yes. I want that also. *Cara mia,* I wish I could come to you tonight. I will count the days until we are together again. It will only be another week."

"Gianluca. You will tell them. I'm very serious about this."

"I will, *cara mia.* It was too soon to mention marriage. I agree."

"No, you will tell them that we are only friends. Close friends. That's all."

"Of course. Of course." He let his fingers trail over her breasts.

~ * ~

As soon as she came into her room Laise saw the open velvet box with the lavish earrings. She felt a small annoyance that Gianluca hadn't taken them away. And hadn't she closed the box?

As soon as she had left Gianluca, her thoughts turned to the other, the one who had seduced her with his eyes all evening. He would come to her, she knew it. She lashed herself for her weakness, scourged her conscience for her lasciviousness as she saw the pictures in her mind of what she wanted. Craved.

Her movements were languid as she unzipped the white lace dress and let it fall to her ankles. She kicked off her strappy sandals and slid the lacy bikini panties down her legs. She raised her arms, watching herself in the glass as she ran her fingers through her hair, pulling it off her face, letting it fall around her shoulders.

Mesmerized by her reflection, she slowly reached out to the dressing table and picked up one of the topaz earrings. She clipped it to her ear. She turned her head in the mirror, watching the bright diamonds catch the light. She reached for the mate and clipped it to her other ear. Her image gazed back at her, her nakedness enhanced by the large jewels. Slowly she walked over to the lamp beside the bed and extinguished it, then folded back the silky embroidered sheet. The scent of lavender drifted up, a whisper of promise.

The moon's light flooded the room, fuller and brighter than before, casting long, silvery shapes over her body and the billowing pillows. Her breath was shallow as she waited and she could feel a light, rapid pulse in her throat and fingertips.

Light—blazing, glaring brilliance filled the room. Laise blinked at the Venetian glass chandelier, its watery drops aglitter. Ugo stood with his hand on the light switch, then walked to the bed. He was still in his evening clothes, dark, elegant, puissant—a Renaissance prince whose power was absolute. He looked down on her in the white bed, his mouth curved in a sardonic smile when he saw the earrings.

"*Molto bella,* very pretty." Still he did not move, his gaze roving over her body.

Laise felt she could not bear it. She felt she was

drowning in his obsidian eyes. He reached and ran his fingers over her pubis. A scorching current ran through her at his touch. She could not look away.

She opened her legs.

For seconds he watched his fingers stroke her, then abruptly he knelt.

His tongue was thick and powerful and yet like silk. He grasped her knees and roughly flattened her legs apart. Involuntarily her long legs wrapped around his neck and she moved against his insistent mouth as he tantalized her into a series of wracking, shuddering orgasms that tore through her like a volcano. She grasped his thick hair with her fingers and caught a corner of the lace pillow with her teeth to keep her guttural cries muffled as she writhed and twisted with the fiery sensations that flooded her. She fell back as he released her, her eyes closed in anticipation to be filled, stretched, needing the hard pounding maleness of his weight on her and in her.

"Now...now," she gasped.

But it was quiet. Slowly she opened her eyes to the bright glare of the chandelier. He was not there. The quiet, silken room was empty.

She drew herself up on her knees in the middle of the huge bed. The enormity of his insult hit her with the force of a blow. He had not even undressed. He had merely serviced the *putana,* with her *compenso* sparkling in her ears.

She sobbed with frustration and rage, then threw herself off the bed. The earrings flew against the door where they bounced and dropped to the floor. One arm sent flying the array of crystal bottles, boxes, and atomizers on the dressing table, where they made scarcely a tinkle as they hit the thick rug. She turned, furious, looking for something else to fling, to smash, when she caught sight of herself in the full glass. The reflection of her disheveled hair and wild eyes sobered her as hot, angry tears of humiliation sprang in her eyes and spilled down her cheeks.

TWENTY

CHRISTINA

"Goddammit, Christina, if I've told you once I've told you fifty times not to make social engagements for us until this election is over. I'm not sure one week from the next where I'm scheduled to be. Cancel the Heart Ball thing. The last thing I need in the paper is my picture at some big society soirée."

"Oh, for God's sake. Senators are expected to be social. I've reminded you for months. The company's underwritten the favors and the flowers. This *soirée*, as you call it, is no surprise, David." Christina guided the Jaguar through the early morning rush hour traffic onto the drop-off ramp of Barry Goldwater Terminal.

"Cancel us."

"No. I won't. After all, I'm on the committee. You know that. I'm expected to go and besides I've already paid fifty thousand dollars for our table, and don't go pretending this is something I've just thought up."

"Jesus." He stared out the passenger window.

She glared at his turned head. "We go every year. I've been traipsing around to all your fun, fun, fun things since last May and now this is something we're going to go to. We never see our friends anymore. All we ever do is this election garbage, and if you think I enjoy those herds of Elks and

Moose, you're quite wrong. You get all the ooh, Senator this, and aah, Senator that and I have to stand around grinning like some fucking idiot and you're so rotten mean and worn out all the time we haven't made love in weeks and if this is some kind of preview of what our lives are going to be like in Washington, you can count me out."

"What the hell is that supposed to mean?"

"I'll stay here with the kids. They don't want to leave, anyway." She spit the words out. "And I don't either. You can come home when the spirit moves you. We won't see any more of you than we do now."

"Good! Stay here then!" he roared. "Jesus, if this isn't typical of you, Christina. When the going gets a little tough you turn into a roaring A-number one bitch."

"It's always me who's at fault, isn't it?" she fumed as she jockeyed the car through the chaotic mass of early morning traffic at the US Airways drop-off curb. "The whole house has to pussyfoot around you. Nobody knows who's going to get it next. Lupe disappears when you come in the door. At least we'll have some peace and quiet for a week until you come back. Praise the Lord. Boy, it's going to be wonderful when you're here all the time. We can all hardly wait. Even Rosie and Gil cringe when you walk in the door."

"What unmitigated bullshit!"

David jumped from the car before it had fully stopped and flung the back door open for his suit bag. The door slammed with a resounding thwump, and, grim-faced he spun and strode into the terminal to catch the Monday morning flight to Washington.

Her window hummed down. "I'll go by myself," she shouted.

He didn't look back.

Christina squealed the tires of the ordinarily sedate car and blinked back tears of fury.

It had all begun innocently enough. She'd mentioned

they had a table at the Heart Ball a week from Saturday night. She was on the committee and in charge of the favors and the centerpieces, which Merriman & Cross had footed the bill for. They were going to be gorgeous. She and the Martinez brothers had pulled out all the stops with flowers and drapery and specially designed candles.

She and David were always big sponsors and had gone every year forever. She never dreamed he wouldn't want to go. And it wasn't as if one party was all that big a deal. After all, the people who would be at the ball voted, too. Would be much more likely, if truth be told, to vote for him than all those people he schmoozed every weekend.

Her anger began to dissipate and she started to feel a little guilty at fighting with David when he had so much on his mind. They were all under a strain. And maybe the bits about Lupe disappearing when he came home and Rosie and Gil cringing *was* a bit much.

Still, he didn't need to bite her head off at every little thing.

Oh, look. She didn't care that much about the ball. She would have been okay missing it if he hadn't been so shitty about it.

They hadn't had a good weekend. He was cross and irritable when he wasn't on the phone or preoccupied on the computer. When they'd come home after that perfectly awful American Legion dance on Saturday night, she had tried to be funny and laugh about some of the crazy things people said.

Then she'd tried to tease him out of his mood and apologized if she'd been patronizing, which she didn't think she had been, and let's face it, she was feeling a little guilty about Sev Justus kissing her, and…well…kissing him back. In the garage at the Borgata. So she'd put on her sexiest nightie and tickled David where she thought it would do the most good. He'd turned his back and fallen asleep. Again. When *was* the last time they'd made love?

She was still feeling defiant when Sev called at nine o'clock. "I'm going over to the warehouse this morning and look over the paintings and stuff I told you about. Any chance my art expert can come with me?"

She swallowed, her throat suddenly dry. "Sev, I told you I'm not an expert."

"I know you did." The voice was lazy, dismissing her protest. "Can you come?"

"Well..." The heated scene in the car with David swam into her head.

"Christina, please. I apologize for the other morning. I got carried away. I promise I'll behave." There was a pause. "Look, I won't touch you. I'll stay ten feet away. I'll be all business. I really do want your opinion on some of this stuff."

She made up her mind. "What time?"

"An hour? Can I pick you up?"

"An hour's fine. But I...I have things I have to do later. I'll meet you there. Just give me directions."

He told her where to go. "I'll meet you at the gate. Don't wear anything fancy. We may have to climb around a bit."

She had on a silk T-shirt, jeans and loafers. She thought she was dressed about right, and really, she didn't want to look like she'd gone to a lot of trouble for Sev Justus. But she washed her face and redid her makeup and hair.

They got the key from the warehouseman and drove through a complex of large, modern storage buildings just off the freeway near the airport.

"We had to find a place to store everything when the house was sold. We got this place specially climate-controlled, dust filters, all that." Sev unlocked the big rolling door and it screeched along its track when he pulled it back. The light panel was just inside the door and he threw the switch.

"Wow. He wasn't a collector," Christina exclaimed. "He was a big old pack rat." She stepped over the track, excited.

A huge room was hung and stacked with hundreds of paintings of cowboys, Indians, scenes of the west. The middle of the room was crowded with bronzes, marbles, carved wood statuary. There was more. Much more.

"It's a marvelous mess. Surely he had this catalogued," she said.

"Yeah. But there's some question as to the objectivity of the cataloguer. Some relative or another. Dead now. It's out-of-date anyway. The old guy was collecting all the time."

They walked slowly around the room, going through stacks of canvases and prints, examining signatures, labels, picking up pots and sculptures. There was also a section of the room filled with old weapons, saddles worked with turquoise and silver, Navajo rugs, fancifully beaded clothing, headdresses, jewelry, and a dozen or so cigar store Indians. Baskets of all descriptions were stacked in corners and hung from wires on the ceiling. There were also loops and loops of barbed wire.

"What in the hell is this stuff here for?" Sev asked in wonder as he held up a section of rusty wire.

"A lot of people collect it. See, look. There are hundreds of different styles of barbs. You can even buy barbed wire swizzle sticks plated in gold."

"Well, I'll be damned. I would have given it to the junk man,"

"You don't know your kitsch, Sev Justus. Actually, this *junk* is worth a lot more than some of the other things here. Some of the paintings are just a cut above Elvis-painted-on-black-velvet that they sell by the side of the road on weekends."

Sev picked up a flowing eagle headdress and arranged the black-tipped feathers around his head. He pulled a long, beribboned spear from a pile on the floor and struck a warlike pose, dark eyes flashing.

Christina studied him critically. "Definitely the real you. Very chief-y. Are you sure you're not part Indian?"

"Don't think so." He grinned. "But I had some pretty rascally ancestors. Who can say for sure?"

She raised an eyebrow and started to laugh, then thought better of it.

"Left myself wide open with that remark, didn't I? You can go ahead and say it. My feelings won't be hurt."

Her face was innocence itself. "Me? I have no idea what you mean." Her mouth quivered.

He winked and took off the headdress. "You're a better actress than you let on."

They worked their way through the conglomeration, stopping sometimes to admire, sometimes to laugh. They made their way back to the entrance of the crowded storage room.

Christina surveyed the room, brushing back a lock of hair that kept falling in her eyes. "There are wonderful things here. Some of the paintings and sculpture. A lot of the Native American work. A good bit of the other stuff is worthless." She looked at Sev, standing a few feet away, his elbow resting on the back of a large bronze horse. "But you knew that."

"Yes."

"You need an appraiser. A specialist." She picked up a small bronze calf. "And you knew that, too."

"Yes."

"Then, why am I here?"

"I don't know, Christina. Why are you here? That's very important for me to know. I want to know why you came. You had every reason not to." He waited, but she didn't answer. "I know why I asked you. I had to see you again."

Her eyes were downcast and she rubbed the little calf in her hands. "I'm not sure," she whispered.

"I told you when I called you I wouldn't touch you."

"I know." She drew a ragged breath.

"Unless you want me to." He moved closer to her and

she could feel his warmth. He reached and brushed back the loose lock of her hair. "Do you want me to, Christina? I want to. I want to very much."

She watched her thumb slide back and forth over the calf. "I had a fight with David this morning. I left him at the airport to catch his flight back to Washington. He was very angry. So was I. I'm feeling emotional and terribly vulnerable right this minute, Sev. I can't trust myself with you."

"Do you want me to touch you, Christina?"

She didn't answer, but caught her lip in her teeth.

It was a moment before he said, "I don't want you to come to me because you had a fight with David. But you know it's going to happen, don't you?"

She looked up, her ears ringing in dismay, then dropped her head.

He took the little calf from her shaking fingers and placed it carefully on a table. "When you do want me, Christina, I'll know it." He tipped her face up to his. "Don't look away." He rubbed her bottom lip with his thumb. "But you'd better be sure, because next time I won't stop." He picked up her handbag and put it over her shoulder. His voice was rough. "We'd better go, while I'm still in control of myself."

TWENTY ONE

CHRISTINA

"Here are the earrings I'm wearing tonight." Christina held up splashy clusters of diamonds and pearls. "See, they curve up around my ears like this, so my ears will have to show. That's it. I'm not wearing anything else."

"Gorgeous, dear, gorgeous. They should be quite a sensation without shoes. Or a dress." The hairdresser pulled her hair in various directions, his foxy face bright with his joke.

"Hunter, you're an idiot. You want to hear about my dress?"

"Well, of course, dear heart. And you must bring me pictures. You know I get my vicarious jollies hearing about the fabulous parties you go to."

"It's Prada. Very simple. White, clingy charmeuse, soft. To the floor, where it kind of bursts into dozens of little bunches of pleats. Cut down to here in front and waaay down to here in back, where it falls to the floor where the bunches of pleats flare out into a teeny train. I've been pounding my bod at the gym for weeks and weeks because *everything* shows."

"Christina, you make me almost sorry I'm not straight." Hunter studied her in the mirror, then held up an earring. "Let's sweep it back. Very icy, very regal."

"Hunter, I'm counting on you. Are you going to do

sparkle?"

"Too L.A. Let's just do some delicate lowlights." He hurried off to mix the color.

Christina sat back and tried to think if she'd forgotten any of David's clothes. He'd called during the week and apologized for being a bastard and if she didn't mind going alone for awhile, he'd meet her there. There was an American Legion affair he had to stop at. He'd come home and change to the cowboy boots thing. He'd just shake some hands, et cetera, et cetera, come home and change to black tie. Then naturally she said she'd wait for him, and he said she didn't have to—to go ahead to Ting and Jenks's cocktail party before. In other words, they'd pretty much made up their quarrel. She would go ahead and he'd get there when he could.

The Heart Ball was the most lavish and prestigious of all the charity balls and really opened the social season. Women looked all year for the dresses they would wear. Christina had found hers in New York this summer. The Heart Ball was her favorite party, but even so, she would have missed it if David had insisted. Been disappointed, but grown-up about it. She could always wear the Prada to something else. And of course there were all kinds of parties in Washington.

Hunter came back with his little ceramic bowl. He painted some soft streaks through her hair, entertaining her with naughty jokes and sly comments about some of his other customers. Later, when she'd been shampooed and dried, he caught her hair and twirled it into one long curl that he anchored at the back of her head. "Only for you will I surrender these hairpins, love. I had them hand-made a few years back and can't get them anymore." He studied her critically, then said with satisfaction, "I could count the cheekbones on one hand that I could do this hair with." He handed a Chinese lacquer mirror and stood back, almost purring with satisfaction. "Now go over to Cheryl and let her do her makeup magic. You'll be the belle of the ball."

At home Christina fended off the delirious assault of Rosencrantz and Guildenstern, settled a dispute between Caroline and David, Jr. over a Hard Rock Café T-shirt, glanced through a stack of uninteresting mail and escaped to her bedroom, hoping she would have time to doze in the Jacuzzi.

One wall of the tub alcove was glass that edged a sheer drop outside the window. She had thought at first she might be nervous about the cliff right outside her bath, but for some reason the glass between her and the drop-off made her feel secure. Flying in airplanes and looking out of windows in high buildings didn't bother her either. She couldn't explain it— outside, heights terrified her. When she was a kid she'd swung through trees with the best of them, but now her vertigo got worse as she got older. Sometimes she thought she'd go to one of those desensitizing courses, but that was just another of those things that got pushed into the background. It really didn't interfere with her life. David had had that low wall put up along the steep driveway, so now her stomach didn't drop out when she drove up.

One long inside wall of the bath was the actual rock of the mountain where she had trained moss and small plants to grow. It was all kind of greenhousey and she loved to lie in the big tub and gaze at the city that stretched out for miles on a clear day. She supposed people down below had trained telescopes into the glass walled bathroom from time to time. She certainly would have herself. But she and David never bothered to cover up.

What with the rock, plants, mirrors, and the white curly-lamb rug in the center, the room always made Christina feel sexy. She and David had had some memorable times in the tub with nothing but the glass wall between them and the city.

She stepped into the foaming bubbles, careful not to get her hair wet. She heard David come in. Good, he wasn't late. He had to dress in Western clothes for the Legionnaires, then come back home afterward and change into evening clothes.

Lupe was going to tie his tie. She hoped that worked, but she could redo it at the ball if it came out badly.

David came into the bathroom. "Did you pick up my shirt, Christina?"

"Of course I did. I checked it and they'd gotten that crease out of the collar. They apologized that they had to do it over. Everything's hanging in your closet. I took your studs and cufflinks out of the vault and put them on top of the cupboard by your closet door."

David's closet was actually a long, narrowish room with built-in cupboards and shelves. One whole side was for suits and jackets. Christina knew they'd never have a fraction of that space when they went to Washington. Of course, even if David were elected, this would always be their main residence, but still, she was spoiled.

"Please don't dawdle, David. The sooner you get to the Legionnaire barbecue, the sooner you can get back home to change. And you've got that half-hour drive to the Princess. I'll get a ride with Miriam and Jack or somebody. We can pick up my car at Ting's tomorrow."

"Could you manage to do that, Christina? Lupe can go with you. I've got to be at the television station to tape those television spots. I'll probably be there all day." He sounded irritable. "Barney's got some hotshot media guy to work me over."

She could hear slamming drawers and swearing. "David, are you still angry because I'm not waiting to go with you tonight? I said I would. And if you don't want to come at all, it's perfectly all right."

There was a silence, then he appeared at the bathroom door. "I'm not angry, Christina, but let's just say I hope you plan to be with me at these things the rest of the campaign."

"I told you I would." She didn't want another fight. She stood and stepped out of the bathtub.

David watched her wrap herself in the peach bath sheet,

then turned and walked out of the bathroom. She yanked the towel around her and tucked it in. There was a time she would have at least gotten a nice little leer or two when she was naked. "Your son, with some coercion, polished your cowboy boots. He did a fair job," she called after him. "It would be nice to thank him before you go."

After she'd dried herself she reached for the Waterford perfume bottle and trailed the jewel-like stopper over her breasts and down her legs, then behind her ears. A lush jasmine and bergamot filled the bathroom.

"I'm leaving now." David watched her pull on the gossamer panty stockings. "I'll get there when I can. Not too late, I hope. I'm assuming since you paid that ridiculous amount that we've got a ringside seat at this shindig."

She smiled. "Don't be grouchy, David." He always called their table on the dance floor a ringside seat. He was right. Amazing the things you saw going on. "We'll all watch for you,"

He glanced at the bed. "That your dress? You sure it'll stay on?"

She laughed. "No."

"I'll just look for the cheering crowd then."

"Bye. Knock 'em dead."

He stopped at the door. "Christina, maybe it'd be a good idea if you tamed down some of your clothes, at least until after the election."

Stung at his remark, she went back to carefully working the expensive stockings up her legs, afraid she'd poke a fingernail through. They were made with no seams at all so nothing would show through her dress. Screw it, she fumed silently. I'll wear whatever I please. If I want to flop my tits out, that's *my* business.

She crossed to her closet and slid several dresses over, revealing the heavy safe door with the massive combination lock. The small climate-controlled room was cut into the mountain. They kept jewelry and valuables there, as well as Christina's furs. She pulled a long white fox boa from its pink satin hanger and swung the heavy door closed. October brought cool nights and she would need a wrap.

She checked the Judith Lieber jeweled cat *minaudière* for her lipstick and compact, fastened the diamond earrings, then stepped into her dress. It was precarious, she thought, as she put her toes into the silk slippers. Good. She turned and looked at her back. Christina liked her back and the satiny expanse the length of her spine still was honey-colored from the summer sun.

~ * ~

Ting and Jenks greeted their guests in the marble-floored foyer.

"David is so sorry to miss your party, but he'll meet us there. I guess this is something I'll have to get used to. He said to tell you he's happy for you both." Christina gave Jenks a hug and an air kiss. "You caught us all by surprise, running off to Mexico to get married like you did."

"Us, too. We just did it, and it's wonderful." Ting had a rich, plummy voice that spread over her words like jam. She chortled. "We even think it might be legal, Mexico and all. But to be safe we figure we'd better do it again here one of these days. But we had to rush to get this house ready for the party. So, maybe we're still living in sin, but our hearts were in the right place."

"I'm so glad you decided to have the party again, Ting. It wouldn't have been the same if we didn't come to your house before the Heart Ball. It looks fabulous. You and Miriam did miracles."

Christina moved away as other couples arrived to congratulate the newly married Jamesons. The house was new, and Miriam had just been able to get it finished for the party. It arched over a wash that turned into a running stream when it rained. A spreading palo verde tree lived in a glass alcove at the end of the living room. The house had been built around it. Ting and her former husband Jake had been art collectors and Christina noticed that Ting seemed only to have taken the best things when she moved out. Jake probably didn't know the difference.

The evening was still mild and most of the people were out by the pool and bar. Christina started for the open doors, but checked herself. Sev and Hallie Justus were talking to Ann and Bartlett Savage. She knew she would see Sev tonight and told herself how she would behave. Had he told Hallie that she'd gone to the warehouse? She would have to wait to see if Hallie mentioned it. She felt her composure get a little wobbly and decided not to go outside.

Nervous, she absently took a glass of champagne from a passing waiter and crossed the blue and red Oriental to the end of the room. Miriam, Laise and Preston Brock were studying a large Mark Rothko painting, its floating colors shimmering against a brick wall. Miriam was in her usual black. Laise wore a flamboyant emerald gown, pleated and puffed, that Christina knew would look outlandish on anybody else. God, she and Preston were a beautiful couple. Christina couldn't put her finger on why she couldn't warm up to him. He was movie star handsome, with silver hair, kind of a sensual mouth, sleepy eyes. Wonderful nose. She often thought that maybe he was just extra reserved, but that didn't explain why he put her off so. Maybe he just didn't like her. He was certainly doing a superb job as David's finance chairman.

"Is that what I think it is?" Christina joined the other three.

"God, couldn't you die? Yes, it is a Rothko. Jenks bought it for Ting as a wedding present," Miriam said. "I never dreamed I'd get to do a room with a real one. I'm making Ting promise me I can come back when nobody's here and just sit and look at it. She can't refuse. God would strike her down, after I busted my ass to get this place finished." Miriam looked at Christina. "Great dress. Did you forget some of it?"

"What you see is what you get."

"Wow. Is David at that American Legion barbecue thing?"

"Yes." Christina paused. "Miriam, are you really saying I wouldn't wear this if David were here?"

Miriam cocked her head. "Now does that sound like me?"

"No. No, I'm sorry I snapped at you."

"Campaign getting you down tonight?"

Christina took another flute of champagne from the passing waiter. "Oh, I guess. Maybe a little." She made a face. "Why do I drink this stuff?"

"Don't look at me. David coming later? I thought Jack should be at the barbecue hoedown, too, but he's sent along Larry Dawson and a couple of his young press guys to run interference for David." She giggled. "And Jack wouldn't let me come to one of these things by myself. He's afraid I won't behave, if you can imagine. Anyway, he said he'd get more work done here tonight than he would in a week on the phone. So here I am. All dressed up and bitchy as usual. One of the mares is due to foal and I'll kill Jack if I miss it. I've got my phone in my bag and Esteban will call if she goes into labor. But I think I'll check. Excuse me, will you?" She turned back. "And Christina, stay cool. We all love you."

Christina tried to laugh, then turned back to the painting. What a fabulous wedding present.

"I think I'd kill for it, wouldn't you?"

His voice was low, just behind her right ear and sent a shiver down her back. She steeled herself and turned to smile brightly. "Willingly. His things hypnotize me."

Sev's amused eyes bored into hers and made her throat dry.

"David's not with you?"

"He's coming later. He had an American Legion thing."

"Do you need a ride out to the hotel?"

"Um, no. I mean I'm going with Miriam and Jack."

He smiled lazily. "Do they know it?"

"Well, of course." She'd answered too quickly and she knew that he knew she'd forgotten to ask.

He took a swallow of his drink, still watching her. Then he touched her shoulder and turned to go. "I'm not going to bite you, Christina. Not yet, anyway."

She hated it that her heart was pounding.

~ * ~

The Princess Hotel seemed something like a mirage out of Arabian Nights, looming out of the brushy desert, glowing against the night sky. Beautiful cars swam up to the entrance to the ballroom like a school of sleek fish—Mercedes Benzes, Rolls Royces. Jaguars and Lexuses were common, but there were other exotic wonders of the automotive aristocracy—a couple of Ferraris, a Stutz Blackhawk, a Lamborghini, a Maserati. Three television stations had cameramen recording the arrival of the state's most powerful and influential. Christina smiled into the glaring lights as the valet helped her from the car.

Miriam muttered to her from the side of her mouth. "I'm not used to this shit, but you're going to have to be, babe."

"Oh God, Miriam's got on her black tie mouth." Jack grimaced. "Help me keep her tamed down, will you, Christina. Not insult somebody really major that I need to hit up for money. Oh, there goes Barney Bentham. I need to see him while he's still sober."

"Talk about sober, you two go ahead. I need to breathe some air. The champagne really made me fuzzy. I don't know why I drink it." But she did know. Sev had made her tense and she had drunk three, maybe four...or was it five glasses...without tasting, or even realizing it.

She was drawn to the splashing of the softly

illuminated, multi-level waterfall across the terrace. The air was fresh and chilly by the water and she wrapped the white fox around her shoulders and took a deep breath, then another. On three sides, dark steps rose twenty feet. Water cascaded into a pool below and meandered through canal-like passages under bridges and more fountains. Lights played over the moving water in a mesmerizing rush of pattern and sound.

Her eye caught a movement on a small balcony below where she stood. Sev and Hallie Justus were talking. Then it became obvious that they were arguing. Hallie threw up her hands, spun, and disappeared. Sev turned and rested his elbows on the stone railing and frowned at the water sluicing down the opposite wall. Then he looked up and saw Christina watching.

The lights reflected on the water washed them both with a pale eerie light, and to Christina the world seemed to slip away. The sound of the water, the excited chatter of the guests, the music from the cocktail string quartet disappeared and she looked steadily into Sev Justus's dark, hot eyes.

She turned quickly and felt her silk slippers flying over the brick patio, away from the entrance to the ballroom, to the stairs that led below. Halfway down, she froze, gripping the iron railing. Sev was taking the steps two at a time to meet her. The roar of the water was overpowering here. He grabbed her hand and pulled her close, then down the stairs across a walkway, down a corridor that led to the spa.

Sev pulled at the door to the spa, but it was locked. There were other doors, all locked. There was the elevator and he pushed the button impatiently. Silently the door slid open. He pulled Christina inside as he pushed the Close button, then Four. As the elevator moved upward, he searched the instrument panel. The elevator stopped between floors.

They stared at each other, panting from their flight. He raised a hand and traced a finger over her cheek and down her chin, then slipped her dress off her shoulder and traced his finger around her nipple as she trembled under his touch. He raised his eyes and his voice was tight and harsh. "I'm not going to muss your hair or your lipstick, but this is going to be quick and hard. Is that what you want?"

She couldn't speak, but rested her head against the wall of the elevator.

"Say it. Look at me. Say it."

"Yes." She mouthed the words and closed her eyes, felt him pull her dress up over her hips. The sound of his zipper made her eyes fly open and he brought his mouth achingly close to hers.

His fingers rubbed the gossamer barrier of her stockings. "I want to look at you tonight and know what's under that beautiful dress. And that you know I know." His fingers tore the stockings and he pushed against her as she wrapped her arms around his neck. He picked her up, then brought her down hard. Her head spun. Did she cry out? She didn't know, but her legs pulled him into her and she heard the guttural sound that tore from him as he drove her against the elevator's railing.

It was just as he said it would be—quick and hard.

He lifted her from him, then caught her as her legs buckled. He smoothed the dress over her hips and adjusted the dress's top, then bent and picked up the white fox.

She looked at him in shocked silence. Then he reached for her hand and buried his lips in her palm. When he straightened, his voice was ragged. "I'll go up to Four and get off. Take the elevator down."

She got off at the level where they'd begun, sure there must be a powder room near the spa that had looked deserted. She had to have a few minutes alone, get herself together. She stared at the jeweled *minaudière* in her hand. She had clutched it throughout.

The small powder room at the end of a dark corridor was empty. She went into a stall and cleaned herself, trying to ignore the wet, ragged tear in the expensive stockings.

In the mirror her face was flushed. Curiously she slipped her gown off her shoulders. The flush was over her chest and breasts, probably over her whole body. Her makeup was okay, just a few strands of hair out of place. Rather attractive, she decided. Not quite so cool and regal as her hairdresser had wanted her to look. It was sexier.

Sexy. She smiled ruefully in the mirror. That's all she needed right now—to be sexier. What had she done? Had she lost her mind? A surge of heat bloomed between her legs.

Shakily she touched up her lipstick and powdered her nose, then studied her face, her bright eyes. All in all, she thought with a pang, she looked like a million dollars.

When she went upstairs she expected the ball to be in full swing, but though it seemed she had been gone an eternity, it was in reality only twenty minutes. No one had, in fact, even missed her.

"Get me a drink, will you, Jack?" Christina couldn't believe she sounded almost normal.

"You want a martini, right? Champagne buzz worn off?" He looked at her. "You sure you're okay?"

"Yes to all questions."

Miriam came up. "Get me another, too, Jack. We're at table three. A table impressive enough to render us totally deaf from the orchestra before the night is over. If there's anything you want to tell me, do it now. I won't be able to hear you once we get to the table."

Jack grinned. "Then I guess I'd better get in a 'Behave yourself, Miriam' before we go in."

Inside the opulent ballroom was a sea of tables elaborately decorated with sprays of red, amber, and purple flowers in tall columns of twisted gold lamé. Swags of gold swept from hanging baskets cascading with more flowers. The room flickered softly with hundreds of gold heart-shaped candles.

Jack whistled. "This what Merriman & Cross paid for,

Christina?" His eyes swept the room. "I hope we don't have to declare bankruptcy."

"Stop griping, you fabulous philanthropist. You know you write it off," said Miriam.

"Love the favors, Christina," Laise Brock called over from the next table.

Christina had chosen small gold pillboxes in the shape of a heart pavéd with faux rubies. The men got gold business card cases with a tiny ruby heart and the year of the ball engraved in the corner.

The voices, the music, the tinkle of glasses and silver were beginning to focus out of the jumble in Christina's head. She felt like she was beginning to make sense when she talked to people, but her body still held the aching sensations of the cataclysm in the elevator. She knew where Sev's table was across the dance floor and she made her eyes avoid it.

When the first course arrived, her stomach rebelled. She toyed with the pretty plate—a smoked salmon roulade in a purple basil and pine nut mousse resting in a swirling raspberry mayonnaise. The rest of the courses came and went, but her stomach was still flighty. She began to watch the door for David. How could she face him?

People danced throughout the dinner, between the courses, and the rest of the men at the table made sure Christina didn't feel neglected. When dinner was finally over, she fled to the ladies' room. As soon as she got inside, she wished she had gone to the quiet one downstairs. The room was full of chatter and she found herself swept into a group gathered around a vanity. Hallie Justus was showing off her birthday ring, the expensive diamond and emerald that Christina had gone to pick up with Sev. She admired it as best she could and turned to fumble in her evening bag for her lipstick.

"Oh, my dear. You've sat in something, I'm afraid. Here, in the folds in the back of your skirt," Hallie exclaimed.

She brushed her hand over the back of Christina's gown. Christina felt the color drain from her face.

"Here, it's still wet. I'll wipe it off with a damp towel and it'll be dry in a second. It's all kind of hidden in the pleats anyway. Your dress is silk, isn't it? That dries fast."

Shaky, her hands damp, Christina stumbled into a stall and with a handful of tissue tried to wipe the telltale spot dry. When she finally came out and made her way through a new group of chattering women, she checked the full-length mirror. It probably looked all right. No more than a shadow in the soft fold at the back of the gown. A wave of hysteria threatened to engulf her. How would she get through this night?

She prayed Sev wouldn't ask her to dance, but she knew he would. She had steeled herself for it, and behaved with what she thought was a reasonable facsimile of poise when he came to the table.

He moved her away from the table and across the floor in a crush of dancers. He held her lightly, but his words stripped her.

"I can't take my eyes off you and all I want is what we did in the elevator. Can you feel how much I want you? Can you feel how much I want it?" The orchestra's beat pounded as he whispered in her ear. "To pull your dress off. Pull your skirt up over your hips, tear your stockings and feel you ready for me." He pressed her hips to his. "Push into you again and again and again and again and hear you whimper."

She felt a bolt of heat and a gush between her legs as his arms tightened around her. On the crowded dance floor she pressed against him and bit the knuckles of her hand on his shoulder as she stumbled.

"Here you are, Christina. I just got here. You mind, Sev?" David touched her shoulder.

"Not at all." Sev's voice was smooth. "It's good you're here. Christina was saying she doesn't feel well. A little dizzy. Maybe she should go home."

David put an arm around her, concerned. "You do look feverish. Maybe we'd best go."

"Yes." Her voice sounded strange in her ears. "Yes, I think I'd better. I don't know what's wrong with me." She swayed against David, her legs wobbly.

~ * ~

At home, David was solicitous and insisted she go right to bed, but when he stretched out beside her and put his arm around her, she pulled his head down and kissed him with a wildness that surprised him. "Make love to me, David. Please. I've missed you."

Before she slept, she thought how tonight the semen of her lover mingled with her husband's and she buried her face in her pillow and tried to blot out the image.

TWENTY TWO

LAISE

"Why can't you stay?" Gianluca lay stretched out on his bed like an unselfconscious puppy.

"Stop trying to get yourself all worked up again, Gianluca, dear. I've been here three hours already. You know I can't spend evenings with you." Laise worked her stockings up her legs.

He ran his toes invitingly up her back. "You don't have another fancy party to go to, do you?"

"I told you no, but that doesn't mean I don't have to leave."

"You looked very beautiful to go to your ball. Like a queen. When we're married you will wear dresses like that with me."

"We're not getting married. And how do you know what I looked like?"

"I saw you. I came to your house and watched you leave."

Laise got very still. "You did what?" she asked quietly.

"I came to your house. I wanted to see what your husband looked like. He's old."

"How did you get past the gateman?"

"He wouldn't let me in. So I parked a block away and

climbed over your wall."

Laise moved up the bed and looked down at Gianluca. "Don't ever do that again."

"Laise, I love you. Everything you do is important to me," he said petulantly.

"Gianluca, what I do with you is...lovely. I enjoy it. I have fun with you. But this is a separate part of my life. I'm a married woman with two children."

"You don't love your husband."

"That has nothing to do with you."

"You must divorce him soon, and marry me. You love me."

She turned away and started to get up. "Gianluca, you're not being rational."

Without warning she was spun around and pulled to the bed under him, his arms like a vise around her, his face inches from hers. Shocked, she looked into eyes black with a fury that stunned her.

His lips were pulled back in a tense smile over his white teeth. "Don't ever say that." His voice cracked. "Don't ever say that."

"What in the hell do you think you're doing? Get off of me."

Slowly his grip relaxed. "I'm sorry, *cara mia*. I didn't mean to hurt you."

"You didn't hurt me, but I don't like being thrown around. You might remember that." She sat up, rubbing her arms.

"*Mi dispiace.* Sometimes, *cara mia,* you treat me like a bad little boy. I'm a man. It makes me very angry."

She softened. "I think, Gianluca, that's probably the last thing I treat you as—a little boy." She patted his bare knee and stood up. "I'll see you at school on Monday."

"Will you come here in the afternoon?" he asked.

"Not Monday. Maybe Tuesday." She buttoned her skirt

and zipped the fly front. She walked around the familiar room, clipping on earrings, slipping her car keys into her pocket, shrugging her handbag over her shoulder. At the door she turned. He was still lying on the bed, his face unhappy. "*Ciao*, Gianluca. It was good today."

Driving home she made up her mind. She would end this affair with Gianluca. It led nowhere. He had been a good thing in her life, something she needed, her body needed. She had been aimless, drifting, a sexless life in a sexless marriage. He was joyous and exuberant and young. He made her laugh and, of course, he set every sensual wire in her body humming. She had come alive and opened herself to feeling again.

Then she wondered why she had said *again*. She had never really known her womanhood. She had married so young, and Preston had not awakened her. He hadn't known how. Gianluca had sensed her vague yearnings and been young and arrogant enough to challenge her.

That part had all been good. But when she met Will, she knew that she could share her life with a man, not just her bed. It was time she should tell Preston she wanted a divorce. It was time to be free and actively start looking for a whole life. She thought almost daily about calling Will in San Francisco. Her palms would get damp and her heart would pound as she reached for the phone. But then she would pull back. That wasn't the whole life she should look for. He wasn't free, and being his mistress wasn't enough.

Other times she'd think, yes, it would be enough. Simply to see him and be with him would be all she would need.

Oh, God, she was so unhappy. What bad choices she had made with the men in her life. But she was only thirty-three. She could make a new beginning. Maybe she would live in Europe awhile. She had always been happiest there. Jeremiah and John were fourteen and twelve now. They were closer to Preston and could stay here with him. They would live in the same house, attend the same schools. They could visit her in Europe. Travel. It would be good for them. And everything would be fine.

Her thoughts spun like this nearly all the time. The only episode that she shied from was the aberration of Ugo Lucchese. She hadn't understood her visceral reaction to him then and she didn't now. She had felt with him a lust so primitive it still shamed her. And he had trampled on her pride like no one ever had. For what reason? If he had only wanted to humiliate Gianluca, why hadn't he told him about those two nights in her bedroom? The young man obviously didn't know.

She must put the incident behind her—another reason to break with Gianluca. He was a constant reminder of those two dreadful nights in Portofino. She had learned from those nights, more perhaps than she wanted to know about herself. She must now move forward and try to find some peace in her life.

As soon as the election was over, she would tell Preston. That was less than six weeks away. It wouldn't be fair to give him that worry with all he had to think about now. She would give her resignation at school, finish out the semester. The boys were old enough to handle a divorce. Half their friends' parents were divorced. They hardly paid any attention to her now that their lives were so busy. And when they had problems, they went to Preston. He was the important parent, the teacher, the guide.

TWENTY THREE

GIANLUCA

Gianluca got up and closed the curtains against the afternoon sun and returned to the bed and lay down. Maybe it was better that Laise couldn't come to him today. Blue strobe lights streaked behind his eyes. This one was the worst one yet. There had been headaches even before the…trouble in Rome. Even after he had been…sent away. But they had gotten less severe as memories of the *incident* with that *putana* of a girl in Torino had begun to fade. At the Grand Canyon they had disappeared altogether and he had thought he was finally free of the odd control they seemed to have over him.

Then, they'd come back when he was in Italy, when he'd gone back to be with his family in Portofino this summer. They came back after that day his father sneered when he told him he was going to marry Laise Spenser. His mother stood by with her large sad eyes and listened to his father tell him what a fool he was. That she was married. Married and unfaithful to her husband and children. What kind of man was he that he would want such a woman? A woman who was unfaithful to one husband would hardly be faithful to the next. He needed a young Italian virgin, not this arrogant American slut. He had shouted at his father and run from the house. He came back and packed his things the next day. His mother cried and told him to listen to his father. His father!

That had begun the first headache in a long time. The next exploded in his head on the plane bringing him back to the United States.

The next really bad one was last weekend when he watched from behind the big oleander hedge as Laise and her husband came out of their big house dressed so beautifully in their evening clothes and drove away in their Rolls Royce. That night was bad. He didn't like it that she had a life that didn't include him. That would have to change. He must keep pushing her to divorce. When his father saw how much Laise loved him, he would relent and give them money and a beautiful house, like he'd done with his brothers when they married.

A spasm in his head made a white flash so blinding and agonizing that Gianluca shouted in pain as tears streamed down his contorted face. The seizure passed and he lay weak and cold, drenched in sweat. He needed something for times like this. He struggled off the bed, catching himself as a wave of dizziness swept over him.

He'd have to get an amphetamine source. It helped sometimes, revved him up. He wouldn't use it so indiscriminately this time. He was more mature now. But, *Dio,* he needed something for times like this.

Gritting his teeth, he groped around on the floor for his jeans and struggled to pull them over his damp nakedness.

The guy next door knew how to get anything.

TWENTY FOUR

LAISE

The girl swished her ash blonde straight hair at Laise. "It's awful nice of you to give me the test late, Dr. Spenser. I had my grandmother's funeral and just couldn't get back…"

"Yes, Ashley, I understand. We'll just pick up the exam in my office."

Grandmother's funeral. Give me a break! Judging from her tan she's been flopped, probably topless, on a beach in Mexico—Rocky Point, Cabo, or someplace very much like that. Wouldn't you think they'd try to get a little more innovative with their excuses? I can hardly keep a straight face any more with the hordes of unfortunate dead grandmothers. I should announce that there'll be no more makeups. Their grades will depend on how original an excuse they can concoct for missing the exam. Funerals wouldn't count. Also mothers to be met at the airport. Especially around long weekends. God, wouldn't they love that in the Language office. That'd really give them the ammunition to toss me out on my ear.

To the girl she said, "Next time try to get back by Monday, will you? And use a stronger sunscreen at the next funeral."

"Yes, Dr. Spenser." The big blue eyes, lashes lavishly brushed with mascara, blinked innocently, unembarrassed.

It's always "Doctor" when they think they're getting away with something.

The balky elevator creaked to a stop on the fourth floor of the Language-Lit building and Laise motioned the girl to go ahead of her. "Wait here," she said. "I want to pick up my mail."

Laise flipped through the usual junk mail, almost colliding with a student as she made her way down the hall, Ashley tailing obediently behind her. She stuffed the pile absently into her bag and turned the corner to her office. She stopped so suddenly Ashley bumped into her back. Down the hall Will Fowler paced, impatiently checking his watch before looking up to see her. She felt herself walking toward him, aware of only a buzzing in her ears.

He smiled and moved to her. "Hello, Laise."

She was floating, she was sure of it. Her feet weren't touching the ground and her insides were lighter than air.

"Will." *Was that all she could think of to say?*

"I...uh...was waiting for you." He turned his hands up in a helpless gesture.

"It's...wonderful to see you."

The two stood, unable to decide what to do next, lost in the sight of each other.

Laise became aware of Ashley staring at them in fascination, her eyes darting eagerly from one to the other.

"Ashley," Laise said, trying to keep her voice steady, "Let me get your test and then you can take it in the department office. Tell them I said for them to find you a desk. All right?" She hadn't taken her eyes from Will's face and she could feel her own lips in a tremulous smile.

Her hands shook as she unlocked her office. "I'll just be a minute, Will." For a moment she forgot what she was supposed to look for. She simply stood, lost to what to do, trying to think.

"My test, Dr. Spenser." Ashley looked slyly at Will in

the doorway.

"Yes, of course." Laise was all thumbs going through her files, but finally found the exam and tried not to thrust it at the girl as she said, "Take as long as you need."

"Yes, Dr. Spenser. Uh, what if I, like, have any questions?"

Laise thought she would scream. "Ashley, just don't have any questions. Please?"

"Well, like, sure." She sidled out.

Will smiled at the girl and closed the door, then leaned back on it. "I wasn't sure... Was this a very bad idea, Laise?"

"No...oh, no." She found she was wringing her hands.

"I've longed to see you."

She took a tentative step toward him, when he took two strides to enclose her in his arms.

"I'm going to cry." Her voice was muffled against his shirt front.

He tipped her face up. "I know."

"I thought I'd never see you again."

"Yes. And then I found that impossible." He kissed her then and she did cry, with small hiccups and sniffles as she held his face in her hands, smoothing the smile creases in his face with her thumbs.

"We need to talk," he said, taking out his handkerchief and wiping her nose.

"Not here. Let's walk."

"Uh...what about...Ashley, was it?"

She made a sniffly laugh. "I forgot all about her."

Laise stopped in the office and explained about the old friend who had stopped by and would they take Ashley's exam when she was finished and put it in her box?

The office assistant looked Will over with interest, savoring this juicy bit of gossip about the snooty Laise Spenser. "Oh, I'm *so* glad your friend found you. And sure, I'll make sure your student gives her test to me at the bell."

Laise was already flying out the door. "Thanks, Mary."

~ * ~

Outside, tardy students hurried to classes. Will took Laise's hand as they walked down one of the long paths on the campus mall.

"When did you get back from the Middle East?"

"Two weeks ago. We finally got that deal I was working on glued back together without starting another war."

They walked in silence, neither seeming to know where to go next.

Laise cleared her throat. "Then you've been...home?"

"Yes. Laise, that's what we have to talk about. Look. I'm married and I know that bothers the hell out of you, but I've got to tell you that I have the most screwed up marriage there ever was. Actually, I like my wife. She likes me, too. But she came to the conclusion a couple of years ago that a, shall we say, traditional marriage didn't...oh, expand her horizons, or some such rot. You get a lot of that sort of crap when you live in San Francisco. Anyway, she moved out and began expanding her horizons. So things just drifted along, and then I met you."

"Amazing, but my life isn't terribly different. Do you want to divorce her?" Laise could feel a tiny glimmer of hope that she was afraid to let flare too brightly.

"Well, she's divorcing me it turns out. She wants to get married. It seems to another woman. As I said, you get a lot of garbage in San Francisco. She wants me to give her away. Well, I suppose there's a certain logic there. But what I'm really driving at is, you said you and your husband aren't close any more. Do you think there's a possibility for us? I mean, maybe not right away if you don't want. You can take time to get to know me. I...well, I feel we got a fair start on that in Paris, which I can't forget because it's the most momentous thing that ever happened to me. I didn't know what had hit me. I couldn't believe it that you didn't want to see me again and I just couldn't handle that and that's why I'm here." He ran his fingers through his hair. "I'm not making much sense, am I?"

She stopped and turned to him. Her fingers toyed with a button on his suit coat. "Will?" She gathered her courage. "Remember when you called me in Paris the morning you left?"

"How could I ever forget? It was the hardest thing I'd ever done."

She cleared her throat. "When you wanted me to go with you? You told me that you loved me."

He caught her hand. "I know."

"And...and I couldn't say it in English...so I said it in French, too. *Je t'aime.*" Her heart fluttered in her chest like a hummingbird. "But it means the same thing. I love you. From the very beginning, I loved you."

"Yes," he whispered

"I know I do, Will. I tried to tell myself that it wasn't possible. I hardly knew you. That I..."

He silenced her with his kiss, a hard joyous kiss that went on and on as they lost sense of time and place, and the river of students changing classes parted to go around them and close again.

TWENTY FIVE

CHRISTINA

Christina sat on the bed watching David straighten his tie in the big cheval mirror.

"It's a coincidence," he commented, "but it'll look good. I'll get Dick Johnson to alert the press that you're on jury duty. Maybe we'll get a picture of you in the paper, taking your, quote, civic responsibility seriously, unquote. Can't hurt."

"Oh, David," Christina groaned. "I don't mind jury duty. I've liked it when I've done it before. But do you have to tell anybody? Can't I do my civic responsibility, as you call it, quietly? Does everything have to be skewed to the campaign? Can't I just be in the background? Nobody cares what I do."

"That's not true and you know it. But about the jury duty thing, we'll see. Dick will know whether it's something he wants."

Christina stood in the closet, trying to decide what to wear. "If I have to have my picture taken, do you think my gray Oscar de la Renta looks serious enough?" she asked, a touch of sarcasm curling around her words. "Can't be, quote, over the top, unquote, when I'm doing my civic duty."

"Christina, I haven't the foggiest idea what you're talking about. Oscar what? Is it a dress?"

"A suit. You know. The gray one you like."

"Uh, yeah. I suppose a suit'd be good. Serious." He gave a last tug to his tie. "Gotta run. Chamber of Commerce breakfast. I'll be late tonight. Big Motorola dinner."

"How did I get out of that?" she muttered.

"No spouses."

"Hallelujah."

"Don't be such a smartass. We're in this together, remember?"

"How could I forget?"

"Keep it up, Christina. Keep it up. When I need all your support."

"Sorry." She sighed. "I hope your day goes well." She slowly worked the tiny buttons on the white crepe blouse, then twisted her hair into a coil in the back, fastening it with her hairdresser Hunter's special handmade hairpins. She felt a little guilty about that. She hadn't given them back after the Heart Ball.

In the kitchen Lupe fixed the children's breakfast while they stared at cartoons on the television set. Christina automatically snapped it off. "I've told you no television on school mornings. Stop conning Lupe. You know the rules. Put some toast in for me, will you, Caroline?" She poured a cup of coffee and went into the library to find a book to take with her. There would be all kinds of time to kill at the courthouse.

A short while later, she backed the Jaguar out of the garage, her stomach doing its tiny flip-flop when she had to back close to the drop of the mountain to turn the car. David's low reinforced wall on the edge helped a lot, but there was always that few seconds when the rearview mirror showed nothing but clouds and sky.

At the gate she waved to Charlie the gateman and beat the oncoming traffic onto Tatum Boulevard. She noted with disgust that smog hung heavily over the city. Could David do something about legislation to clean up the air? Polls showed people were concerned about pollution.

David was in Phoenix now until the election. Maybe now she could feel more a part of it all. Somehow she'd felt detached—like an observer. The whole thing, from that first evening when David told her he'd been appointed to fill Doug Purcell's Senate seat, there had been an unreal texture to their lives. She'd gone to Washington with David a couple of times this summer, but that had only heightened her sense of the unreality of it. Of course everybody said Washington in the summer was only a shadow of what it was ordinarily. Other people said it was like Oz all four seasons and it was time to worry if you thought it was the real world.

When Christina got downtown she realized she only had a vague idea where she was going. She rarely had a reason to go to the central city. She was to go to Superior Court—David had tried to tell her where to park, but she didn't pay attention. He had a tendency to micro-manage the details of her life—if they happened to fall under his notice, that is. She had answered that she thought she could probably swing finding a place to put her car, then tuned him out.

She locked her car in a county lot the summons had mentioned and hurried up Jefferson Street. It really was a beautiful morning. *When you're right in the smog you don't notice it as much,* she thought.

She went through the security scanner. "Do you always screen everybody?" she asked the guard.

"For awhile now. World's a nutty place. You're Mrs. Cross, aren't you?"

How did he know that? "Yes?"

"Reporter from the *Republic's* been looking for you."

She laughed. "Oh, dear. I wish I could hide somewhere. Got any ideas?"

"I'll say there wasn't much chance of you gettin' away." He grinned. "The lady's a terrier."

As if on cue, the *Republic* reporter and a photographer

found her as she started down the corridor to the jury assembly room.

"Mrs. Cross? I'm Carrie Foster of the *Republic*. This is Joe Morgan. We won't take much of your time, but that's kind of newsy when a member of a Senator's family comes down here. It'll make a good picture."

"I'm surprised they allow you to take pictures of jurors," Christina commented.

"They think it's good for the public to see that important people do the jury thing, too."

Christina smiled, wanting to be friendly, but she felt people beginning to look. "I'm nobody important. Look. I don't mind, but this makes me uncomfortable. I mean, I feel I should be anonymous, just like everybody else."

The young woman gave her a foxy smile. "But you're not." Then she put on her professional face. "A lot of people in your position could have asked to be excused. Why didn't you? Or do you think it's good publicity for your husband?"

Christina beamed. The little baby-faced bitch, she thought. "Not at all. I've done this several times before. I enjoy the experience. It's sad that not everybody feels it's a privilege. It is, you know." *Write that down, honey.*

"Do you think Senator Cross will win in November?"

"I know he will."

"How will you feel about uprooting your family to move to Washington? If he wins."

"Why, it'll be a challenge, of course, but that's what makes life interesting, right? Now, I must go. They start at nine o'clock pretty promptly."

"One picture, Mrs. Cross."

Christina got the feeling that politician's wives weren't high on Carrie what's-her-name's list. "Okay. One."

"Just approach the assembly room door and push it open. Joe will get a quick one. Thank you very much, Mrs. Cross."

Christina did as she was told. The photographer asked for two or three more shots, and by now, Christina felt every eye in the big, crowded room on her when she finally entered and found a seat.

When Christina's name was called on the third go-around, she was assigned to a fourth floor courtroom. A young man with a ponytail walked alongside her. "I saw them take your picture. Are you somebody important?"

"No. I'm not. My husband is a U.S senator. They thought that made me worth taking a picture of."

"Which one?"

"David Cross. I hope you'll vote for him in November."

"No kidding? I will. Nice to meet you Mrs. Cross."

I must remember to tell David I got him one vote today. That's probably more help than I've been so far.

A young bailiff was waiting at the open door to the courtroom. The prospective jurors filed in and were directed onto long benches. Christina happened to be at the end of the first row. The lawyers were sitting at tables in front of the bench, conferring with their clients. Christina's eyes swept curiously over the scene.

Her heart stopped. Severance Justus, his dark head bent, was listening to something his client was saying. She hadn't seen him since the night of the ball. She had tried to block out that whole evening, but it sneaked up on her and she hated the way it made her feel. Hot and aching. He had called her once, at home, but she wasn't there. He left a number, but she didn't call back.

There was a flurry as the clerk called for everyone to rise as the judge came in. He nodded pleasantly to the assembly. When everyone was seated he welcomed the prospective jurors and spoke of the procedure. Christina barely followed what he was saying.

"I will ask a series of questions," he explained. "If you have a yes answer, raise your hand."

When he had gone over the routine, the lawyers and their clients stood and faced the prospective panel, to be introduced. Sev saw her then, but his face remained impassive. Christina dimly heard the judge ask, "Do any of you prospective jurors know any of the attorneys or their clients that you see before you?"

Christina glanced at the others. She was the only one. She raised her hand.

The judge acknowledged her, "Please stand. You are acquainted with someone before you?"

"Yes. I know Mr. Justus."

"What is your relationship with Mr. Justus?"

Christina's hands were wet and she clung to the railing in front of her. "I...he is a business associate of my husband's. Our...our families are social friends."

"Thank you. You may be seated." The judge looked over his glasses at her with interest, then a glimmer of recognition. "You will be excused from serving on this case. You may return to the jury assembly room at the conclusion of my questions."

She sat quickly. When she glanced at Sev, his face was serious, but he winked ever so slightly. Christina's face was hot. She knew she was blushing. *Be composed, Christina*, she thought with desperation.

When the questioning was finished she wanted to run from the room and only forced herself to walk out slowly with the others who had been excused.

She returned to the assembly room shaken and nervous and trying to be inconspicuous in case the reporter came back with her idiotic questions. The words in her book swam around under her eyes. After a time there was some sense to it.

To Christina's surprise, she was empaneled on a jury on the third try. She had expected to be excused when she told that her husband was the state's U.S. Senator, but for some reason this hadn't bothered the attorneys or the judge in the case she was chosen to hear—an insignificant civil case involving a workman's compensation claim. Well, it would be dull, but shouldn't last very long.

The opposing lawyers made their opening statements and the judge recessed until the following morning. It was four o'clock. By the time she got her car she'd be in the middle of rush hour traffic.

Christina hurried up Jefferson Street, gradually becoming aware of quick steps behind her.

"Christina." Sev caught her arm and she stopped and turned.

He searched her face. "I wanted you to call. Why didn't you?"

She looked at him more steadily than she felt. "I thought a long time about it. I decided not to."

"Come, have a drink with me, or we could just sit somewhere. I need to talk to you."

"No. Please, Sev...it...it's all too complicated. It would be dangerous. You know that."

"At least come with me now. You owe me that much."

Christina raised an eyebrow. "I owe it to you? What an odd thing to say."

Sev smiled. "You don't, of course. I thought if I said it you'd believe it. Would you come and talk to me, now that you don't owe it to me? Please?

"No...I..."

"I need to say some things. Please."

Christina was silent.

His voice was lower, softer. "Please." He started to touch her face, but dropped his hand.

"All right." She whispered.

"Where did you park?"

"Just up the street. Not far."

They turned and started up Fourth Avenue. After a couple of blocks Sev said, "Good Lord. I'll have to show you a closer place to park than this. Are you on a trial? For how long?"

"I don't know. They just did the opening arguments before the judge dismissed us for the day. Four days, maybe."

When they got to the Jaguar, Sev took the keys from her hand. "I'll drive."

He drove up Jefferson, talking about the new building going on downtown. "Everything's been torn up for so long. Offices, garages, the arena, Symphony Hall and the Conference Center. Things are changing. But it's beginning to happen. Condos going up. Downtown is a lot more exciting than it used to be." He turned the car onto First Street, past Adams, and turned into the Sheraton garage. "You probably don't come down here much. Hallie never does. The election night headquarters will be here at the Sheraton. I thought you might like to see it. But otherwise this is a businessmen's hotel. Conventions and the like."

He found a space on the second level by the elevator. "Remember where the car is. I'll walk back to the courthouse."

A small garage elevator took them down to the lobby. Neither spoke, but she knew they were remembering the last time they'd been in an elevator. She was careful not to look at him.

Sev touched her arm. "The bar's down this way. It's usually quiet."

There were a few men at the dark paneled bar when they came in, nursing drinks, staring at the glittery bank of liquor bottles in front of the big mirror. Christina wondered whether other lawyers came here much; it wasn't far from the courthouse. She was regretting she'd consented to come. It wouldn't do to be seen in a hotel bar with Sev Justus.

They sat, not saying anything. A waitress came over and put a bowl with some kind of pretzel and peanut mix in the middle of the table. The bar smelled of liquor and ancient cigarette smoke. Christina fiddled with the little plastic drink advertisement. She knew he was watching her and she glanced up, then back down at her hands, twisting her gold wedding band nervously. He reached over and put his hands over hers.

"You're fidgeting."

"I shouldn't be here. I'm nervous."

"You don't have to be nervous with me."

"Yes, I do. I need to be nervous with you more than anyone else."

He brought one of her hands to his mouth and rubbed her fingers softly against his lips.

She caught her breath and tried to pull away, but he didn't let her go.

"Have you thought about me?"

She tried to keep the anguish from her voice. "Yes."

"Are you sorry about what we did?"

"Yes."

"I don't mean guilty. Sorry."

"Severance Justus, lawyer. What difference is there?"

"You know very well what I mean. If you could change that night, would you?"

She looked at him helplessly. The moment stretched. She wanted to say she deeply regretted what had happened. That she'd do anything to erase it all. That it had never happened. The words formed and whirled around, but wouldn't make a cohesive sentence.

Sev stood. "I'll be back in a minute."

There was a drink in front of her. When had it come? She took a swallow, grateful for its icy coldness.

Sev stood over her. "1602. I'll wait for you." He laid a key card on the table and was gone.

Christina stared at the little white card. She wouldn't go to him. He was gone and she could walk away. It was only when he was with her that she weakened. Felt so overpowered. 1602. She got up, leaving the plastic card on the table.

She waited for the small elevator to the parking garage,

pacing nervously, her eyes on the ugly blue carpeting. Behind her two men got off one of the big, brass elevator doors to the upper floors. The door stayed open. Christina turned and stared at it, then slowly walked over. Her head buzzed. She stepped in. She heard the ding of the garage elevator as its door slid open at the same moment the brass doors closed behind her.

1602. Her hand trembled as she pushed the sixteenth floor button. She could no longer deny she was aroused. She'd caught fire the moment he'd touched her down at the table and now she couldn't bear waiting to be with him. She paced in the elevator in an agony that someone would stop its rush upward. Wind whooshed in the airshaft, and then the car slowed and stopped, the doors sliding open silently. Frantic she searched the number printed on the walls. Which way? Which way?

1602.

She had left the key card on the table in the bar. She raised her hand to tap on the door. There was one more chance to stop the insanity. She rested her head on the door, breathing in short gasps.

Then it was open and he was there and she was in his arms, opening her mouth to his, wanting him more than she'd ever wanted anything. Her fingers tore at his tie, unbuttoned his shirt, her mouth drinking in the taste of his throat, the black springy whorls on his chest.

He took her face in his hands. "Shhh. We have time. We have time for it all," he whispered.

He slid her jacket from her shoulders and began to unbutton her blouse.

All those buttons, she thought frantically. "Tear it," she begged.

"No. Not at all. It's...incredibly...erotic." He touched her, stroked her, kissed her as he slowly got the buttons undone. At last he opened her blouse and slipped it off her shoulders. Her bra fastened in front and he unhooked it.

He carried her to the bed and she watched him pull his

clothes off. She writhed with impatience. His eyes glittered as he watched her open to him. He moved over her, then paused and their eyes met before he finally thrust in.

Slowly she became aware of the smooth sheet under her fingers, the soft afternoon light in the room. She held him between her legs as residual spasms clenched at him.

Slowly he withdrew from her, his gaze dark and soft. Then he rolled over on his back. "Mrs. Cross…you are an incredible fuck. David is a lucky man."

She buried her face in his chest. "Don't. You make me feel like…I don't know…"

He tipped her face up. "Christina, look. You're not going to divorce David. I'm not going to divorce Hallie. But we've had the hots for each other for a long time. Let's enjoy what we do and leave the guilt trip somewhere else. All right? I know you enjoy it. I want you to have fun doing it. You're so serious. I've thought to myself, why is this spectacular woman not having any fun in her life?"

"I *haven't* had the hots for you for a long time."

"Haven't you? I've felt it. What is it? You've almost…hummed whenever I've come near you."

"Well, that's an interesting way of putting it. Here I am, not having any fun in my life and humming when the great Severance Justus approaches. So now you're going to kiss it and make it all better."

"For as long as I can."

Christina sat up and looked down at him. "It can't be a long time, Sev. You know that," she whispered. "That night…at the Heart Ball…that was an aberration. Today was…I don't know what today was."

"Today was inevitable."

She slid off the bed. "I've got to go. It's getting late."

"You dress. I want to watch you," he called after her as she disappeared into the bathroom.

When she came out she began gathering up her

scattered clothes.

He laid back against the pillows, his arms in back of his head, his tanned furred body dark against the white sheets. "How long did the judge say the trial would be?"

"Four days, he thought," she answered. Her eyes traveled over him. "You're looking very...male.

He grinned. "I'll keep this room."

It was not a question. He was expecting her to come to him again.

She hooked the pale blue lace bra. "Sev, I can't come here. People have begun to recognize me when I go out. I hate it. But there it is."

"Then I'll find someplace else. Safe."

"Sev...I..."

"Just come here tomorrow. I know Judge Wightman. He starts getting restless for that Scotch and soda about 3:30. We can meet at 4:30. We'll have those days of your trial. Then we'll work something else out."

We. She brushed aside the qualm the word gave her. It was too late for squeamishness. She could rationalize their lovemaking at the Heart Ball. But not this. She had come to him openly, willingly, and practically torn his clothes off in her fever to have him inside her. Until she had turned from the parking garage elevator, there was the chance for sanity. "You're sure I'll do this again."

His eyes held hers. "Yes. Christina. I'm very sure."

"Sev, this is so crazy. So dangerous. I can't. I won't. Please." There was a dark bottomless chasm opening at her feet and she was struggling to keep from falling over the edge.

"Just come tomorrow. You can make up your mind then. But I'll be waiting for you. Wanting you."

Christina looked at him helplessly. Then her hand flew to her hair. "Oh, damn. Hunter's hairpins. They're everywhere. I've got to get my hair up like it was when I left this morning. I can't go home with it falling in my face." She fell to her knees on the sand-colored carpeting, searching for the long, gold pins. "Oh, I can't lose them. Come help look. There were about ten, I think."

Sev got down on the floor. "Here's one. Here's another. How many does that make?"

"I've got five...and here's one. Do you have any more?" She looked up, on hands and knees. He was watching her intently.

"You've got a beautiful ass."

"Sev...Sev, I've got to go."

"In a minute," he said roughly. "No, stay that way."

She was still on her hands and knees and he moved in back of her.

"Sev, don't. I don't like..."

"Shhh. Yes you will."

She felt the roughness of his beard, his lips on her back, then her panties were pulled off. He pushed into her. The motion was gentle and erotic as she forgot the roughness of the carpet on her knees. She curled down and laid her cheek against it as she pushed back into him. He pulled from her and there was a sharp pain between her buttocks and she came up on her knees wanting to escape it, but he held her and in a moment the sensation changed into such searing pleasure that she heard herself making small animal noises until she could bear it no longer. Her orgasm was so powerful she didn't know where it came from—it seemed to explode through her whole body.

She lay in the curve of his arm, still on the floor. She felt such a lassitude that she thought she might never move again. "I've never done that before."

"Did you like it?"

"You know I did." And she knew she was lost. That she would go to him whenever and wherever he wanted.

His fingers stroked her back. "Don't fall asleep."

"I know. I'll get up in a minute and get dressed."

He kissed the top of her head. "Yes. I want to watch you button those damned buttons."

TWENTY SIX

LAISE

The summer heat had faded, and the golden light of autumn suffused the landscape. Laise crossed the campus from the parking lot, her mood brighter than it had been in a long time. She'd spent the weekend with Will in San Francisco and was convinced more than ever that she and Will could look forward to the future. She would have to let the school know that she wouldn't be back next semester. Now she must tell Gianluca and it made her uneasy that he seemed different since the time in Italy, his demeanor clouded with a sort of desperation.

When she found a frantic note from him on her office door, she opened it with a trepidation she couldn't explain. The note told her Donatella had been diagnosed with breast cancer. His father had called him to tell him to come home, that she wanted to see him before her surgery. Ugo had specifically made it understood that it would just be for a visit to his mother. They would discuss the possibility of his returning for Italy for good.

She stopped in Gianluca's office after her class, anxious to reassure the young man. "I'm so sorry to hear about your mother, Gianluca. I'm sure she'll be fine, but it will help her if you go. I could see how devoted you are to her, and she to you. When is the surgery scheduled?"

Usually so neat, his clothes were disheveled. "Monday.

I will leave Friday after classes and stay next week until she is recovering. You are very kind to take my nine o'clock class. Everybody has been so generous."

"Well, of course. Please don't think any more about it. I think my Italian's good enough for a freshman class for one week." She smiled, trying to lighten his mood. She knew he was worried sick about his mother, but Laise had tried to convince him that Donatella's breast tumor had been discovered early and he should be very optimistic.

He ran his fingers through his thick hair, then massaged his temples. "Laise, when I come back, you must divorce your husband. I'm tired of being just your lover, not having a home with you. I want you to become the mother of my children. We haven't been together for three weeks. Where were you the last few days? The office said you were out of town. Why didn't you tell me?"

"Yes, I was in San Francisco."

"You mustn't have secrets from me. I want to tell my mother when I am home when we plan to marry. It will make her happy. We can live part of the time in Italy, part of the time here, if that's what you want. When we marry, my father will give me a large sum—he did with my brothers when they married. And he gave them houses. We won't need your money at all."

"Gianluca, I'd rather we talked about this when you got back, but maybe now is the time after all." She stood and walked over to the door of Gianluca's small office and closed it. "It is a good thing that you will talk with your father about going home to Italy for good." She leaned her back against the door. "This will be my last semester teaching. I'm going to divorce Preston and marry someone else. A man I met this summer."

Gianluca rose from his desk, his face drained of color. "But...but that's not possible. You're in love with me. You are going to marry me."

"Gianluca, no. I'm terribly fond of you. You were good for me. I needed what you gave me. But I don't love you like that. I've never led you to believe I did. I always told you there was nothing permanent for us. I begged you to correct any misconceptions you might have given your family. I never misled you. Never."

"But you did. You knew I loved you. That I wanted to marry you. I told my father."

"I was afraid you had. It made him angry with me. He knew I was married."

"How could he know that? I didn't tell him."

"No. I told him myself. That first night...the night of the party in Portofino. I met him in the galleria. He called me *signorina,* and I corrected him. He's always known I was married. Gianluca, he wants someone else for you, I know he does. An Italian girl. Someone your own age."

"My father adored you. Think of the beautiful gift he wanted me to give you."

How could he know that Ugo Lucchese had given her the ultimate insult with those topaz and diamond earrings? And with his contemptuous *servicing* of her that terrible night in her villa bedroom in Portofino.

Gianluca slumped down at his desk, his fingers pressed to his eyes.

"Gianluca, I've seen you doing that more and more. Is the light bothering you? Do you have headaches?"

"No!"

She walked behind him and gently massaged his shoulders. "My dear, I think you do. I think you should see your family doctor when you're home. Headaches aren't really something to ignore."

His hands were like a vise on her forearms and he yanked her around and slammed her onto the top of the desk, his face inches from hers.

Shocked, she tried to stay calm in the face of his fury.

"Gianluca, you're hurting me. Please let me up."

His eyes blazed and she could feel flecks of saliva as he hissed, "Who is this man you say you will marry instead of me?"

"Gianluca, I won't talk to you when you're acting like this. Let me up, please."

"Who is he?"

"I won't tell you unless you let me get up." The edge of the desk was digging into her back and his weight was oppressive. She began to struggle.

With a sudden twist she was jerked off the desk and a blow sent her spinning across the small office. She hit the wall and her knees buckled under her, her ears ringing as the room faded to a fuzzy gray.

She didn't go completely under, aware of Gianluca kneeling beside her, then gathering her in his arms and crooning to her in Italian. When her head cleared, she saw his face, brown eyes filled with tears that spilled down his cheeks as he wept.

"Cara mia, cara mia, bellisima. What have I done? What have I done to you? *Per piacere, per piacere.* Forgive me," he sobbed. "How could you love someone else? You love me. You love me." He sniffled into her neck.

She struggled out of his embrace and he made no move to stop her, only wringing his hands and weeping Italian endearments. She swayed when she got to her feet, but managed to make it to the door, opening it carefully, looking out. A single student in the corridor looked through a handful of papers, stuffed them in a backpack and moved away. Then there was no one. Her steps were shaky so she kept her hand to the wall. When she made it to her office, she locked the door.

She took a mirror from her desk drawer and examined her face. She didn't think he'd struck her eye, but her cheek was red, beginning to swell. It would undoubtedly bruise. Her skin was fine and fair; the slightest discoloration would show.

A heavy makeup would cover that. Her inner lip bled and her mouth was getting puffy, but that would go down. She wished she had some ice.

Laise rose and went to the window and stared at her palm tree, noting absently how its shiny fronds caught the bright October sunlight. She had always known that Gianluca was high-strung and emotional. He'd shown as much that day in Portofino when he'd confronted the man flirting with her.

Now, recently, she felt he was becoming increasingly unstable. Perhaps the headaches meant something. He missed Italy, he needed a girl his own age, but more than anything, Gianluca needed to be with his family. Being so far away was affecting him emotionally. He should have some counseling. For her to write to Ugo Lucchese would be unthinkable. His mother was ill. There was his uncle in Tucson. Perhaps she should write a letter to him asking his advice.

Laise considered what to do. Gianluca was dear to her. He had, in a sense, freed her from the sterility of her life. She owed him something.

She wavered. Should she write to his uncle? No, it wasn't fair to do that, behind Gianluca's back. *I'll write him a note and leave it on his desk before he leaves, encouraging him to see a doctor. Then he'll know that I've forgiven him for his outburst today.*

She could talk to him when he returned from Italy. By then he would be calmed down.

There were only six more weeks or so of the semester. Then she would be gone to San Francisco to begin a new life. She had planned to tell Preston after the election, but when Will reappeared in her life, she couldn't wait. Preston cried, saying he would miss her, that he did love her. But he did understand about Will, even though he hoped she would change her mind. Keep things the same.

She wouldn't change her mind. Not ever. She had gone to San Francisco to be with Will several weekends. The magic was even greater than Paris because they planned a future together.

TWENTY SEVEN

CHRISTINA

"The plaintiff has agreed to a settlement, ladies and gentlemen of the jury. Your services will no longer be required. The court appreciates the time and effort you have made here. Thank you. Court is adjourned." The judge rapped his gavel and left the bench.

Christina felt a surge of relief. Her eyes had been glued to her watch for the last hour. Four o'clock. She'd be only a little late meeting Sev.

As she hurried from the courthouse, it hit her. She ran to meet her lover. The night of the ball, well, that had been a mad impulse. Yesterday, too. But today she had no excuses. She knew exactly what she was doing and in a frenzy of excitement to do it. And she planned to do it again as soon as possible.

They would have to find someplace else. She felt uneasy about the Sheraton. The danger of seeing someone they knew was too great. Yesterday from the window she had looked down on the *Arizona Republic* news building. Sev had said the press didn't hang out at the hotel bar, but who knew?

She had a key card so she could go directly from the parking garage. She worried about having the plastic hotel card, so buried it in the dozen other cards she carried in her billfold. David would never look there.

She put the key in the door and it swung open. He pulled her into his arms.

"I'm late," she said breathlessly.

"I was afraid you weren't coming," He brushed his knuckles over her breasts and began unbuttoning her dress. "Not so many, this time."

She untied his tie and pulled it off. "Were you here long?"

He kissed her. "No. It only seemed long. Actually I just got here."

"I missed you."

"All I could think of was you." They fell on the bed.

"I know. Oh, yes, yes, yes."

Afterwards he lay on his back and she stretched on her stomach between his legs, her arms crossed over him.

"I've got us an out-of-the-way room at Westcliffs. Off the freeway. Nobody we know would ever go there." He stroked her hair. "I have to leave in a minute. I'm sorry. I have a meeting."

"It's all right." She ran her fingers through the thick black curls. "I love your chest. It's so furry."

An amused grunt rumbled under her cheek.

She licked his nipple and felt it harden. "What's your meeting? Could you be a little late?"

He cleared his throat. "No. It's a campaign meeting." He was quiet a moment. "David will be there."

She swallowed hard. "What will you do?"

"What do you mean, what will I do?"

"I mean, how will you act? You've just made love to his wife."

Sev flipped her over and gripped her shoulders. She averted her face.

"Christina. Look at me. No, don't look over my shoulder. Look at me."

Reluctantly she raised her eyes to his.

"We have to handle it. It's inevitable, and we don't have to hurt anybody if we're careful. Now that this has begun, can you stop it?"

She turned her head away, but he took her chin and forced it back and kissed her roughly. "Can you stop it?"

"No," she whispered.

His mouth found hers and he thrust his knee between her legs. "In case you have second thoughts, I'll be a little late," he muttered.

TWENTY EIGHT

CHRISTINA
Two weeks later

    The meeting with the teacher's union broke up around ten o'clock. David was surrounded by a group unhappy with some of the proposals he had made tonight. Christina stood smiling off to the side, making polite remarks to the ones who wanted to argue with her. David hadn't made this crowd happy, but she knew the points he wanted to get out weren't always to groups that would approve. The crowd might be against his views, but he would be on record and hope the press got it right. He had just finished telling the teachers that throwing more money at school problems hadn't worked and they would have to find new and innovative ways to bring up the state's student test scores. Even though he insisted higher salaries for them were essential, a lot of the teachers were hostile.

    Finally David was able to break away. "Whew. I wouldn't want to do that every day. Thanks for staying. I wish you didn't have to take some heat when it's me they're mad at. Run along home. I have to do a couple of those television spots over. Dick Johnson has some new ideas. I should be home about eleven." He gave her a quick kiss. "I'll walk you to the car."

    As Christina slid into the Jaguar, David turned to go,

then stopped. "Oh, I almost forgot. Sev is going to stop by tonight to bring those revised financial disclosures. We went over them at the meeting today and there were some changes. He'll probably finish late, but I asked him to drop them off on the way home. Tell him we can go over them when I get there. You don't have to wait up. Give him a drink and put him in the library. I'll be along."

Her voice was steady. "All right. See you later." She started the car. "Oh, David," she called out the car window.

He turned. "Yeah?"

"You were very good tonight. In there, talking to the teachers."

He smiled distractedly. "Oh, thanks."

~ * ~

It was almost eleven when she answered the door.

Her heart jumped. "Hello."

Sev glanced over her shoulder. "Is David here yet?"

"No."

"I hoped I might have a chance to see you alone."

"I know."

He grinned. "You going to let me in?"

She gave a start. "Oh. Sorry." Just having him look at her had always affected her. Now it turned her inside out. She floated ahead of him into the living room, his closeness scalding her.

"Is there anyone around?"

"The children are asleep. The dogs are with them. Lupe has gone to her quarters."

He pulled her to him. "Just one kiss." He bent and rubbed his mouth softly on hers, then rubbed his knuckles over her nipples, making them tighten under the voile caftan she wore.

Reluctantly she pulled away and took a long shaky breath, then led him into the living room. She curled up at the end of the long white sofa. He sat at the other.

Neither spoke, but they looked at each other, not knowing what to say. Christina followed her finger across the welting of the cushion. Sev rested his arm against the back of the sofa and rubbed his hand over his mouth. His voice was ragged when he spoke.

"I want you, Christina, right now, this minute. Do you have any idea what it's doing to me to sit here and not be able to touch you?"

"Yes."

Abruptly he took his hand from his mouth and loosened his tie. "I need a drink."

Christina didn't take her eyes from his face. Her voice was soft. "Drink me."

He looked at her sharply.

She lay back on the couch and pulled the caftan over her hips, then slid her panties off and put them in the pocket of the caftan.

His voice was hoarse. "David's due any minute."

A whisper. "It won't take very long,"

How to describe the thick hot rush that filled her. His late day beard scratched her inner thighs. The room spun around as she curled her fingers in his hair. Distantly the sound of a car on the drive came to her. Headlights flashed across the window. The dogs barked back in the children's rooms. The garage door rumbled open.

"Don't stop, don't stop now," she cried.

Voices sounded in the garage. There were footsteps up the stairs.

When David and Jack Merriman came into the living room, Christina stood at the bar. "Sev just got here. I'm making him a drink. Can I get you guys anything?" Were her eyes too bright, her face too flushed?

"Give me a triple quadruple Jack Daniels," begged Jack.

"A Scotch, Christina. A good belt. God, I'm beat," said

David. "Let's try to get this wrapped up tonight, Sev. I've got a helluva day tomorrow. Sorry you had to take your evening to do this. I really appreciate it."

"Happy to do it, David."

Christina walked across the room to Sev and handed him the heavy crystal tumbler. Casually she reached up and brushed a blond curl from the corner of his mouth, caught in the shadow of his beard.

She made David's and Jack's drinks, then excused herself. "I've got an early tennis game with Ting, so I'll leave you all to your business. Nice to have seen you, Sev. Jack. Say hi to Miriam. Hallie, too, Sev."

"Will do," Jack answered and took a slug of his drink.

Sev gave her a small wave. "I'll tell Hallie. Glad to have seen you, Christina. Thanks for the drink."

TWENTY NINE

CHRISTINA

"You were too good for me today, Ting. I need to play more. God, this has been a hectic autumn. Iced tea all right?"

"Perfect." Ting pulled a white sweater over her head as she sat.

Christina and Ting Jameson were on the patio at Paradise Valley Country Club. The tennis courts were full and the hollow plonks of tennis balls mixed pleasantly with the voices of the players, mostly female. The morning air was crystalline sharp.

"The wind last night blew all the smog away. Nice to have a clear morning for a change," Christina remarked.

"Yes, it is." Ting spun her iced tea glass. She looked up suddenly. "Christina, I asked you to play this morning because I wanted to talk to you."

"Oh?" Christina's smile faded when she saw the expression on her friend's face.

"Shit, I don't know how to begin, really…except, well…" Ting took a deep breath. "Christina, the night of the Heart Ball, when we were sitting at our table by the dance floor? I…I saw you dancing with Sev Justus." She waited.

Christina felt the blood drain from her face.

"Tell me to mind my own business, or go to hell, or

anything you want, and I'll stop."

"Go on." A heaviness stole over Christina.

"Christina, don't get involved with Sev." Christina said nothing, so Ting rushed on. "Take it from somebody who's been there. Sev is a fascinating man. He has enormous magnetism. He can be irresistible. He also uses people. I fell for him in the blackest days with Jake, when I knew I was going to leave him. I don't know. Sev seems to sense when a woman is vulnerable and he charmed me right into bed. I won't go into it any more than that, but I was hurt by him, badly. It doesn't matter any more, and at the time I had nothing to lose."

Ting leaned over and uncurled Christina's fingers from around her glass and held her hand. "Christina, you do. You and David both. This isn't the time to put your life...or David's...into Sev Justus's hands." Ting sat back, obviously drained and shaken by her words. "Now, lecture is over. You don't have to say anything, or explain anything. I...just wanted to be a friend to you." She stood up quickly and patted Christina's shoulder. "Have to run, sweetie. Got a meeting with some damned committee that I couldn't say no to. I'm so weak. You'd think I'd know better by now. Hordes of people think since I married a black man I've got a whole new set of pet causes. Jenks just shakes his head."

After Ting had gone, Christina sat, making rings on the table with the sweating iced tea glass. So Ting had been involved with Sev. Christina had never guessed. And Ting had seen her on the dance floor with Sev. No need to wonder if she'd seen Sev's hands on her buttocks as she...came.

She buried her face in her hands.

Alicia Bentham's horsey face loomed over her. "Well hello, Christina. Don't tell me you lost that badly."

"What? Oh...no. No. I'm...just sitting here trying to figure out what I should be doing next." *Oh, God, don't let her sit down. I'll never get away.*

Alicia Bentham sat down. "Barney says the campaign is

going fabulously. It should be a shoo-in unless some absolute disaster strikes. He said, just the other night what a marvel you've been…just the perfect candidate's wife. It'll be good to have the campaign over, won't it?" She simpered. "Get our men back."

The woman prattled on, barely penetrating the red haze in Christina's head. She endured it for another minute, then stood. "It's been so nice to talk to you, Alicia, but I've got to run. Seems there aren't enough hours in the day anymore. I know you understand that, as busy as you are." Christina scooped up her racket and ball bag. "My best to Barney. David's just so pleased how he's helped him. Said he's been simply indispensable."

She really did have to run, she thought with a rush of anticipation, or she wouldn't have time for all her errands before she had to meet Sev.

THIRTY

JACK

"So, did you enjoy the fabulous cooking, the wine, the candles, the soft music—everything to make this an A-number-one-for-the-books romantic evening?"

Jack and Miriam were curled up on their library couch in front of a flickering fire. Soft guitar music played in the background. George Strait sang a plaintive lament. They both loved Country Western.

Jack nuzzled his nose in her silvery hair. "You bet. But that didn't stop me from wondering what you're going to hit me up for. Are you going to tell me how much those sexy pajamas cost?"

"No." Miriam wiggled against him, barely able to contain herself. "I wanted to lull you before I told...ask you how you'd feel about being a new father at the creaky age of thirty-nine."

Miriam heard a low rumble in his chest as his arms tightened around her. He started to speak, cleared his throat and started again. "I think...oh, Miriam." He tipped her face up and looked at her, his eyes crinkling with delight.

"I just found out today for sure," she said blissfully. "I couldn't wait to tell you, but somehow I didn't know when to say it. Isn't that silly?" She wiggled with excitement.

"Yes. No." He eased her down and put an ear on her belly.

"You nut, there's nothing to hear yet. It's only the size of a bumble bee....I'm not due until the middle of June."

"I plan to keep checking"

"Do you think we should find out if it's going to be a boy or a girl?"

"Let's not. Unless you want to."

"No, you're right. Let's not. Let's buy all pink frilly clothes and have a boy. The old-fashioned way.""

"Do you think the imminent addition to the family will object right now to a little zigzig?"

"Baby better not. Maybe we should establish who's boss early on. What do you think?"

"An excellent idea. I wouldn't want you to think those pajamas were a waste of money." His fingers found the waistband and pulled them over her hips.

~ * ~

"Now that I've wined you, dined you, given you the news," Miriam crooned against his chest, "plus all the extra stuff at the end, do you want to tell me what's been bothering you for the last several days?"

"Miriam, I don't know. Somehow I don't want to think about it. Tonight."

"Tell me. I'm tired of having you look off into space and drum your fingers. Is it something about the campaign that's gone wrong?"

Jack was quiet a moment. "I don't know. Maybe." He didn't speak, frowning.

Miriam sat up. "Jack, what is it?"

"Miriam, has Christina said anything to you about Sev Justus?"

"Sev? No. Why?"

"Not that she's been seeing him or anything?"

"Oh, Jack. Christina wouldn't do anything like that.

Where would you get such an idea."

"It's not an idea," Jack said unhappily. "The other night when David and I went back to their house after re-taping those commercials at the television station?"

"Yes, what of it?"

"We, David and I, pulled into their garage. We started up those back stairs, but David forgot some papers and went back down. I walked through the kitchen to go into the living room. I saw…Christina and Sev on the couch…in a very compromising situation…to put it mildly."

"Jack, you know Sev. He's such a chaser. He'd probably wrestled Christina to the couch."

"Miriam, her pants were off and his head was between her legs and she sure didn't look like she minded what he was doing. She was, how shall I say it…in the throes. I think I would say that it looked like something they'd done more than once."

Miriam stood up in agitation and began to pace, wringing her hands in disbelief. "My God, Jack, how could she be such a fool?"

"You tell me. Here David's coming up to the last days before the election and she's running around. Scandal would wreck the campaign and I've never trusted Sev Justus. That he would betray David's trust like this, the treacherous shit. That he sits in those meetings with David…"

"What should we do?"

"That's what's been tearing me up. David's my partner, my best friend. He's a brother. Plus I'm his campaign manager. Miriam, what should I do? I've played this every way I can think of and I can't see myself telling David. And yet I'm sitting on a time bomb." Jack slammed his fist into the arm of the couch. "When I think of him sitting in those meetings, so glib, so sincere…the sonofabitch."

"How did Christina act when you came into the living room? Had she seen you?"

"No." His voice was bitter. "But of course her mind was very occupied at that minute. I backed up real quick and went down to make very loud conversation with David and stomped up the stairs. When we came in Christina was at the bar, making Sev a drink, as cool as you please. She even brushed a curly hair off his mouth with her fingers when she handed him his glass. She made each of us a drink and excused herself. If I hadn't seen what had gone on a few minutes before, I would have never dreamt it."

"Well, she was an actress at one time, you know. Maybe better than she led us all to believe." Miriam was quiet for several minutes. "I think you should forget what you saw. If no one finds out, and nothing happens…that's that. If it comes out somehow, well, so be it. The damage has already been done and nothing will change that." She looked at Jack. "And I'm so sad about that."

"Do you know how relieved I am I won't have to tell David? Do you know how shitty I feel that I'm relieved?"

"Oh, Jack. You're damned if you do, and damned if you don't. Unfortunately I could with equal conviction say that you should warn David, if for no other reason than it could be a campaign issue. But look, in the end it's a personal problem between them."

"God, I wish the election were tomorrow."

THIRTY ONE

CHRISTINA

Christina unlocked the door to the room and slipped inside. The walk from the parking lot always made her uncomfortable and she was relieved to close the door behind her. She always parked the Jaguar in an inconspicuous place down at the end of the parking spaces, even though she knew it was highly unlikely anyone who knew her car would ever see it here. The Westcliffs Hotel was near the freeway and had a transient clientele—travelers, businessmen, football fans who flocked to the nearby university stadium. There was a game this weekend and the place was busier than usual.

Sev had gotten a room for them toward the back, off a garden near the kitchen. The hotel had a restaurant as well as a night club that featured loud musical groups. She and Sev had made love more than once to the rhythms of rock, or rap or reggae—whatever was rehearsing for that night's program.

The musicians usually stayed in the rooms back here and she'd see them lounging outside, smoking pot, or doing coke, she supposed. She didn't know much about drugs. Whenever she passed them she'd try to be inconspicuous, though she often heard whistles and catcalls. They always seemed to know she was going to her lover.

It gave her a frisson of adventure to think she was Sev

Justus's mistress.

She undressed and hung her clothes in the closet, then took off the floral print bedspread and turned back the covers on the bed. She slid between the slick cool sheets and shivered. Sev loved to come in and find her waiting for him, naked and warm and inviting.

She heard the key card insert in the lock and felt a rush of anticipation.

He threw his briefcase on the couch and smiled. "I missed you." He stripped off his clothes and came to the bed.

The sheet slipped to her hips as she knelt on the bed and wrapped her arms around his waist.

He kissed the top of her head. "Miss me?"

"Yes. Don't move just yet."

Afterwards, she lay back on the pillows as he lazily ran his lips over her breasts. "How did you know that was just what I wanted? I could hardly walk here from the parking lot."

"It wasn't very hard to figure out. I do have eyes, you know."

"Beautiful eyes. They're what made me want you so much. Not to mention your mouth, your tits, your ass and your legs."

"Why do you use vulgar words with me?"

He grinned. "Because it turns you on." He moved over her.

"You turn me on," she breathed.

"Yes, and do you have any idea how that excites me?" he murmured into her hair as she arched to him.

After he'd gone, she dozed a little, dreading the thought of having to go home and dress for one of those endless campaign dinners. The group for this one escaped her, but it didn't matter. They all blended into one long parade of stringy chicken, peas, lumpy mashed potatoes and grainy chocolate mousse. Now that the election was so close they went to one almost every night.

Finally she got up and dressed. She usually left the room by the arcadia doors to the parking lot, only a short distance to her car. She still worried about being seen, though they were miles from where she could be recognized. It was later than she thought. Close to four o'clock. She'd have to hurry. She glanced over and noticed that the present rock group was standing outside one of the rooms, the sliding glass doors open—a mixed group of black and white men, long greasy hair, boots, lots of tattoos, piercings and leather. She and Sev had heard an undercurrent of their music. She didn't know what it was—rock or rap...something.

She left the walk and started across the parking lot. From the corner of her eye she noticed one of the group move toward her. It wasn't until he stopped dead in front of her that she knew he meant to block her way.

She tried to walk around him, but he dodged in front of her again, a lascivious grin showing through his wispy dishwater beard. "Where're you goin', pretty lady?"

"To my car. Get out of my way."

"Whoo-oosh. Listen to the rich lady attitude. The rich lady got a boyfriend. Your husband know you got a boyfriend, rich lady?"

Another member of the group sidled over. "Who you got here, man?" He joined the game of dodging and weaving around Christina.

She began to be frightened. *What did they tell you? Don't act like a victim.* "Get the hell out of my way," she hissed.

The first man gave her a playful shove into the hands of the second. His eyes glittered dangerously, pupils black and large.

Christina felt a bubble of fear in her throat. *They must be high on something.* She tried to fight down the panic welling up inside her.

Without warning she was whirled over to the open door

of the hotel room and thrown inside.

A shadowy figure in the corner said, "Hey man, you crazy on the stuff? C'mon. Let her go. She wasn't bothering us."

Christina tried to turn to the man in the corner. "No, I wasn't bothering anyone. Please, help me."

She screamed in pain when her arm was jerked back by the greasy-haired one. "Bitch, whore," he said with contempt.

Christina gasped and turned her head aside. The nightmare that followed was a whirl of dizzying pain. No part of her was left untouched as she choked and wept, and tried to hold onto her self that was being destroyed.

At some time she lost consciousness. When she came to, she saw numbly that it was still day. Her ordeal had seemed an eternity. She lay still, afraid they would notice that she was awake. But as the silence in the room crept into her, she knew they had gone.

Moving was painful, but she struggled up. She was still on the bed. She looked for her clothes. She didn't see them. Frantic now, she jumped up and scoured the room and the bathroom. They had taken her clothes. Her handbag was on the dresser, contents scattered, along with her car keys, but she had nothing to put on. It was a last vicious joke.

Sobbing, she fell to the bed. What could she do? She had to get to her car. She had to escape in case they came back. In a panic she yanked the spread from the bed and wrapped it around her, sarong-style. The parking lot was usually deserted, but it had been busier than usual when she came in. If she ran fast, she might make it before anyone noticed anything amiss. How she was going to get home, or into the house, she couldn't think. All she wanted now was to get away.

She pulled open the sliding door and looked out. Everything was quiet. She clutched her handbag and ran.

A car pulled around the corner at the far end and approached her. She kept her head down, praying.

The car pulled alongside just as she reached her car.

"Christina? Is that you? What brings you over to this part of town?"

It was Jenks Jameson. She felt her control spin out and a sob caught in her throat.

"Christina?" The he saw. "Oh, my God." He slammed on the brakes and jumped out. He wrapped his arms around her. "It'll be all right now. Now it'll be fine. You just come on. Get in my car. Everything's all right now."

Christina collapsed against his shoulder and let herself be led around to the other side of the big Mercedes. Jenks tucked her into the seat and crooned gently. "It'll be fine, you'll see."

He slid behind the wheel and turned to run his eyes over her. Her teeth chattered and she clutched convulsively at the bedspread covering her. "You don't have to say anything, Christina. I know it was bad, but I don't need to know anything you don't want to tell me. I'm going to take you to St. Joe's emergency room. You need to be looked at."

"No, no, no. I won't go," Christina said, her voice shrill. "I can't, I won't." She pawed at the door latch.

Jenks slammed the door lock on. "All right, all right. I think you should, but that's up to you. How does this sound? I'll take you home with me. Ting will find some clothes for you, then we'll call David."

At the mention of David's name, Christina began to sob. There was the dinner tonight. David would be so furious with her. Maybe if she had a few minutes at the Jameson's to get herself together, then she could go home and dress and only be a little late to the dinner. Yes, she would do that and then everything would be all right. Then David would only be a little mad that she was late.

Not angry like he would be about...this. No, not just angry. Terribly, terribly angry.

"I have to know one thing, Christina. Just nod your

head yes or no. Do you want me to call the police?"

She shook her head, as a fresh spate of tears rushed down her cheeks.

~ * ~

Jenks pulled the car into the garage and the automatic door rumbled down behind them. "Just sit tight for a minute. I'll make sure no one else is around. Get Ting."

Christina nodded, hugging her misery to herself.

In a minute Ting opened the car door and helped her out. She held her around the shoulders as they made their way into the kitchen and through the house to the master bedroom where Ting sat her down gently on the big bed.

"I'll get you a robe."

"Ting, I have to take a shower. I'm dirty. I have to, right now. Right now." Her voice spiraled out of control.

Ting sat down and took her hand. "Christina, I understand that you want to. And I know that's all you want to do, but I've worked with...assaulted women. They tell you...well, that you shouldn't. A doctor should examine you first. You can't face the idea, right now, of telling anyone. But later on you will, and there'll be no evidence. Let me call our doctor. I'll sit with you until he comes. I'll stay with you if you want. It will be best. And no one has to know anything."

Christina voice was shrill, hysteria surging into her throat. "No one. No one will ever know this. You must forget. I'll never tell anyone. I'll make myself forget. Oh, what will David say? He'll never forgive me for any scandal. I know you know why I was there...at that hotel. You warned me and I didn't listen. How do you possibly think I could call the police, or see a doctor?"

"David will know, too," Ting said quietly. "He may not know who, but he'll know it was someone." She waited, but Christina stared at the floor. "Come with me. I'll get you towels and things."

It was hard to leave the rushing water, knowing that her

most difficult ordeal lay ahead. Ting brought her jeans and a sweatshirt.

"I don't think they knew who I was," Christina said dully. "But they took all my clothes. There may have been something in a pocket. I don't remember. They probably looked through my handbag, though they didn't take anything. They could blackmail me. Or David, rather."

"Jenks went back to get your clothes back. Christina. He knows who they were. It's a group he's just begun to handle. Don't worry. He'll take care of it. Jenks knows how to do a lot of things I don't ask him much about." She smiled. "He says there are some things I'm too white to understand." She took a deep breath. "I've called David, Christina. He'll be here soon."

Christina buried her face in her hands.

"I know, I know. But, oh my dear, you've got to face him. He's got to know. I'll stay with you or leave you alone. Whatever you want me to do. I told him as little as I possibly could."

~ * ~

His face grim, David's voice was tight with control as he thanked Ting and Jenks. Without turning to Christina, he said, "Get in the car. I'm late enough as it is."

Christina bit her lip swollen lip, determined not to cry. With a last glance at her friends, she followed. His fingers dug into her arm through Ting's sweatshirt as he opened the door of the Mercedes and threw her onto the seat. She huddled against the door as he stormed around to the driver's side, slid in and started the engine with a roar. Her head was thrown back as the car careened out of the driveway and on to the quiet street.

White-faced, David braked the car hard on a gravel side-road and turned off the ignition. "Now you're going to tell me what the hell has been going on, Christina. What is this gang rape business at some freeway motel? What kind of story is this?" He slammed his hand on the steering wheel.

Christina tried to keep a lid on her hysteria, but she couldn't keep the weepiness from her voice. "It...it isn't a story. There was a group of them, they threw me into a room and...and...they did things..."

"And what were you doing there? Tell me, Christina. Tell me what you were doing at some freeway motel that you got grabbed and gang-raped. The election just over a week away, and you've been fucking some guy and managed to get yourself gang-raped in the process." He gripped her shoulders. "Who is it, Christina?"

She began to whimper, her eyes squeezed closed as she tried to blot out the sound of his voice and his awful question.

"Tell me who it is, Christina, or by God I'll throw you out of the car and you can get home however you can. You'd destroy what we have just because you got an itch for some guy and I want to know who it is."

She didn't open her eyes. "Sev Justus."

"Sev!" He pounded the steering wheel. "You've been fucking Sev Justus? Oh, that's just beautiful. My personal lawyer, the legal adviser to my campaign and you—sneaking around behind my back."

He spit out the words, started the car and spun the wheels off the gravel. The car careened down the side road and onto Tatum Boulevard.

He pulled into the garage moments later, leaned across Christina and flung her door open. "Get out. I have things to do."

She swallowed hard. "Where are you going?"

"You may forget," he said with sarcasm, "that we had an appearance to make tonight. I've undoubtedly pissed off the crowd so much at this point that none of them will vote for me, but better late than never. I also have to discuss this unfortunate disaster with my campaign manager to see if we can anticipate and put out any fires. You're not exactly unknown in this town, Christina, seedy motels notwithstanding. Did this bunch that knocked you around go through your billfold? Did they know they were fucking the ass of the loving wife of Senator Cross?"

"Oh, David. Don't tell Jack. I beg you."

"Get in the house, Christina, and take care of your children. Or have you forgotten you're a mother, too?"

Christina stumbled from the car and nearly fell, her legs rubbery and her body painfully sore. *Oh please, let Lupe be in her room. Let the children be wrapped up in the television. I can't let them see me.*

But Lupe was still in the kitchen, cleaning up from the dinner Christina had missed.

"Oh, Mrs. Cross, there are a couple of messages for you. I said I expected you any..." Lupe stopped, the shock on her face obvious.

"It's all right, Lupe. I had...an accident. I...I just want to get to bed. Please don't bother the children. I'll just find my way up." Her voice wavered at the last words and she fell against the counter. "I'll...I'll tell you in the morning."

Lupe went to her. "You just lean on me, Mrs. Cross. We'll just get you to bed. No matter. You can tell me another time." She put her arm around Christina and led her up the short flight to the bedrooms.

Her kindess and tact broke Christina's defenses and she began to cry, softly at first, then with deep retching sobs. Numbly she let Lupe take her clothes off and put a nightie over her head. The woman said nothing about the bruises on her body.

Helped into bed, Christina slipped between the cool silky sheets and buried her head in the pillows, her heart split in fragments at the anger and contempt that David had shown her.

She felt a cool cloth wipe her face and then Lupe's strong hands arranging her arms and legs, covers tucked around her shoulders.

"Would you like a drink, Missus?"

"No. You're very kind."

Lupe patted her cheek. "I'll just turn the light off and you go to sleep now. Everything is better in the morning."

But Christina knew it wouldn't be. Nothing would ever be the same again. What had she done?

~ * ~

When David came in hours later, he stood at the end of the bed.

Christina lay with the lights out. She had taken a sleeping pill, but it hadn't done much good. She had stood for long minutes with the pills in her hand, wondering if it wouldn't be the easiest thing to just take the whole bottle and go to sleep forever. Not have to face tomorrow. But in the end, she'd taken one and poured the rest back in the bottle. Then she went and huddled in the bed.

"I don't know whether you were getting even with me for that business I had with Hallie several years ago or not. It really doesn't matter, does it?" he said wearily. "I regretted that whole episode, Christina, and I thought we'd put it behind us. What I can't forgive you for is your rotten timing. This could blow up my whole campaign—all the time and effort, the money people trusted me with, their faith in me. If it does, it does. I'll just have to accept what happens. We'll have to go on. In the meantime, I'll just handle it. But you can't see him again. If you do, it's all over, Christina."

"I'll see him one more time to tell him." Her voice was expressionless.

"I mean it, Christina."

"I let you see Hallie again. To tell her it was over."

"I'm not saying I'm as fair as you were. Don't see him."

Christina didn't answer.

The room went dark as David closed the door.

THIRTY TWO

DAVID

Jenks set the bag on David's desk. "I know she won't want to look at these things, but it might be a good idea, just to make sure it's all of it. I don't think these guys are jerking me around. They know better. And don't worry, David. They didn't know who she was. They were high. Feelin' mean. Christina just walked by at a very unlucky time." Jenks shifted in his chair uncomfortably. "This is a new group to me. I'd heard them, of course. Their lyrics are violent, but so many are these days. I wish I could have anticipated something like this."

All David could think of was that Christina didn't have to be there at that particular unlucky moment. The pain twisted in him. "I hate it that they'll get away with it, Jenks." David's face was tight with his effort to control a muscle that twitched at the corner of his mouth.

"They are not going...unpunished. I can tell you that. Don't ask me how. You don't want to know." Jenks's face was grim. "It isn't enough, but it will be, shall we say...discouraging to them. You might want to keep Christina's picture out of the paper for the foreseeable future. From what they tell me they were pretty strung out. I don't know how much they remember. This group is from L.A. Politics here mean nothing to them. They were just over here for the gig at the Westcliffs. I know Christina's picture was in the *Republic* for the museum thing several weeks ago, and then they ran that story about her on jury duty. None of these guys would have seen either. All the same, keep her picture out of the paper, for any reason. I don't think there'll be any problems. I've made…arrangements so that there won't *be* a problem," Jenks said blandly. "I believe you can count on that."

"I don't know how to thank you, Jenks. You've been a real friend." David tried to smile, but gave up and stared at his hands clasped on the desk in front of him.

"I'm happy I was able to help. You and Christina have been good to me. And Ting. You accepted me, welcomed me from the very beginning, no questions asked. That meant an awful lot. I don't think you'll ever know how much." He stood and reached across the desk to shake hands. "Be seein' you. Anything else you can think of, just call me. Ting will stop by and see Christina today. Good luck next Tuesday."

David stood and gripped Jenks's hand. "Thanks. I'll need it."

At the door, Jenks turned. "David, Christina…she's been through a terrible thing. And, well, this is hard to bring up…but you should have her tested. These guys, from what I could find out, weren't into needles, but you never know. It's a lousy world."

David stared at the plastic bag on his desk that held Christina's clothes. "Yes."

After Jenks had gone, David tentatively stretched out his hand and touched the bag, then pulled it across the desk and emptied the contents. He picked up a gray suede shoe, trimmed in silver snakeskin. It had a fancy curved heel. He looked inside. Manolo Blahnik, 7AA. A pretty shoe. It matched the gray sheer stockings, snagged and torn. There was a gray wool dress he didn't remember seeing before. Had she bought a new dress to go to Sev? He straightened it out. The buttons down the front had been torn off. Miserable, he picked up the filmy cream lace bra. The hook was bent out and dangled on a single thread. David picked it up and pressed it to his mouth. It smelled faintly of Christina's perfume. Like roses, he thought. He put his head down on the desk and let the floodgate open to the grief he had dammed within himself.

The telephone roused him and he sat up slowly, rubbing the tears from his face. "This is David Cross." He took a breath. "Yes, Preston." He tucked the phone under his chin and slowly replaced Christina's clothes in the plastic bag. "Yes, it's a good idea. Put it together, will you?"

~ * ~

"You no-good bastard. What the hell are you doing in my office?"

Sev closed the door behind him and walked over to the chair in front of David's desk and sat down. "I'm sitting down, David, because I know you won't ask me to and what I've got to say will take too long to stand."

"You son-of-bitch." David half rose from his chair.

"Why, yes. One son-of-bitch to another, as it were."

"What do you mean by that crack?" His voice was tight with anger.

"I've talked to Christina," Sev said wearily. "Oh, sit down, David. You look ridiculous, ready to come at me across the desk."

"I told her she wasn't to contact you again or it was over for us."

"Yes, so she said. Not very practical, eh, David? How would I know what was going on? But enough of this crap. That's not why I'm here. Christina told me what happened to her. Oh, not all of it, but enough that I can fill in the gaps." His voice shook and he cleared his throat. "For that I am so very, very sorry. I would do anything to erase that from her life. I wish I could comfort her, because I think she's getting very little of that from you. Regardless of what you think of me, and we'll get to that, Christina is having to bear the effects of this attack alone. I couldn't be that strong and neither could you. I take the blame for her being there. For this whole thing, if you like."

"It's a little late for that now," David said bitterly. Impulsively he dumped Christina's clothes out on his desk. "See these?"

Sev glanced down. "What is it?"

David picked up the dress. "What do you mean, what is it? It's the dress they tore off of her."

Sev winced.

"See? Her stockings." He held up the torn fragments. "Her shoes."

"I'm sorry. I never saw...I didn't recognize..." He stopped.

They both realized what Sev had said. He had not seen what Christina was wearing because she had nothing on when she was with him.

David stuffed the clothes back in the bag, slumped in his chair and turned to look out the window.

Traffic sounds drifted up from the street. A telephone rang somewhere in another office. After a moment Sev spoke. "You know, for a long time I wondered what it would be like, how sweet it would feel, to be able to say, now, you son-of-a-bitch, see how it feels to have your wife screwing somebody you thought was a friend. And not only that. In love with that friend. I know you considered it just a little fling. But, yes, Hallie was in love with you. She still is for that matter. You left her in pretty bad shape when you dumped her. I'll never forgive you for the way you handled that. And now, these days, I see you getting real chummy with her again and I see her looking all starry-eyed when she's around you, like she was before. I don't know what you have in mind, David. But don't."

"I don't have anything in mind, Sev. I just thought it

was time to treat that as water over the dam."

"God, you are a heartless son-of-a-bitch. But I knew that. I swore I was going to get you." Sev's voice was harsh. "But it didn't turn out like I'd planned it. Oh, yes, I'd planned it all right. I must say it took me a whole lot longer to break down Christina's resistance than I'd thought it would." He gave a small smile. "I usually don't have that much of a problem with women."

"What a smirking bastard you are."

"Yes. Well, as I said, that's neither here nor there. I must say it made it a hell of a lot easier when you went off to Washington." Sev steepled his hands in front of his mouth. "I should have gotten that appointment, you know. Our honorable governor promised it to me."

"What are you talking about?"

Sev raised an eyebrow. "So you really didn't know?"

"Stop talking in riddles."

"We knew Doug Purcell was ill. He was going to resign his Senate seat this summer, while Congress was in recess. I was to have been appointed. Our fine Governor Holliman promised it to me. He owed me, big time. Then Purcell dropped dead and Holliman double-crossed me and gave the appointment to you. Well, nobody ever said you could trust a politician, but you can see I had another reason to hate you, David Cross. You steal my wife, then you steal my job. You're one of those golden boys, David. Things just fall into place for your type. You go along, blissfully unaware of the wreckage you leave behind you." He made a wry smile. "It's the bastards like me who sometimes have to get our hands dirty."

"You're crazy. Holliman would never have given that job to you."

He shrugged. "You can think what you like. But then, I guess you're probably right, since he didn't. I probably wouldn't have been very good in Washington, in any case. It doesn't change anything though, does it? However, I was going to have my revenge. What's the old saying? Revenge is a dish best eaten cold? As it turned out it didn't taste very good to me after all, hot or cold. You see, I fell in love with Christina. That wasn't part of the plan at all."

David stared into the black, intense eyes. Pain was etched on Sev's face.

"You can't have her, Sev," he said, his voice hoarse with anger.

"Oh, that was never a question. I fell in love with Christina, but she doesn't love me. She was infatuated, excited by the forbidden fruit aspect of it all, the sex, flattered by the attention, perhaps, while you were preoccupied elsewhere. All the things that make a woman vulnerable. But, no. She doesn't love me. And that's what I came to tell you. You're a hypocritical prick to be giving her a hard time over this when she desperately needs someone to get her through this ordeal." His voice broke. "And I wish to hell it could be me."

THIRTY THREE

MIRIAM

Miriam knocked softly on the door, then turned the knob and pushed it open. "Christina? It's me. Miriam." The room was dark, but she heard a stirring from the big canopied bed.

Christina struggled to sit up and ran her fingers through her tangled hair.

"Let me open the curtains just a teensy. It's dark as a cave in here."

"Oh, Miriam." The voice was groggy. "I told Lupe I wasn't up to seeing anybody. I don't want to hurt your feelings, but I'm not very good company." Her eyes looked scraped and swollen.

"I talked Lupe into it. She's worried about you, too." Miriam sat on the edge of the bed, her eyes bright with concern.

"I'm a sight, I know."

"Not too bad." Miriam reached over and poured out a glass of water from a carafe on the bedside table. "Here."

It was a relief to see that Christina's eyes weren't blacked. Makeup would cover the bruise on her cheek. Eyes were harder, Miriam knew. She'd patched up enough of her own when Jonas Laird got in an ugly mood. "But you look kinda woolly. Been taking sleeping pills, huh?"

Christina handed the glass back and looked away.

"Christina, I know what happened. Jack told me. I know you're not happy about that. Please don't mind. You need to have people caring about you. Ting and Jenks. Jack and me." She looked at the averted face. "But I wish you'd stop with the sleeping pills. They can be very tempting when the world looks like it's coming to an end."

"And David? Do I need David caring about me?" Christina asked bitterly, swallowing a sob.

Miriam crawled up on the bed on her knees and wrapped her arms around Christina. She tucked the tangled blonde head between her ear and her shoulder and stroked and patted until she felt Christina relax a little.

"David will be fine. He's kind of in shock, too, and well, we know men just aren't very resilient, but they do get around to being understanding when their feelings get over being hurt. Men just fall apart and you just have to be strong and patient, which is very hard for you to do right now, all things considered."

"Miriam, I can't even get out of bed. The thought of facing anybody overwhelms me. I feel dirty and degraded. So guilty. A zero. You'd be so shocked if you really knew everything." Christina's voice was full of unshed tears.

Miriam settled against the big, padded headboard and rearranged Christina's head. "Are you comfy? I want to tell you a story."

Dispirited, she mumbled, "Yes, I guess so."

"You don't know much about me, really, any of my life before I met Jack. Which is one of the reasons I love you. You just opened your heart to me when I was just coming out of zero myself."

"I knew only that you had a disastrous marriage to a guy who was weird and you were very bitter."

"That's all true. As far as it goes." She was quiet a

moment. "I know all about degradation and feeling dirty. The last two years of my marriage to Jonas Laird I felt that every day—because I *was* degraded and dirty. I look back now and ask myself how I allowed it to happen. But it was an insidious thing. You begin to think you deserve it. That you brought it all on yourself. You probably feel that a little bit, too."

"A lot."

"You didn't deserve it, Christina. Remember that. Sure, you did a foolish thing, but we all do foolish things we wish we could take back. You were in the wrong place at an unfortunate time. Why you were there had nothing to do with what happened to you."

"I think it does. David does, too. He can't forgive me."

"He will."

"I forgave him for Hallie," she murmured into Miriam's shoulder. "Did you know he had an affair with Hallie Justus three years ago?"

"Well no, I didn't, but of course, then, that's part of why he's

so angry. He's feeling guilty, too. Like if he hadn't done that, you'd not have done this, and then you wouldn't have been where you were. Guilt makes people very defensive."

Christina sat up and her shoulders drooped as she played with the lace on the blanket cover. "I...didn't tell David what they did to me."

"Do you want to?"

"No."

"Do you want to tell me?"

"I don't know. I can't get it out of my mind. It goes around and around. I have nightmares and wake up crying and screaming."

"What does David do?"

"David doesn't know. He's been sleeping in the guest room on the other side of the house."

Miriam was quiet for awhile, trying to control her anger

at David's insensitivity. "Let me tell you a little about what happened to me," she began.

In a soft monotone, Miriam matter-of-factly described her married life with Jonas Laird.

Christina sat with her head down, crying quietly as Miriam's story unfolded. Then haltingly, she described the afternoon of pain and horror at the Westcliffs. She sat very still when she'd finished and Miriam gently rubbed her back.

"It was a small suggestion by a lovely man who worked for me that sent me to Aaron Shulman. He was a psychiatrist that I went to. Maybe it wouldn't be a practical thing for you to go to Denver. Then again, maybe it would be a good thing. Would you like to see Dr. Shulman? He's the gentlest man. Jack can fly you up anytime you want, as often as you want. Let me call Dr. Shulman. He helped me find my...I think I'd call it my humanity, again. I didn't know at the time if I would ever find my way back. But I did. You will, too. I thought my life was absolutely over, that there was no future at all out there for me. I was only twenty-six, and thought there was nothing left. But there was. I met Jack, my dearest, dearest love, and..." She had wondered whether it was a good idea to deliver happy news to the distraught Christina, then decided it was. "...and now, we're going to have a child. It's wonderful. I could have missed so much."

Christina gasped, turned and flung her arms around Miriam. Her face was alight for the first time and the tears were not for herself.

Miriam laughed. "You're the first to know. But it isn't really a secret. You can tell if you want to."

"When is it?"

"June."

"David...David doesn't know?"

"No," Miriam answered.

"Maybe...maybe I'll tell him."

"That would be nice."

"Miriam? I'm glad you came today. I needed you."

"I know," Miriam said.

"I probably will be all right. In time. It may take awhile."

"Yes, I expect so. Do you want me to call Dr. Shulman?"

"He won't make me go out and climb any mountains like he did you, will he?"

"No. But maybe he'll throw in an acrophobia cure, just for kicks. Then Jack and I can take you along when we go climbing in the Himalayas."

"The doctor would win the Nobel prize if you ever got me on a Himalaya." Christina tried to smile.

"I have to run. I have to meet that awful woman who sends everything back that we've spent months picking out. I'm seriously thinking about murder. I'll stop by tomorrow." Miriam picked up her handbag from the floor and stood up. "You'll be lots better. You'll see."

THIRTY FOUR

DAVID

David walked across the dimly lit bedroom. Christina was asleep, almost lost in the stacks of big, square European pillows she loved. He looked down at the golden hair that fell over her face and fanned out over the pillows, her cheeks flushed. The bruises on her face were fading a little. He'd missed her these past days, missed talking to her, telling her things. It angered him that she couldn't seem to get out of bed. He started to reach down and brush her hair from her face, but his hand stopped.

The afternoon Sev came to his office began playing out in his mind. Sev had made sure to bring up the sex. That she'd enjoyed it. A picture of Christina, naked and smiling, her eyes that passionate blue they got...reaching out her arms. To Sev Justus.

David's hand went to his eyes instead, and he rubbed hard, trying to erase the picture. Did she make those same little sounds with him? Toss her head around when she came? Squeeze her fingers on his back? Did she call out his name—over and over? Not David. Sev?

David's face hardened as a coldness stole into his chest around his heart.

Christina stirred and sighed, then turned on her back.

Her eyes fluttered open. "David?" Her hand tentatively reached out to him.

"I was just leaving for the television station. The debate is tonight."

"I'm, sorry. I forgot. I'll have to dress." Christina struggled out of the pillows.

"Don't bother. You're not in any shape to go anywhere. But do you think you could pull yourself together enough to go to Laise and Preston's for dinner Saturday night? He wants to entertain the big contributors to the campaign. A lot of people we know will be there."

"Yes. Yes, of course. I'll...I'll be fine then. Yes."

"You'd better be."

Christina sank back down in the pillows and stared at the ceiling. "I'm so sorry. I forgot about tonight."

David turned on his heel and left the room.

THIRTY FIVE

GIANLUCA

The plane from Rome was late getting into Kennedy and Gianluca's headache had reached epic proportions. He'd exhausted his small supply of amphetamines about the time they passed over Newfoundland. He had been careful to bring only what he needed for the flight. He didn't want to risk being searched at Customs. He'd also left the gun he'd stolen from his father. It would have been foolish to bring it in. He would get that in Phoenix. He knew where to go. His supplier could get him anything. Gianluca was proud that he had figured things out so carefully.

As the plane began to descend, He gritted his teeth as his headache moved to another plane of agony. Dimly through the red fog of pain, he went over that last scene with his father. He had boasted that Laise had declared her love for him and that soon they would be free to marry. Ugo berated him for his foolishness and, when Gianluca persisted, Ugo told him of his nights in Laise's bedroom. Gianluca screamed that it wasn't true, but Ugo described the scene in shattering detail. He told of Laise, stretched out on the bed, waiting for him, naked and smiling, writhing for him, with the diamond and topaz earrings blazing in the lights from the chandelier that they had left burning, the better to see one another's passion.

Gianluca had become hysterical and lunged at his father, but Ugo had simply slapped him, a resounding cuff that had thrown him against the wall.

"A *buffone* and his *putana*," he had sneered. "Wipe your nose."

Gianluca had rushed to his room and packed his things. He demanded the chauffeur take him to the hospital where, full of emotion, he kissed his mother goodbye, all in the exploding sun of his headache.

His father didn't think he was smart, but he was. Look how he'd gotten somebody brilliant like Laise to promise to marry him. No, that wasn't right. She was his father's whore. He had to remember that.

Gianluca found he had missed his flight to Phoenix, but maybe that was okay. He went through Customs, then went outside to get a taxi.

He gave the cab driver fifty dollars and told him what he needed. The sour-faced cabbie only grunted. They pulled off the expressway at Aqueduct Racetrack. It wasn't long before the cab pulled into the parking lot of a dilapidated market on a seedy, garbage-strewn street. He told the cabbie to wait. He got out and pulled his windbreaker around his ears. The November wind was raw and cold off Jamaica Bay and the late afternoon light was gray and bleak. Trash and dead leaves blew in swirls around his ankles. Gianluca glanced back at the cabbie, but he was slumped down in the seat with his eyes closed, apparently bored with one more fare who needed a hit.

Inside, fly-specked displays of old cereal and canned goods led back to a counter. Gianluca told the strapping Hispanic man behind the counter what he needed.

The big man studied him for a moment, then he disappeared for several minutes and came back with two envelopes in his stained fingers. "Ten milligram blacks, a hundred dollars," he muttered. The whites of his eyes were the bloodshot brownish yellow of an exhausted liver.

Gianluca paid him and went back to the cab, feeling the eyes of the proprietor boring into his back. He tossed down two tablets before he got into the taxi. "Back to Kennedy. American Airlines."

His headache felt better already. Soon his heart would start pumping that elation of energy through his body. He put the white envelopes in his pocket and took out his billfold. He had almost seven hundred dollars left of the thousand his mother had given him. He should be able to get all the stuff he needed. There was some money—a few hundred dollars, in his account in Phoenix. He thought it was probably not a good idea to use his credit cards unless he absolutely had to.

Look at how smart he was being. What a pity his father couldn't see how clever he was.

THIRTY SIX

LAISE

"Preston, I wish you wouldn't go into this now. I need you to go down and supervise setting up the heaters and the two bars. You know if you're not right there, they'll always put a bar too close to the pool and we'll wind up with somebody falling in."

Laise finished buckling the tiny straps of her sandals, stood up from the bed and adjusted her French cut lace panties, then unzipped the back zipper and stepped into the aubergine velvet jumpsuit.

Preston automatically moved to her and zipped up the back. "Is that why you went to San Francisco over the weekend? To see this Will what's-his-name?"

"Thank you." She flounced the big poofed shoulders studded with seed pearls. "Yes." She held up a pair of elaborate antique gold and pearl earrings, shook her head and put them back in her jewelry box and took out simple pearl studs. "And it's Will Fowler." She turned. "I think you'll like him."

Preston smiled weakly. "Do I have to?"

"I'll see a lawyer this week. I suppose you'll want to use Sev. We don't have anything to quarrel over. I want you to have this house. I hope you'll keep it at least as long as the boys are minors. I want the ranch, but you can go there as usual. Look, things are really not going to change all that much. I can't figure out why you're so unhappy. I've never made any secret that our situation could change any time. We haven't done a bad job of keeping up appearances, but now I want out. I want to marry Will. The boys are old enough now that I can think about leaving. You've raised them mostly anyway. And done a wonderful job."

"Laise...I'm...I'm sorry about Bartlett Savage coming tonight.
But he's a big contributor. He was on David's list."

Laise turned. "It really doesn't matter any more about him, does it? Preston, we're friends, you and I. We'll always be friends. More than that. You're dear to me. Do you want me to tie your tie?"

"Would you?"

Laise crossed the bedroom and stood in front of Preston, looping the silk ends around with the expertise of long practice.

"I'll have to learn to do this myself," he said, wincing as she pulled the tie tight.

She smiled and straightened the bow. "I'll teach you before I go." She patted his cheek. "It'll be fine, Preston. You'll see. Now, hurry, will you? I've got to show Arnaud's people where things are and cut some roses for the powder room.

~ * ~

After she'd gone Preston walked over to her mirror and started to brush his hair, but when he caught sight of his face, he put the brush down and stared at himself. Why had he been sent this aberration, this pain? His eyes stung and he pulled a tissue from a gold-filigree box on the dressing table and blew his nose. So it was going to end. He'd been lulled by the passage of five years since Laise had found him with Bartlett Savage. He'd begun to think their lives could continue, tranquil and platonic. But now he'd lost her for good.

Oh, God, don't let me cry.

THIRTY SEVEN

CHRISTINA

Christina hadn't been to the Brock's house in a while, but it hadn't changed. Laise never changed anything, preferring to keep the rooms filled with antiques and European paintings the same as they were when she was growing up. The Spanish style house had a formal, old-fashioned ambience. There was even a long solarium with dozens of Boston ferns, that capricious plant that detested the dry desert air. Laise had told Christina that she loved them, just like her mother had, and when they looked droopy she just threw that batch away and got new.

Guests were gathered outside by the pool and Christina mentally squared her shoulders. She had gritted her teeth and given herself a long pep talk while she dressed for this evening. It was so important that she not let David down tonight. She was sure her absence from campaign events of the past couple of weeks had caused comment. She simply had to carry this off, no matter how shaky she felt. David's hand touched her elbow and they stepped outside.

It was a chilly night, but Arnaud had set up enough heaters that it was comfortable enough. Christina wore a simple red crepe Chanel with a matching sheared red mink bomber jacket, hoping the color would impart some vibrancy that she did not feel. She knew she looked terribly pale and had tried her best with Miriam's coaching and her own theater makeup skills on the dark smudges under her eyes. The bruise on her cheek had faded to an ugly, yellowish color that had actually been easier to cover than she'd expected.

Buried deep was the anxiety that Sev and Hallie would come tonight. They ordinarily would be expected. Could she face him? With David here? She simply did not know what either one would do and she had to handle it, whatever way it played out.

"You look wonderful, sweetie. Good for you for coming." Miriam squeezed Christina's hand. "So sweet of Laise to do this party. I was afraid I was going to have to." She winked. "Jack and Preston want to clean up the campaign debt and get started on building the kitty for the next election. It's money, money, money, all the time. Got to cosset all the Big Enchiladas with the deep pockets. I'm told I even have to be nice tonight."

Christina laughed. "Maybe the evening won't be so hard if I can remember you're trying to be nice for four hours."

Miriam made a long face. "Four hours! I thought I could get away with three. Do you think I could play expectant mommy and faint along about ten o'clock? Aren't pregger ladies always passing out in the movies?"

"Right now you could probably get away with anything with Jack."

Miriam's face brightened. "You really think so? Maybe if I work hard early I can get time off for good behavior. Come with me. Let's go enchant that old fart Boren Whitelaw. Maybe we can get fifty thousand dollars out of him."

"Miriam, I don't think that's how it works. Are you sure you feel okay?"

"Oh, I won't mention money." She gazed down at her cleavage fondly. "I'll just rub my burgeoning boobs— aren't they gorgeous?—on his dried up old arm. He'll remember me kindly when Jack hits him up."

David came up. "I'd like you to talk to Bartlett and Ann Savage, Christina. They've pitched in a bundle."

"Yes, of course. Should I mention their contribution, or just be nice?"

"Just be nice. You behaving yourself, Miriam? Delighted about the baby. Jack told me."

Miriam glanced at Christina briefly. "I'm being an angel. Run along with David, Christina. I'll handle Whitlaw myself. It would be a sin against nature to waste these tits."

"What was that all about?" David asked.

"Miriam is going to do some fundraising."

"God help us." He took her arm and they moved across the room.

Christina suddenly felt bereft without Miriam.

So far, Sev and Hallie hadn't come. She felt a surge of relief. She would make it through the evening.

~ * ~

From time to time during dinner David glanced uneasily down the table at Christina. He had felt her agitation during cocktails as they made their way around the patio greeting people. He had felt her icy hands. But her voice was warm and steady, a beautiful voice that had never failed to thrill him in all the years they'd been married. Her smile was bright, and probably only he could tell it was forced.

It hit him suddenly that she'd lost weight. And she wasn't quite successful in covering up the dark shadows under her eyes. He caught his breath. He had never seen her so…luminous. She glanced up once when she felt him watching her, and her eyes filled with such anguish that he felt scalded. He had to turn away or he would break down. He knew then what this evening cost her—the gracious smile, the lighthearted conversation, the smooth and charming performance of the candidate's wife. His heart constricted and he felt ill. The beautiful woman at the end of the table was his wife and he loved her and had let her down. He'd always thought of himself as a nice guy. And once, he was. When had that changed? When had he become what he was now? A self-centered, self-righteous miserable sonofabitch.

He was in a fever now for this party to end. In the car he would hold her and kiss her and tell her that Sev Justus didn't matter, none of it mattered except that she had come back to him.

~ * ~

All of the supplies were in the car. Now all he had to do was wait. He hadn't counted on there being a party at Laise's tonight, and it made him terribly nervous to have to sit in the car. But it would be over soon. These weren't young people. He had looked in the window. They wouldn't stay late. Pretty soon he would climb the wall and wait in the oleander bushes until the servants were finished cleaning up and guests had left. He would go into the house by the pool.

He was sorry about that mix-up with the gateman down at the entrance to this enclave of rich houses, but the man didn't understand Gianluca needed to see Laise even if his name wasn't on the list. The man wanted to call the house and ask about him, but Gianluca couldn't have that. He couldn't just go over the wall like the last time. He needed to get his car through the gate. People leaving the party wouldn't notice that the gateman didn't seem to be in his little house. The exit opened automatically.

~ * ~

Laise and Preston, Christina and David sat in the living room in front of the dying fire while the four decided on the wording of a follow-up letter to major contributors that they wanted hand-delivered Sunday, the next day. The men had taken their jackets off, relieved to have the evening over.

Preston was saying, "That way they'll get your thank you two days before the election. Good psychology, I think."

"I agree. Can't thank you enough for all your work,

your expertise, Preston. If I win Tuesday, it'll be in no small part through your efforts." He turned to Laise. "Beautiful party, Laise. Perfect, as usual. Now I think we'd better let you all get some sleep."

"Finish your drink, David," Preston said. "No rush."

"I have, thanks." He leaned forward to put his glass on the table and stopped, puzzled.

Christina saw David's look and turned to see an intruder, shoulders hunched in a windbreaker in front of the big French doors. Was he part of the caterer's help? Why was he so wild looking?

Laise turned in her chair and gasped. "Gianluca! What in God's name are you doing here?"

"Who the hell are you?" demanded Preston.

The man ignored everyone but Laise. His voice was high and thin, and his eyes glittered huge and black. "It was necessary to come. You see my father told me how you made love to him. You promised me you loved me and we would get married, but you let my father lick you and fuck you. You were going to be my wife, and now you're my father's whore."

Laise started to stand, but a bullet, then another, spun her back and she flew over the big coffee table where a spatter of blood traced over the fine wood from the small holes punctured in the aubergine velvet.

Preston tried to catch her, screaming, "No, Laise, no, no…no!"

The mass of red hair slipped through his hands as two more shots cracked.

The scene unfolded in slow motion to Christina. A red splash appeared on Preston's forehead and David floated through the air to shield her, but two large red stars bloomed on his white shirtfront. She fell on her knees to David. His eyes looked amazed, then they closed. He didn't move.

Christina raised her head to find the ghastly gun pointing straight at her, the metallic circle of the muzzle wavering slightly as it grew larger coming toward her.

She stared at the cold blue O, then raised her eyes to meet Gianluca's, now streaming with tears. He stared down at David, then his hand shot out and seized her hair. There was a long stream of voluble Italian, and numbly Christina realized he wanted her to get up and go with him. She still clutched her red mink jacket. It had been in her lap while she was waiting for David to get ready to leave.

Gianluca laid the gun along her cheek and yanked her hair. She cried out and he pushed her roughly to the front door. Christina knew that all the catering people had gone. That's what the Italian had been waiting for; indeed, he seemed surprised to find her and David still there. There would be no one to help her. She tried to look back at the bloody scene, at David lying on the floor, praying David survived, but then her mind saw the red starbursts on his white shirt front. The cold steel of the gun pressed against her cheek.

She was hurried down the long front walk and down the drive. In the street there was a small Japanese car. The man opened the door on the driver's side and threw her across the seat.

~ * ~

Christina huddled against the car door. David was dead. David lay back there on the floor with Laise and Preston. He had not forgiven her and now it was too late. The emptiness spread through Christina as she convulsively gripped the red mink jacket in her lap. At first she watched Gianluca in terror, expecting him to shoot her as well, but as the small car got farther and farther away from the house, his agitation seemed to calm. He appeared to have a direction to his plans.

When he turned onto I-17, she knew they were going north, but by now she had lost interest. It didn't matter where they were going. He would kill her and it really didn't matter. She supposed she was a hostage and that he would need her for a while, but then there would come the time that she had no value. He had killed three people, one more would make no difference.

As they approached the big rest area at Sunset Point on the freeway, a glimmer of self-preservation fluttered. There would be people there.

"I have to go to the bathroom."

"You will have to wait."

"I can't. We drank wine and coffee tonight. I can't wait."

He swore under his breath in Italian, but he pulled off the freeway to the rest area. It was a main stop on the way to Flagstaff and was generally busy. Even at this hour, after midnight, there were still cars, campers, and the big semis parked along the well-lit parking lot. Gianluca parked next to the women's bathroom and went around to let Christina out. He held her arm and walked her swiftly into the bathroom, shoved her into a cubicle and stepped in with her, leaving the door partly ajar, his body blocking the lock, the gun pointing at her head.

A woman and her teenage daughter had looked on in amazement, then outrage. "You shouldn't be in there." The woman's voice was shrill. "This is the 'ladies.' Melissa, go get Daddy."

"My friend, she is sick. I'm afraid to leave her alone. Please understand." He moved the gun to the crack at the door.

Christina stared at it, at Gianluca, then called out, "Please don't be angry at my friend. I really do need his help. I'm sick."

Her heart sank when the woman's voice answered, now full of sympathy. "Well, then. That's different. Aren't you a nice man to take care of her. Can we do anything?"

Gianluca's voice was warm, gentle. "You are very kind. No."

"Then come along, Melissa. We'll leave these folks be."

Resigned, Christina pulled up her skirt and closed her eyes. She would pretend he wasn't there. Bitterly she thought how she'd gotten good at making her mind blank.

The gun pressed against her back as Gianluca pushed her out of the stall. He watched as she washed her hands. "You are a nice woman. I would have killed them." He took her arm as they left, the gun in her ribs, and walked her down to the scenic lookout point—a rocky promontory with a panoramic view of the valley and surrounding mountains. There was a three quarter moon that washed the valley in silver and made the dark mountains loom against the sky. A chill wind whipped around them as Gianluca relieved himself over the iron railing, then pushed her back to the car.

"My name is Gianluca. What may I call you?"

An infinitesimal crack in the numbness that enveloped Christina slowly opened enough to admit a wisp of hope. This man who would stop and let her go to the bathroom, ask her name, might have some feeling after all. But when she began to think what she might do, the events of the past two weeks crushed her. Her husband had discovered her infidelity, she had been gang-raped, seen her husband and friends murdered, and was speeding north with the killer who would certainly put a bullet into her as soon as she was no longer useful. She clamped down on the waves of nausea that swept over her.

"Christina. My name is Christina."

He grunted in approval. "A beautiful name. Our Lord's name."

She stared at him.

As they drove, she found if she concentrated on the white ribbon of highway, her stomach gradually eased. She found that the broken white line in the middle of the road soothed her if she stared at it, and gradually her mind closed down. In a trance, her eyes drooped and she dozed, her mind numb.

Consciousness seeped into Christina's stupor as the

little car began laboring up the long inclines as they came into the high mountains. The rest had sharpened her awareness and she could think of what had happened. She played in her mind the bloody scene, as Laise spun over the coffee table and Preston, horrified, had tried to catch her, the beautiful red hair spilling through his hands. And David. David had tried to shield her with his body, and now he was dead. Had he forgiven her? Yes, he must have. He'd wanted to protect her. She began to cry, softly at first, until her wrenching sobs became long wails of terrible grief.

"Why? Why? Why?" she whimpered, her control slipping away. "Why did you kill them all? Oh, David...David..."

Gianluca gripped the steering wheel with one hand. His other whipped over and glanced a blow off of Christina's cheek. *"Silenzio!"*

Her sobs continued, but began to grow quieter as she tried to calm herself, not provoke him. She must stay controlled. She rubbed her cheek where he had hit her and thought: *I, who have never been struck by anyone, hurt by anyone in my entire life, look at me now. I've been raped. Beaten.* She squeezed her eyes shut, trying to stop the tears.

~ * ~

Gianluca was alarmed. The woman had been so docile. He had even congratulated himself at his acuity at taking her as a hostage. He had started to shoot her, too. But she was very pretty. Of course, if she had screamed or gotten hysterical, he would have, but when she'd looked at him, her beautiful face without hope, with a calm acceptance, he couldn't spoil it by shooting. He hadn't wanted to kill any of them except for Laise, but it had been necessary. Anybody could see that it had been necessary. It would be hours before the bodies were found and he wouldn't have to worry for awhile about being hunted. Who would ever connect him to Laise in the first place? He had taken care of the guard at the security gate when the man became…difficult, and there was no one else who had seen him near the house.

But a hysterical woman would be an awful lot of trouble. He really should have killed her. She was a witness. He should have thought of that. Oh, he was so confused. He probably would kill her, otherwise she'd have to go all the way into the canyon with him. He would find peace there. Like the first time. When the headaches went away.

Her sobs had gone into dry hiccups. He looked over and assessed how she was dressed. The skirt of the dress was tight. Her shoes were some gold leather strap things, ridiculously high. *Basta!* If he kept her he'd have to get her something else to wear. The fur jacket was warm, but she'd need cover on her legs. It would be cold at the canyon.

~ * ~

As Christina's sobs subsided she leaned her head against the cold window, welcoming the shock to her feverish forehead. She had to pull herself together. She had two children. They would need her.

"The last man I shot. He was your husband?"

His voice filtered through the oppressive whine of the old car's little engine. Christina, startled, swung her head away from the window to stare at the handsome dark face, now so full of sympathy.

She choked. "Yes."

"I am sorry. I didn't mean to kill anyone but Laise. She deceived me, you know?"

Maybe if he talked, she thought. *Maybe I can get him to be my friend. Maybe he won't kill me. Maybe he will let me go. The children will need me. I've got to try.*

"No, I didn't know. How did she deceive you? She was a very honest person. How were you her friend?"

Gianluca began a long, disjointed tale, mixed with English and Italian, about how Laise had fallen in love with him and how they had been lovers. That Laise was going to marry him and when she went to Italy, she had fallen under the spell of his father. They had fucked together. He had had to kill her, of course, to save his honor. To save his father's honor. Laise had wickedly seduced his father. She was evil. She was a whore.

It was nearly four in the morning when they reached Flagstaff. Gianluca stopped for gas at a large truck stop, its garish lights visible for miles. He made her get out and go with him into the big chrome and Formica restaurant, smelling of warmed-over coffee and a dirty grill. He got them both coffee and took her over to the gift shop, manned by a sleepy, pudgy-faced girl with bad skin, yawning over a comic book. They went back to a wall hung with T-shirts and sweatshirts. There was a bin full of cheap sneakers.

"What size do you wear?"

"A seven."

"Find a pair."

Christina looked at him warily. "Why?"

"Because where we go you can't walk in those shoes." He shoved her. "Look."

Dispirited, she fumbled through the pungent rubbery mass and extracted a white pair and handed them to Gianluca. He pulled a sweatshirt and sweatpants off hangers and they went up to the girl at the cash register.

Before they pulled back on the highway, he stopped the car. He pulled the sweatshirt and pants from their plastic bag, brought them around and opened her door. "Get out. Take off your dress and shoes and put these on."

She stared at him for a moment and then got out and took off the red mink jacket. She unbuttoned the dress at the back of her neck, pulled it over her head and handed it to him.

Gianluca licked his lips as he stared at her breasts, the nipples pale and tight in the cold. "You are a very beautiful woman."

Christina said nothing, looking steadily at a point over his shoulder.

He handed her the sweatshirt and she shrugged into it. He handed her the pants. She kicked off her gold sandals and stepped into the gray baggy pants, pulling the drawstring tight. The air was frosty and the soft cotton fleece inside the knits felt good on her skin.

"I can put the sneakers on in the car." She leaned to pick up her sandals. And hesitated.

He was impatient. "*Si.* Get in the car. Let's go." He shoved her onto the seat and went around to the driver's side.

They drove away. He had not noticed her gold sandals in the grass by the side of the road, now glinting red in the taillights of the car.

THIRTY EIGHT

CHRISTINA AND GIANLUCA

Up until Flagstaff, Christina had vaguely thought that Gianluca was simply fleeing the bloody scene in Phoenix. But when they left the mountain town heading due north on Highway 180, she knew that he had a destination. When he came to a turnoff, he had not hesitated, sure of where he was going. The narrow road across the high Coconino Plateau was deserted. It would be two, two and a half hours until dawn and the black landscape was unrelieved. Had Gianluca a hideaway somewhere out in this desolate land?

Christina sank deeper into the red mink jacket. Gianluca's car didn't have a heater and the weather was getting colder as they went north. "Where are we going?"

"You don't need to know," he said irritably.

~ * ~

He was beginning to have misgivings about Christina, realizing he had panicked when he forced her to come with him. He had half-expected to be run down by the police before he got out of the city, but he'd just breezed along without a sign of trouble and now he was stuck with a witness he would have to drag along on the difficult trails. Well, he would play it by ear, as the Americans say. He could always get rid of her.

Still, she was very pretty and if she didn't give him any

trouble he kind of liked the idea of having a woman along with him. To tell the truth he'd felt sexually aroused ever since he'd killed Laise and those others. When she'd taken off her dress he had been tempted to take her into the back seat to relieve this thick ache that the rough-riding little car only aggravated. He would have to see how compliant she was after they got to the safety of the canyon. He had the gun if she got difficult, though it was nicer when they wanted it. Once he had her, there wouldn't be any trouble. That was one thing he knew—he could satisfy a woman.

His jeans got uncomfortably tight at the prospect and he shifted his weight in the small bucket seat.

~ * ~

Christina now thought they must be headed for the Grand Canyon. This far on Highway 180 there was really no other destination. She and David had brought the children several times and David had taken them on mule rides down Bright Angel trail. She hadn't gone, of course—hadn't even been able to watch the mule train with her husband and children disappear down the trailhead. But what would a desperate Italian killer want to go there for? Didn't he realize it was crowded with people? It was overrun in summer, but tourists came from all over the world even in cold weather. The canyon was breathtaking when a storm frosted it with snow.

She tried to think if she'd heard what the weather was this weekend over the canyon, but she simply hadn't had any reason to pay attention. It would surely be crowded though and that was a break for her. Surely she'd be able to escape, find someone to help her. In the meantime she would talk to this Gianluca. Appear docile and engage his sympathy if she could.

I've got to try. Italians have a strong sense of family. They adore their mothers.

"I have small children, you know." Her voice wavered. "You've...you've killed their father. They will be lost. They will need me." Desperately. She fought down the panic that those words brought—the tears that sprang to her eyes.

Gianluca gripped the steering wheel and scowled. "*Silenzio!* I told you before. Just shut up!"

That's too accusatory, she thought frantically. *I've upset him.*

She closed her eyes and tried to think of nothing until she could be calm. Surely there was some sort of plan she could think of, just to keep her sanity, if nothing else. Her mind was clearer now—not the jumble it had been. She was glad she was rid of the tight skirt and flimsy shoes. He'd helped her there.

There began to be signs for the entrance to the canyon. It was still dark when the ranger booth loomed up and Gianluca slammed on the brakes. A sign indicated the park didn't open until eight o'clock and there was a heavy chain across the entrance. He backed up, shifted to his lowest gear and the little car bucked and ground up the rocky embankment, bouncing down on the roadway on the other side.

Christina could feel his excitement and knew they were nearing the end of their journey. Uneasily she watched the piñon pines flash by the headlights. They passed through Grand Canyon Village, silent in the pre-dawn, lights showing only from the kitchens of the old El Tovar and Bright Angel Lodge. The lots seemed nearly full.

But Gianluca sped on around wooded curves, to the west. She wasn't so familiar with this part of the park, but they passed groups of dark buildings. There were small rustic cabins to rent in some areas, some quite isolated. Perhaps he planned to hole up in one of those. He had planned this carefully, she thought. Who would ever think to look here? Maybe it wasn't such a strange place for a hideout. Crowded yet isolated. Christina's heart sank as she gripped her knees and fought down a bubble of hysteria.

The sky was beginning to lighten faintly when they came to the end of the gravel road. The car lights picked out a sign that said Hermit's Rest. There was a stone and log lookout building with a curio shop and a parking lot. Gianluca pulled the car into a grouping of wind-twisted pine and cypress so that branches partially obscured the car. He opened the door and got out, stretching, then motioned for her to get out. He carried the gun in his windbreaker pocket, but now pushed it into his belt. He looked to see if she got the point.

"The trailhead is down that service road." He indicated a sign that said Hermit's Trail. "I will carry most of the equipment and provisions. But you will have to carry something. There is no water on the trail and we must carry what we will need. *Capisce?*"

Christina had slowly backed up to the side of the car, her heart a trip hammer in her chest. "No...no, I don't understand."

Through the trees she could see the blush of the sunrise beginning to tint the startling rock formations of the canyon into deep roses and lavenders, illuminating the abyss.

"This is the end of the journey. Now we go down," Gianluca said shortly. "Come here. *Ho fretto.* I'm in a hurry."

Christina stared at him. He expected her to go down that precipitous trail! "But I can't. It's impossible, don't you see? I can't bear heights. They...paralyze me. You must understand, I'd only hold you back." Her hands had turned to ice and she could feel sweat beginning to sting her armpits.

Gianluca looked at her, his handsome face unreadable. Then he walked slowly back and stood directly in front of her. "Ah, Christina." His voice was soft, conversational. He pulled the gun from his belt and pointed it directly between her eyes, four inches away. "It would be a shame to shoot the beautiful woman who has the Lord's name."

Her mind spinning out of control, Christina went to the back of the car. She had to get away. It was unthinkable that she would...would disappear over the edge of the cliff and begin that dizzying, terrifying trail into the massive gorge.

307

Gianluca put the gun back in his belt. He handed her a water canteen and showed her how to strap it over her shoulder. He buckled a second canteen to himself. He handed her a small blue backpack. "This isn't heavy. Your arms go through here."

Christina looked numbly at the backpack in her hands.

"Like this."

He grunted and hoisted a much larger one over his shoulders and crossed the straps over his chest. It was awkward to hook and she stepped to him slowly and took the hook from his hand and fastened it.

"*Grazie.*" He turned to close the trunk.

Then she ran. The forest here was not thick, the floor covered with soft grass, and as she ran her mind adjusted to the primary need to save herself. Behind her she could hear Gianluca cursing in Italian as he wrestled to divest himself of the heavy, encumbering knapsack. She would have only seconds before he freed himself and he came after her. Would he shoot her? She blessed the hours she had labored at the spa—the aerobics classes, the Pilates classes, the stair machines, the stationary bicycles—all for the perfect figure to wear her perfect clothes. It was those hours that might give her the strength to save her life.

She ran lightly, sure-footed, her heart beating strong and regular in her chest. Elation filled her as she listened to her breath coming in calm, almost syncopated rhythm as it matched her foot strikes against the sandy, pine-needled floor of the of the piñon forest.

She had gotten away. He had to come for her, but her freedom gave her a chance. She was covering ground. Maybe it would be enough. By necessity she had darted away from Gianluca, away from Grand Canyon Village and its more peopled area. She would try to make a sweep around him in hopes of hitting the road and its possibility of tourists. She remembered the Hermit's Trail was not regularly traveled by hikers. It wasn't a maintained trail and, as Gianluca had said, there was no water until one reached the floor of the canyon.

She strained her ears, hoping to hear a vehicle, or perhaps voices, but there was only the morning breeze breathing softly through the pines, and the harsh cries of jays and ravens.

But isn't that what he would expect her to do? Head away from the canyon, since he now knew she was afraid of heights? Christina slowed slightly at her indecision.

Abruptly she felt the sharp jab in her right foot and the jolt as she fell sprawling across a fallen pine log. Through the haze of pain she saw the small jutting rock that had tripped her. Her heart was pounding now at the surprise of it. She reached down and rubbed her foot vigorously, taking the chance to look back to see if Gianluca followed her. She realized she was sweating hard. The mink jacket was too warm for this kind of exertion. She would do better without it. She pulled it off, then had an idea. She tucked it behind the pine log, with only a little bit of sleeve showing. Gianluca might catch sight of the small, brilliant spot of red and be fooled. He would come to investigate. When he found the jacket he would be angry, but he would head toward the road. She would go the other way. She had time to make only one plan and act on it. She would pray it was the right one.

Christina trotted off in the direction of the canyon. She would follow the edge of it, far enough away that she wouldn't get dizzy, and eventually come to the village, or cabins. Something, surely. Within minutes she caught a glimpse through the trees ahead of blue sky, and then the multi-colored limestone and sandstone walls, buttes and spires. She veered to the right, and then heard shots behind her. She ran faster. Gianluca had seen the red jacket, she guessed. He would go to see if his shots had hit her. Would he then do what she hoped?

She tried to maintain an even pace, looking ahead for obstacles, planning her course to cover the most ground. It had been seven or eight miles from Grand Canyon Village proper, but maybe she could come on a cabin. Or cars if she could find the road. She wished she had a watch, but she hadn't worn one last evening. She had lost track of time. It seemed she had been running forever, but it was probably closer to half an hour.

She was tiring and her breath was beginning to catch in her throat. She took deep gulps of air, afraid she might get a cramp in her side, afraid to admit how much those shots had frightened her.

Christina kept glancing to the left, keeping the canyon just in her peripheral vision, her ears trying to pick out any sounds of pursuit. She startled a doe and fawn, which leaped off into the woods, their white undertails flashing. She heard another shot. Closer this time. He hadn't gone the other way! He was following her and shooting the gun to panic her. She tried to run faster and for awhile the adrenalin surge she got from the gunshot increased her speed, but gradually her pace wore down and her breath came in short, harsh gasps. She had to veer to the right, then veer to the right again. The canyon was scooping inward.

Suddenly the canyon edge was in every direction but toward Gianluca. The awful realization came that she had run into a promontory and there was only one way out.

The shot was very close this time and made the hairs on her neck crawl. She forced it out of her mind. Her eyes flew right, then left. Perhaps she could edge around his right. Christina stopped running and began to ease herself from tree to boulder to tree. Her gray sweatshirt and pants would not be easy to see. She knew her hair was too bright, particularly when it caught a shaft of sunlight, now creeping over the grassy forest floor as the sun rose higher. She had nothing to cover it with.

She stopped abruptly and scooped up handfuls of sandy dirt and pine needles and rubbed them into her hair. What she couldn't do with speed she might now do with stealth. She glided along the needle-carpeted forest floor, acutely aware of every movement, every sound. Surely the road must be ahead. Her heart lurched when she picked up the crunch and crackles of Gianluca's boots in the silent morning air, though she couldn't see him.

And then she did. He was moving quickly, crouching close to the ground. He hadn't seen her yet, but a patch of sunlight through the trees caught the glint of the gun he carried. Christina froze behind a tree. She could hear him thrashing around now, moving away from her.

Silently she slipped from behind the tree. She was sure she saw the cliff edge turn away straight ahead. She would be off the promontory and headed toward the road. Her throat was deadly dry, and her breath came in deep ragged gasps. But she didn't hear the footsteps any longer.

"*Ciao*, Christina."

Gianluca stepped from behind a cluster of boulders, the gun pointed straight at her heart, a half-smile of triumph on his beautiful mouth.

She slowed her steps, then came to a halt, overwhelmed with the ghastly injustice of this. The she simply stood, her head down, long dry sobs shaking her body, her tears blinding her eyes.

Gianluca walked to her. "I ought to kill you right here. You have cost me an hour already and we still have to get back to the car. The park will be open soon and others might be at the trailhead."

He slapped her hard enough to stagger her and she caught at a tree trunk to steady herself. She spat at him, full of hate, bereft of hope.

He tossed the red jacket at her. "Hurry up."

Slowly she shuffled ahead of him, beginning to tremble at the thought of each step taking her toward the terrifying trail into the mile-deep, ancient gorge.

I've got to pull myself together, she thought, as she

stumbled ahead of Gianluca. *I must or I will not survive. Christina, Christina, David is dead—you're alive and the children need you. You must hold on to this.*

She stifled a sob.

Her mind raced. This fear of heights is only that. Fear. *You can overcome it*, she argued with herself. *It can be cured with special therapy. I know this. I don't have that luxury now, but the fear can be conquered. I must cure myself, conquer it myself. I must learn not to be afraid. They say if you keep saying things, believing things, they will come true. I am alive and the children need me and I will survive this horror. I will make the canyon my friend . The river at the bottom is my friend. I must believe this. I can do this. I will do this. I will see Caroline and Davey again. They need me. I can't be selfish and give in to this irrational fear. I am healthy, my balance is excellent. I can climb down those walls. They are my friends. I won't look down at first, but I will learn to. I will function and be cooperative. He is angry now, but he must learn to take me for granted, forget about me.*

Then I will kill him.

Christina tried to remember all the things she had ever heard Miriam and Jack say about climbing. You stayed balanced on your feet, you never clung with your hands. Your hands were only aids to your feet and legs. And this was a trail, after all. A path. People climbed down it all the time. It was rugged, yes, but if other people could do it, she could make herself. The only problem was her mind, and she would make her mind strong.

Over and over Christina repeated the phrase. *The canyon is my friend.*

THIRTY NINE

GIANLUCA AND CHRISTINA

When they got back to the parking lot it was about 8:30. The sun had turned the air warmer and there were several cars parked at the lodge. Gianluca eyed them warily as they began to strap on their gear. Christina jumped when a voice hailed them, from the door of the building.

"Mornin'." A park ranger waved and started down the steps.

Gianluca took his gun from his belt and slipped it into his jacket pocket. "If you say anything, I will shoot him, then I will shoot you."

"Sorry I was late gettin' here this mornin'. You folks need a map for the trail?" the ranger called. "Got your permit?"

Gianluca waved a pink piece of paper. "Right here. And we don't need a map," he shouted, his white teeth showing a broad smile and his voice exuding good humor. "I worked here last summer. Went down this trail all the time."

The ranger slowed. "Okay. Enjoy your trip." He turned back to the lodge.

Christina saw a film of perspiration on Gianluca's upper lip. He watched the ranger disappear into the lodge and slipped the gun back in his belt.

"Hurry up. There will be others. It takes all day to reach

the bottom before dark this time of year. If we don't hurry, we won't make it."

"How...how far is it?"

"Nine miles."

Christina squelched a pang of terror. *The canyon is my friend.*

Gianluca locked the car and jerked his head at her toward the service road. She started toward it.

Involuntarily her steps slowed as they came to the beginning of the trail. The vastness of the canyon swam at the edges of her vision. Lightheaded and afraid, she kept her eyes down, narrowing her consciousness, compressing it to what was only under her feet.

Gianluca caught her elbow and shoved her onto the path. One step, her mind willed. One step at a time. The ground was tan, pale, slightly sandy, with small pebbles, a small plant. A tiny beetle skittered under a rock. She had made the beginning of the long descent. A whimper escaped her throat, but she swallowed it, stamped it out, gritted her teeth. She denied her peripheral vision: the immense depth and breadth of the canyon swirling in a haze of rust, lavender, orange, and gold, along with blurs of dark green—the gnarled junipers that clung to variations in the sheer limestone walls. With immense effort she shut out all but what she felt beneath her feet through the soles of the cheap sneakers. Her mind tumbled; her breath came fast and shallow. She counted her steps...twenty, twenty-one...twenty-two.

Gianluca snorted his impatience. She felt the gun press against the back of her neck—the small, cold O.

"*Vada! Vada!* Hurry up!"

She stopped moving and turned into the wall and rested her cheek against its rough, cool surface, her eyes closed, trying to keep her voice steady.

"Gianluca? That's your name, isn't it?"

"*Si.*" The pressure of the gun muzzle increased.

"Gianluca. Please put your gun away. You cannot possibly frighten me more than I already am. If it weren't for my children and the hope that you'll let me go, I wouldn't care if you shot me. I would welcome it. But I will not run away again. You won. I will do everything you tell me. I promise you. I will try to go down this trail as best I can, but I am terrified. You must be patient if I'm to go with you. Especially now, in the beginning. I promise you I will do better, but for now, you must be patient with me." She didn't move her position or open her eyes. She simply waited. Then the gun muzzle went away and she could hear a zipper. He had put the gun in his knapsack.

She turned then, her eyes down on the trail and took another step, then another.

The canyon is my friend. The river is my friend. Gianluca is my enemy.

~ * ~

The trail was sometimes as narrow as three feet, usually it was wider. Christina discovered that sometimes there was a sheer drop down, sometimes it angled gently, with scrubby juniper, pinon, or cactus clinging tenaciously to life where they could find a foothold in the arid miniscule layer of soil that crusted the inner walls of the gorge. The first time she hazarded a glance, her stomach heaved and she clutched the stone cliff. She knew that people thought those afraid of heights were afraid they would fall. It wasn't like that. She felt she *was* falling. But she waited and counted her steps, then she glanced again, a tiny surreptitious dart of her eyes. The degree that it was easier was so minute, so nearly insignificant that she was afraid to hope. But she did. She was triumphant. She would do it.

She tried walking naturally, like strolling along a sidewalk. It wasn't easy, and the fear was still a presence, but now that she knew she could do it, her panic subsided. She watched her feet in the cheap sneakers, now reddish from the pulverized hermit shale of the path. Two thousand three steps, two thousand four. Had she counted accurately? Maybe she should be in the three thousands. Did it matter?

Eventually other thoughts began to seep in. Had anyone found David? And Laise and Preston? Lupe must be worried. Had she called anyone? How would they ever find out who had killed them all and taken her, and where? Who was Gianluca? What had Laise done to him that drove him to kill? His tirade back when he called Laise a whore and that she had seduced his father was such an incomprehensible tangle of English and Italian, she had made little sense of it.

Christina was tired, but she didn't want to stop. The rhythm of her steps and her mindset had moved her into a kind of trance. Was it self-hypnosis? If they stopped she would have to begin her mind games all over. She trudged ahead.

"We can't go around the rockfall. We'll have to climb over it." Gianluca's words filtered into her consciousness.

Christina's eyes crept forward until they came to a section of the trail blocked by a small avalanche of rocks from above. She turned cold. The obstruction was a mix of rubble that looked unstable. The Park Service didn't maintain this trail. There could be dozens like this. They would be scrambling through loose rock with a sheer drop on one side.

Gianluca's voice was directly behind her, his voice surprisingly gentle. "I will go first."

He stepped carefully, testing the stability of the pile. A few rocks tumbled down the cliff. He took another step, but the pile did not shift. He held out a hand to Christina. "Come."

She fought the panic and hesitated, then took his hand. It was warm and firm. Gingerly she stepped up. Another shower of rocks fell and she stifled a scream as she heard them rattle down the canyon wall. She was drenched with sweat and her teeth chattered. Somehow, with her hand in his, she moved across the steeply angled pile of dislodged stones and pieces of the cliff that had broken away to rest precariously across the trail. In what seemed an eternity they reached the other side. Christina's sweat-slick hand still clung to Gianluca's. He loosened her fingers and walked ahead. They came to a wider place in the trail and he stopped.

"We need water and something to eat. Also rest for a short time. Both of us would have more energy if you hadn't been so stupid and tried to run away." He pulled out what looked like some kind of energy bars. "Are you hungry?"

She shook her head. She was empty, but she wasn't hungry. The thought of eating made the bile rise in her throat. Her throat was raw with thirst, though. She would like a drink. He had told her to drink from her canteen as she walked along, but she couldn't. Couldn't move any part of her body but her feet, blotting out all but her steps, inching along.

Gianluca sat down near the edge, giving her the space next to the rough wall. She still kept her eyes averted and fumbled with the cap of the canteen, concentrating on it furiously, to keep from seeing the huge sweep of the spires and formations of the canyon. The water was warm and stale, but she drank and drank, her eyes closed. It would be a major effort to get up and begin her ordeal again.

"You are so afraid. I didn't believe you. You are being very brave, I think."

Christina didn't answer or open her eyes.

They left their resting place and Christina resumed her concentration. She was functioning on the trail, not at ease, surely, but she was getting accustomed to the steep precipices, even able to take quick looks around her. She was no longer paralyzed with terror.

She thought about Gianluca. He was strung tight and she had learned that any mention of the killings made him explosive. But he had manifested some inkling of gallantry—helping her over the rockfall, sitting closest to the edge when they had stopped. He was becoming more relaxed with her. Less vigilant the deeper they got into the canyon. They were making better time, too, and that lessened his anxiety.

If she could kill him, how would she do it? He was ahead of her now. That was a plus, but she had no weapon. The only possibility would be a rock. Christina thought of herself running up in back of him with a rock big enough to hurt him. A possibility—but she would first have to come upon the rock. The more likely way to kill him would be to push him off the edge. Doing that she would have to come to the edge herself—and she would be off balance. Could she do that? If she faltered it would be too late. He would know and he would kill her. She would have to practice getting closer to the edge. Imperceptibly she moved away from the wall and to the center of the trail. She felt the tugs of fear envelop her, but she held steady to the middle.

She thought of Caroline and David Jr. She thought of the canyon and the mocha ribbon of the Colorado, closer now, and less threatening. She had no idea of Gianluca's destination, wondering if he had friends among the Havasupai Indians whose reservation occupied most of Havasupai Canyon. When he told the ranger he had worked here, was that true? What did he do here? Whatever it was, he knew where he was going.

Her mind less occupied with her fear, Christina began to speculate on Gianluca's motives for the murders. Clearly she and David were accidental victims, there by happenstance to witness Gianluca's revenge on Laise. Was Preston also an accidental victim? What had precipitated the violence? Laise was such a private person. She didn't confide. Where had she so enraged Gianluca that he was driven to kill her? Somehow his father figured in this. An affair with Laise? Would Gianluca confide his reasons? She could never ask him and chance a fit of rage. She needed Gianluca calm.

Who was he? He was Italian, but he spoke an American English easily and idiomatically, with only a slight accent. He had spent a lot of time here.

Christina shook her head. She would never know,

because she planned that Gianluca would not have the chance to tell her. She would have to kill him on the heights. They were the only weapon she had.

Gianluca rounded a curve and disappeared from her sight. Her adrenalin surged at the fleeting freedom, but she knew it was hopeless that he would leave her. Almost in answer to her thoughts, he reappeared, his face troubled. "The trail has washed away ahead. There is a foothold, and enough of a handhold. We will have to cross that way. You will go first."

Tense, Christian moved around the bend and looked, horrified at the passage that Gianluca had described. A gaping hole was all that was left of the trail. The foothold he described seemed almost non-existent. How solid was it? Clearly he didn't know, nor was he overly-confident. That was why she would go first. Gallantry ceased here.

Christina knew, however, it would have to be crossed. Twenty feet of treacherous, possibly shifting sandstone and shale would have to be crossed with fingers and toes because there was no other choice.

"You can do it," Gianluca said, though his tone belied his assurance.

"Yes." She could do it because she had to.

"*Brava!*"

Christina pictured Caroline and David waiting on the other side. She would go to them. She turned her face to the cliff wall. If she waited she would freeze. Tentatively she touched her foot to the small ledge. It held. She tried to remember to balance on her feet, to delicately find a place to curl her fingers, just lightly, patiently. Don't cling, don't cling. Twenty feet. No more than the length of her bathroom. She was crossing her bathroom to turn on the tub that overlooked the valley. She would lie in the water and gaze at the city.

Christina was sweating heavily. When had it gotten so hot? The air was cool but the sun beat down on her back. She must take the mink jacket off when she got to the other side. Tuck it carefully in her backpack. She would need it tonight because it would be very cold. The cliff face felt warm to her touch as her trembling fingers lightly explored its surface, finding small irregularities to hold and keep her balance.

She didn't look ahead to her objective, afraid to find that she had only gone a few feet, so she was several feet beyond the break and back on the trail before she realized it. Relief made her weak and she crouched down, knees trembling, fighting tears.

When she stood she didn't wait for Gianluca. He was halfway across, but he would catch up to her. A hundred feet beyond, there was a wide place in the trail, with a cluster of boulders that gave her a sense of refuge. She sat and took off her jacket, tucking it through the straps in her backpack. She opened the canteen and drank the tepid, plasticky water.

Gianluca came and sat also. "You did very well. I think we should rest here for a short time."

He unstrapped his knapsack and tossed it to the ground, then unzipped a pocket and took out several energy bars. He handed her one. "I must insist you eat this. You will have no strength if you don't eat."

Christina unwrapped the bar and nibbled at the end. It wasn't bad—cheap chocolate on the outside, a kind of syrupy gumminess on the inside with an underlying texture like sawdust. But it was sweet and would give her energy. Gianluca watched her and handed her another.

"It's good you can eat. You are not so frightened now."

After he had eaten, he leaned back against the boulder and closed his eyes. Christina watched him, her heart pounding. How beautiful he was, with his classical face. It was inconceivable that he could be the vicious killer she knew him to be. She surveyed the ground around him for a rock, but there was nothing she could lift. She stirred in her frustration and he opened his eyes slightly. So he was still vigilant with her.

Gianluca rested for perhaps ten minutes, then stood and stretched. He climbed to the top of the boulders and surveyed the trail below. He beckoned her up.

She stared at him, silhouetted against the sapphire sky and the rose and violet spires of the canyon. She finished buckling her backpack and picked her way to just below where he stood.

"We will have to hurry to make it down before dark. Tomorrow we go that way. You can see the beginning of Havasupai Canyon from here. See? Where it begins to get green? There's a trading post at the Supai village. We can get supplies there. The Indians know me."

Christina pulled her way up and stood slightly behind him. "Where? I don't see." She coiled inside.

"There. Follow my finger."

Christina pushed him with all her might and felt him give beneath her hands. He fell off to the side, his arms flailing as he tried to recover his balance. She jumped backward, but he grabbed her ankle as he slipped on the rock. She was thrown off balance and was suddenly in the air, the canyon's colors swimming in her eyes as she spun through space, then scraped and scrabbled down the cliff face, experiencing the nightmare that had haunted her imagination for a lifetime. Her body slammed to a stop and a violent pain shot through her arm. She blacked out, then swam to consciousness only to black out again, her lungs heaving and screaming in the clouds of dust kicked up by her fall.

The throb in her arm seeped into the reddish blackness behind her eyes.

A shot pierced the fog and she tried to clear her head. She struggled to her elbows but the pain was so intense she dropped down again. She raised on her left arm cautiously and her situation came to her in all its horror. She was on a small outcropping of rock that hung out over the river far below, with absolutely no way to get off.

A series of shots fired and this time she heard the ping of a bullet strike on the ledge. Gianluca was firing at her from above. How could he not have fallen? How could she have failed her one chance?

There was a slight bulge in the cliff face of her ledge and she inched her body beneath it as far as she could. A bullet could ricochet, but she didn't think he could get a clear shot at her.

Numb, dry-eyed, she lay there, contemplating the hopelessness of her position. Why didn't she simply roll over a few times into the void? Or let Gianluca kill her. There was no way off this piece of rock, she had only a little water, her small jacket to protect her from the nighttime freezing temperatures. She had tried to kill Gianluca and she had botched it. It was out of her hands now.

She heard the whine of the next bullet, then watched as a chunk of her perch fell away under its impact. Just how strong was her ledge? It might give way any time, but there was nothing she could do. There was nowhere to go.

Her eye caught a movement and she realized Gianluca was no longer above her, but moving down a switchback on the trail to find a spot on a level with her ledge. Why did he want to kill her? She was no longer any threat at all.

She watched him position himself. He fired again, but he was farther away and his shot was wild. He needed a better angle to reach her as she cowered under the slight overhang of the cliff. But he had time. He would find the range soon enough.

She watched his progress to an outcropping of rock as he pulled himself hand over hand until he had a direct line-of-sight to Christina. She could see his dazzling smile as he took careful aim. Somehow she wasn't afraid as she waited. He might miss this time, or the next, but he would find his target. Maybe it was easier this way, to get it over with quickly. It would be bad to be only wounded. Perhaps she would stand to give him a clear shot. But somehow she couldn't abandon the last shred of her life.

The bullet twanged over her head, sending a small shower of dust and small pebbles down on her head. The shot reverberated in the canyon.

It was almost as if she were watching the action in slow motion. Gianluca reloaded his gun and inched a little closer. He took careful aim.

Christina saw his body tilt. He tried to scramble to his feet, but the rocks on which he had lain simply crumbled away as he slid faster and faster, then with a splitting crack, was flung into space. He turned several times in the air and then Christina couldn't see him anymore.

He hadn't screamed. That's odd, she thought. He hadn't made a sound at all as he plummeted into the swift, ropy, brown river.

It was a long time before her mind stirred back to reality. She wished she had something she could splint her arm with, but of course there wasn't anything. Then it began to sink in that she was free of Gianluca. Hope stirred faintly. Maybe someone started down the trail after them. There was perhaps an hour of daylight, maybe less. Once the sun set, darkness would fall quickly. Perhaps someone heard the shots. Maybe she could attract attention if someone was on the trail.

Then she remembered the two washed-out sections of the trail. If a hiker negotiated the first, he would surely abandon the trail when he came to the treacherous second rockfall. But there were people who loved that sort of thing. Weren't there? She had to cling to any sliver of hope.

Christina sat up carefully, cradling her broken arm, and eased herself out of the small backpack Gianluca had made her carry. Pain made her stomach turn, but she fought down the nausea. One-handed she unzipped the backpack and went through the contents. It was mostly a change of clothes for him, a picture of a pretty, dark-haired woman, several packets of twenty dollar bills, and some unidentified white pills. There was a small black velvet box. She snapped the lid open. The last rays of the sun before it dropped behind the ridge of the canyon winked in the diamond petals that surrounded quarter-size topaz jewels. Were these to be a gift for Laise, she wondered? They were worth a fortune. Did he have that kind of money?

She closed the box and returned it to the backpack pocket. It took several agonizing minutes to ease her broken arm into one of Gianluca's cashmere sweaters and the red mink jacket. The cold was becoming sharp. It was unlikely anyone would come down the trail now. Huddled under the rock, with her feet wrapped in Gianluca's jeans, she couldn't hope for anyone now until tomorrow afternoon, and that would be Monday. Her chances were very, very slim.

Twilight deepened colors and shadows picked out fantastic shapes in the rock formations as the temperature dropped. Then the colors faded. The moon rose.

During the long cold night Christina would doze occasionally, but mostly her mind pored over the events of the past months. How empty and foolish her liaison with Sev had been. Just another bored housewife looking for a thrill. She thought of David with sorrow. Perhaps they'd gotten lazy with their marriage because it had all been so easy for them the past few years. She had drifted along with a half-assed writing career, not really trying anything very challenging. She had raised a lot of money for a lot of good causes, but had her commitment been any more than social? *Be honest, now, Christina. You don't have to impress anyone here.*

She'd been a pretty good mother.

That made her cry because deep in her heart she knew she would never see Caroline and David again.

As the night wore on, she put on as many of Gianluca's clothes as there were. She was very cold, her feet especially. Finally she struggled out of the mink jacket, whimpering with the agony of moving her broken arm, and tucked the soft fur around her feet, then wrapped the jeans around her head and shoulders. That seemed marginally warmer and she was able to drift off to sleep, wondering vaguely if she might roll off her ledge, and in her pain and despair, not much caring one way or another.

FORTY

CHRISTINA

The moon still bathed the canyon in a ghostly silver when she awoke, stiff and cold, her arm a pulsing misery. Christina discovered she had scarcely moved in her sleep, still huddled against the wall under the overhang. The sky had paled to the east. Five o'clock, maybe? No, closer to six. It would be a long day. Maybe, maybe someone would come down the trail, but it wouldn't be until this afternoon that they would pass on the trail above her. It would be a hard wait. The moon was somewhere in back of her, but she couldn't see it. She watched as the fantastic towers, buttes, and spires of the canyon became more distinct in the predawn light. Finally a single shaft of light winked over the black rim as the sun gently rose to brush the ancient layers of rock that told of two billion years of the earth's geological history. She could see pockets of mist down along the river and vaguely hear the whisper of rapids in the overwhelming silence of the dawn. The great brooding chasm seemed peaceful to her now, a refuge. There were more terrible places to come to the end of one's life.

God, her arm hurt. She pressed the long bone gently, but it was swollen too much to locate the fracture. She surveyed the ledge. It was about fifteen feet long and about six feet wide. She smiled faintly. About the size of the Oriental rug that ran the length of the upstairs hallway at home.

There was a chunk that had broken away from Gianluca's bullet. She had no desire to walk around, but she should move carefully. She thought of Gianluca's outcropping simply crumbling away.

How long could she survive here? Three days? How long, that is, if she could keep her sanity. She had to keep an iron grip on her emotions just to keep herself from flying apart in all directions. Panic was just under the surface.

She thought about the white pills in the blue nylon backpack. What were they for? She unzipped the bag and got them out again. There were about twenty. She counted them. Twenty-one. Maybe if things got truly unbearable, she could take all of them. See what they would do. Grimly she returned the packet to the backpack. She wouldn't think about them. Until tomorrow. Then she would have to think about them.

She unhooked the canteen and took a long drink of water. There wasn't much left when she was finished. She remembered reading somewhere that in a water-critical situation, it didn't matter much whether you drank what you had all at once or rationed it out a little at a time. You might get so fritched up about rationing it that you wouldn't drink what you had. She looked at the canteen, then put it to her lips and drank what was left. Now she would just forget about it. She was about to toss the canteen off the ledge, but hesitated and set it carefully down at her side. You weren't supposed to litter in the canyon.

Curled up under the overhang she felt almost safe, and she let her eyes roam over the dramatic rock formations. *They're right*, she thought. *There is a haze of pollution over the canyon, washing out the brilliant colors.* One side said it was smog from Los Angeles, another that it was from the Navajo Generating Plant. Whatever, it was truly a shame. Funny, she could look at it calmly now, pick out small details. What would David say if he could see her now, clinging for her life to this precarious ledge and not trembling in abject terror? But maybe he could.

The brutal rape had been the center of her existence a few days ago, and now she scarcely remembered it. It was insignificant.

Another strange thing. She wished she had killed Gianluca. It was a terrible way to feel, but it would have made up a little for David and the others. She wished he had gone to his death knowing that it was Christina Cross who had killed him.

~ * ~

The morning crawled by, with her musings interspersed with periods of dozing. She thought of Caroline and David. Then others. The friends she'd thought she knew so well. Laise and Preston. She'd sensed something wrong there for quite awhile. Miriam and Jack. Thank God they'd gone home before the slaughter. They were so thrilled about the baby coming. She'd known Jack during his breakup with Joanna, saw how sad they both were. And yet, Jack said nothing after Joanna left. Had borne his hurt alone. And during that time Miriam was enduring a hell with her sadistic first husband.

Ting and Jenks were so loving, but what had Ting gone through with Jake? And Ting with Sev? No one had even guessed.

Christina cringed over her liaison with Sev. He had set her on fire and the forbidden sex was thrilling. Was she simply another conquest for him? It had been such a stupid thing for her to do. How did Hallie bear his infidelities? She remembered her own misery over Hallie's affair with David. Was that how Hallie coped? With others?

Alicia Bentham? She had that awful Barney to put up with, the booze and God knew what else. And Ann and Bartlett Savage. Ann, with her facelifts and boob jobs, purple bedroom and purple nighties and pole dances. What did she have to contend with? What went on behind Bartlett's hooded eyes?

How well do we ever really know anyone? Christina thought. *These are people I knew and saw every day. People who I thought were happy and successful. Beautiful people. People who were to be envied, maybe. But were they, after all? Were we? We all hide our troubles so well in the faces we show to our friends.*

But should we? Miriam and Jack, Ting and Jenks...what would I have done without their kindness?

What would have become of David and me if we had survived this horror? Would David have forgiven me? I would like to have known that he did...before he...

Tears welled up and blurred the majestic panorama that would be the final picture in her life.

The sound of a small plane engine intruded, but she'd heard them all day yesterday, tourist overflights too far up to do her any good. Canyon air currents swirled unpredictably and there had been crashes over the years. Finally, flights were limited to only above the canyon rim. This one seemed closer, though, and she roused herself from her lethargy and began to look for it. When it came into view it seemed to be coming right toward her, though that was probably all illusion. But maybe it would get close enough if she could somehow attract attention. She looked at the red mink jacket. It was very bright. She would have to wave it, close to the edge where it would stand out from the rosy canyon wall.

The plane seemed to be coming very close and Christina struggled to her feet. She bumped her head on the overhang and stumbled as her cold legs and feet refused to hold her weight.

The plane passed, not really very close at all. Would it come back on a return trip? She had to be ready, in case. She rubbed her legs with her left hand. She wiggled her toes, then gradually eased to her feet, nervously holding onto the overhang and stifling the vertigo that assailed her. She rubbed new tears from her eyes. She had begun to think she had conquered her fears. Would she be able to go to the edge if the plane came back?

The sound of the plane's engine grew fainter and then disappeared. She made herself stay on her feet, made herself look down until her stomach quieted and the lightheadedness passed. She took several steps back and forth, then moved a little closer to the edge. She moved back and picked up the red jacket and leaned against the rocky overhang to wait. She had to be ready if the plane came back. It might be her only chance.

She squinted down the canyon trying to spot the small single engine plane. Maybe it would go all the way to Lake Mead with its load of tourists before it came back. If it came back. Her ears strained to pick up the bee-like whine, but all she heard was an immense silence that seemed to roar in her head.

Then she heard the motor again and her heart began to race. She clutched the soft fur, grown damp and spiky from her wet hands. There, she could see it. It looked closer to the canyon wall. Closer to her. Carefully she stepped out and began waving her jacket.

"Please, oh, please see me," she begged. "Please. I'm over here."

And then the plane was past her. She didn't know if anyone had seen her or not. Then she saw the plane bank and turn. He was coming back! She waved the jacket frantically.

The plane made two more passes and she was convinced she had been spotted. When it finally flew back down the canyon, Christina crept under her overhang and huddled, her good arm wrapped around her knees. The pilot had dipped his wings before he flew away. She could begin to hope.

~ * ~

"I'm certain of it Senator Cross. I flew by three times. You said she was wearing a red jacket when you saw her last," the pilot said.

Two deputy sheriffs, the pilot and Jack were poring over a map of the canyon.

David grimaced as he jumped up from the chair in the airport office. His chest was wrapped tightly from armpits to waist, immobilizing the wounds and three broken ribs from Gianluca's bullets. "Jack, get ready to go. I'll find out where to look from Bill here." A wave of nausea churned his stomach and he leaned against the desk, fighting the black spots that swam before his eyes.

"We'll be ready," Jack said. He hurried out the door to the company plane Miriam was warming up on the tarmac of Tusayan Grand Canyon Airport.

"I wish you'd let us handle this Senator, sir." The deputy sheriff's voice was sympathetic. "I can understand your concern and all, but she seems pretty much okay. Air Evac's on its way. I don't like the idea of you flying out over the canyon. Those updrafts are very tricky. And you're not in very good shape, if I may say so, sir."

David gritted his teeth against the pain and the exasperation. "Captain, Jack was a Navy pilot on a carrier. I've got over three hundred flying hours and a current license. I'm perfectly qualified and able to fly the right seat. Now if you'll just let Bill here show me the map..."

The pilot hesitated, then leaned over the large map of the canyon. "She's on a small ledge below Hermit's Trail. How she got there is anybody's guess. Probably fell. She was alone. No telling if her captor is around. I didn't see anyone else. I wouldn't fly too close. I can't tell you how stable her situation is and vibrations from the plane's engines could destabilize that rock. It's a combination of shale and sandstone. Very friable, soft."

"We won't be in there long. I want her to know we're here. That we're coming to get her." He turned to the policeman. "Captain, my wife left me for dead. I know she probably won't be able to see me, but she knows the plane.

She'll recognize it. To me that's very important. And I need to see her for myself."

"Yes, sir, remember what the pilot said about getting too close."

~ * ~

It was a different plane, she could tell by the engine. When she spotted it she grabbed the jacket again and stood up to wave it. As it got closer, her eyes narrowed, then widened in disbelief. It was David's and Jack's company plane. She was sure of it. David had come to…no. She had almost forgotten. David was dead. But Jack had come to help her. Yes, there it was. The blue company logo on the side of the plane. It dipped its wings as it flew by, then banked to fly by her again. Joyfully she waved the red jacket as the plane passed her three times.

~ * ~

"We've got to leave her for now, David," Jack said. "She saw us. She knows help is coming. The Air Evac chopper is heading into the airport. Miriam and I will have to be there ready to go. I think we've got enough information now."

Tears streamed down David's face. "Look at her. How is she doing it? She's terrified of heights. When I think…"

Miriam wrapped her arms around David. "She'll be fine. She was always stronger than she knew. I can't wait to tell her you're alive and kicking. That you're waiting for her."

"What do you mean, you'll tell her?" David turned to stare at Miriam.

"Why, I'll be the first to reach her. Look, that ledge may be a little shaky. I'm small. I'm the best person to go to her."

David's voice was shaky. "I won't have it. You're pregnant. It's much too dangerous."

"Oh, it isn't. I've done this so many times I can do it in my sleep. Right, Jack?"

Jack hesitated then gave a nod. "She's right, David. God knows I wouldn't do anything to jeopardize Miriam, but it really is a fairly simple operation. And Miriam wants to do it. Think of what support that will be for Christina. She's been through such a helluva lot."

"I feel very strongly about this, David," Miriam said. She petted his head as he cried on her shoulder. "We'll see you at the hospital in Flagstaff. Which is where you ought to be anyway. Tell them to put you to bed. Tell them I said so."

~ * ~

When the plane disappeared, Christina felt a sense of loss so vast, an emptiness so painful that she fell on her knees in despair. The events of the past hours had been so bizarre, so unreal that she felt sometimes that she was a character in some monstrous play. Her situation had been so without hope that her mind had formed a protective cocoon around her that pushed these happenings into the realm of make-believe.

But when she saw the company plane, she was thrown back into her world, where David had been killed and she would never see him again. She had not had the chance to tell him how sorry she was and how much she loved him. An aching loneliness fell over her, even as she knew that now she would be rescued. She would live again, but David would not be there when she went back to that life.

She had no idea when her rescuers would come. Dazed, she went about getting ready. It was awkward with her useless right arm, but she stuffed Gianluca's clothes into the backpack. The police would probably want these things. Curiously she looked at the diamond and topaz earrings, then zipped them into a side pocket. She studied the woman's picture. There was a resemblance. It was probably his mother. She looked about the right age.

The police would analyze the white pills. She wondered if they would tell her what they were—find out what would have happened if she had taken them in her desperation.

No. No, she didn't want to know.

~ * ~

The helicopter was able to set down on a point about 500 yards above the trail. There were four in the rescue team—two from the Air Evac team, Jack and Miriam—plus the pilot.

"It'll take about twenty minutes to get down to the trail," Jack said. "From there we'll lower Miriam down to Christina. Miriam'll get her hooked up to the line you drop and you can pull her up. You want to take Miriam out, too? We'll be walking out on the trail."

"Up to you," the pilot said.

"I'll go with Christina," Miriam said, "to the Flagstaff Hospital. David will be there, but until then she'll need some moral support. She'll be scared getting pulled into the chopper. Hell, it makes my eyes get big."

"Twenty minutes it is. I'll watch for you, then throw down the line. Soon's we get her in we'll throw down a line for you."

The rescue team moved off to begin the climb down, setting up belays as they rappelled down the cliff face to the trail. When they were above Christina, Jack shouted down, "We're coming. Hang on."

They saw Christina cautiously look up from below the overhang. She looked small and frightened, about fifty feet down.

"I can't climb or anything," she called. "My arm is broken."

"Damn, that complicates things a bit. Does that first aid box have anything for a splint, Miriam?"

"Yes. I can take care of an arm."

"Joe, let's get this belay going. That rock looks good." Jack straddled a rock and the other man secured his waist loop to a rock behind Jack. He passed Miriam's climbing rope around his waist above the tie-in rope and braced his feet. He would be the one to keep Miriam safe.

"Ready." Miriam looked over.

"Be careful. I wish you hadn't talked me into this. Go."

Miriam grinned and moved below the rocks, out of Jack's sight.

"Belay on?" she called.

"Belay on."

"Testing." Miriam jerked the line to indicate the direction of the pull. "Ready to go."

"Go."

Miriam leaned back over the edge of the cliff, keeping a tight grip on the rope with her right hand. Feet well apart, she stepped off into the sky. Keeping her body perpendicular to the cliff face, she walked backward down to Christina's ledge.

"Down rope. Twenty five feet." Then, "ten feet."

Her feet found the ledge. "I'm down," she yelled.

Smiling, she moved to Christina. "Hi, babe. Good to see you. We don't have a lot of time. Let me do the talking while you give me your arm"

"Miriam, you shouldn't have done this. It's too dangerous. Oh, God, I'm so glad to see you." Tears spilled down her cheeks.

"Shut up, dear heart. First thing, David is okay. Banged up, but okay. The shots broke his ribs but passed on through—he had a medium concussion from falling. But he's waiting for you at the hospital in Flag."

Christina caught her breath, then dropped her head onto her good hand and began to cry.

"Now, go ahead and cry while I splint your arm. They'll give you a shot for the pain upstairs. This little orchestra seat you have is liable to fall off at any time." She worked quickly. "What happened to the guy?"

"He was shooting at me and the cliff he was on gave way."

"Jesus God. Why was he shooting at you?"

"I tried to kill him."

Miriam stared at Christina. Then she cleared her throat. "We'd better hurry. They said this rock is touchy."

"How did you know where to look?"

"David was able to call 911 when he came to. Lucchese also killed the security guard at the Brock's gatehouse."

"Was that his name?"

"Yes. The media have gone crazy, as you can well imagine. It's all over the papers and TV. The lady at the Sunset Point bathroom remembered him taking you into the bathroom. She called 911. There was a big deal astro-physicist down in Tucson who was afraid it was his nephew. Then the girl at the truck stop remembered you. Or your coat, to be exact. And she also thought you had the most beautiful blonde hair. Next they found your gold sandals. Everything pointed to the canyon. Then they did some checking. Some of the faculty at ASU said there had been some gossip that Laise had been chummy with this young Italian instructor, Gianluca Lucchese. David remembered Laise calling him Gianluca. Turns out he'd worked here a year or so ago. Took hikers, mule trains into the canyon. It began to add up. The park ranger at Hermit's Point remembered the guy who said he'd worked here. Then we knew which trail to search."

The sound of the helicopter droned near. "Now I'm going to hook you into this harness. I'm sorry and you'll be scared shitless, but it can't be helped. You'll have to be hauled out by chopper. Think you can handle it?"

Christina nodded. "Will you be with me?"

"I'll be right behind you." Miriam straightened and watched the helicopter begin to hover overhead. A line snaked out of the open door and fell on the ledge. Miriam anchored the line to Christina's harness.

"How are the children?"

"Great. Worried about you. They'll be happy kids, I'll tell you."

"How...how is David?"

"David is so crazy beside himself with worrying about you he hardly knows where he is."

"Laise and Preston?"

Miriam shook her head, checked the knot. She put her hand on Christina's shoulder. "Don't worry about that other...uh, little thing, hm? David wanted you to know that's all past. Wanted you to know he was going to tell you that...before the...business at the Brock's. You ready?"

Christina swallowed hard. "Yes. I've got to get back to vote for David. Tomorrow's election day."

"By God it is." She patted Christina's shoulder. "Bon voyage. Close your eyes and think of England." She gave two jerks of the line and Christina rose from the ledge. Miriam watched with concern. Acrophobics sometimes started thrashing around. Christina looked all right.

Just as Christina was being pulled into the chopper, Miriam felt a shifting under her feet and heard a shower of rocks into the canyon. "Hurry up, you guys," she muttered uneasily as she gathered the backpack and the red mink. She looked up and saw the rope fall from the chopper, but it fell short of the ledge. The ground beneath her tipped as the pilot maneuvered the chopper closer. The rope dangled tantalizingly close, but it was still beyond her fingertips.

The helicopter hovered, then inched closer, the rotors spinning perilously close to the cliff face. The rope brushed the ledge and Miriam grabbed it. She quickly looped the rope to her harness then looped it into a knot. The ledge gave way and Miriam stumbled, then the rope tightened and she swung out, dangling over the canyon before the winch began to pull her to safety as the ledge crumbled and with a roar plummeted into the river below.

Fifty feet above, the two men of the rescue team leaned over Jack, who lay sprawled on his back. "I'll be damned, Joe. He's fainted."

EPILOGUE

David Cross won his Senate seat and was reelected for three more terms. A year after the election, Christina and he had a baby girl they named Miriam.

Laise and Preston's boys, Jeremy and John, were raised by their great uncle, John Spenser. Jeremy studied finance at Stanford and eventually took over the family's fortune. John became the ranch's manager.

Miriam and Jack went on to have four boys. The third boy's hair turned white when he was sixteen.

Will Fowler remarried his wife three years after Laise's death.

Sev and Hallie Justus stayed together. Sev ran for governor three years after the events here, was elected and served two terms. For political reasons, the Crosses and Justuses came to maintain a surface cordiality.

Ting and Jenks had twin girls two years later.

Bartlett Savage divorced Ann and became openly involved with a young man.

Barney Bentham remained party chairman through David's first term in office, then died of liver complications.

About Virginia

Virginia Nosky is a prize winning author, poet and screenwriter. The settings of her work, with the exception of some side ventures into Boston, New York, Paris and the Mediterranean, are in the Southwest where the dramatic scenery and violent weather add another dimension to her stories. She lives in Paradise Valley, Arizona with her husband Richard and two rescued retrievers, Barkis and Peaches.

Visit our website for our growing catalogue of quality books.
www.champagnebooks.com

Made in the USA
Lexington, KY
30 October 2013